THE CRITICS LOVE
JOHN GRISHAM

"With every new book I appreciate John Grisham a little more, for his feisty critiques of the legal system, his compassion for the underdog, and his willingness to strike out in new directions."
—*Entertainment Weekly*

" John Grisham is exceptionally good at what he does. . . . Grisham's books are also smart, imaginative, and funny, populated by complex, interesting people, written by a man who is driven not merely by the desire to entertain but also by genuine (if understated) outrages at human cupidity and venality."
—*The Washington Post*

" John Grisham is about as good a storyteller as we've got in the United States these days."
—*The New York Times Book Review*

" John Grisham owns the legal thriller."
—*The Denver Post*

By John Grisham

THEODORE BOONE BOOKS

JOHN GRISHAM

CAMINO ISLAND

A NOVEL

DELL BOOKS · NEW YORK

Camino Island is a work of fiction. Names, characters, businesses, organizations, places, events, and incidents are the product of the author's imagination or are used fictitiously. Any resemblance to actual persons, living or dead, or locales is entirely coincidental.

2020 Dell Mass Market Edition

Copyright © 2017 by Belfry Holdings, Inc.
Excerpt from *The Rooster Bar* by John Grisham
copyright © 2017 by Belfry Holdings, Inc.

Published in the United States by Dell, an imprint of Random House, a division of Penguin Random House LLC, New York.

DELL and the HOUSE colophon are registered trademarks of Penguin Random House LLC.

Originally published in hardcover in the United States by Doubleday, a division of Penguin Random House LLC, in 2017.

ISBN 978-1-5247-9715-7
Ebook ISBN 978-0-385-54305-7

Cover design: John Fontana
Cover photograph: Birgit Tyrell/Arcangel Images

Printed in the United States of America

randomhousebooks.com

4 6 8 10 12 11 9 7 5

Dell mass market edition: April 2020

TO RENÉE

Thanks for the story

CAMINO ISLAND

CHAPTER ONE
THE HEIST

1.

The imposter borrowed the name of Neville Manchin, an actual professor of American literature at Portland State and soon-to-be doctoral student at Stanford. In his letter, on perfectly forged college stationery, "Professor Manchin" claimed to be a budding scholar of F. Scott Fitzgerald and was keen to see the great writer's "manuscripts and papers" during a forthcoming trip to the East Coast. The letter was addressed to Dr. Jeffrey Brown, Director of Manuscripts Division, Department of Rare Books and Special Collections, Firestone Library, Princeton University. It arrived with a few others, was duly sorted and passed along, and eventually landed on the desk of Ed Folk, a career junior librarian whose task, among several other monotonous ones, was to verify the credentials of the person who wrote the letter.

Ed received several of these letters each week, all in many ways the same, all from self-proclaimed Fitzgerald buffs and experts, and even from the occasional true scholar. In the previous calendar year, Ed had cleared and logged in 190 of these people through the library. They came from all over the world and arrived wide-eyed and humbled, like pilgrims before a shrine. In his thirty-four years at the same desk, Ed had processed all of them. And, they were not going away. F. Scott Fitzgerald continued to fascinate. The traffic was as heavy now as it had been three decades earlier. These days, though, Ed was wondering what could possibly be left of the great writer's life that had not been pored over, studied at great length, and written about. Not long ago, a true scholar told Ed that there were now at least a hundred books and over ten thousand published academic articles on Fitzgerald the man, the writer, his works, and his crazy wife.

And he drank himself to death at forty-four! What if he'd lived into old age and kept writing? Ed would need an assistant, maybe two, perhaps even an entire staff. But then Ed knew that an early death was often the key to later acclaim (not to mention greater royalties).

After a few days, Ed finally got around to dealing with Professor Manchin. A quick review of the library's register revealed that this was a new person, a new request. Some of the veterans had been to Princeton so many times they simply called his number and said, "Hey, Ed, I'll be there next Tuesday." Which was fine with Ed. Not so with Manchin. Ed went through the Portland State website and found his man. Undergraduate degree in American lit from the University of Oregon; master's from UCLA; adjunct gig now for three years. His photo revealed a rather plain-looking young man of perhaps thirty-five, the makings of a beard that was probably temporary, and narrow frameless eyeglasses.

In his letter, Professor Manchin asked whoever responded to do so by e-mail, and gave a private Gmail address. He said he rarely checked his university address. Ed thought, "That's because you're just a lowly adjunct professor and probably don't even have a real office." He often had these thoughts, but, of course, was too professional to utter them to anyone else. Out of caution, the next day he sent a response through the Portland State server. He thanked Professor Manchin for his letter and invited him to the Princeton campus. He asked for a general idea of when he might arrive and laid out a few of the basic rules regarding the Fitzgerald collection. There were many, and he suggested that Professor Manchin study them on the library's website.

The reply was automatic and informed Ed that Manchin was out of pocket for a few days. One of Manchin's partners had hacked into the Portland State directory just deep enough to tamper with the English department's e-mail server; easy work for a sophisticated hacker. He and the imposter knew immediately that Ed had responded.

Ho hum, thought Ed. The next day he sent the same message to Professor Manchin's private Gmail address. Within an hour, Manchin replied with an enthusiastic thank-you, said he couldn't wait to get there, and so on. He gushed on about how he had studied the library's website, had spent hours with the Fitzgerald digital archives, had owned for years the multivolume series containing facsimile editions of the great author's handwritten first drafts, and had a particular interest in the critical reviews of the first novel, *This Side of Paradise*.

Great, said Ed. He'd seen it all before. The guy was trying to impress him before he even got there, which was not at all unusual.

2.

F. Scott Fitzgerald enrolled in Princeton in the fall of 1913. At the age of sixteen, he was dreaming of writing the great American novel, and had indeed begun working on an early version of *This Side of Paradise*. He dropped out four years later to join the Army and go to war, but it ended before he was deployed. His classic, *The Great Gatsby*, was published in 1925 but did not become popular until after his death. He struggled financially throughout his career, and by 1940 was working in Hollywood, cranking out bad screenplays, failing physically and creatively. On December 21, he died of a heart attack, brought on by years of severe alcoholism.

In 1950, Scottie, his daughter and only child, gave his original manuscripts, notes, and letters—his "papers"— to the Firestone Library at Princeton. His five novels were handwritten on inexpensive paper that did not age well. The library quickly realized that it would be unwise to allow researchers to physically handle them. High-quality copies were made, and the originals were locked away in a secured basement vault where the air, light, and temperature were carefully controlled. Over the years, they had been removed only a handful of times.

3.

The man posing as Professor Neville Manchin arrived at Princeton on a beautiful fall day in early October. He was directed to Rare Books and Special Collections, where he met Ed Folk, who then passed him along to another assistant librarian who examined and copied his Oregon driver's license. It was, of course, a forgery, but a perfect one. The forger, who was also the hacker, had been trained by the CIA and had a long history in the murky world of private espionage. Breaching a bit of campus security was hardly a challenge.

Professor Manchin was then photographed and given a security badge that had to be displayed at all times. He followed the assistant librarian to the second floor, to a large room with two long tables and walls lined with retractable steel drawers, each of which was locked. Manchin noticed at least four surveillance cameras high in the corners, cameras that were supposed to be seen. He suspected others were well hidden. He attempted to chat up the assistant librarian but got little in return. He jokingly asked if he could see the original manuscript for *This Side of Paradise*. The assistant librarian offered a smug grin and said that would not be possible.

"Have you ever seen the originals?" Manchin asked.

"Only once."

A pause as Manchin waited for more, then he asked, "And what was the occasion?"

"Well, a certain famous scholar wished to see them. We accompanied him down to the vault and gave him a look. He didn't touch the papers, though. Only our head librarian is allowed to do so, and only with special gloves."

"Of course. Oh well, let's get to work."

The assistant opened two of the large drawers, both labeled "This Side of Paradise," and withdrew thick, oversized notebooks. He said, "These contain the reviews of the book when it was first published. We have many other samples of later reviews."

"Perfect," Manchin said with a grin. He opened his briefcase, took out a notepad, and seemed ready to pounce on everything laid on the table. Half an hour later, with Manchin deep in his work, the assistant librarian excused himself and disappeared. For the benefit of the cameras, Manchin never looked up. Eventually, he needed to find the men's room and wandered away. He took a wrong turn here and another one there, got himself lost, and eased through Collections, avoiding contact with anyone. There were surveillance cameras everywhere. He doubted that anyone at that moment was watching the footage, but it could certainly be retrieved if needed. He found an elevator, avoided it, and took the nearby stairs. The first level below was similar to the ground floor. Below it, the stairs stopped at B2 (Basement 2), where a large thick door waited with "Emergencies Only" painted in bold letters. A keypad was next to the door, and another sign warned that an alarm would sound the instant the door was opened without "proper authorization." Two security cameras watched the door and the area around it.

Manchin backed away and retraced his steps. When he returned to his workroom, the assistant was waiting. "Is everything okay, Professor Manchin?" he asked.

"Oh yes. Just a bit of a stomach bug, I'm afraid. Hope it's not contagious." The assistant librarian left immediately, and Manchin hung around all day, digging through materials from the steel drawers and reading old reviews he cared nothing about. Several times he wandered off, poking around, looking, measuring, and memorizing.

4.

Manchin returned three weeks later and he was no longer pretending to be a professor. He was clean shaven, his hair was colored a sandy blond, he wore fake eyeglasses with red frames, and he carried a bogus student card with a photo. If someone asked, which he certainly didn't expect, his story was that he was a grad student from Iowa. In real life his name was Mark and his occupation, if one could call it that, was professional thievery. High-dollar, world-class, elaborately planned smash-and-grab jobs that specialized in art and rare artifacts that could be sold back to the desperate victims for ransom. His was a gang of five, led by Denny, a former Army Ranger who had turned to crime after being kicked out of the military. So far, Denny had not been caught and had no record; nor did Mark. However, two of the others did. Trey had two convictions and two escapes, his last the year before from a federal prison in Ohio. It was there he'd met Jerry, a petty art thief now on parole. Another art thief, a onetime cell-mate serving a long sentence, had first mentioned the Fitzgerald manuscripts to Jerry.

The setup was perfect. There were only five manuscripts, all handwritten, all in one place. And to Princeton they were priceless.

The fifth member of the team preferred to work at home. Ahmed was the hacker, the forger, the creator of all illusions, but he didn't have the nerve to carry guns and such. He worked from his basement in Buffalo and had never been caught or arrested. He left no trails. His 5 percent would come off the top. The other four would take the rest in equal shares.

By nine o'clock on a Tuesday night, Denny, Mark, and Jerry were inside the Firestone Library posing as grad students and watching the clock. Their fake student IDs had worked perfectly; not a single eyebrow had been raised. Denny found his hiding place in a third-floor women's restroom. He lifted a panel in the ceiling above the toilet, tossed up his student backpack, and settled in for a few hours of hot and cramped waiting. Mark picked the lock of the main mechanical room on the first level of the basement and waited for alarms. He heard none, nor did Ahmed, who had easily hacked into the university's security systems. Mark proceeded to dismantle the fuel injectors of the library's backup electrical generator. Jerry found a spot in a study carrel hidden among rows of stacked tiers holding books that had not been touched in decades.

Trey was drifting around the campus, dressed like a student, lugging his backpack, scoping out places for his bombs.

The library closed at midnight. The four team members, as well as Ahmed in his basement in Buffalo, were in radio contact. Denny, the leader, announced at 12:15 that all was proceeding as planned. At 12:20, Trey, dressed like a student and hauling a bulky backpack, entered the McCarren Residential College in the heart of the campus. He saw the same surveillance cameras he had seen the previous week. He took the unwatched stairs to the second floor, ducked into a coed restroom, and locked himself in a stall. At 12:40, he reached into his backpack and removed a tin can about the size of a twenty-ounce bottle of soda. He set a delayed starter and hid it behind the toilet. He left the restroom, went to the third floor, and set another bomb in an empty shower stall. At 12:45, he found a semi-dark hallway on the second floor of a dormitory and nonchalantly tossed a string of ten jumbo Black Cat firecrackers down the hall. As he scrambled down the stairwell, the explosions boomed through the air. Seconds later, both smoke bombs erupted, sending thick clouds of rancid fog into the hallways. As Trey left the building he heard the first wave of panicked voices. He stepped behind some shrubs near the dorm, pulled a disposable phone out of his pocket, called Princeton's 911 service, and delivered the horrifying news: "There's a guy with a gun on the second floor of McCarren. He's firing shots."

Smoke was drifting from a second-floor window. Jerry, sitting in the dark study carrel in the library, made a similar call from his prepaid cell phone. Soon, calls were pouring in as panic gripped the campus.

Every American college has elaborate plans to handle a situation involving an "active gunman," but no one wants to implement them. It took a few dumbstruck seconds for the officer in charge to push the right buttons, but when she did, sirens began wailing. Every Princeton student, professor, administrator, and employee received a text and e-mail alert. All doors were to be closed and locked. All buildings were to be secured.

Jerry made another call to 911 and reported that two students had been shot. Smoke boiled out of McCarren Hall. Trey dropped three more smoke bombs into trash cans. A few students ran through the smoke as they went from building to building, not sure where exactly the safe places were. Campus security and the City of Princeton police raced onto the scene, followed closely by half a dozen fire trucks. Then ambulances. The first of many patrol cars from the New Jersey State Police arrived.

Trey left his backpack at the door of an office building, then called 911 to report how suspicious it looked. The timer on the last smoke bomb inside the backpack was set to go off in ten minutes, just as the demolition experts would be staring at it from a distance.

At 1:05, Trey radioed the gang: "A perfect panic out here. Smoke everywhere. Tons of cops. Go for it."

Denny replied, "Cut the lights."

Ahmed, sipping strong tea in Buffalo and sitting on go, quickly routed through the school's security panel, entered the electrical grid, and cut the electricity not only to the Firestone Library but to half a dozen nearby buildings as well. For good measure, Mark, now wearing night vision goggles, pulled the main cutoff switch in the mechanical room. He waited and held his breath, then breathed easier when the backup generator did not engage.

The power outage triggered alarms at the central monitoring station inside the campus security complex, but no one was paying attention. There was an active gunman on the loose. There was no time to worry about other alarms.

Jerry had spent two nights inside the Firestone Library in the past week and was confident there were no guards stationed within the building while it was closed. During the night, a uniformed officer walked around the building once or twice, shined his flashlight at the doors, and kept walking. A marked patrol car made its rounds too, but it was primarily concerned with drunk students. Generally, the campus was like any other—dead between the hours of 1:00 and 8:00 a.m.

On this night, however, Princeton was in the midst of a frantic emergency as America's finest were being shot. Trey reported to his gang that the scene was total chaos with cops scrambling about, SWAT boys throwing on their gear, sirens screaming, radios squawking, and a million red and blue emergency lights flashing. Smoke hung by the trees like a fog. A helicopter could be heard hovering somewhere close. Total chaos.

Denny, Jerry, and Mark hustled through the dark and took the stairs down to the basement under Special Collections. Each wore night vision goggles and a miner's lamp strapped to his forehead. Each carried a heavy backpack, and Jerry hauled a small Army duffel he'd hidden in the library two nights earlier. At the third and final level down, they stopped at a thick metal door, blacked out the surveillance cameras, and waited for Ahmed and his magic. Calmly, he worked his way through the library's alarm system and deactivated the door's four sensors. There was a loud clicking noise. Denny pressed down on the handle and pulled the door open. Inside they found a narrow square of space with two more metal doors. Using a flashlight, Mark scanned the ceiling and spotted a surveillance camera. "There," he said. "Only one." Jerry, the tallest at six feet three inches, took a small can of black paint and sprayed the lens of the camera.

Denny looked at the two doors and said, "Wanna flip a coin?"

"What do you see?" Ahmed asked from Buffalo.

"Two metal doors, identical," Denny replied.

"I got nothing here, fellas," Ahmed replied. "There's nothing in the system beyond the first door. Start cutting."

From his duffel Jerry removed two eighteen-inch canisters, one filled with oxygen, the other with acetylene. Denny situated himself before the door on the left, lit a cutting torch with a sparker, and began heating a spot six inches above the keyhole and latch. Within seconds, sparks were flying.

Meanwhile, Trey had drifted away from the chaos around McCarren and was hiding in the blackness across the street from the library. Sirens were screaming as more emergency vehicles responded. Helicopters were thumping the air loudly above the campus, though Trey could not see them. Around him, even the streetlights were out. There was not another soul near the library. All hands were needed elsewhere.

"All's quiet outside the library," he reported. "Any progress?"

"We're cutting now," came the terse reply from Mark. All five members knew that chatter should be limited. Denny slowly and skillfully cut through the metal with the torch tip that emitted eight hundred degrees of oxygenated heat. Minutes passed as molten metal dripped to the floor and red and yellow sparks flew from the door. At one point Denny said, "It's an inch thick." He finished the top edge of the square and began cutting straight down. The work was slow, the minutes dragged on, and the tension mounted but they kept their cool. Jerry and Mark crouched behind Denny, watching his every move. When the bottom cut line was finished, Denny rattled the latch and it came loose, though something hung. "It's a bolt," he said. "I'll cut it."

Five minutes later, the door swung open. Ahmed, staring at his laptop, noticed nothing unusual from the library's security system. "Nothing here," he said. Denny, Mark, and Jerry entered the room and immediately filled it. A narrow table, two feet wide at most, ran the length, about ten feet. Four large wooden drawers covered one side; four on the other. Mark, the lock picker, flipped up his goggles, adjusted his headlight, and inspected one of the locks. He shook his head and said, "No surprise. Combination locks, probably with computerized codes that change every day. There's no way to pick it. We gotta drill."

"Go for it," Denny said. "Start drilling and I'll cut the other door."

Jerry produced a three-quarter drive battery-powered drill with bracing bars on both sides. He zeroed in on the lock and he and Mark applied as much pressure as possible. The drill whined and slid off the brass, which at first seemed impenetrable. But a shaving spun off, then another, and as the men shoved the bracing bars the drill bit ground deeper into the lock. When it gave way the drawer still would not open. Mark managed to slide a thin pry bar into the gap above the lock and yanked down violently. The wood frame split and the drawer opened. Inside was an archival storage box with black metal edges, seventeen inches by twenty-two and three inches deep.

"Careful," Jerry said as Mark opened the box and gently lifted a thin hardback volume. Mark read slowly, "The collected poems of Dolph McKenzie. Just what I always wanted."

"Who the hell?"

"Don't know but we ain't here for poetry."

Denny entered behind them and said, "Okay, get on with it. Seven more drawers in here. I'm almost inside the other room."

They returned to their labors as Trey casually smoked a cigarette on a park bench across the street and glanced repeatedly at his watch. The frenzy across the campus showed no signs of dying down, but it wouldn't last forever.

The second and third drawers in the first room revealed more rare books by authors unknown to the gang. When Denny finished cutting his way into the second room, he told Jerry and Mark to bring the drill. This room, too, had eight large drawers, seemingly identical to the first room. At 2:15, Trey checked in with a report that the campus was still in lockdown, but curious students were beginning to gather on the lawn in front of McCarren to watch the show. Police with bullhorns had ordered them back to their rooms, but there were too many to handle. At least two news helicopters were hovering and complicating things. He was watching CNN on his smart phone and the Princeton story was *the* story at the moment. A frantic reporter "on the scene" continually referred to "unconfirmed casualties," and managed to convey the impression that numerous students had been shot "by at least one gunman."

"At least one gunman?" Trey mumbled. Doesn't every shooting require at least one gunman?

Denny, Mark, and Jerry discussed the idea of cutting into the drawers with the blowtorch, but decided against it, for the moment anyway. The risk of fire would be high, and what good would the manuscripts be if they were damaged. Instead, Denny pulled out a smaller one-quarter drive drill and began drilling. Mark and Jerry bored away with the larger one. The first drawer in the second room produced stacks of delicate papers handwritten by another long-forgotten poet, one they'd never heard of but hated nonetheless.

At 2:30, CNN confirmed that two students were dead and at least two more were injured. The word "carnage" was introduced.

5.

When the second floor of McCarren was secured, the police noticed the remnants of what appeared to be firecrackers. The empty smoke bomb canisters were found in the restroom and the shower. Trey's abandoned backpack was opened by a demolition crew and the spent smoke bomb was removed. At 3:10, the commander first mentioned the word "prank," but the adrenaline was still pumping so fast no one thought of the word "diversion."

The rest of McCarren was quickly secured and all students were accounted for. The campus was still locked down and would remain so for hours as the nearby buildings were searched.

6.

At 3:30, Trey reported, "Things seem to be settling down out here. Three hours in, fellas, how's the drilling?"

"Slow," came the one-word response from Denny.

Inside the vault, the work was indeed slow, but determined. The first four opened drawers revealed more old manuscripts, some handwritten, some typed, all by important writers who didn't matter at the moment. They finally struck gold in the fifth drawer when Denny removed an archival storage box identical to the others. He carefully opened it. A reference page inserted by the library read, "Original Handwritten Manuscript of The Beautiful and Damned—F. Scott Fitzgerald."

"Bingo," Denny said calmly. He removed two identical boxes from the fifth drawer, delicately placed them on the narrow table, and opened them. Inside were original manuscripts of Tender Is the Night and The Last Tycoon.

Ahmed, still glued to his laptop and now drinking a highly caffeinated energy drink, heard the beautiful words: "Okay, boys, we have three out of five. *Gatsby's* here somewhere, along with *Paradise*."

Trey asked, "How much longer?"

"Twenty minutes," Denny said. "Get the van."

Trey casually strode across the campus, mixed in with a crowd of the curious, and watched for a moment as the small army of policemen milled about. They were no longer ducking, covering, running, and dashing behind cars with loaded weapons. The danger had clearly passed, though the area was still ablaze with flashing lights. Trey eased away, walked half a mile, left the campus, and stopped at John Street, where he got into a white cargo van with the words "Princeton University Printing" stenciled on both front doors. It was number 12, whatever that meant, and it was very similar to a van Trey had photographed a week earlier. He drove it back onto campus, avoided the commotion around McCarren, and parked it by a loading ramp at the rear of the library. "Van in place," he reported.

"We're just opening the sixth drawer," Denny replied.

As Jerry and Mark flipped up their goggles and moved their lights closer to the table, Denny gently opened the archival storage box. Its reference sheet read, "Original Handwritten Manuscript of The Great Gatsby—F. Scott Fitzgerald."

"Bingo," he said calmly. "We got Gatsby, that old son of a bitch."

"Whoopee," Mark said, though their excitement was thoroughly contained. Jerry lifted out the only other box in the drawer. It was the manuscript for *This Side of Paradise*, Fitzgerald's first novel, published in 1920.

"We have all five," Denny said calmly. "Let's get outta here."

Jerry repacked the drills, the cutting torch, the canisters of oxygen and acetylene, and the pry bars. As he bent to lift the duffel, a piece of the splintered wood from the third drawer nicked him above his left wrist. In the excitement, he barely noticed and just rubbed it for a split second as he removed his backpack. Denny and Mark carefully placed the five priceless manuscripts into their three student backpacks. The thieves hustled from the vault, laden with their loot and tools, and scampered up the stairs to the main floor. They left the library through a service entrance near a delivery ramp, one hidden from view by a thick, long hedge. They jumped through the rear doors of the van and Trey pulled away from the ramp. As he did so, he passed two campus security guards in a patrol car. He flicked a casual wave; they did not respond.

Trey noted the time: 3:42 a.m. He reported, "All clear, leaving the campus now with Mr. Gatsby and friends."

7.

The power outage triggered several alarms in the affected buildings. By 4:00 a.m., an electrical engineer had worked his way through the school's computer grid and found the problem. Electricity was restored in all buildings except the library. The chief of security sent three officers to the library. It took them ten minutes to find the cause of the alarm.

By then, the gang had stopped at a cheap motel off Interstate 295 near Philadelphia. Trey parked the van beside an 18-wheeler and away from the lone camera monitoring the parking lot. Mark took a can of white spray paint and covered the "Princeton University Printing" on both of the van's doors. In a room where he and Trey had stayed the night before, the men quickly changed into hunting outfits and crammed everything they'd worn for the job—jeans, sneakers, sweatshirts, black gloves—into another duffel. In the bathroom, Jerry noticed the small cut on his left wrist. He had kept a thumb on it during the ride and noted that there was more blood than he'd realized. He wiped it clean with a bath cloth and debated whether to mention it to the others. Not now, maybe later.

They quietly removed all their stuff from the room, turned off the lights, and left. Mark and Jerry got into a pickup truck—a fancy club cab leased and driven by Denny—and they followed Trey and the van out of the parking lot, onto the street, then back onto the interstate. They skirted the northern edge of the Philadelphia suburbs, and, using state highways, disappeared into the Pennsylvania countryside. Near Quakertown, they found the county road they had chosen and followed it for a mile until it turned to gravel. There were no houses in the area. Trey parked the van in a shallow ravine; removed the stolen license plates; poured a gallon of gasoline over their bags filled with tools, cell phones, radio equipment, and clothing; and lit a match. The fireball was instant, and as they drove away in the pickup they were confident they had destroyed all possible evidence. The manuscripts were safely tucked between Trey and Mark on the rear seat of the pickup.

As daylight slowly crept over the hills, they rode in silence, each of the four observing everything around them, which was very little. An occasional vehicle passing in the other direction, a farmer headed to his barn and not looking at the highway, an old woman collecting a cat off the front porch. Near Bethlehem, they merged onto Interstate 78 and headed west. Denny stayed well under the speed limit. They had not seen a police car since leaving the Princeton campus. They stopped at a drive-thru for chicken biscuits and coffee, then headed north on Interstate 81 toward the Scranton area.

8.

The first pair of FBI agents arrived at the Firestone Library just after 7:00 a.m. They were briefed by campus security and the Princeton city police. They took a look at the crime scene and suggested strongly that the library remain closed indefinitely. Investigators and technicians from the Trenton office were hurrying to the school.

The president of the university had just returned to his home on campus, after a very long night, when he got the news that some valuables were missing. He raced to the library, where he met with the chief librarian, the FBI, and the local police. Together, they made the decision to keep a lid on the story for as long as possible. The head of the FBI's Rare Asset Recovery Unit in

Washington was on the way, and it was his opinion that the thieves might contact the school quickly and want a deal. Publicity, and there would be an avalanche of it, would only complicate matters.

9.

The celebration was postponed until the four hunters arrived at the cabin, deep in the Poconos. Denny had leased the small A-frame for the hunting season, with funds that would be repaid when they cashed in, and had been living there for two months. Of the four, only Jerry had a permanent address. He'd been renting a small apartment with his girlfriend in Rochester, New York. Trey, as an escapee, had been living on the run most of his adult life. Mark lived part-time with an ex-wife near Baltimore, but there were no records to prove it.

All four had multiple forms of fake identification, including passports that would fool any customs agent.

Three bottles of cheap champagne were in the fridge. Denny opened one, emptied it into four mismatched coffee cups, and offered a hearty "Cheers, boys, and congratulations. We did it!" The three bottles were gone in half an hour and the weary hunters fell into long naps. The manuscripts, still in the identical archival storage boxes, were stacked like bricks of gold in a gun safe in a storage room, where they would be guarded by Denny and Trey for the next few days. Tomorrow, Jerry and Mark would drift back home, exhausted from a long week in the woods hunting deer.

10.

While Jerry slept, the full weight and fury of the federal government was moving rapidly against him. An FBI technician noticed a tiny spot on the first step of the stairway leading to and from the library's vault. She thought, correctly, that it was a drop of blood and that it had not been there long enough to turn dark maroon, almost black. She gathered it, told her supervisor, and the sample was rushed to an FBI lab in Philadelphia. DNA testing was done immediately, and the results were rammed into the national data bank. In less than an hour, it tagged a match in Massachusetts: one Gerald A. Steengarden, a paroled felon convicted seven years earlier of stealing paintings from an art dealer in Boston. A squad of analysts worked feverishly to find any trace of Mr. Steengarden. There were at least five in the U.S. Four were quickly eliminated. Search warrants for the apartment, cell phone records, and credit card records of the fifth Mr. Steengarden were obtained. When Jerry woke up from his long nap deep in the Poconos, the FBI was already watching his apartment in Rochester. The decision was made not to go in with a warrant, but to watch and wait.

Maybe, just maybe, Mr. Steengarden would lead them to the others.

Back at Princeton, lists were being made of all students who had used the library in the past week. Their

ID cards recorded each visit to any of the libraries on campus. The fake ones stood out because in college fake IDs were used for the underage purchase of alcohol, not to sneak into libraries. The exact times of their use were determined, then matched against video footage from the library's surveillance cameras. By noon the FBI had clear images of Denny, Jerry, and Mark, though these would prove to be of little value at the moment. All were well disguised.

In Rare Books and Special Collections, old Ed Folk snapped into high gear for the first time in decades. Surrounded by FBI agents, he raced through the log-in registers and security photos of his recent visitors. Each one was called for verification, and when Adjunct Professor Neville Manchin at Portland State spoke to the FBI he assured them he had never been near the Princeton campus. The FBI had a clear photo of Mark, though they did not know his real name.

Less than twelve hours after the heist was successfully completed, forty FBI agents were grinding away, poring over videos and analyzing data.

11.

Late in the afternoon, the four hunters gathered around a card table and opened beers. Denny rambled on and covered ground they had gone over a dozen times. The heist was over, it was a success, but in any crime clues are left behind. Mistakes are always made, and if you can think of half of them, then you're a genius. The fake IDs would soon be discovered and picked over. The cops would know they had cased the library for days before the heist. Who knew how much damning video footage existed? There could be fibers from their clothing, prints from their sneakers, and so on. They were confident they'd left no fingerprints behind, but there was always that possibility. The four were seasoned thieves and they knew all this.

The small Band-Aid above Jerry's left wrist had not been noticed, and he had decided to ignore it too. He had convinced himself it was of no consequence.

Mark produced four devices identical to the Apple iPhone 5, complete with the company's logo, but they were not phones. Instead, they were known as Sat-Traks, tracking devices tied to a satellite system with instant coverage anywhere in the world. There was no cell phone network, no way for the cops to track them or eavesdrop in any way. Mark explained, again, that it was imperative for the four, plus Ahmed, to remain in constant contact over the next few weeks. Ahmed had obtained the devices from one of his many sources. There was no on/off switch, but instead a three-digit code to activate the Sat-Traks. Once the device was turned on, each user punched in his own five-digit password to gain access. Twice each day, at exactly 8:00 a.m. and 8:00 p.m., the five would hook up through the devices with the simple message of "Clear." Delays were inexcusable and perhaps catastrophic. A delay meant the Sat-Trak, and especially its user, had been compromised in some manner. A delay of fifteen minutes activated Plan B, which called for Denny and Trey to grab the manuscripts and move to a second safe house. If either Denny or Trey failed to report, the entire operation, or what was left of it, was to be aborted. Jerry, Mark, and Ahmed were to leave the country immediately.

Bad news was transmitted by the simple message "Red." "Red" meant, with no questions asked and no time for delay, that (1) something has gone wrong, (2) if possible get the manuscripts to the third safe house, and (3) by all means get out of the country as quickly as possible.

If anyone was nabbed by the cops, silence was expected. The five had memorized the names of family members and their addresses to ensure complete loyalty to the cause and to each other. Retaliation was guaranteed. No one would talk. Ever.

As ominous as these preparations were, the mood was still light, even celebratory. They had pulled off a brilliant crime and made a perfect escape.

Trey, the serial escapee, relished telling his stories. He was successful because he had a plan after each escape, whereas most guys spent their time thinking only of getting out. Same with a crime. You spend days and weeks planning and plotting, then when it's done you're not sure what to do next. They needed a plan.

But they couldn't agree on one. Denny and Mark favored the quick strike, which entailed making contact with Princeton within a week and demanding a ransom. They could get rid of the manuscripts and not have to worry about protecting and moving them, and they could get their cash.

Jerry and Trey, with more experience, favored a patient approach. Let the dust settle; let the reality set in as word crept through the black market; allow some time to pass so they could be certain they were not suspects. Princeton was not the only possible buyer. Indeed, there would be others.

The discussion was long and often tense, but also punctuated with jokes and laughter and no shortage of beer. They finally agreed on a temporary plan. Jerry and Mark would leave the following morning for home: Jerry to Rochester, Mark to Baltimore by way of Rochester. They would lie low and watch the news for the next week, and of course check in with the team twice a day. Denny and Trey would handle the manuscripts and move them in a week or so to the second safe house, a cheap apartment in a grungy section of Allentown, Pennsylvania. In ten days, they would reunite with Jerry and Mark at the safe house, and the four would hammer out a definite plan. In the meantime, Mark would contact a potential middleman he had known for many years, a player in the shady world of stolen art and artifacts. Speaking in the hushed code of the trade, he would let it be known that he knew something about the Fitzgerald manuscripts. But nothing more would be said until they met again.

12.

Carole, the woman living in Jerry's apartment, left at 4:30, alone. She was followed to a grocery store a few blocks away. The quick decision was made not to enter the apartment, not at that time. There were too many neighbors nearby. One word from one of them and their surveillance could be compromised. Carole had no idea how closely she was being watched. While she shopped, agents placed two tracking devices inside the bumpers of her car. Two more agents—females in jogging suits—monitored what she purchased (nothing of interest). When she texted her mother, the text was read and recorded. When she called her friend, agents listened to every word. When she stopped at a bar an agent in jeans offered to buy her a drink. When she returned home just after 9:00, every step was watched, filmed, and recorded.

13.

Meanwhile, her boyfriend sipped beer and read *The Great Gatsby* in a hammock on the rear porch, with the beautiful pond just a few feet away. Mark and Trey were out there in a boat, quietly fishing for bream, while Denny tended to the steaks on the grill. At sunset, a cold wind arrived and the four hunters gathered in the den, where a fire was crackling away. At precisely 8:00 p.m., they pulled out their new Sat-Traks and punched in their codes, everybody pecked in the word "Clear," including Ahmed in Buffalo, and life was secure.

Life was indeed good. Less than twenty-four hours earlier, they were on the campus, hiding in the dark, nervous as hell but also loving the thrill of the chase. Their plan had worked to perfection, they had the priceless manuscripts, and soon they would have the cash. That transfer would not be easy, but they would deal with it later.

14.

The booze helped but sleep was difficult, for all four of them. Early the following morning, as Denny cooked eggs and bacon and guzzled black coffee, Mark sat at the counter with a laptop, scanning headlines from up and down the East Coast. "Nothing," he said. "Plenty of stuff about the ruckus on campus, now officially labeled as a prank, but not a word about the manuscripts."

"I'm sure they're trying to keep it quiet," Denny said.

"Yes, but for how long?"

"Not long at all. You can't keep the press away from a story like this. There'll be a leak today or tomorrow."

"Can't decide if that's good or bad."

"Neither."

Trey walked into the kitchen, with a freshly shaved head. He rubbed it proudly and said, "What do you think?"

"Gorgeous," said Mark.

"Nothing helps," said Denny.

None of the four looked the same as they had twenty-four hours earlier. Trey and Mark had shaved everything—beard, hair, eyebrows. Denny and Jerry had lost their beards but changed hair colors. Denny had gone from sandy blond to dark brown. Jerry was a soft ginger. All four would be wearing caps and glasses that changed daily. They knew they had been captured on video and they knew about the FBI's facial recognition technology and its capabilities. They had made mistakes, but their efforts to remember them were rapidly diminishing. It was time to get on with the next phase.

There was also a cockiness that was the natural after-effect of such a perfect crime. They had first met a year earlier, when Trey and Jerry, the two felons and the most experienced, had been introduced to Denny, who knew Mark, who knew Ahmed. They had spent hours planning and plotting, arguing about who would do what, and when was the best time, and where would they go afterward. A hundred details, some huge, some tiny, but all crucial. Now that the heist was over, all that was history. Before them now lay only the task of collecting the money.

At 8:00 a.m. Thursday, they watched each other go through the Sat-Trak ritual. Ahmed was alive and well. All present and accounted for. Jerry and Mark said good-bye and drove away from the cabin, away from the Poconos, and four hours later entered the outskirts of Rochester. They had no way of knowing the sheer number of FBI agents patiently waiting and watching for the 2010 Toyota pickup truck leased three months earlier. When Jerry parked it near his apartment, hidden cameras zoomed in on him and Mark as they nonchalantly walked across the parking lot and climbed the stairs to the third floor.

The digital photos were instantly streamed to the FBI lab in Trenton. By the time Jerry kissed Carole hello the photos had been matched to the frozen shots taken from the Princeton library surveillance videos. The FBI's imaging technology nailed Jerry, or Mr. Gerald A. Steengarden, and it verified the identity of Mark as the imposter who borrowed the name of Professor Neville

Manchin. Since Mark had no criminal record, he had no data in the national crime network. The FBI knew he was in the library; they just didn't know his name.

But it wouldn't take long.

The decision was made to watch and wait. Jerry had already delivered Mark; perhaps he could give them another one. After lunch, the two left the apartment and returned to the Toyota. Mark was carrying a cheap maroon nylon gym bag. Jerry was carrying nothing. They headed downtown and Jerry drove at a leisurely pace, careful to obey all traffic laws and steer clear of any policemen.

15.

They were watching everything. Every car, every face, every old man sitting on a park bench hiding behind a newspaper. They were certain they were not being followed, but in their business one never rested. They could neither see nor hear the helicopter hovering benignly in the distance, following them three thousand feet in the air.

At the Amtrak station, Mark got out of the truck without a word, grabbed his bag from the back, and hustled along the sidewalk to the entrance. Inside, he bought an economy ticket for the 2:13 train to Penn Station in Manhattan. As he waited, he read an old paperback edition of *The Last Tycoon*. He was not much of a reader but was suddenly obsessing over Fitzgerald. He suppressed a grin when he thought of the handwritten manuscript and where it was now hidden.

Jerry stopped at a liquor store for a bottle of vodka. As he left the store, three rather large young men in dark suits stepped in front of him, said hello, flashed their badges, and said they'd like to talk. Jerry said no thanks. He had things to do. So did they. One produced some handcuffs, another took the vodka, and the third went through his pockets and removed his wallet, keys, and Sat-Trak. Jerry was escorted to a long black Suburban and driven to the city jail less than four blocks away. During the short drive, no one said a word. He was placed in an empty cell, again without a word. He didn't ask; they didn't offer. When a city jailer stopped by to say hello, Jerry said, "Say, man, any idea what's going on here?"

The jailer looked up and down the hall, leaned closer to the bars, and said, "Don't know, pal, but you have sure pissed off the big boys." As Jerry stretched out on the bunk in the dark cell, he stared at the dirty ceiling and asked himself if this was really happening. How in hell? What went wrong?

As the room spun around him, Carole answered the front door and was greeted by half a dozen agents. One produced a search warrant. One told her to leave the apartment and go sit in her car but not to start the engine.

Mark boarded the train at 2:00 and took a seat. The doors closed at 2:13, but the train didn't move. At 2:30, the doors opened and two men in matching navy trench coats stepped on board and looked sternly at him. At that awful moment, Mark knew things were deteriorating.

They quietly identified themselves and asked him to

step off the train. One led him by the elbow while the other grabbed his bag from the overhead rack. Driving to the jail, they said nothing. Bored with silence, Mark asked, "So, fellas, am I under arrest?"

Without turning around, the driver said, "We don't normally put handcuffs on random civilians."

"Okay. And what am I being arrested for?"

"They'll explain things at the jail."

"I thought you boys had to name the charges when you read me my rights."

"You're not much of a criminal, are you? We don't have to read you your rights until we start asking questions. Right now we're just trying to enjoy some peace and quiet."

Mark clammed up and watched the traffic. He assumed they had nabbed Jerry; otherwise they would not have known he, Mark, was at the train station. Was it possible they had grabbed Jerry and he was already spilling his guts and cutting deals? Surely not.

Jerry had not said a word, had not been given the chance. At 5:15, he was fetched from the jail and taken to the FBI office a few blocks away. He was led to an interrogation room and placed at a table. His handcuffs were removed and he was given a cup of coffee. An agent named McGregor entered, took off his jacket, took a seat, and began chatting. He was a friendly type and eventually got around to the *Miranda* warnings.

"Been arrested before?" McGregor asked.

Jerry had in fact, and because of this experience he knew that his pal McGregor here had a copy of his rap sheet. "Yes," he said.

"How many times?"

"Look, Mr. Agent. You just told me I have the right to remain silent. I ain't saying a word and I want a lawyer right now. Got it?"

McGregor said, "Sure," and left the room.

Around the corner, Mark was being situated in another room. McGregor walked in and went through the same ritual. They sipped coffee for a while and talked about the *Miranda* rights. With a warrant, they had searched Mark's bag and found all sorts of interesting items. McGregor opened a large envelope, pulled out some plastic cards, and began arranging them on the table. He said, "Got these from your wallet, Mr. Mark Driscoll. Maryland driver's license, bad photo but with plenty of hair and even eyebrows, two valid credit cards, temporary hunting license issued by Pennsylvania." More cards for the display. "And we got these from your bag. Kentucky driver's license issued to Arnold Sawyer, again with lots of hair. One bogus credit card." He slowly produced more cards. "Bogus Florida driver's license, eyeglasses and beard. Mr. Luther Banahan. And this really high-quality passport issued in Houston to Clyde D. Mazy, along with driver's license and three bogus credit cards."

The table was covered. Mark wanted to vomit but clenched his jaws and tried to shrug. So what?

McGregor said, "Pretty impressive. We've checked them out and we know you're really Mr. Driscoll, address uncertain because you move around."

"Is that a question?"

"No, not yet."

"Good, because I'm not saying anything. I have the right to a lawyer, so you'd better find me one."

"Okay. Odd that in all these photos you got plenty of hair, even some whiskers, and always the eyebrows. Now everything's gone. You hiding from something, Mark?"

"I want a lawyer."

"Sure thing. Say, Mark, we haven't found any papers for Professor Neville Manchin, from out at Portland State. Name ring a bell?"

A bell? What about a sledgehammer to the head?

Through one-way glass, a high-resolution camera was aimed at Mark. In another room, two interrogation experts, both trained in the detection of untruthful suspects and witnesses, were watching the pupils of the eyes, the upper lip, the muscles in the jaw, the position of the head. The mention of Neville Manchin jolted the suspect. When Mark responded with a lame "Uh, I ain't talking, and I want a lawyer," both experts nodded and smiled. Got him.

McGregor left the room, chatted with his colleagues, then entered Jerry's room. He sat down, smiled, waited a long time, and said, "So, Jerry, still not talking, huh?"

"I want a lawyer."

"Sure, right, we're trying to find you one. Not very talkative, are you?"

"I want a lawyer."

"Your buddy Mark is far more cooperative than you are."

Jerry swallowed hard. He was hoping Mark had managed to leave town on the Amtrak. Guess not. What the hell happened? How could they get caught so quickly? This time yesterday they were sitting around the cabin playing cards, drinking beer, savoring their perfect crime.

Surely Mark was not already singing.

McGregor pointed to Jerry's left hand and asked, "You got a Band-Aid there. Cut yourself?"

"I want a lawyer."

"You need a doctor?"

"A lawyer."

"Okay, okay. I'll go find you a lawyer."

He slammed the door as he left. Jerry looked at his wrist. It couldn't be possible.

16.

Shadows fell across the pond, and Denny reeled in his line and began paddling toward the cabin. As the chill off the water cut through his light jacket, he thought about Trey, and, frankly, how little he trusted him. Trey was forty-one years old, had been caught twice with his stolen goods, served four years the first time before escaping and two years the second time before going over the wall. What was so troubling about Trey was that in both cases he'd flipped, sang, ratted on his buddies for lesser sentences. For a professional, that was a cardinal sin.

Of the five in their gang, there was no doubt in Denny's mind that Trey was the weakest. As a Ranger, Denny had fought in wars and survived the gun battles. He'd lost friends and killed many. He understood fear. What he hated was weakness.

17.

At eight o'clock Thursday evening, Denny and Trey were playing gin rummy and drinking beer. They stopped, pulled out their Sat-Traks, pecked in their numbers, and waited. Within seconds, Ahmed chimed in with a "Clear" from Buffalo. Nothing from Mark or Jerry. Mark was supposed to be on a train, enduring the six-hour ride from Rochester to Penn Station. Jerry was supposed to be in his apartment.

The next five minutes passed very slowly, or perhaps they raced by. Things weren't clear. The devices were working, right? They were CIA quality and cost a fortune. For two to go silent at the same time meant . . . well, what did it mean? At 8:06, Denny stood and said, "Let's take the first few steps. Pack our bags with the essentials and plan to haul ass, okay?"

"Got it," Trey replied, obviously concerned. They ran to their rooms and began throwing clothes into duffel bags. A few minutes later, Denny said, "It's eleven minutes after eight. I say at eight-twenty, we're outta here. Right?"

"Agreed," Trey said as he paused to look at his Sat-Trak. Nothing. At 8:20, Denny opened the storage room door and unlocked the gun safe. They stuffed the five manuscripts into two green Army duffels padded with clothing, and carried them to Denny's truck. They returned to the cabin to turn off lights and make one last frantic inspection.

"Should we burn it?" Trey asked.

"Hell no," Denny snapped, irritated at his stupidity.

"That'll just attract attention. So they prove we were here. Big deal. We're long gone and there's no sign of the books."

They turned off the lights, locked both doors, and as they stepped off the porch Denny hesitated a second so Trey could move a step ahead. Then he sprung, slapping both hands tightly around Trey's neck, his thumbs jammed into the carotid pressure points. Trey—older, slightly built, out of shape, and unsuspecting—was no match for the ex-Ranger's death grip around his neck. He wiggled and flailed for a few seconds, then went limp. Denny tossed him to the ground and took off his belt.

18.

He stopped for gas and coffee near Scranton and headed west on Interstate 80. The speed limit was seventy miles per hour. His cruise control was on sixty-eight. He'd had a few beers earlier in the evening but all was clear now. His Sat-Trak was on the console and he glanced at it every mile or so. He knew by now that the screen would remain dark; no one would be checking in. He assumed Mark and Jerry had been nabbed together and their Sat-Traks were being taken apart by some very smart people. Trey's was at the bottom of the pond, along with Trey, both waterlogged and already decomposing.

If he, Denny, could survive the next twenty-four hours and get out of the country, the fortune would be his and his alone.

At an all-night pancake house he parked close to the front door and took a table with his truck in sight. He opened his laptop, ordered coffee, asked about Wi-Fi. The girl said of course and gave him the password. He decided to stay for a spell and ordered waffles and bacon. Online he checked flights out of Pittsburgh, and booked one to Chicago, and from there a nonstop to Mexico City. He searched for storage units that were climate controlled and made a list. He ate slowly, ordered more coffee, killed as much time as possible. He pulled up the *New York Times* and was startled by the lead story, one posted about four hours earlier. The headline read, "Princeton Confirms Theft of Fitzgerald Manuscripts."

After a day of offering no comments and suspicious denials, officials at the university had finally issued a statement confirming the rumors. On the previous Tuesday night, thieves had broken into the Firestone Library while the campus was responding to 911 reports of an active gunman. It was evidently a diversion, and one that worked. The university would not disclose how much of its Fitzgerald collection had been stolen, only that it was "substantial." The FBI was investigating, and so on. Details were scarce.

There was no mention of Mark and Jerry. Denny was suddenly anxious and wanted to hit the road. He paid his check, and as he left the restaurant he dropped his Sat-Trak into a waste can outside the front door. There were no more ties to the past. He was alone and free and excited about the turn of events, but also nervous now that the news was breaking. Getting out of the country was imperative. That was not what he had planned, but things could not be lining up more perfectly. Plans—

nothing ever goes as planned, and the survivors are the ones who can adapt on the fly.

Trey was trouble. He would have quickly become a nuisance, then baggage, then a liability. Denny thought of him only in passing now. As darkness began to dissipate and he entered the northern sprawl of Pittsburgh, Denny slammed the door on any memory of Trey. Another perfect crime.

At 9:00 a.m. he walked into the office of the East Mills Secured Storage operation in the Pittsburgh suburb of Oakmont. He explained to the clerk that he needed to store some fine wine for a few months and was looking for a small space where the temperature and humidity were controlled and monitored. The clerk showed him a twelve-by-twelve unit on the ground floor. The rate was $250 a month for a minimum of a year. Denny said no thanks, he wouldn't need the space for that long. They agreed on $300 a month for six months. He produced a New Jersey driver's license, signed the contract in the name of Paul Rafferty, and paid in cash. He took the key back to the storage unit, unlocked it, set the temperature on fifty-five degrees and the humidity at 40 percent, and turned off the light. He walked the hallways taking note of the surveillance cameras and eventually left without being seen by the clerk.

At 10:00 a.m. the discount wine warehouse opened, and Denny was its first customer of the day. He paid cash for four cases of rotgut chardonnay, talked the clerk out of two empty cardboard boxes, and left the store. He drove around for half an hour looking for a spot to hide, away from traffic and surveillance cameras. He ran his truck through a cheap car wash and parked by the vacuum machines. *This Side of Paradise* and *The Beautiful and Damned* fit nicely in one of the empty wine boxes. *Tender Is the Night* and *The Last Tycoon* were placed in another. Gatsby got a box of his own, once the twelve bottles were removed and left on the rear seat.

By eleven o'clock, Denny had hauled the six boxes inside the storage unit at East Mills. As he left, he bumped into the clerk and said he'd be back tomorrow with some more wine. Fine, whatever, the clerk couldn't care less. As he drove away, he passed rows and rows of storage units and wondered what other stolen loot could be hidden behind those doors. Probably a lot, but nothing as valuable as his.

He drifted through downtown Pittsburgh and finally found a rough section. He parked in front of a pharmacy, one with thick bars over the windows. He rolled down his windows, left the keys in the ignition, left twelve bottles of bad wine on the rear floorboard, grabbed his bag, and walked away. It was almost noon, on a clear and bright fall day, and he felt relatively safe. He found a pay phone, called a cab, and waited outside a soul food café. Forty-five minutes later, the cab dropped him off at the Departures ramp at Pittsburgh International Airport. He picked up his ticket, eased through security without a hitch, and walked to a coffee shop near his gate. At a newsstand he bought a *New York Times* and a *Washington Post*. On the front page of the *Post*, below the fold, the headline yelled at him, "Two Arrested in Princeton Library Heist." No photos and no names were given, and it was obvious Princeton and the FBI were trying to control the story. According to the brief article, the two men were picked up in Rochester the day before.

The search was on for others "involved in the spectacular burglary."

19.

While Denny waited for his flight to Chicago, Ahmed caught a flight from Buffalo to Toronto, where he booked a one-way flight to Amsterdam. With four hours to kill, he parked himself at the bar in an airport lounge, hid his face behind a menu, and started drinking.

20.

The following Monday, Mark Driscoll and Gerald Steengarden waived extradition and were driven to Trenton, New Jersey. They appeared before a federal magistrate, swore in writing that they had no assets, and were assigned counsel. Because of their affinity for fake documents, they were deemed flight risks and denied bail.

Another week passed, then a month, and the investigation began losing steam. What at first had looked so promising gradually began to look hopeless. Other than the drop of blood and the photos of the well-disguised thieves, and of course the missing manuscripts, there was no evidence. The burned-out van, their escape vehicle, was found but no one knew where it came from. Denny's rented pickup was stolen, stripped, and devoured by a chop shop. He went from Mexico City to Panama, where he had friends who knew how to hide.

The evidence was clear that Jerry and Mark had used fake student IDs to visit the library several times. Mark had even posed as a Fitzgerald scholar. On the night of the theft, it was clear the two had entered the library, along with a third accomplice, but there was no indication of when or how they left.

Without the stolen goods, the U.S. Attorney delayed the indictment. Attorneys for Jerry and Mark moved to dismiss the charges, but the judge refused. They stayed in jail, without bail, and without saying a word. The silence held. Three months after the theft, the U.S. Attorney offered Mark the deal of all deals: spill your guts and walk away. With no criminal record, and with no DNA from the crime scene, Mark was the better choice to deal with. Just talk and you're a free man.

He declined for two reasons. First, his lawyer assured him the government would have difficulty proving a case at trial, and because of this he would probably continue to dodge an indictment. Second, and more important, Denny and Trey were out there. That meant the manuscripts were well hidden, and it also meant that retaliation was likely. Furthermore, even if Mark gave them Denny's and Trey's full names, the FBI would have trouble finding them. Obviously, Mark had no idea where the manuscripts were. He knew the locations of the second and third safe houses, but he also knew that in all likelihood they had not been used.

21.

All trails became dead ends. Tips that had at first seemed urgent now faded away. The waiting game began. Whoever had the manuscripts would want money, and a lot of it. They would surface eventually, but where and when, and how much would they want?

CHAPTER TWO
THE DEALER

1.

When Bruce Cable was twenty-three years old, and still classified as a junior at Auburn, his father died suddenly. The two had been feuding over Bruce's lack of academic progress, and things had gotten so bad that Mr. Cable had threatened more than once to cut young Bruce out of his will. Some ancient relative had made a fortune in gravel, and, following bad legal advice, had set up a scheme of misguided and complicated trusts that had strewn money over generations of undeserving kinfolks. The family had for years lived behind the facade of fine wealth while watching it slowly drip away. Threatening to modify wills and trusts was a favorite ploy used against the young, and it had never worked.

Mr. Cable, though, died before he made it to his lawyer's office, so Bruce woke up one day with the promise of a quick $300,000, a beautiful windfall but not quite retirement money. He thought about investing it, and doing so conservatively might net him an annual return of between 5 and 10 percent, hardly enough to sustain the lifestyle Bruce was suddenly contemplating. Investing in a more daring way would be far riskier, and Bruce really wanted to hang on to the money. It did strange things to him. Perhaps the strangest was his decision to walk away from Auburn, after five years, and never look back.

Eventually, a girl enticed him to a Florida beach on Camino Island, a ten-mile-long barrier strip just north of Jacksonville. In a nice condo she was paying for, he spent a month sleeping, drinking beer, strolling in the surf, staring at the Atlantic for hours, and reading *War and Peace*. He'd been an English major and was bothered by the great books he had never read.

To protect the money, and hopefully watch it grow, he considered a number of ventures as he roamed the beach. He had wisely kept the news of his good fortune to himself—the money, after all, had been buried for decades—so he was not pestered by friends offering all manner of advice or looking for loans. The girl certainly knew nothing about the money. After a week together, he knew she would soon be history. In no particular order, he thought about investing in a chicken sandwich franchise, and some raw Florida land, and a condo in a nearby high-rise, and several dot-com start-ups in Silicon Valley, and a strip mall in Nashville, and so on. He read dozens of financial magazines, and the more he read the more he realized he had no patience for investing. It was all a hopeless maze of numbers and strategies. There was a reason he'd chosen English over economics.

Every other day he and the girl wandered into the quaint village of Santa Rosa, to have lunch in the cafés or drinks in the bars along Main Street. There was a decent bookstore with a coffee shop, and they fell into the habit of settling in with an afternoon latte and the *New York Times*. The barista was also the owner, an older guy named Tim, and Tim was a chatterbox. One day he let it slip that he was thinking about selling out and moving to Key West. The following day, Bruce managed to shake the girl and enjoy the latte by himself. He took a seat at the coffee bar and proceeded to prod Tim about his plans for the bookstore.

Selling books was a tough business, Tim explained. The big chains were deep discounting all bestsellers, some offering 50 percent off, and now with the Internet and Amazon folks were shopping from home. In the past five years, over 700 independent bookstores had closed. Only a few were making money. The more he talked the more somber he became. "Retail is brutal," he said at least three times. "And no matter what you do today, you gotta start all over again tomorrow."

Bruce admired his honesty but questioned his savviness. Was he trying to entice a buyer?

Tim said he made decent money with the store. The island had an established literary community, with some active writers, a book festival, and good libraries. Retirees still enjoyed reading and spent money on books. There were about forty thousand permanent residents, plus a million tourists each year, so there was plenty of traffic. What was his price? Bruce finally asked. Tim said he would take $150,000 cash, no owner financing, with the assumption of the lease of the building. Somewhat timidly, Bruce asked if he could see the store's financials, just the basic balance sheet and profit and loss, nothing complicated. Tim didn't like the idea. He didn't know Bruce and thought the kid was just another twentysomething loafing at the beach and spending Daddy's money. Tim said, "Okay, you show me your financials and I'll show you mine."

"Fair enough," said Bruce. He left, promising to return, but got sidetracked by an idea for a road trip. Three days later he said good-bye to the girl and drove to Jacksonville to shop for a new car. He coveted a sparkling-new Porsche 911 Carrera, and the fact that he could simply write a check for one made the temptation painful. He stood his ground, though, and after a long day of horse-trading he surrendered his well-used Jeep Cherokee for a brand-new one. He might need the space to haul things. The Porsche could always wait, perhaps until he'd earned the money to buy one.

With a new set of wheels, and money in the bank, Bruce left Florida for a literary adventure that he anticipated more with each passing mile. He had no itinerary. He headed west, and planned to one day turn north at the Pacific, then back east, then south. Time meant nothing; there were no deadlines. He searched for independent bookstores, and when he found one he decamped for a day or two of browsing, drinking coffee, reading, maybe even lunch if the place had a café. He usually managed to corner the owners and gently poke around for information. He told them he was thinking about buying a bookstore and, frankly, needed their advice. The responses varied. Most seemed to enjoy their work, even those who were wary of the future. There was great uncertainty in the business, with the chains expanding and the Internet filled with unknowns. There were horror stories of established bookshops driven out of business when large discount stores popped up just down the street. Some of the independents, especially those in college towns too small for the chains, appeared to be thriving. Others, even in cities, were practically deserted. A few were new and enthusiastically bucking the trend. The advice was inconsistent and wide-ranging, from the standard "Retail is brutal" to "Go for it, you're only twenty-three years old." But the one constant was that those giving advice enjoyed what they were doing. They loved books, and literature, and writers, the whole publishing scene, and they were willing to put in long hours and deal with customers because they considered theirs to be a noble calling.

For two months, Bruce drifted across the country, zigzagging aimlessly in pursuit of the next independent bookstore. The owner in one town might know three others across the state, and so on. Bruce consumed gallons of strong coffee, hung out with authors on tour, bought dozens of autographed books, slept in cheap motels, occasionally with another bookworm he'd just met, spent hours with booksellers willing to share their knowledge and advice, sipped a lot of bad wine at signings where only a handful of customers showed up, took hundreds of interior and exterior photographs, took pages of notes, and kept a log. By the time his adventure was over, and he was finished and tired of driving, he had covered almost eight thousand miles in seventy-four days and visited sixty-one independent bookstores, no two even remotely similar. He thought he had a plan.

He returned to Camino Island and found Tim where he'd left him, at the coffee bar, sipping espresso and reading a newspaper, looking even more haggard than before. At first, Tim did not remember him, but then Bruce said, "I was thinking about buying the store a couple of months ago. You were asking one-fifty."

"Sure," Tim said, perking up only slightly. "You find the money?"

"Some of it. I'll write a check today for a hundred thousand, and twenty-five grand a year from now."

"Nice, but that's twenty-five short, the way I count."

"That's all I have, Tim. Take it or leave it. I've found another store on the market."

Tim thought for a second, then slowly shoved forward his right hand. They shook on the deal. Tim called his lawyer and told him to speed things along. Three days later the paperwork was signed and the money changed hands. Bruce closed the store for a month for renovations, and used the downtime for a crash course on bookselling. Tim was happy to hang around and share his knowledge on every aspect of the trade, as well as the gossip on customers and most of the other downtown merchants. He had a lot of opinions on most matters, and after a couple of weeks Bruce was ready for him to leave.

On August 1, 1996, the store reopened with as much fanfare as Bruce could possibly drum up. A nice crowd sipped champagne and beer and listened to reggae and jazz while Bruce relished the moment. His grand adven-

ture had been launched, and Bay Books—New and Rare
was in business.

2.

His interest in rare books was accidental. Upon hearing the awful news that his father had dropped dead
of a heart attack, Bruce went home to Atlanta. It wasn't
really his home—he'd never spent much time there—but
rather the current and last home of his father, a man
who moved often and usually with a frightening woman
in tow. Mr. Cable had married twice, and badly, and had
sworn off the institution, but he couldn't seem to exist
without the presence of some wretched woman to complicate his life. They were attracted to him because of
his apparent wealth, but over time each had realized he
was hopelessly scarred by two horrific divorces. Luckily,
at least for Bruce, the latest girlfriend had just moved
out and the place was free from prying eyes and hands.

Until Bruce arrived. The house, a baffling, cutting-
edge pile of steel and glass in a hip section of downtown, had a large studio on the third level where Mr.
Cable liked to paint when he wasn't investing. He had
never really pursued a career, and since he lived off his
inheritance he had always referred to himself as an "in-
vestor." Later, he'd turned to painting, but his oils were
so dreadful that he'd been shooed away from every gallery in Atlanta. One wall of the studio was covered with
books, hundreds of them, and at first Bruce hardly noticed the collection. He assumed they were just window
dressing, another part of the act, another lame effort by

his father to seem deep, complicated, and well read. But upon closer observation, Bruce realized that two shelves held some older books with familiar titles. He began pulling them off the upper shelf, one by one, and examining them. His casual curiosity quickly turned to something else.

The books were all first editions, some autographed by the authors. Joseph Heller's *Catch-22*, published in 1961; Norman Mailer's *The Naked and the Dead* (1948); John Updike's *Rabbit, Run* (1960); Ralph Ellison's *Invisible Man* (1952); Walker Percy's *The Moviegoer* (1961); Philip Roth's *Goodbye, Columbus* (1959); William Styron's *The Confessions of Nat Turner* (1967); Dashiell Hammett's *The Maltese Falcon* (1929); Truman Capote's *In Cold Blood* (1965); and J. D. Salinger's *The Catcher in the Rye* (1951).

After the first dozen or so, Bruce began placing the books on a table rather than returning them to the shelves. His initial curiosity was overwhelmed by a heady wave of excitement, then greed. On the lower shelf he ran across books and authors he'd never heard of until he made an even more startling discovery. Hidden behind a thick three-volume biography of Churchill were four books: William Faulkner's *The Sound and the Fury* (1929); Steinbeck's *Cup of Gold* (1929); F. Scott Fitzgerald's *This Side of Paradise* (1920); and Ernest Hemingway's *A Farewell to Arms* (1929). All were first editions in excellent condition and signed by the authors.

Bruce fished around some more, found nothing else of interest, then fell into his father's old recliner and stared at the wall of books. Sitting there, in a house he'd never really known, looking at wretched oils done by an artist with an obvious lack of talent, wondering where the books came from, and pondering what he would do when Molly, his sister, arrived and they would be expected to plan a funeral service, Bruce was struck by how little he knew about his late father. And why should he know more? His father had never spent time with him. Mr. Cable shipped Bruce off to boarding school when he was fourteen. During the summers, the kid was sent to a sailing camp for six weeks and a dude ranch for six more, anything to keep him away from home. Bruce knew of nothing his father enjoyed collecting, other than a string of miserable women. Mr. Cable played golf and tennis and traveled, but never with Bruce and his sister; always with the latest girlfriend.

So where did the books come from? How long had he been collecting them? Were there old invoices lying around, written proof of their existence? Would the executor of his father's estate be required to lump them in with his other assets and give them, along with the bulk, to Emory University?

Leaving the bulk of the estate to Emory was something else that irked Bruce. His father had talked about it occasionally, without giving too many details. Mr. Cable was of the lofty opinion that his money should be invested in education and not left for children to squander. On several occasions Bruce had been tempted to remind his father that he'd spent his entire life pissing away money earned by someone else, but squabbling over such matters would not benefit Bruce.

At that moment, he really wanted those books. He

decided to keep eighteen of the best and leave the rest behind. If he got greedy and left gaps, someone might notice. He fit them neatly in a cardboard box that had once held a case of wine. His father had battled the bottle for years and finally reached a truce that allowed him a few glasses of red wine each night. There were several empty boxes in the garage. Bruce spent hours rearranging the shelves to give the impression that nothing was missing. And who would know? As far as he knew, Molly read nothing, and, more important, avoided their father because she hated his girlfriends. To Bruce's knowledge, Molly had never spent a night in the house. She would know nothing of her father's personal effects. (However, two months later, she asked him on the phone if he knew anything about "Daddy's old books." Bruce assured her he knew nothing.)

He waited until dark and carried the box to his Jeep. There were at least three surveillance cameras watching the patio, driveway, and garage, and if anyone asked questions, he would simply say he was taking away some of his own stuff. Videos, CDs, whatever. If the executor of the estate later asked about the missing first editions, Bruce would, of course, know nothing. Go quiz the housekeeper.

As things evolved, it was the perfect crime, if, indeed, it was a crime at all. Bruce really didn't think so. In his opinion, he should be receiving far more. Thanks to thick wills and family lawyers, his father's estate was wrapped up efficiently and his library was never mentioned.

Bruce Cable's unplanned entry into the world of rare books was off to a fine start. He plunged himself into the study of the trade and realized that the value of his first collection, the eighteen taken from his father's house, was around $200,000. He was afraid to sell the books, though, afraid someone somewhere might recognize one and ask questions. Since he did not know how his father had gained possession of the books, it was best to wait. Allow some time to pass, for memories to fade. As he would quickly learn in the business, patience was imperative.

3.

The building was on the corner of Third and Main Street in the heart of Santa Rosa. It was a hundred years old and originally built to house the town's leading bank, one that collapsed in the Depression. Then it was a pharmacy, then another bank, then a bookshop. The second floor stored boxes and trunks and file cabinets, all laden with dust and utterly worthless. Up there Bruce managed to stake out a claim, clear some space, throw up a couple of walls, move in a bed, and call it an apartment. He lived there for the first ten years Bay Books was in business. When he wasn't downstairs peddling books, he was upstairs clearing, cleaning, painting, renovating, and eventually decorating.

The bookstore's first month was August 1996. After the wine-and-cheese opening, the place was busy for a few days, but the curiosity began to wear off. The traffic slowed considerably. After three weeks in business, Bruce was beginning to wonder if he'd blundered badly. August saw a net profit of only two thousand dollars, and Bruce was ready to panic. It was, after all, the high season for tourism on Camino Island. He decided to begin discounting, something the majority of independent owners advised against. Big new releases and bestsellers were marked down 25 percent. He pushed the closing time back from seven to nine and put in fifteen hours a day. He worked the front like a politician, memorizing the names of the regular customers and noting what they bought. He was soon an accomplished barista. He could brew an espresso while hustling to the front to check out a customer. He removed shelves of old books, mainly classics that were not too popular, and put in a small café. Closing time went from nine to ten. He cranked out dozens of handwritten notes to customers, and to writers and booksellers he'd met on his coast-to-coast adventure. At midnight, he was often at the computer, updating the Bay Books newsletter. He wrestled with the idea of opening on Sunday, something most of the independents did. He didn't want to, because he needed the rest, and he was also afraid of possible backlash. Camino Island was in the Bible Belt; one could easily walk to a dozen churches from the bookstore. But it was also a vacation spot and almost none of the tourists seemed interested in Sunday morning worship. So in September he said to hell with it and opened at 9:00 a.m. Sunday, with the *New York Times, Washington Post, Boston Globe,* and *Chicago Tribune* hot off the press, along with fresh chicken biscuits from a café three doors down. By the third Sunday, the place was packed.

The store netted four thousand dollars in September and October and doubled that after six months. Bruce stopped worrying. Within a year Bay Books was the hub of downtown, by far the busiest store. Publishers and sales reps succumbed to his constant badgering and began to include Camino Island on author tours. Bruce joined the American Booksellers Association and immersed himself in its causes, issues, and committees. In the winter of 1997, at an ABA convention, he met Stephen King and convinced him to pop over for a book party. Mr. King signed for nine hours as fans waited in lines that wrapped around the block. The store sold twenty-two hundred copies of his various titles and grossed seventy thousand dollars in sales. It was a glorious day that put Bay Books on the map. Three years later it was voted Best Independent Bookstore in Florida, and in 2004 *Publishers Weekly* named it Bookstore of the Year. In 2005, after nine hard years in the trenches, Bruce Cable was elected to the ABA Board of Directors.

4.

By then Bruce was quite the figure around town. He owned a dozen seersucker suits, each a different shade or color, and he wore one every day, along with a starched white shirt with a spread collar, and a loud bow tie, usually either red or yellow. His ensemble was completed with a pair of dirty buckskins, no socks. He never wore socks, not even in January when the temperatures dipped into the forties. His hair was thick and wavy, and he wore it long, almost to his shoulders. He shaved once a week on Sunday morning. By the time he was thirty, some gray was working itself into the picture, a few whiskers and a few strands of the long hair, and it was quite becoming.

Each day, when things slowed a bit in the store, Bruce hit the street. He walked to the post office and flirted with the clerks. He went to the bank and flirted with the tellers. If a new retail shop opened downtown, Bruce was there for the grand opening, and he returned soon afterward to flirt with the salesgirls. Lunch was a major production for Bruce, and he dined out six days a week, always with someone else so he could write it off as a business expense. When a new café opened, Bruce was first in line, sampling everything on the menu and flirting with the waitresses. He usually drank a bottle of wine for lunch and slept it off with a little siesta in the upstairs apartment.

Often, with Bruce, there was a fine line between flirting and stalking. He had an eye for the ladies, as they did for him, and he played the game beautifully. He hit pay dirt when Bay Books became a popular stop on the author circuit. Half the writers who came to town were women, most under forty, all obviously away from home, most of them single and traveling alone and looking for some fun. They were easy and willing targets when they arrived at the bookstore and stepped into his world. After a reading and signing session, then a long dinner, they often retired to the apartment upstairs with Bruce for "a deeper search for human emotion." He had his favorites, especially two young ladies who were doing well with erotic mysteries. And they published every year!

Despite his efforts to carefully groom his image as a well-read playboy, Bruce was at his core an ambitious businessman. The store provided a healthy income, but that was not by accident. Regardless of how late his night had been, he was at the store before seven each morning, in shorts and a T-shirt, unloading and un-boxing books, stocking shelves, taking inventory, even sweeping the floors. He loved the feel and smell of new books as they came out of the box. He found the per-fect spot for each new edition. He touched every book that came into the store, and, sadly, every book that was re-boxed and returned to the publisher for credit. He hated returns and viewed each one as a failure, a missed opportunity. He purged the inventory of stuff that didn't sell, and after a few years settled on about twelve thousand titles. Sections of the store were cramped spaces with saggy old shelves and books stacked on the floors, but Bruce knew where to find anything. After all, he had carefully placed them all. At 8:45 each morn-ing, he hurried upstairs to the apartment, showered, and changed into his seersucker of the day, and at pre-cisely 9:00 a.m. he opened the doors and greeted his customers.

He rarely took a day off. For Bruce, the idea of a va-cation was a trip to New England to meet antiquarian book dealers in their old dusty shops and talk about the market. He loved rare books, especially those by twentieth-century American authors, and he collected them with a passion. His collection grew, primarily be-cause he wanted to buy so much, but also because he found it painful to sell anything. He was a dealer for sure, but one who always bought and almost never sold. The eighteen of "Daddy's old books" he'd filched be-came a wonderful foundation, and by the time Bruce was forty years old he valued his rare collection at two million dollars.

5.

While he served on the ABA Board, the owner of his building died. Bruce bought it from the estate and began expanding the store. He shrunk the size of his apartment and moved the coffee bar and café to the second floor. He knocked out a wall and doubled the size of his children's section. On Saturday mornings, the store was filled with kids buying books and listening to story time while their young moms were upstairs sipping lattes under the watchful eye of the friendly owner. His rare book section received a lot of his attention. On the main floor, he knocked out another wall and built a First Editions Room with handsome oak shelves, paneling, and expensive rugs. He built a vault in the basement to protect his rarest books.

After ten years of apartment living, Bruce was ready for something grander. He'd kept his eye on several of the old Victorians in historic downtown Santa Rosa, and had even made offers to purchase two of them. In both cases he failed to offer enough, and the homes quickly sold to other buyers. The magnificent homes, built by turn-of-the-century railroad magnates and shippers and doctors and politicians, were beautifully preserved and sat timelessly on streets shaded with ancient oaks and Spanish moss. When Mrs. Marchbanks died at the age of 103, Bruce approached her daughter, age 81 and living in Texas. He paid too much for the house, but then he was determined not to lose a third time.

Two blocks north and three blocks east of the store, the Marchbanks House was built in 1890 by a doctor as a gift to his pretty new wife, and had been in the family ever since. It was huge, over eight thousand square feet sprawled over four levels, with a soaring tower on the south side and a turret on the north, and a sweeping veranda wrapped around the ground floor. It had a roof deck, a variety of gables, fish-scale shingles, and bay windows, many of which were adorned with stained glass. It covered a small corner lot that was lined with white picket fences and shaded by three ancient oaks and Spanish moss.

Bruce found the interior depressing, with its dark wood floors, even darker painted walls, well-worn rugs, sagging, dusty drapes, and abundance of brown-brick hearths. Much of the furniture came with the deal, and he immediately began selling it. The ancient rugs that were not too threadbare were moved to the bookstore and added decades to its ambience. The old drapes and curtains were worthless and thrown away. When the house was empty, he hired a paint crew that spent two months brightening up the interior walls. When they were gone he hired a local artisan who spent another two months refinishing every square inch of the oak and heart pine flooring.

He bought the house because its systems worked— plumbing, electrical, water, heating, and air. He had neither the patience nor the stomach for a renovation, one that would virtually bankrupt a new buyer. He had little talent with a hammer and better ways to spend his time. For the next year, he continued to live in his apartment above the store as he pondered the furnishing and decorating of the house. It sat empty, bright, and beautiful, while the task of molding it into his livable space became intimidating. It was a majestic example of Victorian architecture and thoroughly unsuited for the modern and minimalist decor he preferred. He considered the period pieces fussy and frilly and just not his style.

What was wrong with having a grand old home that stayed true to its origins, at least on the outside, while jazzing up the interior with modern furniture and art? Something was not right with that, though, and he became handcuffed with ideas of a decorating scheme.

He walked to the house every day and stood in every room, perplexed and uncertain. Was it becoming his folly, an empty house much too large and complicated for his uncertain tastes?

6.

To the rescue came one Noelle Bonnet, a New Orleans antiques dealer who was touring with her latest book, a fifty-dollar coffee-table tome. He had seen Noelle's publisher's catalog months earlier and was captivated by her photograph. Doing his homework, as always, he learned that she was thirty-seven years old, divorced with no kids, a native of New Orleans, though her mother was French, and well regarded as an expert on Provençal antiques. Her shop was on Royal Street in the Quarter, and according to her bio she spent half the year in southern and southwest France scouring for old furniture. She had published two previous books on the subject and Bruce studied both of them.

This was a habit if not a calling. His store did two and sometimes three signing events each week, and by the time an author arrived Bruce had read everything he or she had published. He read voraciously, and while he preferred novels by living authors, people he could meet, promote, befriend, and follow, he also devoured biographies, self-help, cookbooks, histories, anything and everything. It was the least he could do. He admired all writers, and if one took the time to visit his store, and have dinner and drinks and so on, then he was determined to be able to discuss his or her works.

He read deep into the night and often fell asleep with an open book in the bed. He read early in the morning, alone in the store with strong coffee, long before it opened if he wasn't packing and unpacking. He read constantly throughout the day, and over time developed the curious routine of standing in the same spot by a front window, near the biographies, leaning casually on a full-sized wood sculpture of a Timucuan Indian chief, sipping espresso nonstop, with one eye on the page and the other on the front door. He greeted customers, found books for them, chatted with anyone who wanted to chat, occasionally helped at the coffee bar or front register when things were busy, but always eased back to his spot by the chief, where he picked up his book and resumed his reading. He claimed to average four books per week and no one doubted this. If a prospective clerk did not read at least two per week, there was no job offer.

At any rate, Noelle Bonnet's visit was a great success, if not for the revenue it generated, then certainly for its lasting impact on Bruce and Bay Books. The attraction was mutual, immediate, and intense. After a quick, even abbreviated dinner, they retired to his apartment up-stairs and enjoyed one hell of a romp. Claiming to be ill, she canceled the rest of her tour and stayed in town for a week. On the third day, Bruce walked her over to the Marchbanks House and proudly displayed his trophy. Noelle was overwhelmed. For a world-class designer/decorator/dealer, the presentation of eight thousand square feet of empty floors and walls behind the facade of such a grand Victorian was breathtaking. As they drifted from room to room, she began having visions of how each should be painted, wallpapered, and fur-nished.

Bruce offered a couple of modest suggestions, such as a big-screen TV here and pool table over there, but these were not well received. The artist was at work, suddenly painting on a canvas with no borders. Noelle spent the following day alone in the house, measuring and photographing and simply sitting in its vast empti-ness. Bruce tended the store, thoroughly smitten with her but also having the first tremors of a pending finan-cial nightmare.

She cajoled him into leaving the store over the week-end and they flew to New Orleans. She walked him through her stylish, though cluttered, store, where every table, lamp, four-poster bed, chest, chaise, trunk, rug, commode, and armoire not only had rich origins in some Provençal village but was destined for the perfect spot in the Marchbanks House. They roamed the French Quarter, dined in her favorite local bistros, hung out with her friends, spent plenty of time in bed, and after three days Bruce flew home alone, exhausted, but also, for the first time, admittedly in love. Damn the expense. Noelle Bonnet was a woman he could not live without.

7.

A week later, a large truck arrived in Santa Rosa and parked in front of the Marchbanks House. The following day, Noelle was there directing the movers. Bruce walked back and forth from the store, watching with great interest and a touch of trepidation. The artist was lost in her own creative world, buzzing from room to room, moving each piece at least three times, and realizing she needed more. A second truck arrived not long after the first one left. Bruce, walking back to the store, mumbled to himself that there could be little left in her shop on Royal Street. Over dinner that night, she confirmed this, and begged him to leave for France in just a few days for another shopping adventure. He declined, saying he had some important authors on the way and had to tend to the store. That night, they slept in the house for the first time, in a wrought-iron contraption of a bed she had found near Avignon, where she kept a small apartment. Every stick of furniture, every accessory, every rug and pot and painting had a history, and her love for the stuff was contagious.

Early the following morning, they sipped coffee on the back porch and talked about the future, which, at the moment, was uncertain. She had her life in New

Orleans and he had his on the island, and neither seemed suited for a long, permanent relationship that involved pulling up stakes. It was awkward and they soon changed the subject. Bruce admitted he'd never been to France and they began planning a vacation there.

Not long after Noelle left town, the first invoice arrived. It came with a note, handwritten in her beautiful script, in which she explained that she was forgoing her usual markup and basically selling the stuff at cost. Thank God for small miracles, he mumbled. And now she's headed back to France for more!

She returned to New Orleans from Avignon three days before Hurricane Katrina. Neither her store in the French Quarter nor her apartment in the Garden District was damaged, but the city was mortally wounded. She locked her doors and fled to Camino Island, where Bruce was waiting to soothe and calm her. For days they watched the horror on television—the flooded streets, the floating bodies, the oil-stained waters, the frantic flight of half the population, the panicked rescue workers, the bumbling politicians.

Noelle doubted she could return. She wasn't sure she wanted to.

Gradually, she began to talk of relocating. About half of her customers were from New Orleans, and with so many of them now in exile she was worried about her business. The other half was spread throughout the country. Her reputation was wide and well known and she shipped antiques everywhere. Her website was a success. Her books were popular and many of her fans were serious collectors. With Bruce's gentle prodding, she convinced herself she could move her business to the island and not only rebuild what had been lost but prosper.

Six weeks after the storm, Noelle signed a lease for a small space on Main Street in Santa Rosa, three doors down from Bay Books. She closed her shop on Royal Street and moved what was left of her inventory to her new store, Noelle's Provence. When a new shipment from France arrived, she opened the doors with a champagne-and-caviar party, and Bruce helped her work the crowd.

She had a great idea for a new book: the transformation of the Marchbanks House as it filled up with Provençal antiques. She had photographed the home extensively as it sat empty, and now she would document her triumphant renovation. Bruce doubted the book would sell enough to cover its costs, but what the hell? Whatever Noelle wanted.

At some point the invoices had stopped arriving. Timidly, he broached this subject, and she explained with great drama that he was now getting the ultimate discount: Her! He might own the house, but everything in it would be theirs together.

8.

In April 2006, they spent two weeks in the South of France. Using her apartment in Avignon as home base, they roamed from village to village, market to market, eating food that Bruce had only seen photos of, drinking great local wines not available back home, staying in quaint hotels, seeing the sights, catching up with her friends, and, of course, loading up with more inventory for her store. Bruce, always the researcher, thrust himself into the world of rustic French furniture and artifacts and could soon spot a bargain.

They were in Nice when they decided to get married, right then and there.

CHAPTER THREE
THE RECRUIT

1.

On a perfect spring day in late April, Mercer Mann walked with some anxiety across the Chapel Hill campus of the University of North Carolina. She had agreed to meet a stranger for a quick lunch, but only because of the prospect of a job. Her current one, adjunct professor of freshman literature, would expire in two weeks, courtesy of budget cuts brought on by a state legislature dominated by those rabid about tax and spending cuts. She had lobbied hard for a new contract but didn't get one. She would soon be out of work, still in debt, homeless, and out of print. She was thirty-one years old, quite single, and, well, her life was not exactly going as planned.

The first e-mail, one of two from the stranger, a Donna Watson, had arrived the day before and had been about as vague as an e-mail could be. Ms. Watson claimed to

be a consultant hired by a private academy to locate a
new teacher of creative writing for high school seniors.
She was in the area and could meet for coffee. The salary was in the range of seventy-five thousand dollars
a year, on the high side, but the school's headmaster
loved literature and was determined to hire a teacher
who had actually published a novel or two.

Mercer had one novel under her belt, along with a
collection of stories. The salary was indeed impressive
and more than she was currently making. No other details were offered. Mercer responded favorably and asked
a few questions about the school, specifically what was
its name and where was it located.

The second e-mail was only slightly less vague than
the first, but did reveal the school to be in New England.
And the meeting over coffee had been elevated to a
"quick lunch." Could Mercer meet her at a place called
Spanky's, just off campus on Franklin Street, at noon?

Mercer was ashamed to admit that at the moment
the idea of a nice lunch was more appealing than that
of teaching a bunch of privileged high school seniors.
In spite of the lofty salary, the job was definitely a step
down. She had arrived in Chapel Hill three years earlier
with the intention of throwing herself into teaching
while, and much more important, finishing her current
novel. Three years later, she was being terminated, and
the novel was as unfinished as it had been when she arrived in Chapel Hill.

As soon as she walked into the restaurant, a well-
dressed and perfectly put-together woman of about
fifty waved her over, thrust out a hand, and said, "I'm
Donna Watson. Nice to meet you." Mercer sat across the

table and thanked her for the invitation. A waiter dropped menus on the table.

Without wasting any time, Donna Watson became someone else. She said, "I must tell you that I'm here under false pretenses, okay? My name is not Donna Watson but Elaine Shelby. I work for a company based in Bethesda."

Mercer gave her a blank look, glanced away, looked back, and tried gamely to think of an appropriate response.

Elaine pressed on. "I lied. I apologize, and I promise I will not lie again. However, I'm serious about lunch and I'm getting the check, so please hear me out."

"I suppose you have a good reason for lying," Mercer said cautiously.

"A very good one, and if you'll forgive this one offense, and hear me out, I promise I can explain."

Mercer shrugged and said, "I'm hungry, so I'll just listen until I'm not hungry anymore, and if by then you haven't cleared things up I'll take a walk."

Elaine flashed a smile that anyone would trust. She had dark eyes and dark skin, maybe of some Middle Eastern extraction, possibly Italian or Greek, Mercer thought, though her accent was upper Midwest, definitely American. Her short gray hair was cut in a style so smart that a couple of men had already looked twice. She was a beautiful woman and impeccably dressed, far out of place among the casual college crowd.

She said, "Though I didn't lie about the job. That's why I'm here, to convince you to take a job, one with better terms and benefits than I put in the e-mail."

"Doing what?"

"Writing, finishing your novel."

"Which one?"

The waiter was back, and they quickly ordered matching grilled chicken salads with sparkling water. He snatched the menus, disappeared, and after a pause Mercer said, "I'm listening."

"It's a long story."

"Let's start with the obvious challenge—you."

"Okay. I work for a company that specializes in security and investigations. An established company that you've never heard of because we don't advertise, don't have a website."

"We're getting nowhere."

"Please, hang on. It gets better. Six months ago, a gang of thieves stole the Fitzgerald manuscripts from the Firestone Library at Princeton. Two were caught and are still in jail, waiting. The others have disappeared. The manuscripts have not been found."

Mercer nodded and said, "It was widely reported."

"It was. The manuscripts, all five of them, were insured by our client, a large private company that insures art and treasures and rare assets. I doubt you've heard of it either."

"I don't follow insurance companies."

"Lucky you. Anyway, we have been digging for six months, working closely with the FBI and its Rare Asset Recovery Unit. The pressure is on because in six months our client will be forced to write a check to Princeton for twenty-five million dollars. Princeton really doesn't want the money; it wants the manuscripts, which, as you might guess, are priceless. We've had a few leads but nothing exciting until now. Luckily, there aren't too many players in the murky world of stolen books and manuscripts, and we think we might have picked up the trail of a particular dealer."

The waiter set a tall bottle of Pellegrino between them, with two glasses with ice and lemon.

When he left, Elaine continued, "It's someone you may know."

Mercer stared at her, offered half a grunt, shrugged, and said, "That would be a shock."

"You have a long history with Camino Island. You spent summers there as a kid, with your grandmother, in her beach cottage."

"How do you know this?"

"You've written about it."

Mercer sighed and grabbed the bottle. She slowly filled both glasses as her mind spun away. "Let me guess. You've read everything I've written."

"No, just everything you've published. It's part of our preparation, and it's been quite enjoyable."

"Thanks. Sorry there hasn't been more."

"You're young and talented and just getting started."

"Let's hear it. Let's see if you've done your homework."

"Gladly. Your first novel, *October Rain*, was published by Newcombe Press in 2008, when you were only twenty-four years old. Its sales were respectable—eight thousand copies in hardback, double that in paper, a few e-books—not exactly a bestseller, but the critics loved it."

"The kiss of death."

"It was nominated for the National Book Award and a finalist for PEN/Faulkner."

"And won neither."

"No, but few first novels get that much respect, especially from such a young writer. The *Times* chose it as one of its ten best books of the year. You followed it with a collection of stories, *The Music of Waves,* which the critics also praised, but, as you know, stories don't sell that well."

"Yes, I know."

"After that you changed agents and publishers, and, well, the world is still waiting for the next novel. Meanwhile, you've published three stories in literary magazines, including one about guarding turtle eggs on the beach with your grandmother Tessa."

"So you know about Tessa?"

"Look, Mercer, we know all there is to know, and our sources are public records. Yes, we've done a great deal of snooping, but we haven't dug into your personal life beyond what is available to anyone else. With the Internet these days there's not a lot of privacy."

The salads arrived and Mercer picked up her knife and fork. She ate a few bites as Elaine sipped water and watched her. Finally, Mercer asked, "Are you going to eat?"

"Sure."

"So what do you know about Tessa?"

"Your maternal grandmother. She and her husband built the beach cottage on Camino Island in 1980. They were from Memphis, where you were born, and spent their vacations there. He, your grandfather, died in 1985, and Tessa left Memphis and moved to the beach. As a little girl and as a teenager, you spent long summers with her there. Again, this is what you wrote."

"It's true."

"Tessa died in a sailing accident in 2005. Her body was found on the beach two days after the storm. Neither her sailing companion nor his boat was ever found. This was all in the newspapers, primarily the *Times-Union* out of Jacksonville. According to the public records, Tessa's will left everything, including the cottage, to her three children, one being your mother. It's still in the family."

"It is. I own one-half of one-third, and I haven't seen the cottage since she died. I'd like to sell it but the family agrees on nothing."

"Is it used at all?"

"Oh yes. My aunt spends the winter there."

"Jane."

"That's her. And my sister vacations there in the summer. Just curious, what do you know about my sister?"

"Connie lives in Nashville with her husband and two teenage girls. She's forty and works in the family business. Her husband owns a string of frozen yogurt shops and is doing quite well. Connie has a degree in psychology from SMU. Evidently, she met her husband there."

"And my father?"

"Herbert Mann once owned the largest Ford dealership in the Memphis area. It looks like there was some money, enough to afford Connie's private tuition at SMU, debt-free. The business went south for some reason, Herbert lost it, and for the past ten years he's worked as a part-time scout for the Baltimore Orioles. He now lives in Texas."

Mercer placed her knife and fork on the table and took a deep breath. "I'm sorry, but this is unsettling. I can't help but feel as though I'm being stalked. What do you want?"

"Please, Mercer, our information was compiled by old-fashioned detective work. We have not seen anything that we were not supposed to see."

"It's creepy, okay? Professional spies digging through my past. What about the present? How much do you know about my employment situation?"

"Your position is being terminated."

"So I need a job?"

"I suppose."

"This is not public record. How do you know who's being hired or fired at the University of North Carolina?"

"We have our sources."

Mercer frowned and shoved her salad an inch or two away, as if she were finished. She folded her arms across her chest and scowled at Ms. Shelby. "I can't help but feel, well, violated."

"Please, Mercer, hear me out. It's important that we have as much information as possible."

"For what?"

"For the job we are proposing. If you say no, then we'll simply go away and toss the file on you. We'll never divulge any of our information."

"What's the job?"

Elaine took a small bite and chewed for a long time. After a sip of water, she said, "Back to the Fitzgerald manuscripts. We think they're being hidden on Camino Island."

"And who might be hiding them?"

"I need your assurance that what we discuss from

this point on is extremely confidential. There's a lot at stake here, and a loose word could cause irreparable damage, not just to our client, and not just to Princeton, but to the manuscripts themselves."

"Who in hell might I tell about this?"

"Please, just give me your word."

"Confidentiality requires trust. Why on earth should I trust you? Right now I find you and your company to be very suspicious."

"I understand. But please hear the rest of the story."

"Okay, I'm listening, but I'm not hungry anymore. You'd better talk fast."

"Fair enough. You've been to the bookstore in downtown Santa Rosa, Bay Books. It's owned by a man named Bruce Cable."

Mercer shrugged and said, "I guess. I went there a few times with Tessa when I was a kid. Again, I haven't been back to the island since she died and that was eleven years ago."

"It's a successful store, one of the best independents in the country. Cable is well known in the business and is quite the hustler. He's connected and gets a lot of authors on their tours."

"I was supposed to go there with *October Rain*, but that's another story."

"Right, well, Cable is also an aggressive collector of modern first editions. He trades a lot, and we suspect he makes serious money with that part of his business. He's also known to deal in stolen books, one of the few in that rather dark business. Two months ago we picked up his trail after a tip from a source close to another collector. We think Cable has the Fitzgerald manuscripts, purchased for cash from a middleman who was desperate to get rid of them."

"My appetite has really disappeared."

"We can't get near the guy. We've had people in the store for the past month, watching, snooping, taking secret photos and videos, but we've hit a brick wall. He has a large, handsome room on the main floor where he keeps shelves of rare books, primarily those of twentieth-century American authors, and he'll gladly show these to a serious buyer. We've even tried to sell him a rare book, a signed and personalized copy of Faulkner's first novel, *Soldiers' Pay*. Cable knew immediately that there are only a few copies in the world, including three in a college library in Missouri, one owned by a Faulkner scholar, and one still held by Faulkner's descendants. The market price was somewhere in the forty-thousand-dollar range, and we offered it to Cable for twenty-five thousand. At first he seemed interested but then started asking a lot of questions about the book's provenance. Really good questions. He eventually got cold feet and said no. By then he was overly cautious, and this raised even more suspicions. We've made little progress getting into his world and we need someone inside."

"Me?"

"Yes, you. As you know, writers often take sabbaticals and go away to do their work. You have the perfect cover. You practically grew up on the island. You still have an ownership interest in the cottage. You have the literary reputation. Your story is completely plausible. You're back at the beach for six months to finish the book everybody has been waiting for."

"I can think of perhaps three people who might be waiting for it."

"We'll pay a hundred thousand dollars for the six months."

For a moment Mercer was speechless. She shook her head, pushed her salad farther away, and took a sip of water. "I'm sorry but I'm not a spy."

"And we're not asking you to spy, only to observe. You're doing something that is completely natural and believable. Cable loves writers. He wines them and dines them, supports them. Many of the touring authors stay at his home, and it is spectacular, by the way. He and his wife enjoy hosting long dinners with their friends and writers."

"And I'm supposed to waltz right in, gain his confidence, and ask him where he's hiding the Fitzgerald manuscripts."

Elaine smiled and let it pass. "We're under a lot of pressure, okay? I have no idea what you might learn, but at this point anything could be helpful. There's a good chance Cable and his wife will reach out to you, perhaps even befriend you. You could slowly work your way into their inner circle. He also drinks a lot. Maybe he'll let something slip; maybe one of his friends will mention the vault in the basement below the store."

"A vault?"

"Just a rumor, that's all. But we can't exactly pop in and ask him about it."

"How do you know he drinks too much?"

"A lot of writers pass through and, evidently, writers are horrible gossips. Word gets around. As you know, publishing is a very small world."

Mercer raised both hands, showed both her palms, and slid her chair back. "I'm sorry. This is not for me. I have my faults, but I am not a deceitful person. I have trouble lying and there's no way I could fake my way through something like this. You have the wrong person."

"Please."

Mercer stood as if to leave and said, "Thanks for lunch."

"Please, Mercer."

But she was gone.

2.

At some point during the abbreviated lunch, the sun disappeared and the wind picked up. A spring shower was on the way, and Mercer, always without an umbrella, walked home as fast as possible. She lived half a mile away, in the historic section of Chapel Hill, near the campus, in a small rental house on a shaded, unpaved alley behind a fine old home. Her landlord, the owner of the old home, rented only to grad students and starving, untenured professors.

With perfect timing, she stepped onto her narrow front porch just as the first drops of rain landed hard on her tin roof. She couldn't help but glance around, just to make sure no one was watching. Who were those people? Forget about it, she told herself. Inside, she kicked off her shoes, made a cup of tea, and for a long time sat on the sofa, taking deep breaths and listening to the music of the rain while replaying the conversation over lunch.

The initial shock of being watched began to fade. Elaine was right—nothing is really private these days with the Internet and social media and hackers everywhere and all the talk about transparency. Mercer had to admit the plan was pretty clever. She was the perfect recruit: a writer with a long history on the island; even a stake in the cottage; an unfinished novel with a deadline far in the past; a lonely soul looking for new friends. Bruce Cable would never suspect her of being a plant.

She remembered him well, the handsome guy with the cool suit and bow tie and no socks, and long wavy hair, a perpetual Florida tan. She could see him standing near the front door, always with a book in hand, sipping coffee, watching everything while he read. For some reason Tessa didn't like him and seldom went to the store. She didn't buy books either. Why buy books when you could get them for free at the library?

Book signings and book tours. Mercer could only wish she had a new novel to promote.

When *October Rain* was published in 2008, Newcombe Press had no money for publicity and travel. The company went bankrupt three years later. But after a rave review in the *Times,* a few bookstores called with inquiries about her tour. One was hastily put together, and Mercer's ninth stop was scheduled to be Bay Books. But the tour went off the rails almost immediately when, at her first signing, in D.C., eleven people showed up and only five bought a book. And that was her biggest crowd! At her second signing, in Philadelphia, four fans stood in line and Mercer spent the last hour chatting with the staff. Her third and, as it turned out, final book signing was at a large store in Hartford. In a bar across the street, she had two martinis while she watched and waited for the crowd to materialize. It did not. She finally crossed the street, walked in ten minutes late, and was demoralized when she realized that everyone waiting was an employee. Not a single fan showed up. Zero.

Her humiliation was complete. She would never again subject herself to the embarrassment of sitting at a lonely table with a stack of pretty books and trying to avoid eye contact with customers trying not to get too close. She knew other writers, a few anyway, and she had heard the horror stories of showing up at a bookstore and being greeted by the friendly faces of the employees and volunteers, and wondering how many of them might actually be customers and book buyers, and watching them glance around nervously in search of potential fans, and then seeing them drift away forever when it became apparent that the beloved author was about to lay an egg. A big fat goose egg.

At any rate, she had canceled the rest of her tour. She had not been too keen on the idea of returning to Camino Island anyway. She had many wonderful memories from there, but they would always be overshadowed by the horror and tragedy of her grandmother's death.

The rain made her sleepy and she drifted into a long nap.

3.

Footsteps awakened her. At 3:00 p.m., like clockwork, the postman rumbled across her creaky porch and left her mail in the small box next to her front door. She waited a moment until he was gone, then retrieved the daily delivery, always a dismal collection of junk and bills. She flung the junk onto a coffee table and opened a letter from UNC. It was from the chair of the English department and, despite pleasant and verbose wordage, informed her, officially, that her position was gone. She had been a "valuable asset" to the staff, a "gifted teacher" who had been "admired by her colleagues" and "adored by her students," and so on. The "entire department" wanted her to stay and viewed her as a "great addition," but, sadly, there was simply no room in the budget. He offered her his best wishes and left the door open with the slight hope of "another position" should next year's appropriation "return to normal levels of funding."

Most of the letter was true. The chairman had been an ally, at times even a mentor, and Mercer had managed to survive the minefield of academia by keeping her mouth shut and avoiding, as much as possible, the tenured faculty.

But she was a writer, not a teacher, and it was time to move on. To where, she wasn't certain, but after three years in the classroom she longed for the freedom of facing each day with nothing to do but write her novels and stories.

The second envelope contained her credit card statement. It showed a balance that reflected her frugal life-style and daily efforts to cut all corners. This allowed her to pay off each monthly balance and avoid the usurious rates the bank was eager to heap onto the carry-overs. Her salary barely covered these balances, along with rent, auto insurance, auto repairs, and a bare-bones health insurance policy, one that she considered dropping each month when she wrote the check. She would have been financially stable, and with a little spare cash to buy a better wardrobe and perhaps have some fun, but for the contents in the third envelope.

It was from the National Student Loan Corporation, a wretched outfit that had been hounding her for the past eight years. Her father had managed to cover the first year of her private education at Sewanee, but his sudden bankruptcy and emotional crack-up had left her high and dry. Mercer had managed to squeak through her last three years with student loans, grants, jobs, and a modest inheritance from Tessa's estate. She used the small advances from *October Rain* and *The Music of Waves* to pay down the interest on her student loans but hardly touched the principal.

Between jobs, she had refinanced and restructured her loans, and with each new scheme the horrendous balances grew even as she worked two and three jobs to stay current. The truth was, and she had told no one the truth, she found it impossible to express herself creatively while straining under a mountain of debt. Each morning, each blank page held not the promise of another chapter in a great novel, but rather another lame effort to produce something that might satisfy her creditors.

She had even talked to a lawyer friend about bankruptcy, only to learn that the banks and student loan companies had convinced Congress that such debts should be given special protection and not exempted. She remembered him saying, "Hell, even gamblers can go bankrupt and walk away."

Did her stalkers know about her student debt? It was all private, right? But something told her that professionals could dig deep enough to find almost anything. She had read horror stories of even the most sensitive medical records being leaked to the wrong people. And credit card companies were notorious for selling information about their customers. Was anything really buried and safe?

She picked up the junk mail, tossed it in the wastebasket, filed away the final letter from UNC, and placed the two bills in a rack by the toaster. She made another cup of tea and was about to stick her nose in a novel when her cell phone buzzed.

Elaine was back.

4.

She began with "Look, I'm very sorry about lunch. I didn't intend to ambush you, but there was no other way to start the conversation. What was I supposed to do? Grab you on the campus and spill my guts?"

Mercer closed her eyes and leaned on a kitchen counter. "It's all right. I'm fine. It was just so unexpected, you know?"

"I know, I know, and I'm very sorry. Look, Mercer, I'm

in town until tomorrow morning, when I fly back to Washington. I'd love to finish our conversation over dinner."

"No thanks. You've got the wrong person for this."

"Mercer, we have the perfect person, and, frankly, there is no one else. Please give me the time to explain everything. You didn't hear it all, and as I said, we are in a very tough position right now. We're trying to save the manuscripts before they're either damaged or, worse, sold piecemeal to foreign collectors and lost for good. Please, one more chance."

Mercer could not deny, to herself anyway, that the money was an issue. A really big issue. She wavered for a second and said, "So what's the rest of the story?"

"It will take some time. I have a car and a driver and I'll pick you up at seven. I don't know the town but I've heard that the best restaurant is a place called The Lantern. Have you been there?"

Mercer knew the place but couldn't afford it. "You know where I live?" she asked, and was immediately embarrassed by how innocent she sounded.

"Oh sure. I'll see you at seven."

5.

The car was, of course, a black sedan and looked thoroughly suspicious in her part of town. She met it at the drive and quickly hopped into the rear seat with Elaine. As it drove away, Mercer, sitting low, glanced around and saw no one looking. Why did she care? Her lease was up in three weeks and she would be leaving for good. Her shaky exit plan included a temporary stay in the garage apartment of an old girlfriend in Charleston.

Elaine, now dressed casually in jeans, a navy blazer, and expensive pumps, smothered her with a smile and said, "One of my colleagues went to school here and talks of nothing else, especially during basketball season."

"They are indeed rabid, but it's not my thing, not my school."

"Did you enjoy your time here?"

They were on Franklin Street, moving slowly through the historic district, passing lovely homes with manicured lawns, then into Greek territory, where the homes had been converted to sprawling sorority and fraternity houses. The rain was gone and porches and yards were brimming with students drinking beer and listening to music.

"It was okay," Mercer said without a hint of nostalgia. "But I'm not cut out for life in academia. The more I taught the more I wanted to write."

"You said in an interview with the campus paper that you hoped to finish the novel while in Chapel Hill. Any progress?"

"How did you find that? It was three years ago, when I first arrived."

Elaine smiled and looked out a window. "We haven't missed much." She was calm and relaxed, and she spoke in a deep voice that exuded confidence. She and her mysterious company were holding all the cards. Mercer wondered how many of these clandestine missions Elaine had put together and directed during her career.

Surely she had faced foes far more complicated and dangerous than a small-town book dealer.

The Lantern was on Franklin, a few blocks past the hub of student activity. The driver dropped them off at the front door and they went inside, where the cozy dining room was almost empty. Their table was near the window, with the sidewalk and street just a few feet away. In the past three years, Mercer had read many rave reviews of the place in local magazines. The awards were piling up. Mercer had scanned the menu online and was starving again. A waitress greeted them warmly and poured tap water from a pitcher.

"Anything to drink?" she asked.

Elaine yielded to Mercer, who quickly said, "I need a martini. Up with gin, and dirty."

"I'll have a Manhattan," Elaine said.

When the waitress was gone, Mercer said, "I suppose you travel a lot."

"Yes, too much, I guess. I have two kids in college. My husband works for the Department of Energy and is on a plane five days a week. I got tired of sitting in an empty house."

"And this is what you do? You track down stolen goods?"

"We do a lot of things, but, yes, this is my primary area. I've studied art my entire life and sort of stumbled into this line of work. Most of our cases deal with stolen and forged paintings. Occasionally some sculpture, though it's more difficult to steal. There is a lot of theft these days in books, manuscripts, ancient maps. Nothing, though, like the Fitzgerald case. We're throwing all we have at it, and for obvious reasons."

"I have a lot of questions."

Elaine shrugged and said, "I have a lot of time."

"And they're in no particular order. Why doesn't the FBI take the lead in something like this?"

"It does have the lead. Its Rare Asset Recovery Unit is superb and hard at work. The FBI almost broke the case within the first twenty-four hours. One of the thieves, a Mr. Steengarden, left a drop of blood at the crime scene, just outside the vault. The FBI caught him and his part-ner, one Mark Driscoll, and locked them away. We sus-pect that the other thieves got spooked and disappeared, along with the manuscripts. Frankly, we think the FBI moved too fast. Had they kept the first two under in-tense surveillance for a few weeks, they might have led the FBI to the rest of the gang. That seems even more likely now, with the benefit of perfect hindsight."

"Does the FBI know about your efforts to recruit me?"

"No."

"Does the FBI suspect Bruce Cable?"

"No, or at least I don't think so."

"So there are parallel investigations. Yours and theirs."

"To the extent that we don't share all information, then, yes, we are often on two different tracks."

"But why?"

The drinks arrived and the waitress asked if there were any questions. Since neither had touched a menu, they politely shooed her away. The place was filling up quickly, and Mercer glanced around to see if she recog-nized anyone. She did not.

Elaine took a sip, smiled, set her glass on the table, and thought about her answer. "If we suspect a thief has possession of a stolen painting or book or map, then we have ways of verifying this. We use the latest technology, the fanciest gadgets, the smartest people. Some of our technicians are former intelligence agents. If we verify the presence of the stolen object, either we notify the FBI, or we go in. Depends on the case and no two are remotely similar."

"You go in?"

"Yes. Keep in mind, Mercer, we are dealing with a thief who's hiding something valuable, something our client has insured for a lot of money. It doesn't belong to him, and he's always looking for a way to sell it for big money. That makes each situation rather tense. The clock is always ticking, yet we have to show great patience." Another small sip. She was choosing her words carefully. "The police and FBI have to worry about such things as probable cause and search warrants. We're not always constrained by these constitutional formalities."

"So you break and enter?"

"We never break, but sometimes we enter, and only for purposes of verification and retrieval. There are very few buildings that we cannot ease into quietly, and when it comes to hiding their loot a lot of thieves are not nearly as clever as they think they are."

"Do you tap phones, hack into computers?"

"Well, let's say we occasionally listen."

"So you break the law?"

"We call it operating in the gray areas. We listen, we enter, we verify, then, in most cases, we notify the FBI. They do their thing with proper search warrants, and the art is returned to its owner. The thief goes to prison, and the FBI gets all the credit. Everybody is happy, perhaps with the exception of the thief, and we're not too worried about his feelings."

With her third sip, the gin was settling in and Mercer began to relax. "So, if you're so good, why not just sneak into Cable's vault and check it out?"

"Cable is not a thief, and he appears to be smarter than the average suspect. He seems very cautious, and this makes us even more suspicious. A false move here or there, and the manuscripts could vanish again."

"But if you're listening and hacking and watching his movements, why can't you catch him?"

"I didn't say we were doing all that. We may, and soon, but right now we just need more intelligence."

"Has anyone in your company ever been charged with doing something illegal?"

"No, not even close. Again, we play in the gray, and when the crime is solved who cares?"

"Maybe the thief. I'm no lawyer, but couldn't the thief scream about an illegal search?"

"Maybe you should be a lawyer."

"I can't think of anything worse."

"The answer is no. The thief and his lawyer have no clue that we're even involved. They've never heard of us and we leave no fingerprints."

There was a long pause as they concentrated on their cocktails and glanced at the menus. The waitress hustled by and Elaine politely informed her that they were in no hurry. Mercer eventually said, "It looks as though you're asking me to do a job that could possibly involve getting into one of your gray areas, which is a euphemism for breaking the law."

At least she was thinking about it, Elaine thought to

herself. After the abrupt termination of lunch she was convinced Mercer was history. The challenge now was to close the deal.

"Not at all," Elaine reassured her. "And what law might you be breaking?"

"You tell me. You have other people down there. I'm sure they're not going away. I'm sure they'll be watching me as closely as they're watching Cable. So it's a team, of sorts, a group effort, and I'll have no idea what my invisible colleagues might be doing."

"Don't worry about them. They are highly skilled professionals who have never been caught. Listen, Mercer, you have my word. Nothing we ask you to do is even remotely illegal. I promise."

"You and I are not close enough to make promises. I don't know you."

Mercer drained her martini and said, "I need another." Alcohol was always important in these meetings, so Elaine drained hers too and waved at the waitress. When the second round arrived, they asked for an order of Vietnamese-style pork and crab spring rolls.

"Tell me about Noelle Bonnet," Mercer said, easing the tension. "I'm sure you've done your research."

Elaine smiled and said, "Yes, and I'm sure you went online this afternoon and checked her out."

"I did."

"She's published four books now, all on antiques and decorating the Provençal way, so she's revealed something of herself. She tours a lot, speaks a lot, writes a lot, and spends half the year in France. She and Cable have been together about ten years and seem to be quite the pair. No children. She has one prior divorce; none for him. He doesn't go to France much, because he rarely leaves the store. Her shop is now next door to his. He owns the building and three years ago kicked out the haberdashery and gave her the space. Evidently, he has nothing to do with her business and she stays away from his, except for entertaining. Her fourth book is about their home, a Victorian just a few blocks from downtown, and it's worth a look. You want some dirt?"

"Do tell. Who doesn't like dirt?"

"For the past ten years they've told everyone that they're married, got hitched on a hillside above Nice. It's a romantic story but it's not true. They're not married, and they appear to have a rather open marriage. He strays, she strays, but they always find their way back."

"How in the world would you know this?"

"Again, writers are blabbermouths. Evidently, some are rather promiscuous."

"Don't include me."

"I wasn't. I'm speaking in general terms."

"Go on."

"We've checked everywhere and there's no record of a marriage, here or in France. A lot of writers pass through. Bruce plays his games with the women. Noelle does the same with the men. Their home has a tower with a bedroom on the third floor and that's where the visitors sleep over. And not always alone."

"So I'll be expected to give up everything for the team?"

"You'll be expected to get as close as possible. How you choose to do that is up to you."

The spring rolls arrived. Mercer ordered lobster dumplings in broth. Elaine wanted the pepper shrimp, and she chose a bottle of Sancerre. Mercer took two bites and realized the first martini had deadened everything.

Elaine ignored her second drink and eventually said, "May I ask something personal?"

Mercer laughed, perhaps a bit too loud, and said, "Oh why not? Is there something you don't know?"

"Lots. Why haven't you been back to the cottage since Tessa died?"

Mercer looked away, sadly, and thought about her response. "It's too painful. I spent every summer there from the age of six through the age of nineteen, just Tessa and me, roaming the beach, swimming in the ocean, talking and talking and talking. She was much more than a grandmother. She was my rock, my mom, my best friend, my everything. I would spend nine miserable months with my father, counting the days until school was out so I could escape to the beach and hang out with Tessa. I begged my father to let me live with her year-round, but he would not allow it. I suppose you know about my mother."

Elaine shrugged and said, "Just what's in the records."

"She was sent away when I was six, driven crazy by her demons and I suspect by my father as well."

"Did your father get along with Tessa?"

"Don't be ridiculous. Nobody in my family gets along with anybody else. He hated Tessa because she was a snob who thought my mother married badly. Herbert was a poor kid from a bad section of Memphis who made a fortune selling used cars, then new ones. Tessa's family was old Memphis with lots of history and airs and such, but no real money. You've heard the old saying 'Too poor to paint and too proud to whitewash.' That's the perfect description of Tessa's family."

"She had three children."

"Yes. My mother, my aunt Jane, and my uncle Holstead. Who would name a kid Holstead? Tessa. It came from her family."

"And Holstead lives in California?"

"Yes, he fled the South fifty years ago and moved into a commune. He eventually married a druggie and they have four children, all total whack jobs. Because of my mother they think we're all crazy but they're the real loonies. It's a glorious family."

"That's pretty harsh."

"I'm actually being kind. None of them bothered to attend Tessa's funeral, so I haven't seen them since I was a kid. And, believe me, there are no plans for any reunion."

"*October Rain* deals with a dysfunctional family. Was it autobiographical?"

"They certainly thought so. Holstead wrote me a filthy letter that I considered framing. That was the last nail in the coffin." She ate half a spring roll and followed it with water. "Let's talk about something else."

"Good idea. You said you have questions."

"And you asked why I haven't been back to the beach cottage. It will never be the same and the memories will be hard to deal with. Think about it. I'm thirty-one years old and the happiest days of my life are behind me, in that cottage with Tessa. I'm not sure I can go back."

"You don't have to. We'll rent a nice place for six

months. But your cover works better if you use the cottage."

"Assuming I can. My sister uses it for two weeks every July and there may be some other rentals. Aunt Jane takes care of it and occasionally rents it to friends. A Canadian family takes it every November. Jane winters there from January through March."

Elaine took a bite and then a sip of her drink.

"Just curious," Mercer said. "Have you seen it?"

"Yes. Two weeks ago. Part of the preparation."

"How does it look?"

"Pretty. Well cared for. I'd like to stay there."

"Still a bunch of rentals up and down the beach?"

"Sure. I doubt if much has changed in eleven years. The area has sort of an old-time vacation feel to it. The beach is beautiful and not crowded."

"We lived on that beach. Tessa had me up with the sun, checking on the turtles, the new arrivals that made their nests during the night."

"You wrote about that, a lovely story."

"Thank you."

They finished their drinks as the entrées arrived. Elaine approved of the wine and the waitress poured some in both glasses. Mercer took a bite and put down her fork. "Look, Elaine, I'm just not up to this. You've got the wrong person, okay? I'm a terrible liar and I'm just not good at deceiving people. I cannot wiggle my way into the lives of Bruce Cable and Noelle Bonnet and their little literary gang and come away with anything that might be valuable."

"You've already said this. You're a writer living at the beach for a few months in the family cottage. You're hard at work on a novel. It's the perfect story, Mercer, because it's true. And you have the perfect personality because you're genuine. If we needed a con artist we wouldn't be talking right now. Are you afraid?"

"No. I don't know. Should I be?"

"No. I've promised you that nothing we put before you will be illegal, and nothing will be dangerous. I'll see you every week—"

"You'll be there?"

"I'll come and go, and if you need a buddy, male or female, we can arrange to have one nearby."

"I don't need a babysitter, and I'm not afraid of anything but failure. You'd be paying me a lot of money to do something I can't begin to imagine, something important, and you obviously expect results. What if Cable is as smart and tough as you think he is and reveals nothing? What if I do something stupid and he gets suspicious and moves the manuscripts? I can see a lot of ways to screw this up, Elaine. I have no experience and no clue."

"And I love your honesty. That's why you're perfect, Mercer. You're direct, sincere, and transparent. You're also very attractive and Cable will immediately like you."

"Are we back to sex? Is that part of this job description?"

"No. Again, what you do is up to you."

"But I have no idea what to do!" Mercer said, raising her voice and catching a glance from the nearest table. She lowered her head and said, "Sorry." They ate for a few minutes in silence.

"You like the wine?" Elaine asked.

"It's very good, thank you."

"It's one of my favorites."

"What if I say no again? What do you do then?"

Elaine tapped her lips with her napkin and drank some water. "We have a very short list of other possible writers, none as interesting as you. To be honest, Mercer, we're so convinced you're the perfect person that we've put all of our eggs in your basket. If you say no, we'll probably scrap the entire plan and move on to the next one."

"Which is?"

"I can't go into that. We're resourceful and we're under a lot of pressure, so we'll move fast in another direction."

"Is Cable the only suspect?"

"Please, I can't talk about that. I can tell you a lot more when you're down there, when you're good and committed and the two of us are walking on the beach. There's a lot to talk about, including some ideas about how you should proceed. But I won't go into it now. It is, after all, quite confidential."

"I get that. I can keep secrets. That's the first lesson I learned with my family."

Elaine smiled as if she understood, as if she trusted Mercer completely. The waitress poured more wine and they worked on their entrées. After the longest silence of the meal, Mercer swallowed hard, took a deep breath, and said, "I have sixty-one thousand dollars in student debt that I can't get rid of. It's a burden that consumes every waking hour and it's making me crazy."

Elaine smiled again as if she knew. Mercer almost asked if she knew, but really didn't want the answer.

Elaine put down her fork and leaned on her elbows. She tapped her fingertips together softly and said, "We'll take care of the student loans, plus the hundred grand. Fifty now, fifty in six months. Cash, check, gold bars, any way you want it. Off the books, of course."

Lead weights suddenly lifted from Mercer's shoulders and evaporated into the air. She stifled a gasp, put a hand to her mouth, and blinked her eyes as they quickly moistened. She tried to speak but had nothing to say. Her mouth was dry so she sipped water. Elaine watched every move, calculating as always.

Mercer was overwhelmed by the reality of instantly walking away from the bondage of student debt, a nightmare that had burdened her for eight years. She took a deep breath—was it actually easier to breathe now?—and attacked another lobster dumpling. She followed it with wine, which she really tasted for the first time. She would have to try a bottle or two in the coming days.

Elaine smelled a knockout and moved in for the kill. "How soon can you be there?"

"Exams are over in two weeks. But I want to sleep on this."

"Of course." The waitress was hovering, and Elaine said, "I want to try the panna cotta. Mercer?"

"The same. And with a glass of dessert wine."

6.

With little to pack, the move took only a few hours, and with her Volkswagen Beetle stuffed with her clothes, computer and printer, books, and a few pots and pans and utensils, Mercer drove away from Chapel Hill without the slightest trace of nostalgia. She was leaving behind no fond memories and only a couple of girlfriends, the kind who'd keep in touch for a few months and then be gone. She had moved and said good-bye so many times she knew which friendships would endure and which would not. She doubted she would ever see the two again.

She would head south in a couple of days, but not now. Instead, she took the interstate west, stopped in the lovely town of Asheville for lunch and a quick walk around, then chose smaller highways for a winding trip through the mountains and into Tennessee. It was dark when she finally stopped at a motel on the outskirts of Knoxville. She paid cash for a small room and walked next door to a taco franchise for dinner. She slept a proper eight hours without a single interruption, and woke up at dawn ready for another long day.

Hildy Mann had been a patient at Eastern State for the past twenty years. Mercer visited her at least once a year, sometimes twice, never more than that. There were no other visitors. Once Herbert finally realized his wife was not coming home, he quietly went about the process of a divorce. No one could blame him. Though Connie was only three hours away, she had not seen her mother in years. As the oldest, she was Hildy's legal guardian, but much too busy for a visit.

Mercer patiently went through the bureaucratic challenge of getting checked in. She met with a doctor for fifteen minutes and got the same, dismal prognosis. The patient was the victim of a debilitating form of paranoid schizophrenia and separated from rational thought by delusions, voices, and hallucinations. She had not improved in twenty-five years and there was no possible reason for hope. She was heavily medicated, and with each visit Mercer wondered how much damage the drugs had done over the years. But there was no alternative. Hildy was a permanent ward of the mental hospital and would live there until the end.

For the occasion, the nurses had forgone the standard white pullover gown and dressed her in a baby-blue cotton sundress, one of several Mercer had brought over the years. She was sitting on the edge of her bed, barefoot, staring at the floor when Mercer walked in and kissed her on the forehead. Mercer sat beside her, patted her knee, told her how much she'd missed her.

Hildy responded only with a pleasant smile. As always, Mercer marveled at how old she looked. She was only sixty-four but could pass for eighty. She was gaunt, almost emaciated, with snow-white hair and the skin of a ghost. And why not? She never left her room. Years earlier, the nurses had walked her out to the rec yard once a day for an hour or so, but Hildy had eventually balked at that. Something out there terrified her.

Mercer went through the same monologue, rambling on about her life and work and friends and this and that, some true, some fiction, none of it apparently hitting the mark. Hildy seemed to process nothing. Her face was fixed with the same simple smile and her eyes never left the floor. Mercer told herself that Hildy recognized her voice, but she wasn't sure. In fact, she wasn't sure why she even bothered with the visits.

Guilt. Connie could forget about their mother but Mercer felt guilty for not visiting more often.

Five years had passed since Hildy had spoken to her. Back then, she had recognized her, uttered her name, and even thanked her for stopping by. Months later, Hildy had turned loud and angry during a visit and a nurse intervened. Mercer often wondered if the medication was now juiced a bit more when they knew she was coming.

According to Tessa, as a young teenager Hildy had loved the poetry of Emily Dickinson. So Tessa, who visited her daughter often during the early years of her commitment, had always read poetry to her. Back then Hildy would listen and react, but over the years her condition had deteriorated.

"How about some poetry, Mom?" Mercer asked as she pulled out a thick, worn copy of *Collected Poems*. It was the same book Tessa had brought to Eastern State for years. Mercer pulled over a rocking chair and sat close to the bed.

Hildy smiled as she read and said nothing.

7.

In Memphis, Mercer met her father for lunch at a midtown restaurant. Herbert lived somewhere in Texas, and with a new wife whom Mercer had no interest in either meeting or discussing. When he'd sold cars he talked about nothing but cars, and now that he scouted for the Orioles he talked of nothing but baseball. Mercer wasn't sure which subject held less interest, but she gamely hung on and tried to make lunch enjoyable. She saw her father once a year, and after only thirty minutes remembered why. He was in town supposedly checking on some "business interests," but she doubted it. His businesses had flamed out in spectacular fashion after her first year in college, leaving her to the mercy of student lenders.

She still pinched herself to make sure it was true. The debts were gone!

Herbert moved back to baseball and rambled on about this high school prospect and that one, never once inquiring about her latest book or project. If he had read anything she had published, he never said so.

After a long hour, Mercer was almost missing the visits to Eastern State. Unable to speak, her poor mother was not nearly as boring as her windy and self-absorbed father. But they said good-bye with a hug and a kiss and the usual promises to get together more often. She said she'd be at the beach for the next few months finishing a novel, but he was already reaching for his cell phone.

After lunch, she drove to Rosewood Cemetery and put roses on Tessa's grave. She sat with her back against the headstone and had a good cry. Tessa was seventy-four when she died, but youthful in so many ways. She would be eighty-five now, no doubt as fit as ever and busy roaming the beach, collecting shells, guarding the turtle eggs, sweating in her gardens, and waiting for her beloved granddaughter to come play.

It was time to go back, to hear Tessa's voice, to touch her things, to retrace their steps. It would hurt at first, but Mercer had known for eleven years that the day would come.

She had dinner with an old high school friend, slept

in her guest room, and said good-bye early the following morning. Camino Island was fifteen hours away.

8.

She spent the night in a motel near Tallahassee and arrived at the cottage, as planned, around noon. Not much had changed, though it was now painted white and not the soft yellow Tessa had preferred. The narrow drive of oyster shells was lined with neatly trimmed Bermuda grass. According to Aunt Jane, Larry the yard guy was still taking care of the place, and he would stop by later to say hello. The front door was not far from Fernando Street, and for privacy Tessa had lined her boundaries with dwarf palmettos and elderberry shrubs, now so thick and tall that the neighbors' homes could not be seen. The flower beds where Tessa had spent the mornings away from the sun were filled with begonias, catmint, and lavender. The porch columns were covered with ever-creeping wisteria. A sweet gum tree had grown considerably and shaded most of the small front lawn. Jane and Larry were doing a nice job of landscaping. Tessa would be pleased, though she would certainly find ways to improve things.

The key worked but the door was jammed. Mercer shoved it hard with a shoulder and it finally opened. She stepped into the great room, a long wide space filled with an old sofa and chairs in one corner, facing a television, then a rustic dining table that Mercer did not recognize. Behind it was the kitchen area, surrounded by a wall of tall windows with a view of the ocean two hundred feet away, beyond the dunes. All of the furniture was different, as well as the paintings on the walls and the rugs on the floors. It felt more like a rental than a home, but Mercer was prepared for this. Tessa had lived there year-round for almost twenty years and kept it immaculate. Now it was a vacation place and needed a good dusting. Mercer walked through the kitchen and went outside, onto the wide deck filled with aging wicker furniture and surrounded by palm trees and crape myrtles. She brushed dirt and cobwebs off a rocker and sat down, gazing at the dunes and the Atlantic, listening to the waves gently rolling in. She had promised herself she would not cry, so she didn't.

Children were laughing and playing on the beach. She could hear but not see them; the dunes blocked the view of the surf. Gulls and fish crows cawed as they darted high and low above the dunes and the water.

Memories were everywhere, golden and precious thoughts of another life. Tessa had practically adopted her when she became motherless and moved her to the beach, at least for three months each year. For the other nine months Mercer had longed to be at this very spot, sitting in these rockers in the late afternoon as the sun finally faded behind them. Dusk had been their favorite time of the day. The glaring heat was over; the beach was empty. They would walk a mile to the South Pier and back, looking for shells, splashing in the surf, chatting with Tessa's friends, other residents who came out late in the day.

Those friends were now gone too, either dead or sent away to assisted living.

Mercer rocked for a long time, then got up. She

walked through the rest of the house and found little that reminded her of Tessa. And this was a good thing, she decided. There was not a single photo of her grandmother to be found; only a few framed snapshots of Jane and her family in a bedroom. After the funeral, Jane had sent Mercer a box of photos and drawings and puzzles she thought might be of interest. Mercer had kept a few of them in an album. She unpacked it, along with the rest of her assets, and went to the grocery store to get some of the basics. She made lunch, tried to read but couldn't concentrate, then fell asleep in a hammock on the deck.

Larry woke her as he stomped up the side steps. After a quick hug, each commented on how the years were treating the other. He said she was as pretty as ever, now "a fully grown woman." He looked the same, a bit grayer and more wrinkled, his skin even more leathered and beaten by too much time in the sun. He was short and wiry, and he wore what appeared to be the same straw hat she remembered as a child. There was something shady in his past, Mercer couldn't recall it at the moment, and he had fled to Florida from somewhere far up north, maybe Canada. He was a freelance gardener and handyman, and he and Tessa had always bickered over how to care for the flowers.

"You should have come back before now," he said.

"I suppose. You want a beer?"

"No. Stopped drinking a few years back. Wife made me quit."

"Get another wife."

"I've tried that too."

He'd had several wives, as Mercer remembered things,

and he was a terrible flirt, according to Tessa. She moved to a rocker and said, "Sit down. Let's talk."

"Okay, I guess." His sneakers were stained green and his ankles were caked with grass clippings. "Some water would be nice."

Mercer smiled and fetched the drinks. When she returned she twisted off the top of a beer bottle and said, "So what have you been up to?"

"The same, always the same. And you?"

"I've been teaching and writing."

"I read your book. Liked it. I used to look at your picture on the back and say 'Wow, I know her. Known her for a long time.' Tessa would've been so proud, you know?"

"Indeed she would have. So what's the gossip on the island?"

He laughed and said, "You've been gone forever and now you want the gossip."

"What happened to the Bancrofts next door?" she asked, nodding over her shoulder.

"He died a couple of years ago. Cancer. She's still hangin' on but they put her away. Her kids sold the house. New owners didn't like me; I didn't like them." She remembered his bluntness and efficiency with words.

"And the Hendersons across the street?"

"Dead."

"She and I swapped letters for a few years after Tessa died, then we sort of lost interest. Things haven't changed much around here."

"The island doesn't change. Some new homes here and there. All the beach lots have been built up, some fancy condos down by the Ritz. Tourism is up and I guess that's good. Jane says you're gonna be here for a few months."

"That's the plan. We'll see. I'm between jobs and I need to finish a book."

"You always loved books, didn't you? I remember stacks of them all over the house, even when you were a little girl."

"Tessa took me to the library twice a week. When I was in the fifth grade we had a summer reading contest at school. I read ninety-eight that summer and won the trophy. Michael Quon came in second with fifty-three. I really wanted to get to one hundred."

"Tessa always said you were too competitive. Checkers, chess, Monopoly. You always had to win."

"I guess. Seems kind of silly now."

Larry took a drink of water and wiped his mouth on the sleeve of his shirt. Gazing at the ocean, he said, "I really miss the old gal, you know. We bickered nonstop over the flower beds and the fertilizer, but she would do anything for her friends."

Mercer nodded but said nothing. After a long silence, he said, "Sorry to bring it up. I know it's still tough."

"Can I ask you something, Larry? I've never talked to anyone about what happened to Tessa. Later, long after the funeral, I read the newspaper stories and all that, but is there something I don't know? Is there more to the story?"

"No one knows." He nodded at the ocean. "She and Porter were out there, three or four miles, probably within view of land, and the storm came out of nowhere. One of those late summer afternoon jobs, but a pretty nasty one."

"Where were you?"

"At home, puttering. Before you could turn around the sky was black and the wind was screaming. The rain was thick and blowing sideways. Knocked down a bunch of trees. Power was out. They said Porter got off a Mayday but I guess it was too late."

"I was on that boat a dozen times, but sailing was not my thing. I always thought it was too hot and too boring."

"Porter was a good sailor, and as you know, he was crazy about Tessa. Nothing romantic. Hell, he was twenty years younger."

"I'm not so sure about that, Larry. They were awfully friendly, and as I got older I became suspicious. I found a pair of his old deck shoes in her closet one time. I was snooping around, like a kid will do. I didn't say anything, but just listened harder. I got the impression Porter spent a lot of time around here when I was gone."

He was shaking his head. "No. Don't you think I'd know it?"

"I suppose."

"I'm here three times a week and I keep an eye on the place. Some dude hanging around? I wouldn't miss it."

"Okay. But she really liked Porter."

"Everybody did. A good guy. Never found him, never found the boat."

"And they searched?"

"Oh yes, biggest search I ever saw. Every boat on the island was out there, including me. Coast Guard, helicopters. A jogger found Tessa up at the North Pier at sunrise. As I remember, it was two or three days later."

"She was a good swimmer but we never used life jackets."

"It wouldn't matter in that storm. So, no, we'll never know what happened. I'm sorry."

"I asked."

"I'd better go. Anything I can do for you?" He stood slowly and stretched his arms. "You have my phone number."

Mercer stood too and gave him a light hug. "Thanks, Larry. It's good to see you."

"Welcome back."

"Thanks."

9.

Late in the day, Mercer kicked off her sandals and headed for the beach. The boardwalk began at the deck and rose and fell with the dunes, which were off-limits and protected by laws. She ambled along, as always looking for the gopher tortoises. They were endangered, and Tessa had been a fanatic about protecting their habitat. They lived off the sea oats and cordgrass that covered the dunes. By the time she was eight years old, Mercer could identify all the vegetation—the sandburs, beach stars, yuccas, and Spanish bayonets. Tessa had taught her about these plants and expected her to remember from summer to summer. Eleven years later, she still remembered.

Mercer closed the narrow boardwalk gate behind her, walked to the edge of the water, and headed south. She passed a few beachcombers, all of whom nodded and smiled. Most of them had dogs on leashes. Ahead, a woman walked directly toward her. With her perfectly starched khaki shorts and chambray shirt, and cotton sweater draped over her shoulders, she looked like a model straight out of a J.Crew catalog. The face was soon familiar. Elaine Shelby smiled and said hello. They shook hands and walked together, stepping barefoot in the sea foam.

"So how's the cottage?" Elaine asked.

"It's in good shape. Aunt Jane runs a pretty tight ship."

"Did she ask a lot of questions?"

"Not really. She was happy that I wanted to stay here."

"And you're clear until early July?"

"Around July 4. Connie and her family will have it for two weeks then, so I won't be around."

"We'll get you a room nearby. Any other rentals for the cottage?"

"No, not until November."

"You'll be done by then, one way or the other."

"If you say so."

"Two initial ideas," Elaine said, quickly getting down to business. It appeared to be an innocent walk on the beach, but it was actually an important meeting. A golden retriever on a leash wanted to say hello. They rubbed his head and exchanged the usual pleasantries with his owner. Walking again, Elaine said, "First, I'd stay away from the bookstore. It's important that Cable comes to you, not the other way around."

"And how do I arrange that?"

"There's a lady on the island, Myra Beckwith, a writer you might have heard of."

"Nope."

"Didn't think so. She's written a pile of books, really raunchy romance novels, and she uses a dozen pen names. She once sold well in that genre but she's slowed down with age. She lives with her partner in one of the old homes downtown. She's a big woman, six feet tall and broad, a real bruiser. When you meet her you won't believe she's ever had sex with anybody, but she has an impressive imagination. A real character, very eccentric and loud and colorful, and she's sort of the Queen Bee of the literary crowd. Of course, she and Cable are old friends. Drop her a note, make the introduction, tell her what you're doing here, the usual routine. Say you'd like to stop by for a drink and say hello. Cable will know about it within twenty-four hours."

"Who's her partner?"

"Leigh Trane, another writer you might have heard of."

"Nope."

"Didn't think so. She aspires to write literary fiction, really impenetrable stuff that the stores can't give away. Her last book sold three hundred copies and that was eight years ago. They're an odd couple in every sense of the word, but they'll probably be a hoot to hang out with. Once they know you, Cable will not be far behind."

"Simple enough."

"The second idea is a little riskier but I'm certain it will work. There's a young writer named Serena Roach."

"Bingo. Someone I've heard of. Never met her but we have the same publisher."

"Right. Her latest novel came out a few days ago."

"I saw a review. Sounds dreadful."

"That's not important. What's interesting is that she's touring and she'll be here Wednesday of next week. I have her e-mail. Drop her a note, give her the spiel, and say you'd like to have coffee and so on. She's about your age, single, and it could be fun. Her signing will be the perfect reason for you to visit the store."

"And since she's young and single we can expect Cable to be on his best behavior."

"With you in town for a spell, and with Ms. Roach on tour, there's a chance Cable and Noelle might host a dinner after the signing. By the way, Noelle is in town these days."

"I'm not going to ask how you know this."

"Quite simple. We went antiques shopping this afternoon."

"You said this might be risky."

"Well, over drinks it might come out that you and Serena have never met until now. A convenient coincidence, maybe. Maybe not."

"I don't think so," Mercer said. "Since we have the same publisher, it seems believable that I would stop by and say hello."

"Good. There will be a box delivered to your cottage in the morning at ten. It's a pile of books, all four of Noelle's and the three by Serena."

"Homework?"

"You love to read, right?"

"That's part of my job."

"I'll also throw in some of Myra's garbage just for fun. Total trash but quite addictive. I could find only one of Leigh Trane's books and it will be in the collection. I'm sure she's out of print and with good reason. Not sure I'd bother. I couldn't finish chapter 1."

"Can't wait. How long are you here?"

"I leave tomorrow." They walked in silence, still at the water's edge. Two kids on paddleboards splashed nearby. Elaine said, "When we were having dinner in Chapel Hill you had questions about the operation. I can't say much, but we are quietly offering a reward for information. A couple of months ago, we found a woman who lives in the Boston area. She was once married to a book collector who deals in the rare stuff and is known to handle books with shady backgrounds. Evidently, the divorce was fairly recent and she's carrying some baggage. She told us that her ex-husband knows a lot about the Fitzgerald manuscripts. She thinks he bought them from the thieves and quickly flipped them out of fear. She thinks he got a million bucks but we haven't been able to trace the money, nor has she. If it happened, it was probably an offshore deal with hidden accounts and such. We're still digging."

"Have you talked to the ex-husband?"

"Not yet."

"And he flipped them to Bruce Cable?"

"She gave us his name. She worked in the business with her ex until things went sour, so she knows something about the trade."

"Why would he bring them here?"

"Why not? This is home and he feels secure. As of now, we are assuming the manuscripts are here, but that's a rather significant assumption. We could easily be wrong. As I've said, Cable is very smart and clever and knows what he's doing. He's probably too savvy to keep them in a place that would be incriminating. If there's a vault under the bookstore, I doubt he would store them there. But who knows? We're just guessing and will continue to do so until we have better information."

"But what kind of information?"

"We need a set of eyes inside the store, specifically inside his First Editions Room. Once you get to know him and start hanging around the store, buying books, showing up at author events, and so on, you will gradually develop a curiosity about his rare stuff. You'll have some old books that Tessa left behind and these will be your entrée. How much are they worth? Does he want to buy them? We have no idea where these conversations might go, but at least we'll have someone on the inside, someone he does not suspect. At some point, you'll hear something. Who knows what, when, and where. The Fitzgerald heist might be dinner conversation. As I said, he drinks a lot and alcohol causes loose lips. Things slip out."

"It's hard to believe he'd let that slip."

"True, but the slip might come from someone else. What's crucial now is to have eyes and ears on the inside."

They stopped at the South Pier and turned around and headed north. Elaine said, "Follow me," and they walked to a boardwalk. She opened the gate and they climbed the steps to a small landing. She pointed to a two-story triplex at the far end and said, "The one on the right belongs to us, for now anyway. That's where I'm staying. In a couple of days someone else will be there. I'll text you their number."

"Will I be watched?"

"No. You're on your own, but you'll always have a friend just in case. And I'd like an e-mail every night, regardless of what's going on. Okay?"

"Sure."

"I'm leaving now." She held out her right hand and Mercer shook it. "Good luck, Mercer, and try to think of this as a vacation at the beach. Once you get to know Cable and Noelle, you might actually enjoy them and have some fun."

Mercer shrugged and said, "We'll see."

10.

The Dumbarton Gallery was a block off Wisconsin Avenue in Georgetown. It was a small gallery on the ground floor of an old redbrick town house, one in need of a good paint job and perhaps a new roof. Despite the heavy foot traffic only a block away, the gallery was usually deserted, its walls practically bare. It specialized in minimalist modern stuff that, evidently, wasn't too popular, at least not in Georgetown. Its owner didn't really care. His name was Joel Ribikoff, fifty-two years old and a convicted felon, busted twice for dealing in stolen valuables.

His art gallery on the first floor was a front, a ruse designed to convince anyone who might be watching, and after two convictions and eight years in the slammer Joel believed that someone was always watching, that he had gone straight and was now just another struggling gallery owner in Washington. He played the game, had some shows, knew a few artists and even fewer clients, and halfheartedly maintained a website, again for the benefit of watchful eyes.

He lived on the third floor of the town house. On the second he had his office where he tended to his serious business, that of brokering deals for stolen paintings, prints, photographs, books, manuscripts, maps, sculpture, and even forged letters allegedly written by famous dead people. Even with the horrors of two convictions and life in prison, Joel Ribikoff simply could not stick to the rules. For him, living in the underworld was far more exciting, and profitable, than minding a small gallery and pushing art few people wanted. He loved the thrill of connecting thieves to their victims, or thieves to intermediaries, and structuring deals that involved multiple layers and parties with the valuables moving in the dark as money was wired to offshore accounts. He rarely took possession of the loot, but preferred to be the savvy middleman who kept his hands clean.

The FBI had stopped by a month after the Fitzgerald heist at Princeton. Of course, Joel knew nothing. A month later, they were back, and he still knew nothing. After that, though, he learned a lot. Fearing the FBI had tapped his phones, Joel had disappeared from the D.C. area and went under deep cover. Using prepaid and disposable cell phones, he had made contact with the thief and had met him at an interstate motel near Aberdeen, Maryland. The thief had introduced himself as Denny and his accomplice was Rooker. A couple of tough guys. On a cheap bed in a double room that was worth seventy-nine dollars a night, Joel took a look at the five Fitzgerald manuscripts that were worth more than any of the three could imagine.

It had been obvious to Joel that Denny, undoubtedly the leader of the gang or what was left of it, was under enormous pressure to unload them and flee the country. "I want a million dollars," he'd said.

"I can't find that much," Joel had replied. "I have one and only one contact who will even talk about these books. All the boys in my business are extremely spooked right now. The Feds are everywhere. My best, no, my only, deal is half a million."

Denny had cursed and stomped around the room, pausing occasionally to peek through the curtains and glance at the parking lot. Joel got tired of the theatrics and said he was leaving. Denny finally caved and they completed the details. Joel left with nothing but his briefcase. After dark, Denny left with the manuscripts and instructions to drive to Providence and wait. Rooker, an old Army pal who had also turned to crime, met him there. Three days later, and with the assistance of another intermediary, the transfer had been completed.

Now Denny was back in Georgetown, with Rooker, and looking for his treasure. Ribikoff had given him a good screwing the first time around. It would not happen again. As the gallery was closing at 7:00 p.m. on Wednesday, May 25, Denny walked in its front door while Rooker pried open a window to Joel's office. When all doors were locked and all lights were off, they carried Joel to his apartment on the third floor, bound and gagged him, and began the ugly business of extracting information.

CHAPTER FOUR
THE BEACHCOMBER

1.

With Tessa, the day began with the sunrise. She would drag Mercer out of bed and hurry to the deck, where they sipped coffee and waited with great anticipation for the first glimpse of the orange glow rising on the horizon. Once the sun was up, they would hustle down the boardwalk and check out the beach. Later in the morning, as Tessa worked in the flower beds on the west side of the cottage, Mercer would often ease back into bed for a long nap.

With Tessa's consent, Mercer had had her first cup of coffee around the age of ten, and her first martini at fifteen. "Everything in moderation" was one of her grandmother's favorite sayings.

But Tessa was gone now, and Mercer had seen enough sunrises. She slept until after nine and reluctantly got out of bed. As the coffee brewed, she roamed around the cottage in search of the perfect writing space and didn't find one. She felt no pressure and was determined to write only if she had something to say. Her novel was three years past due anyway. If they could wait for three years in New York, then they could certainly handle four. Her agent checked in occasionally, but with less frequency. Their conversations were brief. During her long drives from Chapel Hill to Memphis to Florida, she had loafed and dreamed and plotted and at times felt as though her novel was finding its voice. She planned to toss the scraps that she'd already written and start over, but this time with a serious new beginning. Now that she was no longer in debt, and no longer worried about the next job, her mind was wonderfully uncluttered with the nagging irritations of everyday life. Once she was settled and rested, she would plunge into her work and average at least a thousand words a day.

But for her current job, the one for which she was being handsomely paid, she had no idea what she was doing, and no idea how long it might take to do whatever she was supposed to do, so she decided there was no benefit in wasting a day. She went online and checked her e-mails. Not surprisingly, ever-efficient Elaine had dropped a note during the night with some useful addresses.

Mercer typed an e-mail to the Queen Bee: "Dear Myra Beckwith. I'm Mercer Mann, a novelist house-sitting on the beach for a few months while I work on a book. I know virtually no one here and so I'm taking a chance by saying hello and suggesting we—you, Ms. Trane, me—get together for a drink. I'll bring a bottle of wine."

At ten on the dot, the doorbell rang. When Mercer

opened the front door an unmarked box was on the porch but there was no delivery guy in sight. She took it to the kitchen table, where she opened and unpacked it. As promised, there were the four large picture books by Noelle Bonnet, three novels by Serena Roach, the rather slim literary edition by Leigh Trane, and half a dozen romance novels with artwork that fairly sizzled. All manner of skin was being groped by gorgeous young maidens and their handsome lovers with impossibly flat stomachs. Each was by a different author, though all were written by Myra Beckwith. She would save those for later.

Nothing she saw inspired her to pursue her own novel.

She ate some granola as she flipped through Noelle's book about the Marchbanks House.

At 10:37 her cell phone buzzed, caller unknown. She barely said "Hello" before a frantic, high-pitched voice declared, "We don't drink wine. I do beer and Leigh prefers rum, and the cabinet's stocked full so you don't have to bring your own bottle. Welcome to the island. This is Myra."

Mercer was almost chuckling. "A pleasure, Myra. I didn't expect to hear from you so soon."

"Well, we're bored and always looking for somebody new. Can you hold off till six this afternoon? We never start drinking before six."

"I'll try. See you then."

"And you know where we are?"

"On Ash Street."

"See you."

Mercer put the phone down and tried to place the

accent. Definitely southern, maybe East Texas. She selected one of the paperbacks, one supposedly written
by a Runyon O'Shaughnessy, and began reading. The
"savagely handsome" hero was loose in a castle where
he was not welcome, and by page 4 he had bedded two
chambermaids and was stalking a third. By the end of
the first chapter, everyone was exhausted, including
Mercer. She stopped when she realized her pulse was up
a notch. She did not have the stamina to blitz through
five hundred pages.

She took Leigh Trane's novel to the deck and found a
rocker under an umbrella. It was after eleven, and the
midday Florida sun was beating down. Everything left
unshaded was hot to the touch. Ms. Trane's novel dealt
with a young, unmarried woman who woke up pregnant one day and wasn't sure who the father was. She
had been drinking too much during the past year, had
been rather promiscuous, and her memory was not that
sharp. With a calendar, she tried to retrace her steps,
and finally made a list of the three likeliest suspects.
She vowed to secretly investigate each one with the plan
to one day, after her child arrived, spring a paternity
suit on the real daddy and collect support. It was a nice
setup, but the writing was so convoluted and pretentious
that any reader would have difficulty plowing through.
No scene was clear, so that the reader was never certain
what was going on. Ms. Trane obviously had a pen in one
hand and a thesaurus in the other because Mercer saw
long words for the first time. And, just as frustrating, the
dialogue was not identified with quotation marks, and
often it was not clear who said what.

After twenty minutes of hard work, she was exhausted and fell into a nap.

She woke up sweating, and bored, and boredom was not acceptable. She had always lived alone and had learned to stay busy. The cottage needed a good cleaning but that could wait. Tessa might have been a fastidious housekeeper but Mercer did not inherit that trait. Living alone, why should she care if the place wasn't spotless? She changed into a bathing suit, noted in the mirror her rather pale skin and vowed to work on the tan, and went to the beach. It was Friday, and the weekend renters were arriving, though her stretch of the beach was almost deserted. She took a long swim and short walk, then returned to the cottage and showered and decided to find lunch in town. She put on a light sundress and no makeup, except for lipstick.

Fernando Street ran for five miles along the beach, and next to the dunes and the ocean it was lined with a mix of old and new rentals, budget motels, fine new homes, condos, and an occasional bed-and-breakfast. Across the street, there were more homes and rentals, shops, a few offices, more motels, and restaurants offering up bar food. As she puttered along, adhering to the strict limit of thirty-five miles per hour, Mercer thought nothing had changed. It was exactly as she remembered. The town of Santa Rosa maintained it well and every eighth of a mile there was a small parking lot and boardwalk for public beach access.

Behind her, to the south, there were the big hotels, the Ritz and the Marriott sitting beside high-rise condos, and the more exclusive residential enclaves, developments Tessa had never approved of, because she believed too many lights interfered with the nesting of green and loggerhead turtles. Tessa had been an active member of Turtle Watch, as well as every other conservation and environmental group on the island.

Mercer was not an activist, because she couldn't stand meetings, which was another reason to stay away from campuses and faculties. She entered the town and eased along with the traffic on Main Street, passing the bookstore with Noelle's Provence next door. She parked on a side street and found a small café with courtyard seating. After a long, quiet lunch in the shade, she browsed through the clothing stores and T-shirt shops, mixing with the tourists and buying nothing. She drifted toward the harbor and watched the boats come and go. She and Tessa came here to meet Porter, their sailing friend who owned a thirty-foot sloop and was always eager to take them out. Those had been long days, for Mercer anyway. As she remembered things, there was never enough wind and they baked in the sun. She had always tried to hide in the cabin but the boat had no air-conditioning. Porter had lost his wife to some horrible disease; Tessa said he never talked about it and had moved to Florida to escape the memories. Tessa always said he had the saddest eyes.

Mercer had never blamed Porter for what happened. Tessa loved to sail with him and she understood the risks. Land was never out of sight and there were no thoughts of danger.

To escape the heat, she stepped inside the harbor restaurant and had a glass of iced tea at the empty bar. She gazed at the water and watched a charter boat return with a load of mahimahi and four happy and red-faced fishermen. A gang of jet skiers set off, going much too fast in the no-wake zone. And then she saw a sloop easing away from the pier. It was about the same length and color as Porter's, and there were two people on deck, an older gentleman at the wheel and a lady in a straw hat. For a moment it was Tessa, sitting idly by, drink in hand, perhaps offering unsolicited advice to the captain, and the years disappeared. Tessa was alive again. Mercer longed to see and hold her and laugh about something. A dull pain ached in her stomach, but soon the moment passed. She watched the sloop until it disappeared, then paid for the tea and left the harbor.

At a coffee shop, she sat at a table and watched the bookstore across the street. Its large windows were packed with books. A banner announced an upcoming author signing. Someone was always at the door, coming or going. It was impossible to believe the manuscripts were in there, locked away in some vault hidden in the basement. It was even more far-fetched to think that she was somehow supposed to deliver them.

Elaine had suggested that Mercer stay away from the store and wait until Cable made the first move. However, Mercer was now her own spy, making her own rules, though still without a clue. She wasn't exactly taking orders from anyone. Orders? There was no clear game plan. Mercer had been tossed into battle and expected to adjust and improvise on the fly. At 5:00 p.m., a man in a seersucker suit and bow tie, undoubtedly Bruce Cable, walked out of the store and headed east. Mercer waited until he was gone, then crossed the street and entered Bay Books for the first time in many years.

She could not remember the last visit but guessed she was either seventeen or eighteen, and driving.

As she always did in any bookstore, she drifted aimlessly until she found the shelves for Literary Fiction, then scanned quickly through the alphabet, about midway down to the *M*s, to see if either of her books might be in inventory. She smiled. There was one copy of the trade edition of *October Rain*. There was no sign of *The Music of Waves,* but that was to be expected. She had not found her short story collection in a bookstore since the week it was published.

With a partial victory in hand, she wandered slowly through the store, soaking up the smells of new books, and coffee, and, from somewhere, the hint of pipe smoke. She adored the saggy shelves, the piles of books on the floors, the ancient rugs, the racks of paperbacks, the colorful section for bestsellers at 25 percent off! From across the store she took in the First Editions Room, a handsome paneled area with open windows and hundreds of the more expensive books. Upstairs in the café, she bought a bottle of sparkling water and ventured outside on the porch, where others were drinking coffee and passing the late afternoon. At the far end, a rotund gentleman was smoking a pipe. She flipped through a tourist guide for the island and watched the clock.

At five minutes before six, she went downstairs and spotted Bruce Cable at the front counter chatting with a customer. She seriously doubted if he would recognize her. His only clue would be her black-and-white photo on the dust jacket of *October Rain,* a novel that was now seven years old and had generated only pennies for his store. But she had been scheduled to sign here during her aborted book tour, and he allegedly read everything, and he probably knew her connection to the island, and, most important, at least from his viewpoint, she was an attractive young female writer, so perhaps the odds were even that he would spot her.

He did not.

2.

Ash Street was one block south of Main. The house was on a corner lot at the intersection of Fifth. It was old and historic with gabled roofs and two-storied gallery porches on three sides. It was painted a soft pink and trimmed in dark blue on its doors, shutters, and porches. A small sign over the front door read, "Vicker House 1867."

From her past, Mercer could not remember a pink house in downtown Santa Rosa, not that it mattered. Houses get painted every year.

She tapped on the door and a pack of yappy dogs erupted on the other side. A beast of a woman yanked open the door, thrust out a hand, and said, "I'm Myra. Come in. Don't mind the dogs. Nobody bites around here but me."

"I'm Mercer," she said, shaking hands.

"Of course you are. Come on."

The dogs scattered as Mercer followed Myra into the foyer. In a screech, Myra unloaded a "Leigh! Company's here! Leigh!" When Leigh failed to instantly respond, Myra said, "Stay here. I'll go find her." She disappeared through the living room, leaving Mercer alone with a rat-sized mongrel that cowered under a knitting table and growled at her with all teeth flashing. Mercer tried to ignore him or her as she sized up the place. In the air there was a less than pleasant odor of what seemed to be a mix of stale cigarette smoke and dirty dogs. The furniture was old flea market stuff, but quirky and engaging. The walls were covered with bad oils and watercolors by the dozens, and not a single one depicted anything remotely connected to the ocean.

Somewhere in the depths of the house Myra yelled again. A much smaller woman emerged from the dining room and said softly, "Hello, I'm Leigh Trane," without offering a hand.

"A pleasure. I'm Mercer Mann."

"I'm loving your book," Leigh said with a smile that revealed two perfect rows of tobacco-stained teeth. Mercer had not heard anyone say that in a long time. She hesitated and managed an awkward "Well, thank you."

"Bought a copy two hours ago, from the store, a real book. Myra is addicted to her little device and reads everything on it."

For a second Mercer felt obligated to lie and say something nice about Leigh's book, but Myra saved her the trouble. She lumbered back into the foyer and said, "There you are. Now that we're all good friends, the bar is open and I need a drink. Mercer, what would you like?"

Since they didn't drink wine, she said, "It's hot. I'll take a beer."

Both women recoiled as if offended. Myra said, "Well,

okay, but you should know that I brew my own beer, and it's different."

"It's dreadful," Leigh added. "I used to like beer before she started her own brewery. Now I can't stand the stuff."

"Just gulp your rum, sweetheart, and we'll get along fine." Myra looked at Mercer and said, "It's a spicy ale that's 8 percent alcohol. Knock you on your ass if you're not careful."

"Why are we still standing in the foyer?" Leigh asked.

"Damned good question," Myra said, flinging an arm toward the stairway. "Come with me." From behind she looked like an offensive tackle as she cleared the hallway. They followed in her wake and stopped in a family room with a television and fireplace and, in one corner, a full bar with a marble counter.

"We do have wine," Leigh said.

"Then I'll have some white wine," Mercer said. Anything but the home brew.

Myra went to work behind the bar and began firing questions. "So, where are you staying?"

"I don't suppose you remember my grandmother Tessa Magruder. She lived in a little beach house on Fernando Street."

Both women shook their heads. No. "Name sorta rings a bell," Myra said.

"She passed away eleven years ago."

"We've been here for only ten years," Leigh said.

Mercer said, "The family still owns the cottage and that's where I'm staying."

"For how long?" Myra asked.

"A few months."

"Trying to finish a book, right?"

"Or to start one."

"Aren't we all?" Leigh asked.

"Got one under contract?" Myra asked, rattling bottles.

"Afraid so."

"Be thankful for that. Who's your publisher?"

"Viking."

Myra waddled out from behind the bar and handed drinks to Mercer and Leigh. She grabbed a quart-sized fruit jar of thick ale and said, "Let's go outside so we can smoke." It was obvious that they had been smoking inside for years.

They walked across a plank deck and settled around a pretty wrought-iron table next to a fountain where a pair of bronze frogs spewed water. Old sweet gum trees blanketed the courtyard with a thick layer of shade, and from somewhere a gentle breeze settled in. The door off the porch didn't latch and the dogs came and went as they pleased.

"This is lovely," Mercer said as both hosts fired up cigarettes. Leigh's was long and skinny. Myra's was brown and potent.

"Sorry about the smoke," Myra said, "but we're addicted, can't stop. Once, long ago, we tried to quit, but those days are history. So much work, effort, misery, and finally we said to hell with it. Gotta die of something, you know." She took a long pull from her cigarette, inhaled, exhaled, then washed it all down with a slug of homemade ale. "You want a drink? Come on, try it."

"I wouldn't do that," Leigh said.

Mercer quickly sipped her wine and shook her head. "No thanks."

"This cottage, you say it's been in the family?" Myra asked. "Been coming here for a long time?"

"Yes, since I was a little girl. I spent the summers here with my grandmother Tessa."

"How sweet. I like that." Another slurp of the ale. Myra's head was peeled about an inch above her ears so that her gray hair flopped from side to side when she drank, smoked, and talked. She was completely gray and about Leigh's age. Leigh, though, had long dark hair that was pulled back into a tight ponytail and showing no gray.

Both seemed ready to pounce with questions, so Mercer took the offensive. "What brought you to Camino Island?"

They looked at each other as if the story was long and complicated. Myra said, "We lived in the Fort Lauderdale area for many years and got tired of the traffic and crowds. The pace of life here is much slower. People are nicer. Real estate is cheaper. And you? Where's home for you these days?"

"I've been in Chapel Hill for the past three years, teaching. But now I'm sort of in transition."

"What the hell does that mean?" Myra asked.

"Means I'm basically homeless and unemployed and desperate to finish a book."

Leigh cackled and Myra guffawed as smoke streamed from their noses. "We've been there," Myra said. "We met thirty years ago when neither one of us had two pennies to rub together. I was trying to write historical fiction and Leigh was trying to write that weird literary shit she's still trying to write and nothing was selling. We were on welfare and food stamps and working for minimum wage, and, well, things were not looking too good. One day we were walking down a mall and saw a long line of people, all middle-aged women, waiting for something. Up ahead was a bookstore, one of those Walden bookshops used to be in every mall, and sitting at a table having a grand time was Roberta Doley, back then one of the bestselling romance gals in the business. I got in line—Leigh was too much of a snob— bought the book and we made each other read it. The story was about a pirate who roamed the Caribbean raiding ships and raising hell and running from the Brits, and it just so happened that everywhere he docked there was a gorgeous young virgin just waiting to be deflowered. Total crap. So we conjured up this story about a southern belle who couldn't stay away from her slaves and got herself pregnant. We threw everything at it."

Leigh added, "Had to buy some dirty magazines, you know, for reference materials. A lot of that stuff we didn't know about."

Myra laughed and continued. "We knocked it out in three months and I reluctantly sent it to my agent in New York. A week later she called and said some idiot was offering fifty grand as an advance. We published it under the name of Myra Leigh. Isn't that clever? Within a year we had a pile of cash and never looked back."

"So you write together?" Mercer asked.

"She writes it," Leigh said quickly, as if to distance herself. "We work on the story together, which takes about ten minutes, then she grinds it out. Or we used to."

"Leigh's too much of a snob to touch it. She'll damned sure touch the money, though."

"Now, Myra," Leigh said with a smile.

Myra sucked in a lungful and blew a cloud over her shoulder. "Those were the days. We cranked out a hundred books under a dozen names and couldn't write 'em fast enough. The dirtier the better. You should try one. Pure filth."

"I can't wait," Mercer said.

"Please don't," Leigh said. "You're much too smart for it. I love your writing."

Mercer was touched and quietly said, "Thank you."

"Then we slowed down," Myra continued. "We got sued twice by this crazy bitch up north who claimed we had stolen her stuff. Wasn't true. Our crap was much better than her crap, but our lawyers got nervous and made us settle out of court. That led to a big fight with our publisher, then our agent, and the whole thing sort of knocked us off our stride. Somehow we got the reputation as thieves, or at least I did. Leigh did a good job of hiding behind me and dodging all the mud. Her literary reputation is still intact, such as it is."

"Now, Myra."

"So you stopped writing?" Mercer asked.

"Let's say I slowed down considerably. There's money in the bank and some of the books are still selling."

"I still write, every day," Leigh said. "My life would be empty if I didn't write."

"And it would be a helluva lot emptier if I didn't sell," Myra snarled.

"Now, Myra."

The pack's largest dog, a forty-pound long-haired

mutt, squatted close to the patio and dropped a pile. Myra saw it happen, said nothing, then covered the area with a cloud of smoke when the dog was finished.

Mercer changed the subject with "Are there other writers on the island?"

Leigh nodded with a smile and Myra said, "Oh, far too many." She chugged the fruit jar and smacked her lips.

"There's Jay," Leigh said. "Jay Arklerood."

It was becoming apparent that Leigh's job was to merely suggest so that Myra could then narrate. She said, "You would start with him, wouldn't you? He's another literary snob who can't sell and hates everybody who can. He's also a poet. Do you like poetry, Mercer dear?"

Her tone left no doubt that she had little use for poetry. Mercer said, "Don't read much of it."

"Well, don't read his, if you could even find it."

"I'm afraid I haven't heard of him."

"No one has. He sells less than Leigh."

"Now, Myra."

"What about Andy Adam?" Mercer asked. "Doesn't he live here?"

"When he's not in rehab," Myra said. "He built a fine home down on the south end, then lost it in a divorce. He's a mess but a really good writer. I adore his Captain Clyde series, some of the best crime fiction around. Even Leigh can stoop to enjoy it."

Leigh said, "A lovely man, when he's sober, but a dreadful drunk. He still gets in fights."

Seamlessly taking the handoff, Myra jumped right back in with "Just last month he got in a fight at the saloon on Main Street. Some guy half his age beat the hell out of him and the police hauled him in. Bruce had to post his bond."

"Who's Bruce?" Mercer asked quickly.

Myra and Leigh sighed and took a sip, as if any discussion of Bruce might take hours. Leigh eventually said, "Bruce Cable, he owns the bookstore. You've never met him?"

"Don't think so. I can remember visiting the store a few times when I was a kid, but I can't say that I met him."

Myra said, "When it comes to books and writers, everything revolves around the store. Thus, everything revolves around Bruce. He's the Man."

"And this is a good thing?"

"Oh, we adore Bruce. He has the greatest bookstore in the country and he loves writers. Years ago, before we moved here and back when I was writing and publishing, he invited me to a book signing at his store. It's a bit unusual for a serious bookstore to host a romance writer, but Bruce didn't care. We had a helluva party, sold a bunch of books, got drunk on cheap champagne, and kept the store open until midnight. Hell, he even had a book signing for Leigh."

"Now, Myra."

"It's true, and she sold fourteen books."

"Fifteen. My biggest signing ever."

"My record is five," Mercer said. "And that was my first signing. Sold four at the next, then zero at the third. After that I called New York and canceled everything."

"Go, girl," Myra said. "You quit?"

"I did, and if I ever publish again I will not go on tour."

"Why didn't you come here, to Bay Books?"

"It was on the schedule, but I freaked out and pulled the plug."

"You should've started here. Bruce can always drum up a crowd. Hell, he calls us all the time, says there's a writer coming in and we might really like his or her book. That means get our butts down to the store for the signing and buy the damned book! We never miss."

"And we have a lot of books, all signed by the authors and most unread," Leigh added.

"Have you been to the store?" Myra asked.

"I stopped by on the way here. It's lovely."

"It's civilization, an oasis. Let's meet there for lunch and I'll introduce you to Bruce. You'll like him and I can assure you he'll fancy you. He loves all writers, but the young pretty females get special attention."

"Is he married?"

"Oh yes. His wife is Noelle and she's usually around. A real character."

"I like her," Leigh said, almost defensively, as if most people felt otherwise.

"What does she do?" Mercer asked as innocently as possible.

"She sells French antiques, next door to the book-store," Myra said. "Who needs another drink?"

Mercer and Leigh had hardly touched their drinks. Myra stomped away to refill her fruit jar. At least three dogs followed her. Leigh lit another cigarette and asked, "So tell me about your novel, your work in progress."

Mercer took a sip of warm Chablis and said, "I really

can't talk about it. It's a little rule I have. I hate to hear writers talk about their work, don't you?"

"I suppose. I'd love to discuss my work but she won't listen. It seems as though talking about your work would motivate you to actually write. Me, I've had writer's block for the past eight years." She chuckled and took a quick puff. "But then she's not much help. I'm almost afraid to write because of her."

For a second Mercer felt sorry for her and was almost tempted to volunteer as her reader, but she quickly remembered her tortured prose. Myra stormed back with another quart, kicking at a dog as she sat down.

She said, "And don't forget the vampire girl. Amy what's her name?"

"Amy Slater," Leigh said helpfully.

"That's her. Moved here about five years ago with her husband and some kids. Hit pay dirt with a series about vampires and ghosts and such junk, really awful stuff that sells like crazy. On my worst days, and believe me I've published some dreadful books that were supposed to be dreadful, I can outwrite her with one hand tied behind me."

"Now, Myra. Amy's a lovely person."

"You keep saying that."

"Anybody else?" Mercer asked. So far every other writer had been trashed and Mercer was enjoying the carnage, which was not at all unusual when writers gathered over drinks and talked about each other.

They thought for a second and worked their drinks. Myra said, "Got a bunch of the self-published crowd. They crank 'em out, post 'em online, call themselves writers. They print a few copies and hang around the bookstore, pestering Bruce to put 'em up front by the door and dropping in every other day to check on their royalties. A real pain in the ass. He's got a table where he puts all the self-published stuff and he's always wrangling with one or two of them over placement. With the Internet everybody is now a published author, you know?"

"Oh, I know," Mercer said. "When I was teaching, they would leave books and manuscripts on my front porch, usually with a long letter describing how wonderful their work was and how much they'd appreciate a blurb."

"So tell us about teaching," Leigh said softly.

"Oh, it's much more fun to talk about writers."

"I got one," Myra said. "Guy's name is Bob but he uses the pen name of J. Andrew Cobb. We call him Bob Cobb. He spent six years in a federal pen for some type of bad corporate behavior and learned to write, sort of. He's published four or five books about what he knows best—corporate espionage—and they're fun to read. Not a bad writer."

"I thought he left," Leigh said.

"He keeps a condo down by the Ritz, and in the condo he's always got some young girl he met on the beach. He's pushing fifty, the girls are usually half that. He's a charmer, though, and can tell great stories about prison. Careful when you're on the beach. Bob Cobb is always on the prowl."

"I'll write that down," Mercer said with a smile.

"Who else can we talk about?" Myra asked, chugging.

"That's enough for now," Mercer said. "It will take some work to remember these."

"You'll meet them soon enough. They're in and out

of the bookstore and Bruce is always having folks over for drinks and dinner."

Leigh smiled and set down her drink. "Let's do it here, Myra. Let's throw a dinner party and invite all of these wonderful people we've been trashing for the past hour. We haven't hosted in some time and it's always Bruce and Noelle. We need to officially welcome Mercer to the island. What do you say?"

"Great idea. Lovely idea. I'll get Dora to cater and we'll get the house cleaned. How about it, Mercer?"

Mercer shrugged and realized that it would be foolish to object. Leigh left to refresh her drink and fetch more wine. They spent the next hour talking about the party and haggling over the guest list. With the exception of Bruce Cable and Noelle Bonnet, every other potential invitee had baggage, and the more the better. It promised to be a memorable evening.

It was dark when Mercer finally managed to get away. They practically demanded that she stay for dinner, but when Leigh let it slip that there was nothing in the fridge but leftovers, Mercer knew it was time to go. After three glasses of wine she was not ready to drive. She roamed downtown and drifted with the tourists along Main Street. She found a coffee shop still open and killed an hour at the bar with a latte and a glossy magazine promoting the island, primarily its real estate agents. Across the street the bookstore was busy, and she eventually walked over and stared at the handsome display window but did not go inside. She ventured down to the quiet harbor, where she sat on a bench and watched the sailboats rock gently on the water. Her ears were still ringing from the avalanche of gossip she had just absorbed, and she chuckled at the visual of Myra and Leigh getting drunk and blowing smoke and growing more excited about the dinner party.

It was only her second night on the island, but she felt as though she was settling in. Drinks with Myra and Leigh would have that effect on any visitor. The hot weather and salty air helped ease the transition. And with no home to long for it was impossible to feel homesick. She had asked herself a hundred times what, exactly, she was doing there. The question was still around but it was slowly fading.

3.

High tide was at 3:21 a.m., and when it crested the loggerhead turtle slid onto the beach and paused in the sea foam to look around. She was three and a half feet long and weighed 350 pounds. She had been migrating at sea for over two years and was returning to a spot within fifty yards of where she had made her last nest. Slowly, she began to crawl, a slow, awkward, unnatural movement for her. As she labored along, pulling with her front flippers and pushing with more power with her rear legs, she paused frequently to study the beach, to look for dry land and for danger, for a predator or any unusual movement. Seeing none, she inched ahead, leaving a distinctive trail in the sand, one that would soon be found by her allies. One hundred feet ashore, at the toe of a dune, she found her spot and began flinging away loose sand with her front flippers.

Using her cupped rear flippers as shovels, she began form-
ing the body pit, a round shallow burrow four inches
deep. As she dug she rotated her body to even the in-
dentation. For a creature of the water, it was tedious
work and she paused often to rest. When the body pit
was finished she began digging even deeper to con-
struct the egg cavity, a teardrop-shaped chamber. She
finished, rested some more, then slowly covered the egg
cavity with the rear of her body and faced the dune.
Three eggs dropped at the same time, each shell covered
with mucus and too soft and flexible to break upon
landing. More eggs followed, two and three at a time.
While laying, she didn't move, but appeared to be in a
trance. At the same time she shed tears, excreting salt
that had accumulated.

Mercer saw the tracks from the sea and smiled. She
carefully followed them until she saw the outline of
the loggerhead near the dune. From experience, she knew
that any noise or disturbance during nesting could
cause the mother to abort and return to the water without covering her eggs. Mercer stopped and studied the
outline. A half-moon peeked through the clouds and
helped define the loggerhead.

The trance held; the laying continued without interruption. When the clutch held a hundred eggs, she was
finished for the night and began covering them with
sand. When the cavity was filled, she packed the sand
and used her front flippers to refill the body pit and dis-
guise the nest.

When she began moving, Mercer knew the nesting
was over and the eggs were safe. She gave the mother a

wide berth and settled into a dark spot at the toe of another dune, hidden in the dark. She watched as the turtle carefully spread sand over her nest and scattered it in all directions to fool any predators.

Satisfied her nest was safe, the turtle began her cumbersome crawl back to the water, leaving behind eggs she would never bother with again. She would repeat the nesting once or twice during the season before migrating back to her feeding ground, hundreds of miles away. In a year or two, maybe three or four, she would return to the same beach and nest again.

For five nights a month, from May through August, Tessa had walked this section of the beach looking for the tracks of nesting loggerheads. Her granddaughter had been at her side, thoroughly captivated by the hunt. Discovering the tracks had always been exciting. Finding a mother actually laying her eggs had been an indescribable thrill.

Now Mercer reclined on the dune and waited. The Turtle Watch volunteers would come along soon and do their work. Tessa had been the president of that club for many years. She had fought fiercely to protect the nests and many times had chastised vacationers for tampering with the protected areas. Mercer remembered at least two occasions on which her grandmother had called the police. The law was on her side, and that of the turtles, and she wanted it enforced.

That strong and vibrant voice was now silent, and the beach would never be the same, at least not for Mercer. She gazed at the lights of the shrimp boats on the horizon and smiled at the memories of Tessa and her turtles. The wind picked up and she folded her arms over her chest to stay warm.

In sixty days or so, depending on the temperature of the sand, the hatchlings would come to life. With no help from their mother, they would crack open their shells and dig out in a group effort that could take days. When the time was right, usually at night or in a rainstorm when the temperature was cooler, they would make a run for it. Together they would burst from the cavity, take a second to get oriented, then hustle down to the water and swim away. The odds were stacked against them. The ocean was a minefield with so many predators that only one baby turtle in a thousand would see adulthood.

Two figures were approaching at the shoreline. They stopped when they saw the tracks, then slowly followed them to the nest. When they were certain the mother was gone and the eggs had been laid, they studied the site with flashlights, made a circle in the sand around it, and sunk a small stake with yellow tape. Mercer could hear their soft voices—two women—but was safely hidden from their view. They would return at daylight to secure the nest with wire fencing and signage, something she and Tessa had done many times. As they walked away, they carefully kicked sand over the turtle's tracks to make them disappear.

Long after they were gone, Mercer decided to wait for the sun. She had never spent the night on the beach, so she nestled into the sand, reclined comfortably against the dune, and eventually fell asleep.

4.

Evidently, the island's literary gang was too afraid of Myra Beckwith to say no to a last-minute invitation to dinner. No one wanted to offend her. And, Mercer suspected, no one wanted to risk missing a gathering where they would almost certainly be talked about in their absence. Out of self-defense, and curiosity, they began arriving at the Vicker House late Sunday afternoon for drinks and dinner to honor their newest member, albeit a temporary one. It was Memorial Day weekend, the start of summer. The invitation by e-mail said 6:00 p.m., but for a bunch of writers that hour meant nothing. No one was on time.

Bob Cobb arrived first and immediately cornered Mercer on the back porch and began asking questions about her work. He had long gray hair and the bronze tan of a man who spent too much time outside, and he wore a gaudy floral-print shirt with the top buttons open to reveal a brown chest with matching gray hair. According to Myra, the rumor was that Cobb had just submitted his latest novel and his editor wasn't happy with it. How she knew this she wouldn't say. He sipped her homemade brew from a fruit jar and stood uncomfortably close to Mercer as they talked.

Amy Slater, the "vampire girl," came to her rescue and welcomed her to the island. She went on about her three kids and claimed to be thrilled to get out of the house for the evening. Leigh Trane joined the circle but said little. Myra was stomping around the house in a hot pink flowing dress the size of a small tent, barking instructions to the caterer, fetching drinks, and ignoring the pack of dogs that had the run of the place.

Bruce and Noelle arrived next, and Mercer finally met the man responsible for her little sabbatical. He wore a soft yellow seersucker suit with a bow tie, though the invitation clearly said "extreme casual." But Mercer had long since learned that with a literary crowd anything goes. Cobb was wearing rugby shorts. Noelle was beautiful in a simple white cotton shift, a narrow one that hung perfectly on her slender frame. Damn French, Mercer thought, as she sipped Chablis and tried to keep up her end of the small talk.

Some writers are seasoned raconteurs with an endless supply of stories and quips and one-liners. Others are reclusive and introverted souls who labor in their solitary worlds and struggle to mix and mingle. Mercer was somewhere in between. Her lonely childhood had given her the ability to live in her own world, where little was said. Because of this, she pushed herself to laugh and chatter and enjoy a joke.

Andy Adam showed up and immediately asked for a double vodka on the rocks. Myra handed it to him and cast a wary look at Bruce. They knew Andy was "off the wagon" and this was a concern. When he introduced himself to Mercer she immediately noticed a small scar above his left eye and thought about his penchant for brawling in bars. He and Cobb were about the same age, both divorced, both hard-drinking beach bums who were lucky enough to sell well and enjoy undisciplined lives. They soon gravitated to each other and began talking about fishing.

Jay Arklerood, the brooding poet and frustrated literary star, arrived just after seven, which, according to Myra, was early for him. He took a glass of wine, said hello to Bruce, but did not introduce himself to Mercer. With the gang all there, Myra called for quiet and proposed a toast. "A drink to our new friend, Mercer Mann, who'll be here a spell in the hope that she'll find inspiration in the sun and on the beach and finish that damned novel that's now three years past due. Cheers!"

"Only three years?" Leigh said and got a laugh.

"Mercer," Myra said, prompting.

Mercer smiled and said, "Thank you. I'm delighted to be here. From the age of six I came here every summer to stay with my grandmother Tessa Magruder. Some of you might have known her. The happiest days of my life, so far at least, were spent with her on the beach and on the island. It's been a long time, but I'm delighted to be back. And delighted to be here tonight."

"Welcome," Bob Cobb said as he lifted his drink. The others did too, offered a hearty "Cheers!" and began talking at once.

Bruce stepped closer to Mercer and quietly said, "I knew Tessa. She and Porter died in a storm."

"Yes, eleven years ago," Mercer said.

"I'm sorry," Bruce said, somewhat awkwardly.

"No, it's okay. It has been a long time."

Myra charged in with "Oh well, I'm hungry. Bring your drinks to the table and we'll have dinner."

They made their way inside to the dining room. The table was narrow and not long enough for nine people, but had there been twenty, Myra would have packed them around it anyway. It was surrounded by a collection of mismatched chairs. The setting, though, was beautiful, with a row of short candles down the middle and lots of flowers. The china and stemware were old and smartly matched. The vintage silver was perfectly arranged. The white cloth napkins had just been ironed and folded. Myra held a sheet of paper with the seating arrangement, one that she and Leigh had obviously debated, and barked instructions. Mercer was seated between Bruce and Noelle, and after the usual complaining and grumbling the rest of them fell into place. At least three separate conversations began as Dora, the caterer, poured wine. The air was warm and the windows were open. An old fan rattled not far above them.

Myra said, "Okay, here are the rules. No talking about your own books, and no politics. There are some Republicans here."

"What!" Andy said. "Who invited them?"

"I did, and if you don't like it you can leave now."

"Who are they?" Andy demanded.

"Me," Amy said, raising her hand proudly. It was obvious this had happened before.

"I'm a Republican too," Cobb said. "Even though I've been to prison and roughed up by the FBI, I'm still a loyal Republican."

"God help us," Andy mumbled.

"See what I mean," Myra said. "No politics."

"How about football?" Cobb asked.

"And no football," Myra said with a smile. "Bruce, what would you like to talk about?"

"Politics and football," Bruce said and everyone laughed.

"What's happening at the store this week?"

"Well, Wednesday Serena Roach is back. I expect to see you all at the store for the signing."

"She got trashed in the *Times* this morning," Amy said, with a hint of satisfaction. "Did y'all see it?"

"Who reads the *Times*?" Cobb asked. "Left-wing garbage."

"I'd love to be trashed in the *Times,* or anywhere else for that matter," Leigh said. "What's her book about?"

"It's her fourth novel and it's about a single woman in New York City who's having relationship problems."

"How original," Andy blurted. "Can't wait to read that one." He drained his second double vodka and asked Dora for another. Myra frowned at Bruce, who shrugged as if to say, "He's a grown man."

"Gazpacho," Myra said as she picked up her spoon. "Dig in."

Within seconds they were all chatting at once as separate conversations spun off. Cobb and Andy quietly discussed politics. Leigh and Jay huddled at the end of the table and talked about someone's novel. Myra and Amy were curious about a new restaurant. And in a soft voice Bruce said to Mercer, "I'm sorry I brought up Tessa's death. It was quite rude."

"No, it wasn't," she said. "It was a long time ago."

"I knew Porter well. He was a regular at the store, loved detective stories. Tessa dropped in once a year but didn't buy a lot of books. Seems like I vaguely remember a granddaughter many years ago."

"How long are you here?" Noelle asked.

Mercer was confident that everything she had told Myra had already been relayed to Bruce. "A few months. I'm between jobs, or I should say that I'm out of work.

For the past three years I've been teaching but I hope that's behind me. And you? Tell me about your store."

"I sell French antiques. I have a shop next door to the bookstore. I'm from New Orleans but I met Bruce and moved here. Just after Katrina."

Soft, clear, perfect diction, with no trace of New Orleans. No trace of anything. And no wedding ring but plenty of jewelry.

Mercer said, "That was 2005. A month after Tessa's accident. I remember it well."

Bruce asked, "Were you here when it happened?"

"No, that was the first summer in fourteen years that I did not spend here. I had to get a job to pay for college and I was working in Memphis, my hometown."

Dora was removing the bowls and pouring more wine. Andy was getting louder.

"Do you have children?" Mercer asked.

Both Bruce and Noelle smiled and shook their heads. "We've never had the time," she said. "I travel a lot, buying and selling, mainly to France, and Bruce is at the store seven days a week."

"You don't go with her?" Mercer asked Bruce.

"Not very often. We were married there."

No you weren't. It was such an easy, casual lie, one they had been living for a long time. Mercer took a sip of wine and reminded herself that she was sitting next to one of the most successful dealers of stolen rare books in the country. As they talked about the South of France and the antiques trade there, Mercer wondered how much Noelle knew about his business. If he had really paid a million bucks for the Fitzgerald manuscripts, surely she would know it. Right? He was not a tycoon with interests around the world and ways to move and hide money. He was a small-town bookseller who practically lived in his store. He couldn't hide that much money from her, could he? Noelle had to know.

Bruce admired *October Rain* and was curious about the abrupt end to Mercer's first book tour. Myra overheard this and called for quiet as she prompted Mercer to tell her story. While Dora served baked pompano, the conversation settled on the topic of book tours and everyone had a story. Leigh, Jay, and Cobb confessed that they, too, had wasted an hour or two in the back of stores selling zero copies. Andy drew small crowds with his first book, and, not surprisingly, was kicked out of a bookstore when he got drunk and insulted customers who wouldn't buy it. Even Amy, the bestseller, had a few bad days before she discovered vampires.

During dinner, Andy switched to ice water, and the entire table seemed to relax.

Cobb got wound up with a story from prison. It was about an eighteen-year-old kid who was sexually abused by his cellmate, a real predator. Years later, after both had been paroled, the kid tracked down his old cellie, found him living the quiet life in the suburbs, his past forgotten. Time for revenge.

It was a long, interesting story, and when Cobb finished, Andy said, "What a crock. Pure fiction, right? That's your next novel."

"No, I swear it's true."

"Bullshit. You've done this before, regaled us with a tall tale to see how we react to it, then a year later it's a novel."

"Well, I have thought about it. What do you think? Commercial enough?"

"I like it," Bruce said. "But go easy on the prison rape scenes. You've overplayed those a bit, I think."

"You sound like my agent," Cobb mumbled. He pulled a pen out of his shirt pocket as if he needed to start taking notes. "Anything else? Mercer, what do you think?"

"I get a vote?"

"Sure, why not? Your vote will mean as much as the rest of these hacks."

"I might use the story," Andy said and everyone laughed.

"Well, you damned sure need a good story. Did you make your deadline?"

"Yes, I've sent it in and they've already sent it back. Structural problems."

"Same as your last book, but they published it anyway."

"And a good move on their part. They couldn't print 'em fast enough."

"Now, boys," Myra said. "You're breaking the first rule. No talking about your own books."

"This could go on all night," Bruce whispered to Mercer, just loud enough for the rest to hear. She loved the bantering, as they all did. She had never been with a group of writers so eager to jab each other, but all in fun.

Amy, whose cheeks were red from the wine, said, "What if the kid from prison is really a vampire?" The table erupted with even more laughter.

Cobb quickly replied, "Hey, I hadn't thought about that. We could start a new series about vampires in prison. I like it. You want to collaborate?"

Amy said, "I'll get my agent to call your agent, see if they can work something out."

With perfect timing Leigh said, "And you wonder why books are declining." When the laughter died, Cobb said, "Once again shot down by the literary mafia."

Things were quieter for a few minutes as they worked on dinner. Cobb started chuckling and said, "Structural problems. What does that mean?"

"Means the plot sucks, which it does. I never really felt that good about it, frankly."

"You could always self-publish it, you know. Bruce will put it on that folding card table in the back of the store, his own slush pile."

Bruce replied, "Please. That table is full."

Myra changed the subject by asking, "So, Mercer, you've been here a few days. Can we ask how the writing is going?"

"That's a bad question," Mercer replied with a smile.

"Are you trying to finish a book, or start one?"

"I'm not sure," she said. "The current one will probably get tossed, then I'll start a new one. I'm still undecided."

"Well, if you need any advice whatsoever, about any aspect of writing or publishing, or romance or relationships, food, wine, travel, politics, anything under the sun, you've come to the right place. Just look around this table. Experts everywhere."

"So I gather."

5.

At midnight, Mercer was sitting on the bottom step of the boardwalk, her bare feet in the sand, the waves rolling in. She would never tire of the sound of the ocean, the gentle breaking of the waves with a calm sea, or the crashing surf in a storm. Tonight there was no wind and the tide was low. A lone figure walked south in the distance, at the edge of the water.

She was still amused by the dinner and tried to remember as much as possible. The more she thought the more astonishing it became. A room filled with writers, with their insecurities and egos and jealousies, and with wine flowing, and not a single argument, not even a harsh word. The popular authors—Amy, Cobb, and Andy—longed for critical acclaim, while the literary ones—Leigh, Jay, and Mercer—longed for greater royalties. Myra didn't give a damn one way or the other. Bruce and Noelle were content to stay in the middle and encourage them all.

She wasn't sure what to make of Bruce. The first impression was quite good, but given his good looks and easygoing manner Mercer was certain that everyone liked Bruce, at least initially. He talked enough but not too much, and seemed content to allow Myra to be in charge. It was, after all, her party and she obviously knew what she was doing. He was completely at ease with his crowd and thoroughly enjoyed their stories, jokes, cheap shots, and insults. Mercer got the impression he would do anything to further their careers. They, in turn, were almost deferential to him.

He claimed to be an admirer of Mercer's two books, especially her novel, and they talked about it enough to satisfy her doubts about whether he had actually read it. He said he had done so when it was published and she had been scheduled to sign at Bay Books. That had been seven years earlier, yet he remembered it well. He'd probably skimmed it before the dinner party, but Mercer was impressed nonetheless. He asked her to stop by the store and autograph the two copies in his collection. He had also read her book of short stories. Most important, he was eager to see something else, her next novel perhaps, or more stories.

For Mercer, a once promising writer suffering through an endless drought and handcuffed by the fear that her career might be over, it was comforting to have such a knowledgeable reader say nice things and want more. Over the past few years, only her agent and her editor had offered such encouragement.

He was certainly a charmer, but he said or did nothing out of line, not that she expected anything. His lovely wife was just inches away. When it came to seduction, and assuming the rumors were true, Mercer suspected that Bruce Cable could play the long game as well as the short one.

Several times during the dinner she looked across the table at Cobb and Amy and even Myra and wondered if they had any idea about his dark side. Up front he ran one of the finest bookstores in the country, while at the same time he dealt in stolen goods under deep cover. The bookstore was successful and made him plenty of money. He had a charmed life, a beautiful wife/partner, a fine reputation, and a historic mansion in a lovely town. Was he really willing to risk jail for trading in stolen manuscripts?

Did he have any clue that a professional security team was on his trail? With the FBI not far behind? Any inkling that in just a few months he might be headed to prison for many years?

No, it did not seem possible.

Did he suspect Mercer? No, he did not. Which brought up the obvious question about what to do next. Take it one day at a time, Elaine had said more than once. Make him come to you and ease your way into his life.

Sounds simple, right?

6.

Monday, Memorial Day, Mercer slept late and missed another sunrise. She poured coffee and went to the beach, which was busier because of the holiday but still not crowded. After a long walk, she returned to the cottage, poured more coffee, and took a seat at a small breakfast table with a view of the ocean. She opened her laptop, looked at a blank screen, and managed to type, "Chapter One."

Writers are generally split into two camps: those who carefully outline their stories and know the ending before they begin, and those who refuse to do so upon the theory that once a character is created he or she will do something interesting. The old novel, the one she had just discarded, the one that had tortured her for the past five years, fell into the second category. After five years, nothing of interest had happened and she was sick of the characters. Let it go, she had decided. Let it rest. You can always come back to it. She wrote a rough summary of the first chapter of her new one and went to the second.

By noon she had ground her way through the first five chapter summaries and was exhausted.

7.

Traffic was slow along Main Street, and its sidewalks were crawling with tourists in town for the holiday weekend. Mercer parked on a side street and walked to the bookstore. She managed to avoid Bruce and went to the upstairs café, where she had a sandwich and scanned the *Times*. He walked past her to fetch an espresso and was surprised to see her.

"You have time to sign those books?" he asked.

"That's why I'm here." She followed him downstairs to the First Editions Room, where he closed the door behind them. Two large windows opened onto the first floor and customers browsed through racks of books not far away. In the center of the room was an old table covered with papers and files.

"Is this your office?" she asked.

"One of them. When things are slow I'll ease in here and work a little."

"When are things slow?"

"It's a bookstore. Today it's busy. Tomorrow it will be deserted." He moved a catalog that was hiding two hardback copies of *October Rain*. He handed her a pen and picked up the books.

She said, "I haven't autographed one of these in a long time." He opened the first one to the title page and she scribbled her name, then did the same for the other one. He left one on the table and put one back into its slot on a shelf. The first editions were arranged in alphabetical order by the author's last name.

"So what are these?" she asked, waving a hand at a wall of books.

"All first editions of writers who've signed here. We do about a hundred signings a year, so after twenty years it's a nice collection. I checked the records, and when you were coming through on tour I ordered 120 copies."

"A hundred and twenty? Why so many?"

"I have a First Editions Club, about a hundred of my top customers who buy every autographed book. It's quite a draw, really. If I can guarantee a hundred books, the publishers and writers are pretty eager to put us on the tour."

"And these people show up for every signing?"

"I wish. Usually about half, which makes for a nice crowd. Thirty percent live out of town and collect by mail."

"What happened when I canceled?"

"I returned the books."

"Sorry about that."

"Just part of the business."

Mercer moved along the wall, scanning the rows of books, some of which she recognized. All were single copies. Where were the others? He had put one of hers back and left one on the table. Where were they kept?

"So are any of these valuable?" she asked.

"Not really. It's an impressive collection, and it means a lot to me because I'm attached to each one of them, but they rarely hold their value."

"Why is that?"

"The first-run printings are too large. The first printing for your book was five thousand copies. That's not huge, but to be valuable a book has to be scarce. Sometimes I get lucky, though." He reached high, removed a book, and handed it to her.

"Remember *Drunk in Philly*? J. P. Walthall's masterpiece."

"Of course."

"Won the National Book Award and the Pulitzer in 1999."

"I read it in college."

"I saw an advance reading copy and loved it, knew it had potential, so I ordered a few boxes, and that was before he said he would not be touring. His publisher was broke and not too sharp to begin with, so it did an initial run of six thousand copies. Not bad for a first novel but not nearly enough. Well, the printing got interrupted when the union went on strike. Only twelve hundred copies made it off the press before they shut it down. I got lucky when my supply arrived. The first reviews were insanely good and the second printing, at a different press, was twenty thousand. Double that for the third and so on. The book eventually sold a million copies in hardback."

Mercer opened the book, flipped to the copyright page, and saw the words "First Edition."

"So what's this worth?" she asked.

"I've sold a couple at five thousand dollars. Now I'm asking eight. Still have about twenty-five of them, buried in the basement."

She filed that away but said nothing. She handed the book back to him and walked to another wall covered with books. Bruce said, "More of the collection, but not all of those authors have signed here."

She removed John Irving's *The Cider House Rules* and said, "I'm assuming there are plenty of these on the market."

"It's John Irving. That was seven years after *Garp*, so the first printing was huge. It's worth a few hundred bucks. I have one *Garp*, but it's not for sale."

She returned the book to its slot and quickly scanned the ones next to it. *Garp* was not there. She assumed it too was "buried in the basement," but said nothing. She wanted to ask about his rarest books, but decided to lose interest.

"Did you enjoy dinner last night?" he asked.

She laughed and moved away from the shelves. "Oh yes. I've never had dinner with so many writers. We tend to keep to ourselves, you know?"

"I know. In your honor, everybody behaved. Believe me, it's not always that civilized."

"And why is that?"

"The nature of the breed. Mix together some fragile egos, booze, maybe some politics, and it usually gets rowdier."

"I can't wait. When's the next party?"

"Who knows with that bunch. Noelle mentioned a

dinner party in a couple of weeks. She enjoyed your company."

"Same here. She's lovely."

"She's a lot of fun and she's very good at what she does. You should pop in her store and have a look."

"I'll do that, though I'm not in the market for the high-end stuff."

He laughed and said, "Well, watch out. She's very proud of her inventory."

"I'm meeting Serena Roach for coffee tomorrow before the signing. You've met her?"

"Sure. She's been here twice. She's pretty intense but nice enough. She tours with her boyfriend and her publicist."

"An entourage?"

"I suppose. It's not that unusual. She has battled drugs and appears to be somewhat fragile. Life on the road is unsettling for a lot of writers and they need the security."

"She can't travel by herself?"

Bruce laughed and seemed hesitant to gossip. "I could tell you a lot of stories, okay? Some sad, some hilarious, all colorful. Let's save them for another day, perhaps another long dinner."

"Is it the same boyfriend? The reason I ask is that I'm reading her latest and her character struggles with men, as well as drugs. The author seems to know her material."

"Don't know, but on her last two tours she had the same boyfriend."

"Poor girl is getting roughed up by the critics."

"Yes, and she's not handling it too well. Her publicist called this morning to make sure I don't mention dinner afterward. They're trying to keep her away from the wine bottle."

"And the tour is just starting?"

"We're the third stop. Could be another disaster. I guess she could always quit, like you."

"I highly recommend it."

A clerk stuck her head in the window and said, "Sorry to disturb, but Scott Turow is on the phone."

"I'd better take that," he said.

"See you tomorrow," Mercer said and walked to the door.

"Thanks for signing the books."

"I'll sign all of my books you buy."

8.

Three days later, Mercer waited until dusk and walked to the beach. She removed her sandals and put them into a small shoulder bag. She headed south along the water's edge. The tide was low, the beach wide and deserted but for an occasional couple with their dog. Twenty minutes later, she passed a row of high-rise condos and headed for the Ritz-Carlton next door. At the boardwalk she rinsed her feet, put on the sandals, strolled by the empty pool, and went inside, where she found Elaine waiting at a table in the elegant bar.

Tessa had loved the Ritz bar. Two or three times each summer she and Mercer dressed in their finest and drove to the Ritz, first for drinks and then dinner at the hotel's noted restaurant. Tessa always started with a martini, just one, and until she was fifteen, Mercer ordered a diet soda. When she was fifteen, though, she arrived for the summer with a fake ID and they had martinis together.

By chance, Elaine was sitting at their favorite table, and as Mercer sat down she was hit hard with the memories of her grandmother. Nothing had changed. A guy at the piano was singing softly in the background.

"I got in this afternoon and thought you might enjoy a fine dinner," Elaine said.

"I've been here many times," Mercer said, looking around, soaking in the same smells of salt air and oak paneling. "My grandmother adored this place. It's not for those on a tight budget, but she splurged occasionally."

"So Tessa didn't have money?"

"No. She was comfortable, but she was also frugal. Let's talk about something else."

A waiter stopped by and they ordered drinks.

Elaine said, "I'd say you've had a pretty good week."

Their routine included the nightly e-mail as Mercer recapped things that might be relevant to their search. "I'm not sure I know much more than I did when I got here, but I have made contact with the enemy."

"And?"

"And he's as charming as advertised, very likeable. He stores the good stuff in the basement but did not mention a vault. I get the impression there's quite an inventory down there. His wife is in town and he's done nothing to indicate he has any interest in me, other than his usual attraction to writers."

"You have to tell me about the dinner party with Myra and Leigh."

Mercer smiled and said, "I wish there had been a hidden camera."

CHAPTER FIVE
THE FACILITATOR

1.

For over forty years, the Old Boston Bookshop had occupied the same row house on Wade Street in the Ladder Blocks section of downtown. It was founded by Loyd Stein, a noted antiquarian dealer, and when he died in 1990 his son Oscar took over. Oscar grew up in the store and loved the business, though with time had grown weary of the trade. With the Internet, and with the general decline in all things related to books, he had found it more and more difficult to make a decent profit. His father had been content to peddle used books and hope for the occasional big score with a rare one, but Oscar was losing patience. At the age of fifty-eight, he was quietly looking for a way out.

At 4:00 on a Thursday afternoon, Denny entered the store for the third consecutive day and browsed nonchalantly through the racks and piles of used books.

When the clerk, an elderly lady who had been there for decades, left the front and went upstairs, Denny selected an old paperback copy of *The Great Gatsby* and took it to the register. Oscar smiled and asked, "Find what you're looking for?"

"This will do," Denny replied.

Oscar took the book, opened it to the inside cover, and said, "Four dollars and thirty cents."

Denny laid a five on the counter and said, "Actually, I'm looking for the original."

Oscar took the five and asked, "You mean a first edition? Of *Gatsby*?"

"No. The original manuscript."

Oscar laughed. What an idiot. "I'm afraid I can't help you there, sir."

"Oh, I think you can."

Oscar froze and looked him in the eyes. A cold, hard stare met him. A hard, calculated, knowing stare. Oscar swallowed and asked, "Who are you?"

"You'll never know."

Oscar looked away and put the five in the register. As he did, he realized his hands were shaking. He removed some coins and placed them on the counter. "Seventy cents," he managed to say. "You were here yesterday, weren't you?"

"And the day before."

Oscar looked around. They were indeed alone. He glanced at the small surveillance camera high above, aimed at the register. Denny said quietly, "Don't worry about the camera. I disabled it last night. And the one in your office isn't working either."

Oscar took a deep breath as his shoulders slumped.

After he had spent months living in fear and losing sleep and peeking around corners, the dreaded moment had finally arrived. He asked, in a low, shaky voice, "Are you a cop?"

"No. I'm avoiding cops these days, same as you."

"What do you want?"

"The manuscripts. All five."

"I don't know what you're talking about."

"Is that the best you can do? I was hoping for something a bit more original."

"Get out of here," Oscar hissed, trying to sound as tough as possible.

"I'm leaving. I'll be back at six when you close. You'll lock the door and we'll retire to your office for a little chat. I strongly suggest you play it cool. You have nowhere to run and there's no one who can help you. And we're watching."

Denny picked up the coins and the paperback and left the store.

2.

An hour later, a lawyer named Ron Jazik stepped onto an elevator in the federal building in Trenton, New Jersey, and pushed the button to the ground floor. At the last second, a stranger slid through the doors and pushed the button to the third floor. As soon as the doors closed, and they were alone, the stranger said, "You represent Jerry Steengarden, right? Court appointed."

Jazik sneered and said, "Who the hell are you?"

In a flash, the stranger slapped Jazik across the face, knocking off his glasses. With an iron grip, he grabbed Jazik's throat and rammed his head against the back wall of the elevator. "Don't talk to me like that. A message for your client. One wrong word to the FBI and people will get hurt. We know where his mother lives, and we know where your mother lives too."

Jazik's eyes bulged as he dropped his briefcase. He grabbed the stranger's arm but the death grip just got tighter. Jazik was almost sixty years old and out of shape. The guy with the grip was at least twenty years younger and, at that moment, seemed incredibly strong. He growled, "Am I clear? Do you understand?"

The elevator stopped at the third floor, and as the door opened the stranger let go and shoved Jazik into a corner where he fell to his knees. The stranger walked past him and left as if nothing had happened. No one was waiting to get on, and Jazik quickly got to his feet, found his glasses, picked up his briefcase, and considered his options. His jaw stung and his ears were ringing and his first thought was to call the police and report the assault. There were federal marshals in the lobby and maybe he could wait there with them until his assailant emerged. On the way down, though, he decided it might be best not to overreact. By the time he reached the ground floor, he was breathing again. He found a restroom and splashed water on his face and looked at himself. The right side of his face was red but not swollen.

The physical sensation of taking such a blow was stunning, and painful. He felt something warm in his mouth and spat blood into the sink.

He had not spoken to Jerry Steengarden in over a month. They had little to discuss. Their meetings were always brief because Jerry had nothing to say. The stranger who had just slapped and threatened him had little to worry about.

3.

A few minutes before six, Denny returned to the bookshop and found Oscar waiting nervously at the front counter. The clerk was gone, as were the customers. Without a word Denny flipped the "Open/Closed" sign, locked the door, and turned off the lights. They climbed the stairs to the small cluttered office where Oscar preferred to spend his days while someone else managed the front. He took his seat behind the desk and waved at the only chair not covered with magazines.

Denny sat down and began with "Let's not waste any time here, Oscar. I know you bought the manuscripts for half a million bucks. You wired the money to an account in the Bahamas. From there it went to an account in Panama and that's where I picked it up. Minus, of course, the percentage for our facilitator."

"So you're the thief?" Oscar said calmly. With some pills, he had managed to settle his nerves.

"I'm not saying that."

"How do I know you're not a cop wearing a wire?" Oscar asked.

"You want to frisk me. Go ahead. How would a cop know the price? How would a cop know the details of the money trail?"

"I'm sure the FBI can track anything."

"If they knew what I know they would simply arrest you, Oscar. Relax, you're not going to get arrested. Nor am I. You see, Oscar, I can't go to the cops and you can't either. We're both guilty as hell and looking at a long spell in a federal pen. But it's not going to happen."

Oscar wanted to believe him and was somewhat relieved. However, it was obvious there were a few immediate challenges. He took a deep breath and said, "I don't have them."

"Then where are they?"

"Why did you sell them?"

Denny crossed his legs and relaxed in the old chair. "I got spooked. The FBI grabbed two of my friends the day after the theft. I had to hide the treasure and skip the country. I waited a month, then two. When things settled down, I came back and went to see a dealer in San Francisco. He said he knew a buyer, a Russian who would pay ten million. He was lying. He went to the FBI. We had a meeting scheduled and I was supposed to deliver one manuscript as proof, but the FBI was waiting."

"How did you know?"

"Because we tapped his phones before we went in. We're very good, Oscar. Very patient, very professional. It was a close call and we left the country again so things could cool off. I knew the FBI had a good description of me so I stayed out of the country."

"Are my phones tapped?"

Denny nodded and smiled. "Your landlines. We couldn't hack your cell phone."

"So how did you find me?"

"I went to Georgetown and eventually made contact with Joel Ribikoff, your old pal. Our facilitator. I didn't trust him—who can you trust in this business—and I was desperate back then to unload the manuscripts."

"You and I were never supposed to meet."

"That was the plan, wasn't it? You wired the money, I delivered the goods, then I disappeared again. Now I'm back."

Oscar cracked his knuckles and tried to stay calm. "And Ribikoff? Where is he now?"

"He's gone. He died a horrible death, Oscar, it was awful. But before he died he gave me what I wanted. You."

"I don't have them."

"Fine. So what did you do with them?"

"Sold them. I flipped them as fast as possible."

"Where are they, Oscar? I'm going to find them, and the trail is already bloody."

"I don't know where they are. I swear."

"Then who has them?"

"Look, I need some time to think. You said you're patient, so just give me some time."

"Fair enough. I'll be back in twenty-four hours. And don't do anything stupid like try to run. There's no place to hide and you'll get hurt if you try. We're pros, Oscar, and you don't have a clue."

"I'm not running."

"Twenty-four hours, and I'll be back for the guy's name. Give me his name and you get to keep your money and go on with your life. I'll never tell. You have my word."

Denny jumped to his feet and left the office. Oscar stared at the door and listened to his footsteps as he went down the stairs. He heard the door open, heard its little bell ring, then it closed quietly.

Oscar put his face in his hands and tried not to cry.

4.

Two blocks away, Denny was in a hotel bar eating pizza when his cell phone rattled. It was almost 9:00 p.m. and the call was late. "Talk to me," he said as he glanced around. The place was almost empty.

Rooker said, "Mission accomplished. I caught Jazik in an elevator and had to slap him around. Quite fun, really. Delivered the message and all went well. Petrocelli was more of a problem because he worked late. About an hour ago I caught him in the parking lot outside his office. Scared the shit out of him. A little wimp. At first he denied representing Mark Driscoll but he backed down quickly. Didn't have to hit him but came close."

"No witnesses?"

"None. Clean getaway with both."

"Nice work. Where are you now?"

"Driving. I'll be there in five hours."

"Hurry up. Tomorrow should be fun."

5.

Rooker entered the bookshop at five minutes before six and pretended to browse. There were no other customers. Oscar busied himself nervously behind the front counter but kept his eyes on the man. At six he said, "Sorry, sir, but we're closing." At that moment Denny entered, closed the door behind him, and flipped the "Open/Closed" sign. He looked at Oscar, pointed at Rooker, and said, "He's with me."

"Is anyone here?" Denny asked.

"No. Everyone's gone."

"Good. We'll just stay right here," Denny said as he stepped toward Oscar. Rooker joined him, both within striking distance. They stared at him and no one moved. Denny said, "Okay, Oscar, you've had some time to think. What's it gonna be?"

"You have to promise me you'll protect my identity."

"I don't have to promise anything," Denny snarled. "But I've already said no one will ever know. And what would I gain by revealing your involvement? I want the manuscripts, Oscar, nothing else. Tell me who you sold them to and you'll never see me again. Lie to me, though, and you know I'll be back."

Oscar knew. Oscar believed. At that awful moment the only thing he wanted was to safely get rid of this guy. He closed his eyes and said, "I sold them to a dealer named Bruce Cable, owns a nice bookstore on Camino Island, Florida."

Denny smiled and asked, "How much did he pay?"

"A million."

"Nice job, Oscar. Not a bad flip."

"Would you please leave now?"

Denny and Rooker glared at him without moving a muscle. For ten long seconds Oscar thought he was dead. His heart pounded as he tried to breathe.

Then they left without another word.

CHAPTER SIX
THE FICTION

1.

Entering Noelle's Provence was like walking into the middle of one of her handsome coffee-table books. The front room was filled with rustic country furniture, armoires and dressers and sideboards and armchairs arranged comfortably on ancient stone tile flooring. The side tables were loaded with old jugs and pots and baskets. The plaster walls were peach colored and adorned with sconces and smoky mirrors and dingy framed portraits of long-forgotten barons and their families. Scented candles emitted the thick aroma of vanilla. Chandeliers hung in clusters from the wood-and-plaster ceiling. An opera played softly in the background on hidden speakers. In a side room, Mercer admired a long, narrow wine-tasting table set for dinner with plates and bowls of sun yellow and olive green, the basic colors of rustic Provençal tableware. Against the wall near the front window sat the writer's table, a beautiful hand-painted piece that she was supposed to covet. According to Elaine, it was being offered for three thousand dollars and perfect for their needs.

Mercer had studied all four of Noelle's books and easily identified the furniture and furnishings. She was admiring the writer's table when Noelle entered the room and said, "Well, hello, Mercer. What a nice surprise." She greeted her with the casual French salute of obligatory pecks on both cheeks.

"This place is gorgeous," Mercer said, almost in awe.

"Welcome to Provence. What brings you here?"

"Oh, nothing. Just browsing. I love this table," she said, touching the writer's table. There were at least three featured in her books.

"I found it in a market in the village of Bonnieux, near Avignon. You should have it. It's perfect for what you do."

"I need to sell some books first."

"Come on. I'll show you around." She took Mercer's hand and led her from one room to the next, all filled with furnishings straight from her books. They climbed an elegant staircase of white stone steps and wrought-iron handrails to the second floor, where Noelle modestly showed off her inventory—more armoires and beds and dressers and tables, each with a story. She spoke so affectionately of her collection that she seemed reluctant to part with any of it. Mercer noted that not a single piece on the second floor had a price tag.

Noelle had a small office downstairs in the rear of the store, and beside its door was a small flip-top wine-tasting table. As she described it, Mercer wondered if all

French tables were used for wine tasting. "Let's have some tea," Noelle said and pointed to a chair at the table. Mercer took a seat and they chatted as Noelle boiled water on a small stove next to a marble sink.

"I adore that writer's table," Mercer said. "But I'm afraid to ask its price."

Noelle smiled and said, "For you, dear, it has a special price. For anyone else it's three thousand, but you can have it for half of that."

"That's still a stretch. Let me think about it."

"Where are you writing now?"

"At a small breakfast table in the kitchen, with a view of the ocean, but it's not working. I'm not sure if it's the table or the ocean, but the words are not coming."

"What's the book about?"

"I'm not sure. I'm trying to start a new one but it's not going too well."

"I just finished *October Rain* and think it's brilliant."

"You're very kind." Mercer was touched. Since coming to the island she had now met three people who spoke highly of her first novel, more encouragement than she had received in the past five years.

Noelle placed a porcelain tea service on the table and deftly poured boiling water into matching cups. Both added a cube of sugar but no milk, and as they stirred Noelle asked, "Do you talk about your work? I ask because most writers talk too much about what they've written or want to write, but a few find it difficult for some reason."

"I prefer not to, especially about what I'm doing now. My first novel feels old and dated, like I wrote it many years ago. In many ways, it's a curse to get published so young. Expectations are high, the pressure is on, the literary world is waiting for some great body of work. Then a few years pass and there's no book. The promising star is slowly forgotten. After *October Rain,* my first agent advised me to hurry up and publish my second novel. She said that since the critics loved my first one they would certainly hate my second, whatever it was, so go ahead and get the sophomore jinx over with. Probably good advice, but the problem was I didn't have a second novel. I guess I'm still searching."

"Searching for what?"

"A story."

"Most writers say the people come first. Once they are onstage, they somehow find a plot. Not you?"

"Not yet."

"What inspired *October Rain?*"

"When I was in college I read a story about a missing child, one who was never found, and what it did to the family. It was an incredibly sad, haunting story, but also beautiful in many ways. I couldn't forget about it, so I borrowed the story, fictionalized it thoroughly, and wrote the novel in less than a year. That seems hard to believe now, working that fast. Back then I looked forward to every morning, to the first cup of coffee and the next page. It's not happening now."

"I'm sure it will. You're in the perfect place to do nothing but write."

"We'll see. Frankly, Noelle, I need to sell some books. I don't want to teach and I don't want to find a job. I've even thought about writing under a pen name and cranking out mysteries or something that might sell."

"There's nothing wrong with that. Sell some books and then you can write whatever you want."

"That plan is slowly taking shape."

"Have you thought about talking to Bruce?"

"No. Why would I?"

"He knows the business and the art from every angle. He reads everything, knows hundreds of writers and agents and editors, and they often come to him for his insights, not necessarily his advice. He won't give any, unless he's asked. He likes you and he admires your work and he would probably say something helpful."

Mercer shrugged as if the idea might have merit. The front door opened and Noelle said, "Excuse me, but I may have a customer." She left the table and disappeared. For a few moments, Mercer sipped her tea and felt like a fraud. She wasn't there to shop for furniture or chat about writing or pretend to be another lonely, troubled author trying to make friends. No, she was there snooping for any scrap of information she could hand over to Elaine, who might one day use it against Noelle and Bruce. A sharp pain hit deep in her bowels as a wave of nausea swept over her. She endured it, waited for it to pass, then stood and steadied herself. She walked to the front of the store, where Noelle was helping a customer who appeared to be serious about a dresser.

"I need to be going," Mercer said.

"Of course," Noelle said almost in a whisper. "Bruce and I would love to have you over for dinner soon."

"How lovely. I'm free for the rest of the summer."

"I'll call."

2.

Later in the afternoon, Noelle was arranging a collection of small ceramic urns when a well-dressed couple in their forties entered the store. Her first glance told her they were far more affluent than the average tourists who dropped in from the street, browsed long enough to understand the prices, then hustled away empty-handed.

They introduced themselves as Luke and Carol Massey from Houston and said they were staying at the Ritz for a few days, their first visit to the island. They had heard about the store, had even seen its website, and were immediately attracted to a tile-top dining table that was a hundred years old and, at that moment, the most expensive item in the store. Luke asked for a tape measure and Noelle handed one over. They measured the table from all directions, mumbling between themselves that it would be perfect in the guesthouse dining room. Luke rolled up his sleeves and Carol asked if they could take photos. Of course, Noelle said. They measured two dressers and two large armoires, and in doing so asked intelligent questions about the wood, the finishes, the histories. They were building a new home in Houston and wanted it to look and feel like a Provençal farmhouse, one they had vacationed in the year before near the village of Roussillon in the Vaucluse. The longer they stayed the more enamored they became with virtually everything Noelle had to offer. She took them upstairs to the pricier furniture and their interest intensified. After an hour in the store, and at almost 5:00 p.m.,

Noelle opened a bottle of champagne and poured three glasses. While Luke was measuring a leather chaise and Carol was snapping photos, Noelle excused herself to go downstairs and check on the front. When two stragglers left, she locked the door and returned to the wealthy Texans.

They gathered around an old *comptoir* and got down to business. Luke asked questions about shipping and storage. Their new home was at least six months away from completion and they were using a warehouse to gather furniture and furnishings. Noelle assured them that she shipped all over the country and that was no problem. Carol clicked off the items she wanted to purchase at that moment, one of which was the writer's table. Noelle said no, she was holding it for someone else, but she could easily find another one during her upcoming trip to Provence. They walked downstairs to her office, where she poured more champagne and began working on a bill. The total was $160,000, a figure that didn't faze them. Haggling over prices was part of the business, but the Masseys had no interest in it. Luke laid down a black credit card as if dealing in pocket change, and Carol signed the order.

At the front door, they hugged her like old friends and said they might be back tomorrow. When they were gone, Noelle tried to remember a sale of that magnitude. She could not.

At 10:05 the following morning, Luke and Carol breezed back into the store with bright smiles and high energy. They said they'd spent half the night looking at photos and mentally moving pieces around their unfin-

ished home, and, well, they wanted more. Their architect had e-mailed them scaled drawings of the first two
levels and they had sketched in designs and placements
of where they wanted Noelle's furniture. She couldn't
help but notice that the house covered nineteen thousand square feet. They went to her second floor, spent
the entire morning measuring beds, tables, chairs, and
armoires, and in doing so wiped out her inventory. The
bill for the second day was over $300,000, and Luke
again whipped out the black credit card.

For lunch, Noelle locked the store and took them
to a popular bistro around the corner. While they ate,
her lawyer checked the validity of the credit card and
learned that the Masseys could buy whatever they
wanted. He also dug into their backgrounds but found
little. Why did it matter? If the black card worked, who
cared where the money came from?

Over lunch, Carol asked Noelle, "When will you get
more inventory?"

Noelle laughed and said, "Well, obviously sooner
rather than later. I was planning a trip to France in early
August, but now that I have nothing to sell I need to
move it up."

Carol glanced at Luke, who seemed a bit sheepish for
some reason. He said, "Just curious. We are wondering
if perhaps we could meet you over there and shop together."

Carol added, "We love Provence, and it would be a
blast hunting for antiques with someone like you."

Luke said, "We don't have kids and love to travel, especially to France, and we're really into these antiques.

We're even looking for a new designer who could help with the flooring and wallpaper."

Noelle said, "Well, I happen to know everyone in the business. When would you want to go?"

The Masseys looked at each other as if trying to recall their busy schedules. Luke said, "We're in London on business in two weeks. We could meet you in Provence after that."

"Is that too soon?" Carol asked.

Noelle thought for a second and said, "I can make it work. I go several times a year and even have an apartment in Avignon."

"Awesome," Carol said with great excitement. "It will be an adventure. I can just see our home filled with stuff that we find ourselves in Provence."

Luke raised a wineglass and said, "Here's to antiques hunting in the South of France."

3.

Two days later, the first truck was loaded with most of Noelle's inventory. It left Camino Island bound for a warehouse in Houston where a large space was waiting. A thousand square feet had been leased to Luke and Carol Massey. The bill, though, would eventually cross the desk of Elaine Shelby.

In several months, when the project was over, for better or for worse, the lovely antiques would slowly re-enter the market.

4.

At dusk, Mercer went to the beach, turned south, and drifted along at the water's edge. The Nelsons, from four doors to the south, stopped her for a quick chat as their mutt sniffed her ankles. They were in their seventies and held hands as they walked the beach. They were friendly to the point of being nosy and had already extracted the reason for Mercer's little vacation. "Happy writing," Mr. Nelson said as they left her. A few minutes later she was stopped by Mrs. Alderman, from eight doors to the north, who was walking her twin poodles and always seemed desperate for human contact. Mercer wasn't desperate, but she was enjoying the neighborhood.

Almost to the pier, she left the water and approached a boardwalk. Elaine was back in town and wanted to meet. She was waiting on the small patio outside the triplex she had leased for the operation. Mercer had been there once before and seen no one but Elaine. If there were others involved in the surveillance, or if someone was shadowing her, she was unaware of it. Elaine had been vague when quizzed about it.

They stepped into the kitchen and Elaine asked, "Would you like something to drink?"

"Water is fine."

"Have you had dinner?"

"No."

"Well, we can order a pizza, sushi, or Chinese takeout. What will it be?"

"I'm really not hungry."

"Neither am I. Let's sit here," Elaine said, pointing to a small breakfast table between the kitchen and the den. She opened the fridge and removed two bottles of water. Mercer took a seat and looked around. "Are you staying here?" she asked.

"Yes, for two nights." Elaine sat across from her.

"Alone?"

"Yes. There's no one else on the island as of today. We come and go."

Mercer almost asked about the "we" part but let it pass.

Elaine said, "So, you've seen Noelle's store." Mercer nodded. Her nightly report by e-mail was deliberately vague.

"Tell me about it. Describe the layout."

Mercer walked her through each display room, upstairs and down, adding as much detail as possible. Elaine listened carefully but did not take notes. It was obvious she knew a lot about the store.

"Is there a basement?" Elaine asked.

"Yes, she mentioned it in passing, said she had a workshop down there, but had no interest in showing it to me."

"She's holding the writer's table. We tried to buy it but she said it's not for sale. At some point soon you're going to buy it, but perhaps you'll want it painted. Perhaps she'll do this in the basement, and maybe you'll want to take a look to see a sample of the new color. We need to have a look in the basement because it adjoins the bookstore's."

"Who tried to buy it?"

"We. Us. The good guys, Mercer. You're not alone."

"Why is this not comforting?"

"You're not being watched. We come and go, as I've said."

"Okay. Suppose I get into her basement. Then what?"

"Look. Observe. Take it all in. If we're lucky there might be a door that leads to the bookstore."

"I doubt that."

"I doubt it too but we need to know. Is the wall concrete, brick, wood? We might need to go through it one day, or night. What about the store's video surveillance?"

"Two cameras, one aimed at the front door, the other in the back above the small kitchen area. There could be more but I didn't see any. None on the second floor. I'm sure you already know this."

"Yes, but in this business we triple check everything and we never stop gathering information. How is the front door locked?"

"Dead bolt, with a key. Nothing fancy."

"Did you see a rear door?"

"No, but I didn't go all the way to the rear. I think there are some more rooms back there."

"To the east is the bookstore. To the west is a realtor's office. Any door connecting to it?"

"None that I saw."

"Nice work. You've been here three weeks, Mercer, and you've done a superb job of blending in and not arousing suspicion. You've met the right people, seen all you can see, and we're very pleased. But we need to make something happen."

"I'm sure you have something up your sleeve."

"Indeed." Elaine walked to the sofa, picked up three

books, and placed them in the center of the table. "Here's the story. Tessa left Memphis in 1985 and moved here for good. As we know, her will left her estate to her three children in equal shares. It had a provision leaving you twenty thousand dollars in cash for college. She had six other grandchildren—Connie, Holstead's bunch out in California, and Jane's only child, Sarah. You were the only one who got a specific bequest."

"I was the only one she really loved."

"Right, so our new story goes something like this. After she died, you and Connie were going through her personal items, the small stuff that's not mentioned in the will, and the two of you decided to divide it. A few items of clothing, some old photos, maybe some inexpensive art, whatever. Create the fiction you want. In the deal, you received a box of books, most of them kids' books Tessa had bought for you over the years. At the bottom, though, were these three books, all first editions from the public library in Memphis, all checked out by Tessa in 1985. When Tessa moved to the beach, she either intentionally or inadvertently brought these three books with her. Thirty years later, you have them."

"Are they valuable?"

"Yes and no. Look at the one on top."

Mercer picked it up. *The Convict* by James Lee Burke. It appeared to be in perfect condition, its dust jacket pristine and encased in Mylar. Mercer opened it, turned to the copyright page, and saw the words "First Edition."

Elaine said, "As you probably know, this was a collection of Burke's short stories that got a lot of attention in 1985. The critics loved it and it sold well."

"What's it worth?"

"We bought this one last week for five thousand dollars. The first printing was small and there aren't many of these left in circulation. On the back of the dust jacket you'll see a bar code. That's what the Memphis library was using in 1985, so the book is virtually unmarked. Of course we added the bar code and I'm sure Cable will know someone in the business who can remove it. It's not that difficult."

"Five thousand dollars," Mercer repeated, as if she were holding a gold brick.

"Yes, and from a reputable dealer. The plan is for you to mention this book to Cable. Tell him its story but don't show him the book, at least initially. You're not sure what to do. The book was obviously taken by Tessa and she had no legitimate claim to it. Then it was taken by you, outside her estate, and so you have no legitimate claim to it. The book belongs to the library in Memphis, but after thirty years who really cares? And, of course you need the money."

"We're making Tessa a thief?"

"It's fiction, Mercer."

"I'm not sure I want to defame my deceased grandmother."

"'Deceased' is the key word. Tessa's been dead for eleven years and she didn't steal anything. The fiction you tell Cable will be heard by him only."

Mercer slowly picked up the second book. *Blood Meridian* by Cormac McCarthy, published by Random House, 1985, a first edition with a shiny dust jacket. "What's this one worth?" she asked.

"We paid four thousand a couple of weeks ago."

Mercer laid it down and picked up the third one. *Lonesome Dove* by Larry McMurtry, published by Simon & Schuster, also in 1985. The book had obviously been passed around, though the dust jacket was pristine.

"That one is a little different," Elaine said. "Simon & Schuster was anticipating big numbers and the first printing was around forty thousand, so there are a lot of first editions in the hands of collectors, which, obviously, suppresses the value. We paid five hundred bucks, then put a new dust jacket on it to double the value."

"The dust jacket is a forgery?" Mercer asked.

"Yes, happens all the time in the trade, at least among the crooks. A perfectly forged dust jacket can greatly increase the value. We found a good forger."

Mercer once again caught the "we" angle and marveled at the size of the operation. She laid the book down and gulped some water.

"Is the plan for me to eventually sell these to Cable? If so, I don't like the idea of selling fake stuff."

"The plan, Mercer, is for you to use these books as a means to get closer to Cable. Start off by merely talking about the books. You're not sure what to do with them. It's morally wrong to sell them because they really don't belong to you. Eventually, show him one or two and see how he reacts. Maybe he'll show you his collection in the basement or the vault or whatever he has down there. Who knows where the conversation will go. What we need, Mercer, is for you to get inside his world. He might jump at the chance to buy *The Convict* or *Blood Meridian,* or he may already have them in his collection. If we have him pegged correctly, he'll probably like the idea that the books are not exactly legitimate and want to buy them. Let's see how honest he is with you. We know what the books are worth. Will he give you a low-ball offer? Who knows? The money is not important. The crucial aspect here is to become a small part in his shady business."

"I'm not sure I like this."

"It's harmless, Mercer, and it's all fiction. These books were legitimately purchased by us. If he buys them, we get our money back. If he resells them, he gets his money back. There's nothing wrong or unethical about the plan."

"Okay, but I'm not sure I can play along and be believable."

"Come on, Mercer. You live in a world of fiction. Create some more."

"The fiction is not going too well these days."

"I'm sorry to hear that."

Mercer shrugged and took a sip of water. She stared at the books as her mind raced through various scenarios. Finally, she asked, "What can go wrong?"

"I suppose Cable could contact the library in Memphis and snoop around, but it's a big system and he'd get nowhere. Thirty years have gone by and everything has changed. They lose about a thousand books a year to folks who simply don't return them, and, being a typical library, they have no real interest in tracking them down. Plus, Tessa checked out a lot of books."

"We went to the library every week."

"The story holds together. He'll have no way of knowing the truth."

Mercer picked up *Lonesome Dove* and asked, "What if he spots this forged dust jacket?"

"We've thought about that and we're not sure we'll use it. Last week we showed the book to a couple of old dealers, guys who've seen it all, and neither spotted the forgery. But you're right. It could be a risk we decide not to take. Start with the first two, but make him wait. Drag it out as you struggle with what's right and fair. It's a moral dilemma for you and let's see what kind of advice he gives."

Mercer left with the books in a canvas bag and returned to the beach. The ocean was still and at low tide. A full moon lightened the sand. As she walked she heard voices that slowly grew louder. To her left and halfway to the dunes she saw two young lovers frolicking on a beach towel, their whispered words punctuated by sighs and groans of erotic pleasure. She almost stopped to watch until it was over, until the final heave and thrust, but she managed to move on, absorbing it all as much as possible as she ambled along.

She was consumed with envy. How long had it been?

5.

The second new novel came to an abrupt end after only five thousand words and three chapters, because by then Mercer was already tired of her characters and bored with her plot. Frustrated, depressed, even a bit angry with herself and the entire process, she put on a bikini, the skimpiest one in her growing collection, and went to the beach. It was only 10:00 a.m., but she had learned to avoid the midday sun. From noon until around five it was simply too hot to be outside, whether in the water or not. Her skin was now tanned enough and she worried about too much exposure. Ten o'clock was also about the time that the jogger came by, a stranger about her age. He ran barefoot at the edge of the water, his tall lean frame glistening with sweat. He was obviously an athlete, with a seriously flat stomach and perfect biceps and calves. He ran with an easy, fluid grace, and, she told herself, he seemed to slow just a little as she came into view. They had made eye contact on at least two occasions the previous week, and Mercer was convinced they were ready for the first hello.

She arranged her umbrella and folding chair and covered herself with sunblock, watching all movements to the south as she did so. He always came from the south, from the direction of the Ritz and the fancy condos. She unfolded her beach towel and stretched herself in the sun. She put on her sunglasses and straw hat and waited. As always on weekdays, the beach was practically deserted. Her plan was to see him in the distance and walk casually to the water, timing her movements to coincide with his. She would nail him with a casual "Good morning," the same as everyone else on this friendliest of beaches. She rested on her elbows, and as she waited she tried not to think of herself as just another failed writer. The five thousand words she'd just deleted was the worst junk she'd ever written.

He had been there for at least ten days, too long for a hotel stay. Perhaps he was renting a condo for a month.

She had no idea what to write next.

He was always alone but too far away for her to check on a wedding band.

After five years of lame characters and clunky prose and ideas so bad that she didn't even like them, she was convinced she would never again finish a novel.

Her phone rang and Bruce began with "Hope I'm not interrupting the genius at work."

"Not at all," she said. In fact, I'm lying on the beach practically nude scheming to seduce a stranger. "I'm taking a break," she said.

"Good. Look, we have a signing this afternoon and I'm a bit worried about the crowd. It's an unknown guy with a first novel that's not very good."

What does he look like? How old is he? Straight or gay? But she said, "So this is how you sell books. You rally your writers to come to your rescue."

"You bet. And Noelle is doing a last-minute dinner party at the house, in his honor, of course. Just us, you, him, and Myra and Leigh. Should be fun. Whatta you say?"

"Let me check my calendar. Yes, I'm free. What time?"

"Six, dinner to follow."

"Casual attire?"

"Are you kidding? You're at the beach. Anything goes. Even shoes are optional."

By eleven, the sun was baking the sand and the breeze had moved elsewhere. Evidently, it was too hot for jogging.

6.

The writer's name was Randall Zalinski, and a quick look online revealed little. His brief bio was deliberately vague and intended to give the impression that his career in "dark espionage" had given him rare insights into all manner of terrorism and cyber crime. His novel was about a futuristic showdown between the U.S., Russia, and China. Its two-paragraph summary was sensationalized to the point of being ridiculous, and Mercer found even it to be boring. His doctored photo was of a white male in his early forties. No mention of a wife or family. He lived in Michigan, where, of course, he was at work on a new novel.

His would be the third signing Mercer had attended at Bay Books. The first two had brought back painful memories of her aborted book tour seven years earlier, and she had vowed to avoid the rest, or at least try to. Doing so, though, might be difficult. The signings gave her good reason to hang around the store, something she needed to do and something Elaine strongly suggested. And, it would be next to impossible to tell Bruce she was too busy to support touring authors, especially when he called her with a personal invitation.

Myra had been right; the store had a loyal following and Bruce Cable could organize a crowd. There were about forty of the faithful milling around upstairs near the café when Mercer arrived. For the event, tables and shelves were shoved back to make an open space where chairs were packed haphazardly around a small podium.

At six, the crowd filled the seats and chatted away. Most were drinking cheap wine from plastic cups and everyone seemed relaxed and happy to be there. Myra and Leigh assumed their seats in the front row, just inches from the podium, as if the best seats were always reserved for them. Myra was laughing and cackling and talking to at least three people at once. Leigh sat quietly beside her, chuckling when appropriate. Mercer stood to the side and leaned on a shelf, as if she really didn't belong. The crowd was gray-haired and retired, and she once again noticed that she was the youngest one there. The atmosphere was warm and cozy as a bunch of book lovers gathered to enjoy a new writer.

Mercer admitted she was envious. If she could only finish a damned book then she too could go on tour and draw admirers. Then she remembered her tour, short as it was. It made her appreciate stores like Bay Books and people like Bruce Cable, those rare book-sellers who worked hard to maintain a following.

He stepped to the podium, welcomed his customers, and began a glowing and generous introduction of Randy Zalinski. His years in the "intelligence community" had given him rare insights to the unseen dangers lurking around every corner. And so on.

Zalinski looked more like a spy than a writer. Instead of the usual faded jeans and rumpled jacket, he wore a fine dark suit, white shirt, no tie, and had not a trace of whiskers on a face that was tanned and handsome. And no wedding ring. He spoke off the cuff for thirty minutes and told frightening stories about future cyber wars and how the U.S. was at a great disadvantage in keeping up with our enemies, the Russians and Chinese. Mercer suspected she might hear the same stories over dinner.

He appeared to be touring alone, and as Mercer drifted

away she decided that the guy had potential, though, unfortunately, he was in town for only one night. She also thought about the legend, the one in which Bruce hit on the younger female authors and Noelle did the same with the men. The Writer's Room in their tower was allegedly used for the sleepovers. Now that Mercer had met them, though, she found this hard to believe.

The audience applauded when Zalinski finished, then formed a line in front of a table where his books were stacked. Mercer preferred not to buy one, and had no desire to read it, but really had no choice. She remembered the frustration of sitting at the table and desperately hoping someone would buy a book, plus she was about to spend the next three hours with the author. She felt obliged and waited patiently as the line moved along. Myra saw her and struck up a conversation. They introduced themselves to Zalinski and watched him scribble his autograph in their copies.

As they walked down the stairs, Myra mumbled, almost too loudly, "Thirty bucks down the drain. I'll never read a word of it."

Mercer chuckled and said, "Same here, but we made our bookseller happy."

At the front counter, Bruce whispered to them, "Noelle is at the house. Why don't you head on over?"

Mercer, Myra, and Leigh left the store and walked four blocks to the Marchbanks House. "Have you seen it already?" Myra asked.

"No, but I've seen the book."

"Well, you're in for a treat, and Noelle is the perfect hostess."

7.

The house was much like Noelle's store, filled with rustic country furniture and richly decorated. Noelle gave a quick tour of the downstairs, then hustled off to the kitchen to check on something in the oven. Myra, Leigh, and Mercer took their drinks to the rear veranda and found a cooler spot under a wobbly fan. The night was sticky and Noelle had let it be known that dinner would be indoors.

Dinner took an unexpected twist when Bruce arrived, alone. He said that their guest, Mr. Zalinski, suffered from migraines and was having a bout. Randy sent his apologies but needed to go lie down in a dark hotel room. As soon as Bruce fixed his drink and joined them, Myra went after Zalinski. "I'd like a refund of thirty dollars, please," she said, and it wasn't clear if she was joking. "I wouldn't read his book at gunpoint."

"Careful," Bruce said. "If my little bookshop did refunds you'd owe me a fortune."

"So all sales are final?" Mercer asked.

"Damned right they are."

Myra said, "Well, if you're going to make us buy the books, please get some decent authors in the store."

Bruce smiled and looked at Mercer. "We have this conversation at least three times a year. Myra, the queen of trash, disapproves of almost all other commercial writers."

"Not true," Myra fired back. "I just don't dig espionage and all that military crap. I won't touch the book and don't want it cluttering up my house. I'll sell it back to you for twenty bucks."

"Now, Myra," Leigh said. "You always say that you love the clutter."

Noelle joined them on the veranda with a glass of wine. She was concerned about Zalinski and asked if they should call a doctor friend. Bruce said no, Zalinski was a tough guy who could take care of himself. "And I thought he was quite dull," Bruce added.

"How's his book?" Mercer asked.

"I skimmed a lot. Too much technical stuff, too much of the writer showing off how much he knows about technology and gadgets and the dark web. I put it down several times."

"Well, I'm damned sure not picking it up," Myra said with a laugh. "And, to be honest, I was not looking forward to dinner."

Leigh leaned in and looked at Mercer. "Dear, don't ever turn your back on this crowd."

Noelle said, "Well, now that you're okay with dinner, let's eat."

In a wide rear hallway, somewhere between the veranda and the kitchen, Noelle had decorated her table, a dark, round wooden piece that looked oddly contemporary. Everything else was old, from the mutton-bone chairs to the fine French flatware and large earthen plates. Again, it looked like something lifted straight from one of her books, a setting that was almost too pretty to disturb with a meal.

As they took their places and refilled their glasses, Mercer said, "Noelle, I think I want to buy that writer's table."

"Oh, it's yours. I had to put a sold sign on it because so many folks have been trying to buy it."

"It may take some time to get the money straight, but I must have it."

"And you think that's going to cure your writer's block?" Myra asked. "An old table from France?"

"Who said I had writer's block?" Mercer asked.

"Well, what do you call it then when you can't think of anything to write?"

"How about a 'drought'?"

"Bruce? You're the expert."

Bruce was holding the large salad bowl as Leigh took a serving. He said, "'Block' sounds too severe. I think I prefer 'drought.' But, who am I? Y'all are the word-smiths."

Myra laughed for no apparent reason and blurted, "Leigh, remember the time we wrote three books in a month? We had this slimeball publisher who wouldn't pay us, and so our agent said we couldn't jump to another house because we owed the guy three books. So Leigh and I came up with three of the worst plots ever, really ridiculous stuff, and I banged the typewriter ten hours a day for thirty straight days."

"But we had a great one in the wings," Leigh said, passing along the salad bowl.

Myra said, "Right, right. We had the best idea ever for a semi-serious novel, but we were not about to give it to our jackass publisher. We had to get out of his lousy contract so we could snag a better house, one that would appreciate the genius behind our great idea. That part of it worked. Two years later, the three awful books were still selling like crazy while the great novel flopped. Go figure."

Mercer said, "I think I might want to paint it, though, the writer's table."

"We'll look at some colors," Noelle said. "And make it perfect for the cottage."

"Have you seen the cottage?" Myra asked in mock surprise. "We haven't seen the cottage. When do we see the cottage?"

"Soon," Mercer said. "I'll throw a dinner."

"Tell them the good news, Noelle," Bruce said.

"What good news?"

"Don't be coy. A few days ago a rich couple from Texas bought Noelle's entire inventory. The store is practically empty."

"Too bad they're not book collectors," Leigh said.

"I saved the writer's table," Noelle said to Mercer.

"And Noelle is going to close for a month so she can hustle back to France and restock."

Noelle said, "They're very nice people, and very knowledgeable. I'm meeting them in Provence for more shopping."

"Now, that sounds like fun," Mercer said.

"Why don't you go with me?" Noelle said.

"Might as well," Myra said. "Can't do any more damage to your novel."

"Now, Myra," Leigh said.

"Have you been to Provence?" Noelle asked.

"No, but I've always wanted to see it. How long will you be there?"

Noelle shrugged as if a schedule was not important. "Maybe a month or so." She glanced at Bruce and something passed between them, as if the invitation to Mercer had not been discussed beforehand.

Mercer caught it and said, "I'd better save my money for the writer's table."

"Good call," Myra said. "You'd better stay here and write. Not that you need my advice."

"She doesn't," Leigh said softly.

They passed around a large serving bowl of shrimp risotto and a basket of bread, and after a few bites Myra began looking for trouble. "Here's what I think we should do, if I might say so," she said, chomping away with a mouth full of food. "This is very unusual and I've never done it before, which is all the more reason to do it now, you know, venture into unknown territory. We should have a literary intervention, right now, around this table. Mercer, you've been here for what, a month or so, and haven't written a damned word that might one day be sold, and, frankly, I'm getting kinda tired of your moaning and bellyaching about not making any progress with the novel. So, it's pretty obvious to all of us that you don't have a story, and since you haven't published in, what, ten years—"

"More like five."

"Whatever. It's plain as day that you need some help. So what I propose is that we intervene as your new friends and help you find a story. Just look at all the talent around the table here. Surely we can steer you in the right direction."

Mercer said, "Well, it can't get any worse."

"See what I mean," Myra said. "So, we're here to help." She gulped some beer from a bottle. "Now, for purposes of this intervention, we need to set some parameters.

First and most important is to decide whether you want to write literary fiction, stuff you can't give away, hell, Bruce can't even sell it, or do you want to write something more popular. I've read your novel and your stories and I'm not the least bit surprised they didn't sell. Forgive me, okay? This is, after all, an intervention so we have to be brutally blunt. Okay? Everybody okay with the bluntness thing?"

"Go for it," Mercer said with a smile. The rest nodded. We're all having fun. Let's hear it.

Myra crammed in a fork stuffed with lettuce and kept talking. "I mean, you're a beautiful writer, girl, and some of your sentences just stopped me cold, which, one could argue, is not something a good sentence is supposed to do, but anyway you can write like hell and I think you can write anything. So what's it gonna be— literary fiction or popular fiction?"

"Can't it be both?" Bruce asked, thoroughly enjoying the conversation.

"For a handful of authors, right," Myra replied. "But for the vast majority the answer is no." She looked at Mercer and said, "This is something we've been debating for about ten years, since the first day we met. But, anyway, let's assume that you will probably not be able to write literary fiction that will slay the critics and also rack up impressive royalties. And by the way, there is no envy here. I don't write anymore so my career is over. I'm not sure what Leigh is doing these days but she's damned sure not publishing anything."

"Now, Myra."

"So we can safely say her career is over too, and we don't care. We're old and we have plenty of money, so there's no competition. You're young and gifted and you'll have a future if you can just figure out what to write. Thus this intervention. We're just here to help. By the way, this risotto is delicious, Noelle."

"Am I supposed to respond?" Mercer asked.

"No, it's an intervention. You're supposed to sit there and listen to us as we beat you up. Bruce, you go first. What should Mercer write?"

"I would start by asking what you read."

"Everything by Randy Zalinski," Mercer said and got a laugh.

"Poor guy's laid up with a migraine and we're trashing him over dinner," Myra said.

"God help us," Leigh said quietly.

Bruce asked, "What are the last three novels you read?"

Mercer took a sip of wine and thought for a second. "I loved *The Nightingale* by Kristin Hannah, and I believe it sold well."

Bruce agreed. "Indeed it did. It's out in paperback and still selling."

Myra said, "I liked it, but you can't make a living writing books about the Holocaust. Besides, Mercer, what do you know about the Holocaust?"

"I didn't say I wanted to write about it. She's written twenty books, all different."

"Not sure it qualifies as literary fiction," Myra said.

"Are you sure you would recognize it if you saw it?" Leigh asked with a grin.

"Was that a cheap shot, Leigh?"

"Yes."

Bruce regained control with "Anyway, the other two novels?"

"*A Spool of Blue Thread* by Anne Tyler, one of my favorites, and *LaRose* by Louise Erdrich."

"All girls," Bruce said.

"Yes, I rarely read books written by men."

"Interesting, and smart, since about 70 percent of all novels are purchased by women."

"And all three sell, right?" Noelle asked.

"Oh yes," Bruce said. "They write great books that sell well."

"Bingo," said Mercer. "That's the plan."

Bruce looked at Myra and said, "Well, there you have it. A successful intervention."

"Not so fast. What about murder mysteries?" Myra asked.

"Not really," Mercer replied. "My brain doesn't work like that. I'm not devious enough to drop off clues and pick them up later."

"Suspense? Thrillers?"

"Not really. I can't do intricate plots."

"Spies, espionage?"

"I'm too much of a girl."

"Horror?"

"Are you kidding? After dark I'm afraid of my shadow."

"Romance?"

"Don't know the subject matter."

"Porn?"

"I'm still a virgin."

Bruce added, "Porn doesn't sell anymore. You can get all you want for free online."

Myra exhaled dramatically and said, "Those were the

days. Twenty years ago Leigh and I could make the pages sizzle. Science fiction? Fantasy?"

"Never touch the stuff."

"Westerns?"

"I'm afraid of horses."

"Political intrigue?"

"I'm afraid of politicians."

"Well, that does it. Looks like you're destined to write historical fiction about screwed-up families. Now get to work. We expect some progress from this point on."

"I'll start first thing in the morning," Mercer said. "And thanks."

"Don't mention it," Myra said. "And since we're on the subject of interventions, has anyone seen Andy Adam? Reason I ask is that I bumped into his ex at the grocery store a few days ago and she seemed to think he's not doing too well."

"Let's just say he's not sober these days," Bruce said.

"Anything we can do to help?"

"Nothing I can think of. Right now Andy is just a drunk, and until he decides to sober up he'll be nothing more than a drunk. His publisher will probably turn down his latest, and that will mean more trouble. I'm worried about him."

Mercer was watching Bruce's wineglass. Several times Elaine had said he drank too much, but Mercer had not seen this. At Myra and Leigh's dinner party, and now again tonight, he sipped his wine, was slow to refill, and was in perfect control.

With Andy out of the way, Myra led them through a recap of their other friends' lives. Bob Cobb was on a sailboat down around Aruba. Jay Arklerood was in Canada spending some time isolated in a friend's cabin. Amy Slater was busy with the kids, one of whom was playing T-ball. Bruce grew noticeably quiet. He was careful to absorb the gossip but not repeat any of it.

Noelle seemed excited to be leaving the Florida heat for a month. Provence was warm too, but not as humid, she explained. After dinner, she again asked Mercer to join her there, maybe not for a month, for perhaps a week or so. Mercer thanked her but said she needed to work on the novel. That, plus money was tight and she was saving for the writer's table.

"It's yours, dear," Noelle said. "I'm saving it for you."

Myra and Leigh left at nine and walked home. Mercer helped Bruce and Noelle in the kitchen and managed to say good-bye before ten. When she left, Bruce was sipping coffee in the den, his nose stuck in a book.

8.

Two days later, Mercer ventured downtown and had lunch at a small café with a shaded courtyard. Afterward, she strolled along Main Street and noticed that Noelle's shop was closed. A handwritten sign on the door explained that the owner was in France shopping for antiques. The writer's table was on full display in the front window, in an otherwise empty room. She went next door, said hello to Bruce, and walked upstairs to the café, where she ordered a latte and took it outside to the balcony overhanging Third Street. As expected, he soon joined her.

"What brings you downtown?" he asked.

"Boredom. Another unproductive day at the typewriter."

"I thought Myra had cured your writer's block."

"Wish it could be that simple. Do you have a few minutes, to talk?"

Bruce smiled and said of course. He glanced around and noticed a couple at a nearby table, too close for a serious conversation. "Let's go downstairs," he said. She followed him down to his First Editions Room and he closed the door behind them. "This must be serious," he said with a warm smile.

"It's somewhat delicate," she said. She told him the story of Tessa's old books, the ones she had "borrowed" from the Memphis Public Library in 1985. She had rehearsed the tale a dozen times and seemed genuinely perplexed about what to do. She was not surprised that he enjoyed the story and was interested in the books. In his opinion, there was no need to contact the library in Memphis. Sure, it would love to have the books back, but their losses had been written off decades ago. Besides, the library would have no appreciation for their real values. "They would probably just put them back on the shelves for the next person to steal," he said. "Believe me, nothing good would happen to the books. They should be protected."

"But they're not really mine to sell, right?"

He smiled and shrugged as if this was a technicality of little consequence. "What's the old saying? Possession is nine-tenths of the law. You've had the books for over ten years. I'd say they belong to you."

"I don't know. It just doesn't feel right for some reason."

"Are the books in good shape?"

"They seem to be. I'm no expert. I've taken good care of them. In fact, I've rarely touched them."

"Can I see them?"

"I don't know. This is just the first step. If I show you the books, then we would be getting closer to a transaction."

"At least let me see them."

"I don't know. Do you have the titles in your collection?"

"Yes. I have all of James Lee Burke's books and all of Cormac's."

Mercer glanced at the shelves as if looking for them. "Not here," he said. "They're with the rare books downstairs. Salt air and humidity are brutal on books, so I keep the valuable ones in a vault where the temperature is controlled. Would you like to see them?"

"Maybe later," Mercer managed to say casually. In fact, she was wonderfully indifferent. "Any idea what these two might be worth, you know, just ballpark figures?"

"Sure," he said quickly, as if anticipating the question. He swung around to a desktop computer, hit a few keys, and studied the screen. "I bought the first copy of *The Convict* in 1998 for twenty-five hundred bucks, so it's probably more than doubled in value. It all depends on the condition, which of course I won't know until I actually take a look. I bought another copy in 2003 for thirty-five hundred." He continued scrolling. Mercer couldn't see the screen but it appeared to be loaded with an extensive collection. "I have one copy of *Blood Meridian,* bought it from a dealer pal in San Francisco about ten years ago. Nine to be exact, paid, let's see, two thousand for it but it had a slight chip on the jacket and some aging. Not in great shape."

Well, just buy a forged jacket, Mercer thought, now that she knew so much about the business. Instead, she managed to seem pleasantly surprised. "Are you serious? They're that valuable?"

"Don't doubt me, Mercer, this is my favorite part of the business. I make more money trading rare books than selling new ones. Sorry if that sounds like bragging, but I love this stuff. If you'd like to sell the books I'll be happy to help."

"They have the library's bar codes on the dust jacket. Wouldn't that hurt their value?"

"Not really. They can be removed and I know every restorer in the business."

And probably every forger. "How would I show them to you?" she asked.

"Put 'em in a bag and bring 'em in." He paused and swiveled back to face her. "Or better yet, I'll stop by the cottage. I'd like to see the place. I've driven by it for years and always thought it was one of the prettiest on the beach."

"I really don't want to haul them around."

9.

The afternoon dragged on, and at one point Mercer could not resist the temptation to call Elaine for an update. Their plan was progressing faster than they had imagined, and now Bruce was ready to pounce on the books. The fact that he was stopping by the cottage was almost too good to be true, at least for Elaine.

"Where's Noelle?" she asked.

"Gone to France, I guess. Her store is closed indefinitely while she's off shopping."

"Perfect," Elaine said. She knew that the day before Noelle had flown from Jacksonville to Atlanta, where she boarded an Air France flight at 6:10 p.m. for a nonstop to Paris. She had arrived at Orly at 7:20, on schedule, and caught a 10:40 a.m. flight to Avignon. Their man on the ground there followed her to her apartment on Rue d'Alger in the old section of the city.

When Bruce arrived at the cottage a few minutes after six, Noelle was having a late dinner with a handsome French gentleman at La Fourchette, a famous little restaurant on Rue Racine.

When Bruce arrived at the cottage, Mercer was peeking through the blinds covering a front window. He was driving his convertible Porsche, the one she had seen parked at the Marchbanks House, and he had changed into khaki shorts and a golf shirt. At forty-three, he was lean, fit, and tanned, and though she had yet to hear him reveal the usual boring details of any workout routine, it was obvious he stayed in shape. After two long dinners, she knew that he ate little and drank in moderation. Same for Noelle. Good food was important to them; they just consumed it in small portions.

He was carrying a bottle of champagne, evidence that he was not one to waste time. His wife/partner had left the day before and he was already moving in on his latest prospect. Or so she figured.

Mercer met him at the door and showed him around. On the breakfast table, where she was trying to write her novel, she had placed the two books. "I guess we're having champagne," she said.

"It's just a housewarming gift, maybe for later."

"I'll put it in the fridge."

Bruce sat at the table and stared at the books, as if enthralled. "May I?"

"Of course. They're just old library books, right?" she said with a laugh.

"Hardly." He gently picked up *The Convict* and caressed it as if handling rare jewels. Without opening it, he examined the dust jacket, front, back, and spine. He rubbed the jacket and said, almost mumbling to himself, "First-issue jacket, bright and unfaded, no chips or blemishes anywhere." He slowly turned to the copyright page. "First edition, published by LSU Press in January of 1985." He turned more pages and closed the book. "Very fine copy. I'm impressed. And you've read it?"

"No, but I've read a few of Burke's mysteries."

"I thought you preferred female writers."

"I do, but not exclusively. Do you know him?"

"Oh, yes. He's been to the store twice. Great guy."

"And you have two of these, first editions?"

"Yes, but I'm always looking for more."

"What would you do if you bought it?"

"Is it for sale?"

"Maybe. I had no idea these two were so valuable."

"I would offer five thousand for this, and I would then try to sell it for twice that. I have a number of clients, serious collectors, and I can think of two or three who'd like to add this to their collections. We would haggle for a few weeks. I would come down. They might go up, but I would hold the line at seven thousand. If I couldn't get that, I'd lock it in the basement for five years. First editions are great investments because they can't print any more of them."

"Five thousand dollars," Mercer repeated, apparently stunned.

"On the spot."

"Can I haggle for more?"

"Sure, but six is my top dollar."

"And no one will ever know where it came from? I mean, they can't trace it back to me and Tessa?"

Bruce laughed at the question. "Of course not. This is my world, Mercer, and I've been playing this game for twenty years. These books disappeared decades ago and no one will suspect anything. I'll place them privately with my clients and everyone will be happy."

"There are no records?"

"Where? Who could keep up with all the first editions in the country? Books don't leave trails, Mercer. A lot of them are passed down like jewelry—not always accounted for, if you know what I mean."

"No, I don't."

"Outside of probate."

"Oh, I get it. Are they ever stolen and resold?"

"It happens. I'll turn down a book if its provenance is too shaky, but it's impossible to look at a book and say it's stolen. Take *The Convict*. Its first printing was small. Over time most have disappeared, and as this happens the remaining ones, those in fine condition, become more valuable. But that's still a lot of copies out there in the market and they're identical, or at least they were when they came off the press. Many are passed from one collector to the next. I suppose a few get stolen."

"Can I be downright nosy and ask what's your most valuable first edition?"

Bruce smiled and paused for a second. "You're not being nosy, but let's be discreet. A few years ago I bought a pristine copy of *The Catcher in the Rye* for fifty thousand. Salinger rarely autographed his masterpiece, but he gave this one to his editor, who kept it in his family for years, virtually untouched. Perfect condition."

"How'd you find it? I'm sorry, but this is fascinating."

"For years there were rumors about the book, rumors probably stoked by the editor's family, who smelled a big score. I tracked down a nephew, flew to Cleveland, stalked the guy, and pestered him until he sold me the book. It was never on the market, and as far as I know, no one knows I have it."

"And what will you do with it?"

"Nothing. Just own it."

"Who's seen it?"

"Noelle, a couple of friends. I'll be happy to show it to you, along with the rest of the collection."

"I'd like that. Back to business. Let's talk about Cormac."

Bruce smiled and picked up *Blood Meridian*. "Do you read him?"

"I've tried. He's too violent."

"I find it somewhat unusual that a person like Tessa would be a fan of Cormac McCarthy."

"She read all the time, as long as the books came from the library."

He examined the dust jacket and said, "A couple of

chips here on the spine, probably due to aging, with a bit of fading. Overall, the jacket is in good condition." He opened the book, examined the endpapers, turned to the half-title page and the copyright page, and read it carefully. He turned more pages, almost slowly enough to read the text. Softly, he said, as he flipped through, "I love this book. It's McCarthy's fifth one and his first novel set in the West."

"I hung in there for about fifty pages," she said. "The violence is explicit and gruesome."

"Indeed it is," Bruce said, still turning pages, as if he reveled in the violence. He gently closed the book and said, "A near-fine copy, as we say in the trade. Better than the one I already own."

"And you paid how much for it?"

"Two thousand, nine years ago. I would offer four thousand for this and I would probably just keep it in my collection. Four thousand is the top."

"That's ten thousand for these two books. I had no idea they could be worth that much."

"I know my stuff, Mercer. Ten thousand is a good deal for you, and for me as well. You want to sell?"

"I don't know. I need to think about it."

"Okay. No pressure from me. But, please allow me to keep these in my vault until you decide. As I said, the salt air is brutal."

"Sure. Take them. Give me a couple of days and I'll make up my mind."

"Take your time. No rush. Now, about that champagne."

"Yes, of course. It is pushing seven o'clock."

"I have an idea," Bruce said as he stood and took the

books. "Let's drink it on the beach and go for a walk. I don't get much beach time, not in this business. I love the ocean and most days don't even get the chance to see it."

"Okay," she said with a slight hesitation. Nothing like a romantic stroll in the surf with a man who claimed to be married. Mercer took a small cardboard box from the counter and handed it to him. He placed the books in it as she removed the champagne from the refrigerator.

10.

It took an hour to walk to the Ritz and back, and by the time they returned to the cottage shadows were falling across the dunes. Their glasses were bone dry and Mercer wasted no time refilling them. Bruce fell into a wicker rocker on the deck and she sat nearby.

They had covered his family: the sudden death of his father; the inheritance that bought the bookshop; his mother he hadn't seen in almost thirty years; a distant sister; no contact with aunts, uncles, cousins; grandparents long gone. Mercer had matched him story for story, then went one up with the tragedy of her mother's mental illness and commitment. That was something she told no one, but Bruce was easy to talk to. And to trust. And since both were scarred by the wreckage of abnormal families, they were on common ground and felt comfortable comparing notes and talking about it. The more they revealed, the more they managed to laugh.

Halfway through the second glass of champagne, Bruce said, "I disagree with Myra. You shouldn't write about families. You've done it once, and brilliantly, but once is enough."

"Don't worry. Myra is perhaps the last person I would take advice from."

"Don't you love her, though, crazy as she is?"

"No, not yet, but I'm growing fond of her. Does she really have a lot of money?"

"Who knows? She and Leigh seem to be quite comfortable. They wrote a hundred books together, and by the way Leigh was far more involved in the romance fiction than she will admit. Some of their titles still sell."

"Must be nice."

"It's hard to write when you're broke, Mercer, I know that. I know a lot of writers and very few of them sell enough to write full-time."

"So they teach. They find a campus somewhere and get a steady paycheck. I've done it twice and I'll probably do it again. Either that or sell real estate."

"I don't think that's an option for you."

"Got any other ideas?"

"Actually, I have one great idea. Top me off and I'll tell you a long story." Mercer got the champagne out of the refrigerator and emptied the bottle. Bruce took a long drink, smacked his lips, and said, "I could drink this stuff for breakfast."

"Me too, but coffee's a lot cheaper."

"So I had this girlfriend once, long before Noelle. Her name was Talia, a sweet girl who was gorgeous and talented and really messed up in the head. We dated off and on for about two years, more off than on because she was slowly losing her grip on reality. I couldn't help her and it was painful watching her deteriorate. But she could write, and she was working on a novel that had enormous potential. It was a highly fictionalized story of Charles Dickens and his mistress, a young actress named Ellen Ternan. Dickens was married for twenty years to Catherine, a really stern woman in the Victorian sense. She bore ten children, and in spite of the obvious physical attraction the marriage was notoriously unhappy. When he was forty-five, and perhaps the most famous man in England, he met Ellen, who was eighteen and an aspiring actress. They fell madly in love and he left his wife and kids, though divorce was out of the question in those days. It's never been clear whether he and Ellen actually lived together, and there was even a pretty strong rumor that she had a child that died at birth. Whatever the arrangement, they did a good job of hiding and covering up. However, in Talia's novel, they had a full-blown affair that is narrated by Ellen and no details are spared. The novel got convoluted when Talia introduced another famous affair, one between William Faulkner and Meta Carpenter. Faulkner met her when he was in Hollywood cranking out screenplays for a buck, and from all indications they were in love. This got fictionalized too and was very well done. Then, to make the novel even more complicated, Talia introduced yet another affair between a famous writer and his girlfriend. There was a story, one that was never verified and is probably not true, that Ernest Hemingway had a quick romance with Zelda Fitzgerald when they were living in Paris. As you know, facts often get in the way of a good story, so Talia created her own facts and wrote a highly engaging account of Ernest and Zelda carrying on behind F. Scott's back. So the novel had three sensational, literary love affairs raging by alternating sections, and it was just too much for one book."

"She let you read it?"

"Most of it. She kept changing the stories and rewriting entire sections, and the more she wrote the more muddled it became. She asked for advice, I gave it to her, and she always did the opposite. She was obsessed with it and wrote nonstop for two years. When the manuscript passed a thousand pages I quit reading. We were fighting a lot then."

"What happened to it?"

"Talia said she burned it. She called one day out of her mind and said she had destroyed it for good and would never write another word. Two days later she overdosed in Savannah, where she was living at the time."

"That's terrible."

"Twenty-seven years old and more talent than I've ever seen. A month or so after her funeral, I wrote to her mother and rather gently asked about what, if anything, Talia might have left behind. Never heard a word, and the novel has never been mentioned. I'm convinced she burned it, then killed herself."

"How awful."

"It was tragic."

"You didn't have a copy?"

"Oh no. She would bring the manuscript here for a few days and make me read it while she kept working. She was paranoid about someone stealing her masterpiece and guarded it closely. Poor girl was paranoid about a lot of things. In the end she was off her meds and hearing voices, and there was nothing I could do. Frankly, by then I was trying to avoid her."

They pondered the tragedy for a minute or so, each sipping slowly. The sun was gone and the deck was dark. Neither had mentioned dinner, but Mercer was prepared to say no. They had spent enough time together for one day.

She said, "That's a great story."

"Which one? Dickens, Faulkner, Zelda, or Talia? There's a lot of material there."

"And you're giving it to me?"

Bruce smiled and shrugged. "Take it or leave it."

"And the Dickens and Faulkner stories are true, right?"

"Yes. But the best one is Hemingway and Zelda. It was Paris in the 1920s, the Lost Generation, all that colorful background and history. They certainly knew each other. F. Scott and Hemingway were pals and drinking buddies and the Americans all partied together. Hemingway was always on the prowl—he married four women and had a kinky side. In the right hands, the story could be so salacious that even Myra would approve."

"I could only hope."

"You're not too enthused."

"I'm not sure about historical fiction. Is it history or make-believe? For some reason it seems dishonest to tamper with the lives of real people and make them do things they didn't really do. Sure they're dead, but does that give writers the license to fictionalize their lives? Especially their private matters?"

"Happens all the time, and it sells."

"I guess, but I'm not sure it's for me."

"Do you read them? Faulkner, Hemingway, Fitzgerald?"

"Only if I have to. I try to avoid old dead white men."

"Me too. I prefer to read the people I've met." He drained his glass and set it on the table between them. He said, "I'd better go. Enjoyed the walk."

"Thanks for the champagne," she said. "I'll show you out."

"I can find the door," he said, and as he walked behind her gently kissed her on the top of her head. "See you."

"Good night."

11.

At eight the following morning, Mercer was sitting at the breakfast table, staring at the ocean, ignoring the laptop, daydreaming about something she couldn't describe had she been asked, when she was startled by her cell phone. It was Noelle, calling from France, six hours ahead. She greeted Mercer with a hearty "Bonjour," and apologized for disturbing her creative time, but she needed to check in before the day got away from her. She explained that a man named Jake would be at her store the next day and could meet with Mercer. Jake was her favorite restorer and painter and stopped by periodically. He would be repairing an armoire in the basement workroom, and it would be an excellent time for Mercer to discuss painting the writer's table. The store would be closed and locked, but Jake had a

key and so on. Mercer thanked her and they chatted for
a few minutes about things in France.

As soon as she said good-bye, Mercer called Elaine
Shelby, who was in Washington. Mercer had sent her a
lengthy e-mail the night before with all the details of
the day's events and conversations, so Elaine was fully
briefed. Suddenly it looked as though Mercer might get
to see both basements on the same day.

She called Bruce at noon and said she would take his
offer for the two books. She would be downtown the
following day to see Jake, and she would pop in the bookstore to pick up the check. Plus, she really wanted to see
that copy of *The Catcher in the Rye*.

"Perfect," he said. "How about lunch?"

"Sure."

12.

Elaine and her team arrived after dark and too late
for a meeting. At nine the following morning, Mercer
walked the beach and stopped at the boardwalk leading
to their condo. Elaine was sitting on the steps with a cup
of coffee and sand between her toes. She shook hands
firmly, as always, and said, "Nice work."

"We'll see," Mercer said.

They walked to the condo, where two men were waiting, Graham and Rick. They were sitting at the kitchen
table with their coffee and a large kit or box of some
variety. In it, as Mercer was about to learn, were the
toys of the trade. Mikes and bugs and transmitters and
cameras so small she wondered how they could possi-

bly capture any image. They began pulling out the various devices and discussing the pros and cons and possibilities of each.

At no time had Elaine asked Mercer whether she was willing to wear a hidden camera. It was just assumed that she would, and for a moment this irritated her. As Graham and Rick talked on, Mercer felt a knot in her stomach. She finally blurted, "Is this legal? You know, filming someone without their permission?"

"It's not illegal," Elaine answered with a confident smile. Don't be ridiculous. "No more so than taking a photograph of someone in public. Permission is not required, nor is full disclosure."

Rick, the older of the two, said, "You can't record a telephone conversation without full disclosure, but the government has yet to pass a law prohibiting camera surveillance."

"Anytime, anywhere, except for a private residence," Graham added. "Just look at all the surveillance cameras watching buildings and sidewalks and parking lots. They don't need permission to film anyone."

Elaine, who was very much in charge and outranked the two men, said, "I like this scarf with a buckle ring. Let's try it." The scarf was a flowery mix of colors and appeared to be expensive. Mercer folded it into a trifold and put it around her neck. Rick handed her the buckle ring, a golden clasp with tiny fake jewels, and she slipped the ends of the scarf through it. With a tiny screwdriver, and moving in far too close, Rick examined the buckle ring as he tapped it with the screwdriver.

"We'll put the camera right there and it will be virtually invisible," he said.

"How big is the camera?" Mercer asked.

Graham held it up, a ridiculously tiny device smaller than a raisin. "That's a camera?" she asked.

"High-def. We'll show you. Hand me the buckle ring." Mercer slid it down and gave it to Rick. He and Graham put on matching pairs of surgical magnifying glasses and hovered over their work.

Elaine asked, "Do you know where you're going to lunch?"

"No, he didn't say. I'm meeting Jake at Noelle's store at eleven, then I'll walk next door and see Bruce. Lunch will follow but I don't know where. How am I supposed to use that thing?"

"You don't do anything, just act normally. The camera will be activated remotely by Rick and Graham. They'll be in a van near the store. There's no audio, the camera is too small, so don't worry about what is said. We have no idea what's in either basement so try to scan everything. Look for doors, windows, more cameras."

Rick added, "And look for security sensors on the doors to the basement. We're almost positive there are no doors that lead to the outside. Both basements appear to be completely below ground surface with no stairways on the exterior leading down."

Elaine said, "This is our first look and it could well be the only one. Everything is crucial, but obviously we're looking for the manuscripts, stacks of papers that are larger than printed books."

"I'm familiar with a manuscript."

"Of course you are. Look for drawers, cabinets, anyplace they could possibly fit."

"What if he sees the camera?" Mercer asked, somewhat nervously.

Both men grunted. Impossible. "He won't, because he can't," Elaine said.

Rick handed the buckle ring back and Mercer slid the ends of the scarf through it again. "I'm activating," Graham said as he punched keys on a laptop.

Rick said, "Would you please stand and turn around slowly?"

"Sure." As she did so, Elaine and the boys stared at the laptop. "Pretty amazing," Elaine said, almost to herself. "Take a look, Mercer."

Standing beside the table and facing the front door, Mercer glanced down at the screen and was surprised at the clarity of the image. The sofa, television, armchair, even the cheap rug in front of her were vividly clear. "All from this tiny camera," she said.

"It's a piece of cake, Mercer," Elaine said.

"The scarf really doesn't match anything I have."

"Then what are you wearing?" Elaine asked, reaching for a bag. She pulled out half a dozen scarves.

Mercer said, "Just a little red sundress, I think. Nothing fancy."

13.

Jake opened the front door and locked it behind her. He introduced himself and said he'd known Noelle for many years. He was a craftsman with rough, callused hands and a white beard, and had the look of a hard worker who'd spent a lifetime with hammers and tools.

He was gruff and explained that the writer's desk was already in the basement. She followed him down the steps, slowly and at a distance, trying to remind herself that everything in front of her was being filmed and analyzed. Down ten steps with her hand on the rail and into a long, cluttered room that seemed to run the length of the store, which, as she well knew, was 42 feet wide and 165 feet in depth, same as the bookshop next door. The ceiling was low, no more than eight feet tall, and the flooring was unfinished concrete. All manner of disassembled, broken, unfinished, and mismatched furniture and furnishings were stored haphazardly along the walls. Mercer nonchalantly browsed around, turning slowly in all directions. "So this is where she keeps the good stuff," she said, but Jake had no sense of humor. The basement was well lit and there was a room of some sort near the back. Most important, there was a door in the brick wall between the room and the basement next door, the basement where Elaine Shelby and her mysterious company were betting that Mr. Cable was hiding his treasure. The brick wall was old and had been painted many times, now a dark gray, but the door was much newer. It was metal and solid and there were two security sensors at its top corners.

Elaine's team knew that the two stores were virtually identical in width, length, height, and layout. They were part of the same building, one that had been built a hundred years earlier, and had basically been split in two when the bookstore opened in 1940.

Sitting in a van across the street and staring at their laptops, Rick and Graham were delighted to see that a door connected the two basements. Sitting on a sofa in the condo, Elaine had the same reaction. Go, Mercer!

The writer's table was in the middle of the room, with newspapers spread below it, though the floor had collected paint droppings for years, and Mercer examined it carefully, as if it were some prized possession and not simply a pawn in their game. Jake pulled out a sheet of paint colors and they talked about several, with Mercer being quite hard to please. She eventually settled on a soft pastel blue that Jake would apply with a thin coat to produce the look of something old and distressed. He didn't have that color in his truck and it would take a few days to find it.

Great. She could always come back for the next visit, to monitor his progress. And who knows? With the toys Rick and Graham had in their arsenal she might have cameras in her earrings next time.

She asked if there was a restroom downstairs, and Jake nodded toward the back. She took her time finding it, using it, and strolling back to the front, where he was sanding the top of the writer's table. As he hunched over, she stood directly in front of the metal door for the best footage yet. But there might be a hidden camera watching her, right? She backed away, impressed with her situational awareness and growing experience. She might make a decent spy after all.

She left Jake at the front door and walked around the block to a small Cuban deli where she ordered an iced tea and sat at a table. Within a minute, Rick entered and paid for a soft drink. He sat across from her, smiling, and said almost in a whisper, "Perfect job."

"I guess I'm just a natural at this," she said, the knot in her stomach momentarily gone. "Is the camera on?"

"No, I turned it off. I'll reactivate it when you enter the bookstore. Don't do anything different. The camera is working perfectly and you got us plenty of footage. We are thrilled that there's a door connecting the two basements. Now get as close to it as you can from the other side."

"Nothing to it. I'm assuming we'll leave the store and walk to lunch. Will you keep the camera on?"

"No."

"And I'll be sitting across the table from Cable for at least an hour. You're not worried about him noticing anything?"

"After you've been to the basement, go to the restroom, the one upstairs on the main floor. Take off the scarf and the buckle ring and stick them in your purse. If he says anything, tell him the scarf was too warm."

"I like that. It would be hard to enjoy lunch knowing I was pointing a camera at his face."

"Right. You leave now and I'm right behind you."

Mercer entered the bookstore at 11:50 and saw Bruce rearranging the magazines on a rack near the front. Today's seersucker suit was striped in a soft aqua shade. So far Mercer had noticed at least six different tints to his suits and she suspected there were more. Bow tie of bright yellow paisley. As always, dirty buckskins, no socks. Never. He smiled, pecked her on the cheek, said she looked great. She followed him into the First Editions Room and he picked up an envelope on his desk. "Ten grand for the two books Tessa borrowed thirty years ago. What would she think?"

"She would say, 'Where's my share of the profits?' "

Bruce laughed and said, "We get the profits. I have two clients who want *The Convict*, so I'll play one off the other and clear twenty-five hundred with a few phone calls."

"Just like that?"

"No, not always, just the luck of the day. That's why I love this business."

"A question. That pristine copy of *The Catcher in the Rye* you mentioned. If you decided to sell it, what would you ask?"

"So, you're liking this business too, huh?"

"No, not at all. I have no brain for business. Just curious, that's all."

"Last year I turned down eighty grand. It's not for sale, but if I were somehow forced to put it on the market I would start at one hundred."

"Not a bad deal."

"You said you wanted to see it."

Mercer shrugged as if she were indifferent and offered a casual "Sure, if you're not too busy." It was apparent Bruce wanted to show off his books.

"Never too busy for you. Follow me." They walked past the stairs, through the children's section, and to the very back of the store. The stairs going down were behind a locked door that was out of the way and gave every appearance of being rarely used. A camera watched it from a high corner. A security sensor was attached to its top. With a key, Bruce unlocked a dead bolt and turned an old knob, which was not locked. He pulled the door open and turned on a light. "Careful," he said as he started down. Mercer hung back, careful as he said. He flipped another switch at the bottom of the stairs.

The basement was divided into at least two sections. The front and larger section included the stairs and the metal door that connected to Noelle's, along rows of old wooden shelves sagging with thousands of unwanted books and galleys and advance reading copies. "It's known as the graveyard," Bruce said, waving an arm at the mess. "Every store has a junk room." They took a few steps toward the rear of the basement and stopped at a cinder-block wall that had obviously been added long after the construction of the building. It ran the height and width of the room and seemed to have been wedged snugly into place. It had another metal door with a keypad beside it. As Bruce punched in the code, Mercer noticed a camera hanging from an old rafter and pointed at the door. Something buzzed and clicked, and they stepped through the door as Bruce turned on the lights. The temperature was noticeably cooler.

The room appeared to be completely self-enclosed, with rows of shelves against cinder-block walls, a concrete floor with a slick finish, and a lowered ceiling made of some fibrous material Mercer had no chance of describing. But she filmed it for her experts. Within the hour they would speculate that the room was forty feet in width and about the same in depth; a spacious room with a handsome table in the center; eight-foot ceilings; tight joints; every indication of a room that was airtight, secure, and fireproof.

Bruce said, "Books are damaged by light, heat, and moisture, so all three must be controlled. In here there's almost no humidity and the temperature is always fifty-five degrees. No sunlight, obviously."

The shelves were made of thick metal with glass doors so the spines of the books were visible. There were six shelves in each unit with the bottom about two feet off the floor and the top a few inches above Mercer's head, so about six feet, she guessed. Rick and Graham would agree.

"Where are Tessa's first editions?" she asked.

He stepped to the back wall and put a key into a narrow side panel next to the shelves. When he turned it, something clicked and all six glass doors were released. He opened the second shelf from the top. "Right here," he said, removing the copies of *The Convict* and *Blood Meridian*. "They are safe and sound in their new home."

"Very safe," she said. "This is impressive, Bruce. How many books are down here?"

"Several hundred, but they're not all mine." He pointed to a wall by the door and said, "Those I store for clients and friends. A few are here sort of on consignment. I have one client who's going through a divorce and he's hiding his books right there. I'll probably get a subpoena and get hauled into court, and not for the first time. But I always lie to protect my client."

"And what's that?" she asked, pointing to a tall, bulky, oversized cabinet standing in a corner.

"It's a safe and it's where I keep the really good stuff." He punched in a code on its keypad—Mercer was careful to properly look away—and a thick door unlatched itself. Bruce swung it open. At the top and center there were three shelves, all lined with what appeared to be the spines of fake books, some with titles in gold print. Bruce gently pulled one off the middle shelf and asked, "Are you familiar with a clamshell?"

"No."

"It's this protective box, custom made for each book. Obviously, these books were printed in different sizes, so the clamshells vary. Step over here."

They turned around and moved to the small table in the center of the room. He placed the clamshell on it, opened it, and gently removed the book. Its dust jacket was encased in a clear laminate cover. "This is my first copy of *The Catcher in the Rye*. Got it from my father's estate twenty years ago."

"So you have two copies of it?"

"No, I have four." He opened to the front endpaper and pointed to a slight discoloration. "A little fading here, and a chip or two on the jacket, but a near-fine copy." He left the book and the clamshell on the table and stepped back to the safe. As he did, Mercer turned to it so Rick and Graham would have their full frontal view. At its bottom, below the three shelves of the rarest of books, were what appeared to be four retractable drawers, all closed tightly at the moment.

If Bruce indeed had the manuscripts, then that's where they are. Or so she thought.

He placed another clamshell on the table and said, "This is my most recent edition of the four, the one actually signed by Salinger." He opened the clamshell, withdrew the book, and turned to the title page. "No dedication, no date, just his autograph, which, as I said, is quite rare. He simply refused to sign his books. He went crazy, don't you think?"

"That's what they say," Mercer replied. "These are beautiful."

"They are," he said, still caressing the book. "Sometimes when I'm having a lousy day I sneak down here and lock myself in this room and pull out the books. I try to imagine what it was like being J. D. Salinger in 1951, when this was published, his first novel. He had published a few short stories, a couple in *The New Yorker,* but he wasn't well known. Little, Brown printed ten thousand of these at first, and now the book sells a million copies a year, in sixty-five languages. He had no idea what was coming. It made him rich and famous and he couldn't handle the attention. Most scholars believe he sort of cracked up."

"I taught it in my class two years ago."

"So you know it well?"

"It's not my favorite. Again, I prefer female writers, preferably those still alive."

"And you would like to see the rarest book I have by a woman, dead or alive, right?"

"Sure."

He returned to the safe, with Mercer filming every step and even moving away slightly for another clear frontal assault with her little camera. He found his book and returned to the table. "How about Virginia Woolf, *A Room of One's Own*?" He opened the clamshell and removed the book. "Published in 1929. First edition, near-fine copy. I found it twelve years ago."

"I love this book. I read it in high school and it inspired me to become a writer, or at least give it a shot."

"It's quite rare."

"I'll give you ten thousand for it."

They shared a laugh and he politely said, "Sorry. It's not for sale." He handed it to her. She gently opened it and said, "She was so brave. Her famous line is 'A woman must have money and a room of her own if she is to write fiction.'"

"She was a tortured soul."

"I'll say. She killed herself. Why do writers suffer so much, Bruce?" She closed the book and handed it back to him. "So much destructive behavior, even suicide."

"I can't understand the suicide, but I sort of get the drinking and bad habits. Our friend Andy tried to explain it years ago. He said it's because the writing life is so undisciplined. There's no boss, no supervisor, no time clock to punch or hours to keep. Write in the morning, write at night. Drink when you want to. Andy thinks he writes better with a hangover, but I'm not sure about that." Bruce was fitting the books back into their clamshells. He returned them to the safe.

Impulsively, she asked, "What's in the drawers?"

Without the slightest hesitation, he replied, "Old manuscripts, but they're not worth a lot, not when compared to these books. John D. MacDonald is a favorite of mine, especially his Travis McGee series, and a few years ago I was able to buy two of his original manuscripts from another collector." He was closing the door as he said this. Obviously, the drawers were off-limits.

"Seen enough?" he asked.

"Yes. This is fascinating stuff, Bruce. It's another world I know nothing about."

"I seldom show off these books. The rare book trade is a quiet business. I'm sure no one knows that I have four copies of Catcher, and I'd like to keep it that way.

There is no registry, no one is looking, and many trans-
actions take place in the dark."

"Your secrets are safe. I can't think of a soul I would
want to tell."

"Don't get me wrong, Mercer. This is all legitimate. I
report the profits and pay the taxes, and if I dropped
dead my estate would include these assets."

"All of them?" she asked with a smile.

He returned the smile and said, "Well, most of them."

"Of course."

"Now, how about a business lunch?"

"I'm starving."

14.

The team dined on carryout pizza and washed it
down with soft drinks. At the moment, food was not
important. Rick, Graham, and Elaine sat at the condo's
dining table and reviewed dozens of still photos taken
from Mercer's video. She had produced eighteen minutes of footage from Noelle's store and twenty-two
from Bruce's; forty minutes of precious evidence they
were thrilled to now possess. They had studied it, but
more important it was being analyzed by their lab in
Bethesda. Facts were being established: the size of his
vault, the dimensions of his safe, the presence of surveillance cameras and security sensors; dead bolts on
doors; push-button entry panels. The safe weighed eight
hundred pounds, was made of eleven-gauge steel, and
had been manufactured fifteen years earlier by a factory
in Ohio, sold online, and installed by a contractor out

of Jacksonville. When locked, it was secured by five dead bolts made of lead and sealed by hydraulics. It could withstand heat of 1,550 degrees for two hours. Opening it would not be a problem, but the obvious challenge was getting to it without ringing bells.

They had spent the afternoon around the table, often in long, intense conversations, often on the speakerphone with their colleagues in Bethesda. Elaine was in charge but welcomed collaboration. There were a lot of opinions offered by smart people, and she listened. The FBI consumed most of their time. Was it time to call in the Feds? To introduce them to their favorite suspect? To tell them everything they had learned so far about Bruce Cable? Elaine didn't think so, not yet anyway. And her reason was sound: there was not enough evidence to convince a federal magistrate that Cable had the manuscripts buried in his basement. At the moment, they had a tip from a source in Boston, a forty-minute video of the premises, and some still shots lifted from the video. In the opinions of their two attorneys in Washington, it was simply not enough to get a search warrant.

And, as always, when the Feds entered the picture, they took charge and changed the rules. As of now, they knew nothing of Bruce Cable and had no idea Elaine's little mole had wormed her way inside. Elaine wanted to keep it this way for as long as possible.

One scenario, suggested by Rick but with little enthusiasm, called for the diversion of arson. Start a small fire after midnight on the ground floor of the bookstore, and as alarms wailed and security monitors erupted, enter the basement through Noelle's side and do a smash and grab. The risks were abundant, not the least of which was the commission of several crimes. And what if Gatsby wasn't there? What if Gatsby and friends were being hidden elsewhere, on the island or somewhere else in the country? Cable would be so unnerved he would scatter them across the globe, if he hadn't already done so.

Elaine nixed the plan not long after Rick mentioned it. The clock was ticking but they still had time, and their girl was doing magnificent work. In less than four weeks she had endeared herself to Cable and infiltrated his circle. She had earned his trust and brought them this—forty minutes of valuable footage and hundreds of still shots. They were closing in, or at least they believed so. They would continue to be patient and wait for whatever happened next.

One significant question had been answered. They had debated why a small-town book dealer working in an old building could be such a fanatic about security. And since he was their prime suspect, everything he did was viewed with even more suspicion. The little fortress in his basement was being used to protect the ill-gotten loot of his trade, right? Not necessarily. They now knew that there was a lot of valuable stuff down there. After lunch, Mercer had reported that along with the four copies of *The Catcher in the Rye* and the one of *A Room of One's Own* there were about fifty other books in protective clamshells lined neatly on the shelves of the safe. The vault itself held several hundred books.

Elaine had been in the business for over twenty years and was amazed at Cable's inventory. She had dealt with the established rare book houses and knew them well. Their business was buying and selling and they used catalogs and websites and all manner of marketing to enhance their trade. Their collections were vast and well advertised. She and her team had often wondered if a small-time player like Cable could round up a million dollars for the Fitzgerald manuscripts. Now, though, that question too had been answered. He had the means.

CHAPTER SEVEN
THE WEEKEND GIRL

1.

The invitation was for dinner, a dry one. Dry because Andy Adam was also invited and Bruce was insisting that the night be alcohol-free. Dry also because the touring writer, one Sally Aranca, had kicked the booze a few years back and preferred not to be around the stuff.

Bruce told Mercer on the phone that Andy was about to go away for another detox and was trying desperately to stay sober until he went into lockdown. Mercer was eager to help and happily agreed to the rules.

At the signing, Ms. Aranca charmed her audience of about fifty as she discussed her work and read a brief scene from her latest novel. She was making a name for herself in crime fiction with a series based on a female private investigator in San Francisco, her home. Mercer had skimmed the book during the afternoon, and as she watched and listened to Sally perform she realized that her protagonist was much like Sally herself: early forties, recovering alcoholic, divorced with no kids, quick and witty, savvy and tough, and, of course, quite attractive. She published once a year and toured extensively, always stopping at Bay Books and usually when Noelle was out of town.

After the signing, the four walked down the street to Le Rocher, a small French place with a good reputation. Bruce quickly ordered two bottles of sparkling water and handed the wine list back to the waitress. Andy glanced around a few times at the other tables and seemed eager to snatch a glass of wine, but instead added a slice of lemon to his water and settled down. He was haggling with his publisher over his latest contract, one that included a smaller advance than his last deal. With a fine flair for humor and self-deprecation, he told how he had jumped from publisher to publisher until all of New York was weary of him. He'd burned them all. Over appetizers, Sally recounted her early frustrations at getting published. Her first novel had been rejected by a dozen agents and even more publishers, but she kept writing. And drinking. Her first marriage blew up when she caught her husband cheating, and her life was a mess. Her second and third novels were rejected. Thankfully, some friends intervened and she found the will to stop drinking. With her fourth novel she turned to crime, created her protagonist, and suddenly agents were calling her. The film rights were optioned and she was off and running. Now, eight novels later, the series was established and gaining popularity.

Though she told her stories without a trace of smugness, Mercer could not help but feel a twinge of envy. Sally was writing full-time. Gone were the cheap jobs and loans from her parents, and she was producing a book a year. It all sounded so easy. And Mercer could freely admit to herself that every writer she'd ever met carried a mean streak of envy; it was the nature of the breed.

Over entrées, the conversation suddenly turned to drinking, and Andy admitted he was having problems. Sally was compassionate but tough, and offered advice. She had been sober for seven years and the change had saved her life. She was inspiring, and Andy thanked her for her honesty. At times, Mercer felt as though she was sitting through an AA meeting.

Bruce was obviously quite fond of Ms. Aranca, and as the dinner dragged on Mercer realized she was getting less of his attention. Don't be ridiculous, Mercer thought, they've known each other for years. But once she realized this she couldn't let it go, and it became more obvious, at least to her. Bruce touched Sally a few times, little affectionate pats on the shoulder as his hand lingered.

They skipped dessert and Bruce paid the bill. Walking along Main Street, he said he needed to stop by the bookstore to check on the night clerk. Sally went with him. Everyone said good night and Sally promised to send Mercer an e-mail and stay in touch. As Mercer was walking away, Andy said, "Hey, got time for a drink?"

She stopped and faced him. "No, Andy, that's not a good idea. Not after that dinner."

"Coffee, not booze."

It was just after nine and Mercer had nothing to do at

the cottage. Maybe having a coffee with Andy would help him. They crossed the street and entered an empty coffee bar. The barista said it would close in thirty minutes. They ordered two cups of decaf and took them outside to a table. The bookstore was across the street. After a few minutes, Bruce and Sally left it and disappeared down the street, in the direction of the Marchbanks House.

"She'll stay at his place tonight," Andy said. "A lot of the writers do."

Mercer absorbed this and asked, "Does Noelle figure into their plans?"

"Not at all. Bruce has his favorites. Noelle has hers. At the top of the tower there's a round room, known as the Writer's Room. It sees a lot of activity."

"I'm not sure I understand," Mercer said, though she did so perfectly.

"They have an open marriage, Mercer, and sleeping around is accepted, probably even encouraged. I suppose they love each other but they have no rules."

"That's pretty bizarre."

"Not for them. They seem to be happy."

Finally, some of Elaine's gossip was being verified.

He said, "One reason Noelle spends so much time in France is that she has a longtime boyfriend there. I think he's married too."

"Oh why not. Of course he is."

"And you've never been married, right?"

"Correct."

"Well, I've tried it twice and I'm not sure I can recommend it. Are you dating anyone?"

"No. The last boyfriend hit the road a year ago."

"Met anyone interesting around here?"

"Sure. You, Bruce, Noelle, Myra, Leigh, Bob Cobb. Lots of interesting folks around here."

"Anyone you want to date?"

He was at least fifteen years older, a fierce drinker, a barroom brawler with scars to prove it, a real brute of a man who offered nothing of interest. "Are you trying to pick me up, Andy?"

"No. I was thinking about dinner sometime."

"Aren't you leaving real soon for, how does Myra put it, booze camp?"

"In three days, and I'm trying like hell to stay sober until then. It's not easy. In fact I'm sipping this luke-warm coffee with no caffeine and trying to pretend it's a double vodka on the rocks. I can almost taste it. And I'm killing time because I don't want to go home, even though there's not a drop in the house. On the way there I'll pass two liquor stores, still open, and I'll have to fight myself to keep the car in the road." His voice was fading.

"I'm sorry, Andy."

"Don't be sorry. Just don't get in this shape. It's awful."

"I wish I could help."

"You can. Say a prayer for me, okay? I hate being this weak." As if to get away from the coffee and the conversation, he suddenly stood and began walking. Mercer tried to say something but found no words. She watched him until he turned a corner.

She took the cups to the counter. The streets were quiet; only the bookstore and the fudge shop were still open, along with the coffee bar. Her car was parked on

Third, and for some reason she walked past it. She made the block and kept walking until she passed the Marchbanks House. Up in the tower, a light was on in the Writer's Room. She slowed a step or two, and, as if on cue, the light went off.

She admitted she was curious, but could she also admit to a trace of jealousy?

2.

After five weeks in the cottage, it was time to get away for a few days. Connie and her husband and two teenage girls were on the way for their annual two-week vacation at the beach. Connie had politely, almost dutifully, invited Mercer to join them, but there was no way. Mercer knew the girls would do nothing but stare at their phones all day, and the husband would talk of nothing but his frozen yogurt shops. Though he was modest about his success he worked nonstop. Mercer knew he would be up by five each morning, slugging down coffee as he fired off e-mails and checked shipments and such, and would probably never get his feet wet in the ocean. Connie had joked that he had never lasted the full two weeks. Some crisis would always intervene and he would rush back to Nashville to save his company.

Writing would be out of the question, though at her current pace she couldn't fall much farther behind.

As for Connie, who was nine years older, the two had never been close. With their mother away and their father too self-absorbed, the girls practically raised themselves. Connie fled home at the age of eighteen for college at SMU and never returned. She had spent one summer at the beach with Tessa and Mercer, but by then she was boy crazy and bored with the beach walking and turtle watching and nonstop reading. She left when Tessa caught her smoking pot.

Now the sisters e-mailed once a week; chatted by phone once a month; kept things civil and upbeat. Mercer dropped by occasionally when she was near Nashville, often at a different address. They moved a lot, and always to larger homes in nicer neighborhoods. They were chasing something, a vague dream, and Mercer often wondered where they would be when they found it. The more money they made the more they spent, and Mercer, living in poverty, marveled at their consumption.

There was a backstory that had never been discussed, primarily because a discussion would lead to nothing but hard feelings. Connie had the good fortune of receiving four years of private college education without incurring a dime in student debt, courtesy of their father, Herbert, and his Ford business. However, by the time Mercer enrolled at Sewanee, the old boy was losing his shirt and staring at bankruptcy. For years she had resented her sister's luck, and it was not worth mentioning that Connie had never offered a dime of support. Now that her student debt had miraculously vanished, Mercer was determined to get past the resentment. It might be a challenge, though, with Connie's homes getting grander by the year while Mercer wasn't sure where she'd be sleeping in a few months.

The truth was that Mercer did not want to spend

time with her sister. They were living in different worlds and growing farther apart. So she had thanked Connie for the invitation to stay with her family, and both were relieved when Mercer said no. She said she might be leaving the island for a few days, needed a break and all that, might go here or there to see a friend. Elaine arranged a small suite in a bed-and-breakfast on the beach two miles north of the cottage because Mercer had no plans to go anywhere. The next move was Cable's, and she could not afford to be off the island.

On Friday of July Fourth weekend, Mercer tidied up the cottage and stuffed two canvas bags with her clothes, toiletries, and a few books. As she walked through, turning off lights, she thought of Tessa, and how far she, Mercer, had come in the past five weeks. She had stayed away from the place for eleven years and returned with great trepidation, but in short order she had managed to put aside the awfulness of Tessa's death and dwell on the memories she cherished. She was leaving now, and for good reason, but she would be back in two weeks and again have the place to herself. For how long, no one seemed to know for sure. That would depend on Mr. Cable.

She drove five minutes along Fernando Street to the bed-and-breakfast, a place called the Lighthouse Inn. There was a tall fake lighthouse in the center of the courtyard, one that she remembered well from her childhood. The inn was a rambling Cape Cod–style building with twenty rooms to rent and an all-you-can-eat buffet breakfast. The holiday crowd was descending on the island. A "No Vacancy" sign warned others to stay away.

With a room of her own and some money in her pocket, perhaps she could settle in and write some fiction.

3.

Late Saturday morning, as Main Street was busy with its weekly farmers' market and throngs of vacationers clogged the sidewalks looking for fudge and ice cream and perhaps a table for lunch, Denny entered Bay Books for the third time in a week and browsed through the mystery section. With his flip-flops, camouflage cap, cargo shorts, and torn T-shirt, he easily passed for another badly dressed visitor, one certain to attract the attention of no one else. He and Rooker had been in town for a week, scoping out the points of interest and watching Cable, a little surveillance that hardly posed a challenge. If the book dealer wasn't in his store, he was either somewhere downtown doing lunch or running errands, or he was at his fine home, usually alone. They were being careful, though, because Cable loved security. His store and house were loaded with cameras and sensors and who knew what else. A false move could mean disaster.

They were waiting and watching, reminding themselves to be patient, though their patience was running thin. Torturing information out of Joel Ribikoff, as well as threatening Oscar Stein in Boston, had been easy work compared with what they were facing now. The violence that had worked before might not work so well now. Back then, they needed only a couple of names. Now they wanted the goods. An assault on Cable or his wife or someone he cared for could easily trigger a reaction that could ruin everything.

4.

Tuesday, July 5. The crowds were gone, the beaches empty again. The island woke up slowly, and under a glaring sun tried to shake off the hangover of a long holiday weekend. Mercer was on the narrow sofa, reading a book called *The Paris Wife,* when an e-mail beeped through. It was from Bruce and it read, "Stop by the store next time you're in town."

She replied, "Okay. Anything going on?"

"Always. I have something for you. A little gift."

"I'm bored. Be there in an hour or so."

The bookstore was empty when she strolled in. The clerk at the front counter nodded but seemed too sleepy to speak. She went upstairs and ordered a latte and found a newspaper. Minutes later, she heard footsteps coming up the stairs and knew it was Bruce. Yellow-striped seersucker today, little green and blue bow tie. Always dapper. He got a coffee and they went outside to the balcony overhanging the sidewalk along Third Street. No one else was there. They sat in the shade at a table under a ceiling fan and sipped coffee. Bruce handed over his gift. It was obviously a book that had been wrapped in the store's blue and white paper. Mercer tore the paper off and looked at it. *The Joy Luck Club* by Amy Tan.

"It's a first edition, autographed," he said. "You mentioned her as one of your favorite contemporary writers, so I tracked it down."

Mercer was speechless. She had no idea what the book was worth and was not about to ask, but it was a valuable first edition. "I don't know what to say, Bruce."

"'Thanks' always works."

"It seems inadequate. I really can't accept this."

"Too late. I've already bought it and already given it to you. Call it a welcome-to-the-island gift."

"Then thanks, I guess."

"And you're welcome. The first printing was thirty thousand copies, so it's not that rare. It eventually sold half a million in hardback."

"Has she been here, to the store?"

"No, she doesn't tour much."

"This is incredible, Bruce. You shouldn't have."

"But I did, and now your collection has begun."

Mercer laughed and placed the book on the table. "I don't exactly dream of collecting first editions. They're a bit too pricey for me."

"Well, I didn't dream of being a collector either. It just sort of happened." He glanced at his watch and asked, "Are you in a hurry?"

"I'm a writer with no deadline."

"Good. I haven't told this story in many years, but this is how I started my collection." He took a sip, leaned back in his chair, put an ankle over a knee, and told the story of finding his deceased father's rare books and plucking a few for himself.

5.

Coffee became a lunch date, and they walked to the restaurant at the harbor and sat inside, where the air was substantially cooler. As usual for his business lunches, Bruce ordered a bottle of wine; today's was a Chablis. Mercer approved and they ordered salads and nothing more. He talked about Noelle, said she called every other day, and the search for antiques was going well.

Mercer thought of asking how her French boyfriend was doing. Once again, she found it difficult to believe that they could be so open with their affairs. It might not be unusual in France, but Mercer had never known a couple so willing to share. Sure, she knew people who had cheated, but when they got caught there was everything but acceptance. On the one hand she almost admired their ability to love each other enough to allow the other to stray at will, but on the other hand her southern modesty wanted to judge them for their sleaze.

"I have a question," she said, changing the subject. "In Talia's book, and specifically the story of Zelda Fitzgerald and Hemingway, how did she begin? What was her opening scene?"

Bruce smiled broadly as he wiped his mouth with his napkin. "Well, well, progress at last. Are you serious about the story?"

"Maybe. I've read two books about the Fitzgeralds and the Hemingways in Paris and I've ordered several more."

"Ordered?"

"Yes, from Amazon. Sorry. They're far cheaper, you know?"

"So I hear. Order from me and I'll knock off 30 percent."

"But I like to read e-books too."

"The younger generation." He smiled, took a sip of wine, and said, "Let me think. It's been a long time, twelve, maybe thirteen years. And Talia rewrote the book so many times I was often confused."

"From everything I've read so far, Zelda hated Hemingway, thought he was a bully and a brute and a bad influence on her husband."

"That's probably true. It seems like there was a scene in Talia's novel when the three of them were in the South of France. Hadley, Hemingway's wife, was back in the U.S. for some reason, and Ernest and Scott were really boozing it up. In real life, Hemingway complained several times about Scott's inability to hold his liquor. Half a bottle of wine and he was under the table. Hemingway had a hollow leg and could outdrink anyone. Scott was a severe alcoholic at twenty and never slowed down. Morning, noon, and night, he was always ready for a drink. Zelda and Hemingway were flirting, and they finally got their chance after lunch when Scott passed out in a hammock. Did their business in a guest room not thirty feet from the guy as he snored away. Something like that, but again it's fiction, so write whatever you want. The affair became rather torrid as Ernest drank even more and Scott tried to keep up. When he blacked out, his pal Ernie and his wife, Zelda, would hustle off to the nearest bed for a quick one.

Zelda was smitten with Ernest. Ernest appeared to be crazy about her, but was only leading her on for obvious reasons. By then he was already a serial philanderer. When they returned to Paris, and when Hadley came back from the U.S., Zelda wanted to keep up the fun, but Ernest was tired of her. He said more than once she was crazy. So he stiff-armed her, jilted her, and she hated him from then on. And that, my dear, is the novel in a nutshell."

"And you think that will sell?"

Bruce laughed and said, "My, my, you've become quite mercenary in the past month. You came here with literary ambitions and now you're dreaming of royalties."

"I don't want to go back to the classroom, Bruce, and it's not like I'm being chased by a lot of colleges right now. I have nothing, nothing but ten thousand dollars, courtesy of you and my dear Tessa's sticky fingers. I need to either sell some books or quit writing."

"Yes, it will sell. You mentioned *The Paris Wife*, a fine story about Hadley and Hemingway in those days, and it sold very well. You're a beautiful writer, Mercer, and you can pull it off."

She smiled and took a sip of wine and said, "Thanks. I need the encouragement."

"Don't we all?"

They ate in silence for a few moments. Bruce held up his glass and looked at the wine. "You like the Chablis?"

"It's delicious."

"I love wine, almost too much. For lunch, though, it's a bad habit. It really slows down the afternoon."

"That's why they invented siestas," she said helpfully, easing him along.

"Indeed. I have a little apartment on the second floor, sort of behind the coffee bar, and it's the perfect spot for the post-lunch nap."

"Is this an invitation, Bruce?"

"Could be."

"Is that your best pickup line—'Hey, baby, join me for a nap'?"

"It's worked before."

"Well, it's not working now." She glanced around and touched the corners of her mouth with the napkin. "I don't sleep with married men, Bruce. I mean, I have, on two occasions, and neither was particularly enjoyable. Married men have baggage I don't care to deal with. Plus, I know Noelle and I like her a lot."

"I assure you she doesn't care."

"I find that hard to believe."

He was smiling, almost chuckling, as if she had no idea what she was talking about and he would be pleased to enlighten her. He, too, glanced around to make sure no one could possibly hear. He leaned in and lowered his voice. "Noelle is in France, in Avignon, and when she goes there she stays in her apartment, one she's had for many years. Just down the street is a much larger apartment owned by Jean-Luc, her friend. Jean-Luc is married to an older woman with plenty of money. Jean-Luc and Noelle have been close for at least ten years. In fact, she met him before I met her. They do their siestas, have dinner, hang out, even travel together when his old wife says it's okay."

"So his wife approves?"

"Of course. They're French. It's all quiet and discreet and very civilized."

"And you don't mind? This is really bizarre."

"No, I don't mind at all. That's just the way it is. You see, Mercer, I knew many years ago that I'm simply not cut out for monogamy. I'm not sure any human really is, but I won't argue that. By the time I got to college I realized that there are a lot of beautiful women out there and there's no way I can be happy with just one. I've tried the relationship thing, been through five or six girlfriends, but nothing has ever worked because I can't resist another beautiful woman, regardless of her age. Luckily, I found Noelle, because she feels the same way about men. Her marriage blew up years ago because she had a boyfriend on the side and was sleeping with her doctor."

"So you struck a deal?"

"We didn't shake hands, but by the time we decided to get married we knew the rules. The door is wide open, just be discreet."

Mercer shook her head and looked away. "I'm sorry, I've just never met a couple with such an arrangement."

"I'm not sure it's that unusual."

"Oh, I promise you it's very unusual. You just think it's normal because you're doing it. Look, I caught a boyfriend cheating one time and it took me a year to get over it. I still hate him."

"I rest my case. You take it too serious. What's a little fling now and then?"

"A fling? Your wife has been sleeping with her French boyfriend for at least a decade. You call that a fling?"

"No, that's more than a fling, but Noelle doesn't love him. That's all about companionship."

"I'll say. So the other night when Sally Aranca was in town, was that a fling or companionship?"

"Neither, both, who cares? Sally comes through once a year and we have some fun. Call it whatever you want."

"What if Noelle had been here?"

"She doesn't care, Mercer, listen to me. If you called Noelle right now and told her we're doing lunch and talking about having a nap and what does she think about it, I promise Noelle would laugh and say, 'Hey, I've been gone for two weeks, what's taking so long?' You want to call her?"

"No."

Bruce laughed and said, "You're too uptight."

Mercer had never thought of herself as being uptight; in fact she thought she was fairly laid-back and accepting of most anything. But at the moment she felt like a prude and hated it. "No, I'm not."

"Then let's hop in the sack."

"I'm sorry, I can't be that casual about it."

"Fine. I'm not pushing. I just offered a little nap, that's all."

Both chuckled, but the tension was palpable. And they knew the conversation was not over.

6.

It was dark when they met at the beach end of the cottage boardwalk. The tide was low and the beach was wide and empty. The brightness of a full moon shimmered across the ocean. Elaine was barefoot, and Mercer kicked off her sandals. They walked to the edge of the water and strolled along, just a couple of old friends having a chat.

As instructed, Mercer was being thorough with her nightly e-mails, down to the details of what she was reading and trying to write. Elaine knew almost everything, though Mercer had not mentioned Cable's efforts to get her in bed. Maybe later, depending on what might happen.

"When did you get to the island?" Mercer asked.

"This afternoon. We've spent the last two days at the office with our team, all of our experts—tech guys, operations people, even my boss, the owner of the company."

"You have a boss?"

"Oh yes. I'm directing this project, but my boss will make the final decisions, when we get there."

"Get where?"

"Not sure right now. This is week number six, and, frankly, we're not sure what's next. You've been magnificent, Mercer, and your progress in the first five weeks has been nothing less than astonishing. We are very pleased. But now that we have the photos and videos, and now that you've worked your way into Cable's circle, we're debating our next move. Our confidence level is pretty high, but we have a ways to go."

"We'll get there."

"We adore your confidence."

"Thanks," Mercer said flatly, tired of the praise. "A question. I'm not sure it's wise to pursue the ploy of this novel about Zelda and Hemingway. It just seems too

convenient, with Cable sitting on the Fitzgerald manuscripts. Are we on the right track?"

"But the novel was his idea."

"Maybe it's his bait, his way of testing me."

"Do you have any reason to believe he might suspect
you?"

"Not really. I've been able to spend time with Bruce
and I think I can read him. He's very bright, quick, and
charismatic, and he's also an honest guy who's easy to
talk to. He may be deceptive with some of his business,
but not when he's dealing with his friends. He can be
brutally honest and he doesn't suffer fools, but there's
a sweetness to him that's genuine. I like him, Elaine,
and he likes me and wants to get closer. If he's suspicious, I think I would know it."

"You plan to get closer?"

"We'll see."

"He's lying about his marriage."

"True. He always refers to Noelle as his wife. I'm assuming you're correct when you say they are not really
married."

"I've told you all we know. There are no records in
France or here of them applying for or obtaining a marriage license. I suppose they could've gotten married in
some other country, but that's not their story."

"I don't know how close we'll get and I'm not sure it
can be planned. My point is that I think I know him
well enough to detect any skepticism."

"Then stick with his novel. It will give you the chance
to talk about Fitzgerald. It's even a good idea to write
the first chapter and let him read it. Can you do that?"

"Oh, sure. It's all fiction. Nothing in my life is real these days."

7.

Bruce's next effort was just as casual as his last, but it worked. He called Mercer Thursday afternoon and said that Mort Gasper, the legendary publisher of Ripley Press, was in town, passing through with his latest wife. Gasper came to the island almost every summer and stayed with Bruce and Noelle. It would be a small dinner, just the four of them, late on Friday, a pleasant way to end the week.

After a few days at the bed-and-breakfast, Mercer was claustrophobic and eager to escape. She was desperate to get her cottage back and counting the days until Connie and her gang went home. To keep from writing, Mercer was walking the beach at all hours, careful to stay miles away from the cottage and keeping a sharp eye for anyone who might be related to her.

And meeting Mort Gasper might one day help her waning career. Thirty years ago he had bought Ripley for peanuts and turned the sleepy and unprofitable little house into a major publisher, one that remained defiantly independent. With a brilliant eye for talent, he had collected and promoted a stable of writers known for their diverse literary aspirations, as well as their ability to sell books. A throwback to the golden age of publishing, Mort clung to his traditions of three-hour lunches and late night launch parties at his Upper West Side apartment. He was without a doubt the most colorful figure in publishing and showed no signs of slowing down, even as he approached seventy.

Friday afternoon, Mercer spent two hours online reading old magazine articles about Mort, none of them remotely boring. One from two years earlier told of a two-million-dollar advance Mort paid to an unknown star with a debut novel that sold ten thousand copies. He had no regrets and called it "a bargain." One mentioned his latest marriage, to a woman about Mercer's age. Her name was Phoebe and she was an editor at Ripley.

Phoebe met her at the front door of the Marchbanks House at 8:00 p.m. Friday, and after a pleasant hello warned her that the "boys" were already drinking. As Mercer followed her through the kitchen she heard the humming of a blender. Bruce was concocting lemon daiquiris on the rear porch and had stripped down to shorts and a golf shirt. He pecked Mercer on both cheeks and introduced her to Mort, who greeted her with a fierce hug and contagious smile. He was barefoot and his long shirttail was down to his knees. Bruce handed her a daiquiri and topped off the others, and they sat in wicker chairs around a small table stacked with books and magazines.

It was readily apparent that in situations like this, as in probably all others, Mort was expected to do the talking. This was fine with Mercer. After the third sip she felt a buzz and wondered how much rum Bruce had added to the recipe. Mort was raging about the presidential race and the worrisome state of American politics, a subject Mercer cared little for, but Bruce and

Phoebe seemed engaged and managed to offer enough to keep him going.

"Mind if I smoke?" Mort asked of no one in particular as he reached for a leather case on the table. He and Bruce fired up black cigars and a blue fog soon hovered over them. Bruce got the pitcher and did another round of top-offs. During a rare lull in Mort's monologue, Phoebe managed to inject, "So, Mercer, Bruce says you're here working on a novel."

Mercer knew it would be coming at some point during the evening. She smiled and said, "Bruce is being generous. Right now I'm doing more dreaming than working."

Mort blasted forth a cloud and said, "*October Rain* was a fine debut. Very impressive. Who published it? I can't remember."

With a forgiving smile Mercer said, "Well, Ripley turned it down."

"Indeed we did, a foolish move, but then that's publishing. You guess right on some books and wrong on others, all part of the business."

"It was published by Newcombe, and we had our differences."

He snorted his disapproval and said, "A bunch of clowns. Didn't you leave them?"

"Yes. My current contract is with Viking, if I still have a contract. The last time my editor called she informed me I was three years past due."

Mort roared with laughter and said, "Only three years! To be so lucky. I was yelling at Doug Tannenbaum last week because he was supposed to deliver eight years ago. Writers!"

Phoebe jumped in with "Do you talk about your work?"

Mercer smiled and shook her head. "There's nothing to talk about."

"Who's your agent?" Mort demanded.

"Gilda Savitch."

"Love that gal. I had lunch with her last month."

So glad you approve, Mercer almost said, the rum doing a number. "She didn't mention my name, did she?"

"I can't remember. It was a long lunch." Mort roared again and then gulped his drink. Phoebe asked about Noelle and this occupied them for a few minutes. Mercer noticed there was no activity in the kitchen, no sign of food being prepared. When Mort excused himself for a bathroom break, Bruce went back to the blender for more daiquiris. The girls chatted about the summer and vacations and such. Phoebe and Mort would leave tomorrow and head to the Keys for a month. Publishing was slow in July and thoroughly dormant in August, and, well, since he was the boss they could leave the city for six weeks.

As soon as Mort returned and settled into his chair with his fresh drink and cigar, the doorbell rang and Bruce disappeared. He returned with a large box of carry-out and placed it on the table. "The best fish tacos on the island. Grilled grouper caught this morning."

"You're serving us take-out tacos?" Mort asked in disbelief. "I don't believe this. I take you to the finest restaurants in New York and I get this." As he protested he almost lunged at the tacos.

Bruce said, "The last time we had lunch in the city you took me to that dreadful deli around the corner from your office and my Reuben was so bad I almost puked. And, I picked up the bill."

"You're just a bookseller, Bruce," Mort said, chomping a taco in half. "The writers get the fancy meals. Mercer, next time you're in the city we'll do a three-star."

"A date," she said, knowing it would never happen. At the rate he was draining his glass, he wouldn't remember much by morning. Bruce was letting loose too, drinking far more aggressively than anything she had seen so far. Gone were the thoughtful sips of wine, the measured refills, the chatter about the vintage and producer, the complete self-control. Now, with his hair down and his shoes off, hell it was Friday night after a long week and he was breaking bad with a partner in crime.

Mercer was sipping her icy drink and trying to remember how many she'd had. With Bruce continually topping her glass, it was difficult to keep count. She was buzzed and needed to slow down. She ate a taco and looked around for a bottle of water, or maybe even some wine, but there was nothing else on the porch. Only a fresh pitcher of daiquiris, just sitting there waiting on them.

Bruce topped off their glasses and began telling a story about daiquiris, his favorite summer drink. In 1948, an American writer named A. E. Hotchner went to Cuba to track down Ernest Hemingway, who lived there in the late 1940s and early 1950s. The two became fast friends, and in 1966, a few years after Hemingway's death, Hotchner published a famous book, *Papa Hemingway*.

Predictably, Mort interrupted with "I've met Hotchner, think he's still alive. Must be pushing a hundred."

Bruce replied, "Let's assume you've met everybody, Mort."

Anyway, as the story went, during Hotchner's first visit, which was for some type of interview, Hemingway was reluctant. Hotchner pestered him and they finally met in a bar not far from Hemingway's home. On the phone Hemingway said the place was famous for its daiquiris. Of course, Hemingway was late, so while Hotchner waited he ordered a daiquiri. It was delicious and strong, and since he was not much of a drinker, he took it slow. An hour passed. The bar was hot and sticky so he ordered another. When it was half-gone he realized he was seeing double. When Hemingway finally arrived he was treated like a celebrity. Evidently, he spent a lot of time there. They shook hands and found a table and Ernest ordered daiquiris. Hotchner toyed with his fresh one while Ernest practically drained his. Then he drained another. During his third, Ernest noticed that his new drinking buddy was not drinking, so he challenged his manhood and said that if he wished to hang out with the great Ernest Hemingway he'd better learn to drink like a man. Hotchner manned up, gave it a go, and the room was soon spinning. Later, as Hotchner tried gamely to hold up his head, Ernest lost interest in their conversation and, with a fresh daiquiri, began playing dominoes with the locals. At some point—Hotchner had lost all concept of time—Ernest stood and said it was time for dinner. Hotchner was to follow him. On the way out, Hotchner asked, "How many daiquiris did we drink?"

The bartender thought for a second and said in English, "Four for you, seven for Papa."

"You had seven daiquiris?" Hotchner asked in disbelief.

Ernest laughed, as did the locals. "Seven is nothing, my friend. The record here is sixteen, held by me of course, and I walked home."

Mercer was beginning to feel as though she was on number sixteen.

Mort said, "I remember reading *Papa* when I was in the mail room at Random." Stuffed with tacos, he relit his cigar. "Do you have a first edition, Bruce?"

"I have two, one in fine condition, one not so fine. You don't see many of them these days."

"Any interesting purchases lately?" Phoebe asked.

Other than the Fitzgerald manuscripts stolen from Princeton, Mercer thought to herself, but would never be drunk enough to blurt it. Her eyelids were getting heavier.

"Not really," Bruce said. "Picked up a copy of *The Convict* recently."

Not to be outdone, Mort—and there was probably no one in the history of New York publishing who had either lived through as many drinking stories or heard them from reliable sources—charged in with a windy tale about a drunken brawl in his apartment at two in the morning when Norman Mailer couldn't find any more rum and began throwing empty bottles at George Plimpton. It was hilarious to the point of being hard to believe, and Mort was a seasoned raconteur.

Mercer caught herself nodding off. The last sound she remembered was that of the blender revving up for another batch.

8.

She awoke in a strange bed in a round room, and for the first few seconds she was afraid to move because any movement would sharpen the pounding in her forehead. Her eyes were burning so she closed them. Her mouth and throat were parched. A gentle rolling in her stomach warned that things might get worse. Okay, a hangover; been here before and survived, could be a long day but, hey, what the hell? No one made her drink too much. Own it, girl. The old saying from college: "If you're gonna be stupid you gotta be tough."

She was lying in a cloud, a deep, soft feathery mattress with layers of fine linens all around her. No doubt Noelle's touch. With her newfound cash, Mercer had invested in prettier lingerie, and at that awful moment she was relieved to be wearing it. She hoped Bruce had been impressed. She opened her eyes again, blinked a few times, managed to focus, and saw her shorts and blouse arranged neatly on a nearby chair, his way of saying that there had been an orderly undressing, not a rip-and-tear dash for the bed. Eyes closed again, she dug deeper into the covers.

After the fading sounds of the blender, nothing. So how long had she slept in her chair on the porch while the others swapped stories and kept drinking and winked at each other as they grinned at her? Had she been able to walk away, unsteady and perhaps with a bit of help, or was Bruce forced to lug her up to the third-floor tower? Had she actually blacked out, college style, or had she merely gone to sleep and been put to bed?

Her stomach rolled again. Surely she had not ruined their little porch party with some indescribable up-chucking scene that neither Bruce nor the others would ever mention? The thought of such an awful episode made her even more nauseous. Another glance at her shorts and blouse. They appeared to be free from stains, no signs of a mess.

Then a consoling thought. Mort was forty years older and had made a career out of raising hell. He'd thrown more drunks and suffered through more hangovers than all of his authors combined, so nothing would bother him. He was probably amused by it. Who cared about Phoebe? Mercer would never see her again. Besides, living with Mort she'd seen it all. Bruce certainly had.

A light tap on the door and Bruce eased into the room. He was wearing a white terry-cloth bathrobe and holding a tall bottle of water and two small glasses. "Well, good morning," he said quietly and sat on the edge of the bed.

"Morning," she said. "I really want some of that water."

"I need it too," he said, and filled the glasses. They drained them and he poured more.

"How do you feel?" he asked.

"Not too good. You?"

"A long night."

"How'd I get up here?"

"You fell asleep on the porch, and I helped you to bed. Phoebe was not far behind, then Mort and I lit another cigar and kept drinking."

"Did you beat Hemingway's record?"

"No, but it feels like we got close."

"Tell me, Bruce, did I make an ass of myself?"

"Not at all. You dozed off. You couldn't drive, so I put you to bed."

"Thanks. I don't remember much."

"There's not much to remember. All of us got bombed."

She drained her glass and he refilled it. She nodded at her shorts and blouse and asked, "Who took those off?"

"I did. A real treat."

"Did you molest me?"

"No, but I thought about it."

"Such a gentleman."

"Always. Look, there's a big claw-foot tub in the bathroom. Why don't you take a long hot bath, keep drinking water, and I'll go fix breakfast. I need some eggs and bacon and figure you probably do too. Make yourself at home. Mort and Phoebe are stirring and they'll leave soon. When they're gone, I'll bring you breakfast in bed. A plan?"

She smiled and said, "Sounds nice. Thanks."

He left and closed the door. She had two options. First, she could get dressed, ease downstairs, try to avoid Mort and Phoebe, tell Bruce she needed to leave, and hit the road. But moving quickly was not a good idea. She needed time, time to pull herself together, time to see if her stomach would settle down, time to relax and maybe even sleep it off. And, she wasn't sure she should be driving. The thought of returning to her little suite at the B&B was not appealing either, and the idea of a long hot bath was irresistible at the moment.

The second option was to follow Bruce's plan, one that would eventually land him in the bed with her.

That, she had decided, had reached the point of being inevitable.

She poured another glass of water and eased out of bed. She stretched, took a deep breath, and already felt better. No threats of nausea. She walked to the bathroom, turned on the faucets, and found the bubble bath. A digital clock on the vanity gave the time as 8:20. In spite of her obvious physical problems, she had slept for almost ten hours.

Of course Bruce needed to check on her, to see how the bath was going. He walked in, still in his robe, and placed another bottle of sparkling water next to the tub. "How ya doing?" he asked.

"Much better," she said. The bubbles hid most of her nakedness but not all of it. He took a long approving look and smiled. "Need anything?"

"No, I'm fine."

"I'm busy in the kitchen. Take your time." And he was gone.

9.

She soaked for an hour, then got out and dried off. She found a matching bathrobe hanging on the door and put it on. In a drawer she found a stack of new toothbrushes. She opened one, brushed her teeth, and felt much better. She picked up her lingerie and found her purse next to her shorts and blouse. She removed her iPad, propped up the pillows, got in the bed, made her nest, and returned to her cloud.

She was reading when she heard noises at the door.

Bruce walked in with a breakfast tray, which he placed snugly at her side. "Bacon, scrambled eggs, muffins with jam, strong coffee, and, for good measure, a mimosa."

"I'm not sure I need more booze at this point," she said. The food looked and smelled delicious.

"The hair of the dog. It's good for you." He disappeared for a second and returned with a tray for himself. When he was situated next to her, their trays side by side, in matching bathrobes, he picked up his flute and said, "Cheers." They took a sip and began eating.

"So this is the infamous Writer's Room," she said.

"You've heard of it?"

"The ruin of many a poor girl."

"All of them quite willing."

"So it's true. You get the girls and Noelle gets the boys?"

"True. Who told you about it?"

"Since when do writers keep secrets?"

Bruce laughed and shoved a strip of bacon in his mouth. After two sips of her mimosa, the buzz was back as the remnants of last night's rum mixed with the fresh champagne. Fortunately, the long bath had settled her stomach and the food was delicious. She nodded at a long curved wall with bookshelves from floor to ceiling and asked, "So what are those? More first editions?"

"A mix, nothing of any real value. Odds and ends."

"It's a beautiful room, obviously put together by Noelle."

"Let's forget about her for the time being. She's probably having a late lunch with Jean-Luc."

"And that doesn't bother you?"

"Not in the least. Come on, Mercer, we've had this conversation."

They ate in silence for a few minutes, both ignoring the coffee but not the mimosas. Under the covers, he began gently rubbing her thigh.

She said, "I can't remember the last time I had sex with a hangover."

"Oh, I do it all the time. It's the best cure, actually."

"I guess you should know."

He wiggled out of bed and set his tray on the floor. "Finish your drink," he said, and she did. He lifted her tray and set it aside, then he took off his bathrobe and flung it across the end of the bed. He helped her out of hers, and as soon as they were wonderfully naked they burrowed deep under the covers.

10.

Elaine Shelby was working in her home office late Saturday morning when Graham called from Camino Island. "Touchdown," he announced. "Looks like our girl spent the night in the big house."

"Talk to me," she said.

"She parked across the street around eight last night and her car's still there. Another couple left this morning, don't know their names. Mercer and Cable are inside. It's raining hard here, the perfect morning to shack up. Go, girl."

"It's about time. Keep me posted."

"Will do."

"I'll be down Monday."

Denny and Rooker were watching too. They had traced the North Carolina license plates on Mercer's car and done the background. They knew her name, recent employment history, current lodging at the Lighthouse Inn, publishing résumé, and partial ownership of the beach cottage. They knew Noelle Bonnet was out of town and her store was closed. They knew as much as they could possibly know, except what, exactly, to do next.

11.

The storm lingered and became just another excuse to stay in bed. Mercer, who had not had sex in months, couldn't get enough. Bruce, the seasoned professional, had a drive and stamina that she found amazing at times. After an hour—or was it two?—they finally collapsed and fell asleep. When she awoke, he was gone. She put on her bathrobe, went downstairs, and found him in the kitchen, decked out in the usual seersucker suit and dirty bucks, refreshed and clear-eyed as if ready for another day of rigorous bookselling. They kissed and his hands immediately went inside her bathrobe and grabbed her rear.

"Such a gorgeous body," he said.

"You're leaving me?"

They kissed again in a long, groping embrace. He pulled away slightly and said, "I need to check on the store. Retail's a bitch, you know?"

"When are you coming back?"

"Soon. I'll bring some lunch and we'll eat on the porch."

"I need to go," she said halfheartedly.

"Go where? Back to the Lighthouse? Come on, Mercer, hang around here and I'll be back before you know it. It's raining buckets, the wind's howling, I think we're under a tornado watch. Hell, it's dangerous out there. We'll crawl into bed and read all afternoon."

"I'm sure you're thinking of nothing but reading."

"Keep the bathrobe on and I'll be back."

They kissed again, groped again, and he finally managed to tear himself away. He pecked her on the cheek, said good-bye, and left. Mercer poured a cup of coffee and took it to the back porch, where she rocked in a swing and watched the rain. With some effort, she could almost think of herself as a whore, a bad woman being paid to use her body to further her deception, but her heart wasn't in it. Bruce Cable was a hopeless philanderer who would sleep with anyone regardless of their motives. Now it was her. Next week it would be someone else. He cared nothing for loyalty and trust. Why should she? He asked for no commitment, expected none, gave none in return. For him it was all physical pleasure, and for her, at the moment, the same was true. She shrugged off any hint of guilt and actually smiled at the thought of a vigorous weekend in his bed.

He wasn't gone long. They lunched on salads and wine, and soon made their way back to the tower for another round of lovemaking. During a break, Bruce fetched a bottle of chardonnay and a thick novel. They decided to read on the back porch in wicker rockers and listen to the rain. He had his novel; she, her iPad.

"Can you really enjoy a book on that thing?" he asked.

"Sure. The words are the same. Have you ever tried one?"

"Amazon gave me one of theirs years ago. I just couldn't focus. I could be biased."

"No kidding. I wonder why?"

"What are you reading?"

"*For Whom the Bell Tolls.* I'm alternating between Hemingway and F. Scott, trying to read them all. I finished *The Last Tycoon* yesterday."

"And?"

"It's pretty remarkable, given where he was when he wrote it. In Hollywood, trying to make some money and failing physically and emotionally. And so young. Another tragedy."

"That was his last one, the one he didn't finish?"

"That's what they say. Such a waste of talent."

"Is this homework for the novel?"

"Perhaps. I'm still not sure. What are you reading?"

"It's called *My Favorite Tsunami,* a first novel by a guy who can't write very well."

"What an awful title."

"Yes, and it doesn't get any better. I'm fifty pages in with six hundred to go and I'm struggling. There should be a rule in publishing that debut novels are limited to three hundred pages, don't you think?"

"I suppose. Mine was only 280."

"Yours was perfect."

"Thanks. So will you finish that?"

"I doubt it. I'll give any book a hundred pages, and if by then the writer can't hold my attention I'll put it away. There are too many good books I want to read to waste time with a bad one."

"Same here, but my limit is fifty pages. I've never understood people who grind through a book they don't really like, determined to finish it for some unknown reason. Tessa was like that. She would toss a book after the first chapter, then pick it up and grumble and growl for four hundred pages until the bitter end. Never understood that."

"I don't get it." He took a sip of wine, gazed across the backyard, and picked up the novel. She waited until he had turned a page and asked, "Got any other rules?"

He smiled and laid down the novel. "Oh, Mercer, dear, I have my list. It's called 'Cable's Top Ten Rules for Writing Fiction,' a brilliant how-to guide put together by an expert who's read over four thousand books."

"Do you share this?"

"Occasionally. I'll e-mail it over, but you really don't need it."

"Maybe I do. I need something. Give me a hint or two."

"Okay, I hate prologues. I just finished a novel by a guy who's touring and will stop by next week. He always starts every book with the typical prologue, something dramatic like a killer stalking a woman or a dead body, then will leave the reader hanging, go to chapter 1, which, of course, has nothing to do with the prologue, then to chapter 2, which, of course, has nothing to do with either chapter 1 or the prologue, then after about thirty pages slam the reader back to the action in the prologue, which by then has been forgotten."

"I like this. Keep going."

"Another rookie mistake is to introduce twenty characters in the first chapter. Five's enough and won't confuse your reader. Next, if you feel the need to go to the thesaurus, look for a word with three syllables or fewer. I have a nice vocabulary and nothing ticks me off more than a writer showing off with big words I've never seen before. Next, please, please use quotation marks with dialogue; otherwise it's bewildering. Rule Number Five: Most writers say too much, so always look for things to cut, like throwaway sentences and unnecessary scenes. I could go on."

"Please do. I should be taking notes."

"No, you shouldn't. You don't need advice. You're a beautiful writer, Mercer, you just need a story."

"Thank you, Bruce. I need the encouragement."

"I'm dead serious, and I'm not flattering you because we're in the midst of a little weekend orgy."

"Is that what it's called? Thought it was a fling."

They laughed and took a sip of wine. The rain had stopped and a heavy mist was rolling in. She asked, "Have you ever written?"

He shrugged and looked away. "I've tried, several times, but never finished. It's not my thing. That's why I respect writers, the good ones anyway. I welcome them all and I love to promote all books, but there's a lot of crap on the market. And I'm frustrated with people like Andy Adam who have the talent but squander it with bad habits."

"Have you heard from him?"

"Not yet. He's locked away with no contact. He'll probably call in a week or so. This is either his third or fourth rehab, and I think the odds are against him. Deep inside he really doesn't want to quit."

"It's so sad."

"You look sleepy."

"Must be the wine."

"Let's take a nap."

With some effort, they managed to climb into a hammock and wedge themselves into a tight cuddle. As it rocked gently, they grew still. "Any plans for tonight?" she asked.

"I was thinking more of the same."

"That too, but I'm getting tired of this place."

"Well, dinner is a must."

"But you're a married man, Bruce, and I'm just your weekend girl. What if someone sees us?"

"I don't care, Mercer, and Noelle doesn't care. Why should you?"

"I don't know. It just seems weird having dinner at a nice place on a Saturday night with a married man."

"Who said it was a nice place? It's a dump, a crab shack down by the river, great food, and I assure you no one there buys books."

She kissed him and laid her head on his chest.

12.

Sunday began in much the same fashion as Saturday, without the hangovers. Bruce served breakfast in bed, pancakes and sausage, and they spent two hours scanning the *New York Times*. As noon approached, Mercer needed a break. She was about to begin her farewell when Bruce said, "Look, I'm shorthanded at the store this afternoon and the place will be crawling. I need to go to work."

"Good idea. Now that I know the rules for writing fiction, I need to jot down a few things."

"Always happy to be of service," he said with a smile and pecked her on the cheek. They carried the trays to the kitchen and loaded the dishwasher. Bruce disappeared into the master suite on the second floor, and Mercer returned to the tower, where she dressed quickly and left without another good-bye.

If she had accomplished anything over the weekend, it wasn't obvious. The bedroom antics were certainly enjoyable, and she knew him much better than before, but she wasn't there for sex and she wasn't there to write his novel. She was being paid a lot of money to gather clues and perhaps solve a crime. In that regard, she felt as though she had indeed accomplished little.

In her suite, she changed into a bikini, admired herself in the mirror, and tried to remember all the marvelous things he'd said about her body. It was lean and tanned and she was rather proud she had finally used it. She put on a white cotton shirt, grabbed her sandals, and went for a long walk on the beach.

13.

Bruce called at seven Sunday evening, said he missed her terribly, couldn't imagine getting through the night without her, and could she stop by the store for a drink when he closed?

Sure. What else did she have to do? The walls of her awful little suite were closing in and she had written fewer than a hundred words.

She entered the store a few minutes before nine. Bruce was checking out the last customer and appeared to be working alone. As the customer left, he quickly locked the door and turned off the lights. "Follow me," he said, and he led her up the stairs and through the café, turning off lights as he went. He unlocked a door she had never noticed and they entered his apartment.

"My man cave," he said as he turned on the lights. "I lived here for the first ten years I owned the store. Back then it covered the entire second floor, but then the café came along. Have a seat." He waved at a bulky leather sofa that ran along an entire wall and was covered with pillows and quilts. Opposite the sofa, a large flat-screen TV was mounted on a squat table, and around it were, of course, shelves lined with books.

"Champagne?" he asked as he stepped behind a snack bar and opened the refrigerator.

"Of course."

He removed a bottle, quickly popped the cork, filled two flutes, and said, "Cheers."

They clinked glasses and he gulped most of his. "I really needed a drink," he said as he wiped his mouth with the back of a hand.

"Evidently. You okay?"

"Rough day. One of my clerks called in sick so I worked the floor. It's hard to find good help." He drained his flute and refilled it. He removed his jacket, untied his bow tie, yanked out his shirttail, kicked off his dirty buckskins. They moved to the sofa and fell into it.

"How was your day?" he asked, gulping again.

"The usual. I walked on the beach, got some sun, tried to write, went back to the beach, tried to write some more, took a nap."

"Ah, the writing life. I'm envious."

"I did manage to ditch my prologue, add quotation marks to my dialogue, take out the big words, and I would have cut some more but there's not enough to cut."

Bruce laughed and took another drink. "You're adorable, you know that?"

"And you're such a con man, Bruce. You seduced me yesterday morning and . . ."

"Actually it was morning, noon, and night."

"And here we go again. Have you always been such a ladies' man?"

"Oh yes. Always. I told you, Mercer, I have a fatal weakness for women. When I see a pretty one, I have one thought. It's been that way since college. When I got to Auburn and was suddenly surrounded by thousands of cute girls, I went wild."

"That's not healthy. Have you thought about therapy?"

"What? Who needs it? This is a game for me, and you have to admit I play it rather well."

She nodded and took a sip, her third. His glass was empty so he refilled it again. "Easy, boy," she said but he ignored her. When he was back on the sofa she asked, "Have you ever been in love?"

"I love Noelle. She loves me. We're both very happy."

"But love is about trust and commitment and sharing every aspect of your lives."

"Oh, we're into sharing big-time, believe me."

"You're hopeless."

"Don't be such a sap, Mercer. We're not talking about love; we're talking about sex. Pure physical pleasure. You're not about to get involved with a married man and I don't do relationships. We'll get it on whenever you want or we can stop right now. We'll be friends with no strings attached."

"Friends? How many female friends do you have?"

"None really. A few nice acquaintances, maybe. Look, if I had known you planned to analyze me I wouldn't have called."

"Why did you call?"

"I figured you were missing me."

They managed to laugh. Suddenly Bruce set down his flute, took hers and placed it next to his, grabbed her hand, and said, "Come with me. I have something to show you."

"What is it?"

"A surprise. Come on. It's downstairs."

Still barefoot, he led her out of the apartment, through the café, down to the first floor, and to the door to the basement. He unlocked it, flipped a light switch, and they eased down the wooden steps to the basement. He turned on another light and punched the code that unlocked the vault.

"This better be good," she said, almost under her breath.

"You will not believe it." He pulled open the thick metal door to the vault, stepped inside, and turned on another light. He walked to the safe, entered another pass code, and waited a second for the five hydraulic bolts to release. With a loud clicking sound, the door was free and he gently pulled it open. Mercer watched everything as closely as possible, knowing she would be expected to write down every detail for Elaine and the team. The inside of the vault and the interior of the safe appeared the same as the last time she saw them. Bruce tugged on one of the four lower drawers and slid it open. There were two identical wooden boxes; she would later estimate them to be fourteen inches square and made of what she guessed to be cedar. He removed one and stepped to the small table in the center of the vault. He gave her a smile, as if revealing a rare treasure.

The top of the box was attached by three small hinges, and he gently raised it. Inside was what appeared to be a cardboard box, gray in color. Carefully, he lifted it out and placed it on the table. "This is called an archival storage box, made of acid- and lignin-free board and used by most libraries and serious collectors. This came from Princeton." He opened the box, and announced proudly, "The original manuscript of *The Last Tycoon*."

Mercer's jaw dropped as she stared in disbelief and eased closer. She tried to speak but couldn't find the words.

Inside the box was a stack of faded letter-sized sheets of paper, perhaps four inches thick, obviously well aged and a relic from another time. There was no title page; indeed, it appeared as though Fitzgerald had simply plunged into chapter 1 with the thought of tidying things up later. His cursive was not pretty and hard to read, and he had begun making notes in the margins from the very beginning. Bruce touched the edges of the manuscript and went on, "When he died suddenly in 1940, the novel was far from finished, but he worked from an outline and left behind a considerable amount of notes and summaries. He had a close friend named Edmund Wilson, who was an editor and a critic, and Wilson cobbled the story together and the book was published a year later. Many critics consider it to be Fitzgerald's finest work, which, as you said, is remarkable given his health."

"You are kidding, right?" she managed to say.

"Kidding about what?"

"This manuscript. Is this the one that was stolen?"

"Oh yes, but not by me."

"Okay. What's it doing here?"

"It's a very long story and I won't bore you with the details, many of which I know nothing about. All five were stolen last fall from the Firestone Library at Princeton. There was a gang of thieves and they got spooked when the FBI grabbed two of them almost immediately. The others unloaded their loot and disappeared. The manuscripts quietly entered the black market. From there they were sold off separately. I don't know where the other four are but I suspect they've left the country."

"Why are you involved, Bruce?"

"It's complicated, but I'm really not that involved. You want to touch the pages?"

"No. I don't like being here. This makes me nervous."

"Relax. I'm just hiding this for a friend."

"Must be a helluva friend."

"He is. We've been trading for a long time and I trust him implicitly. He's in the process of brokering a deal with a collector in London."

"What's in it for you?"

"Not much. I'll get a few bucks down the road."

Mercer stepped away and moved to the other side of the table. "For a few bucks it seems like you're assuming a rather significant risk. You're in possession of major stolen property. That's a felony that could get you sent away for a long time."

"It's a felony only if you get caught."

"And now you've made me complicit in this scheme, Bruce. I'd like to leave now."

"Come on, Mercer, you're too uptight. No risk, no reward. And you're not complicit in anything, because no one will ever know. How can anyone possibly prove you ever saw this manuscript?"

"I don't know. Who else has seen this?"

"Only the two of us."

"Noelle doesn't know."

"Of course not. She doesn't care. She runs her business and I run mine."

"And part of your business is trafficking in stolen books and manuscripts?"

"Occasionally." He closed the archival storage box and placed it back in the wooden one. Carefully, he replaced it in the drawer and shoved it closed.

"I really want to go," she said.

"Okay, okay. I didn't think you'd freak out. You said you've just finished *The Last Tycoon* and I thought you'd be impressed."

"Impressed? I might be overwhelmed, bewildered, scared to death, a lot of things right now, but I'm not impressed, Bruce. This is crazy stuff."

He locked the safe, then the vault, and as they started

up the stairs he flipped off the lights. On the ground floor, Mercer headed for the front door. "Where are you going?" he asked.

"I'm leaving. Please unlock the door."

Bruce grabbed her, turned her around, squeezed her tightly, and said, "Look, I'm sorry, okay?"

She pulled back hard and said, "I want to go. I'm not staying in this store."

"Come on, you're overreacting, Mercer. Let's go upstairs and finish the champagne."

"No, Bruce, I'm not in the mood right now. I can't believe this."

"I'm sorry."

"You've already said that; now please unlock the door."

He found a key and unlocked the dead bolt. She hurried through the door without another word and walked around the corner to her car.

14.

The plan had been built on assumptions and speculation and no small measure of hope, but now it had succeeded. They had the proof, the answer they so desperately needed, but could she deliver? Could she take the next crucial step and make the call that would send Bruce to prison for the next ten years? She thought about his downfall, his ruin and humiliation, and his horror of being caught red-handed, arrested, hauled into court, then taken away. What would happen to his beautiful and important bookstore? His home? His friends? His cherished collection of rare books? His money? Her betrayal would have enormous consequences and damage more than one person. Perhaps Cable deserved all that was coming, but not his employees, not his friends, not even Noelle.

At midnight, Mercer was still on the beach, wrapped in a shawl, toes dug into the sand, staring at the moon-lit ocean and asking herself again why she ever said yes to Elaine Shelby. She knew the answer, but the money seemed much less important now. The destruction she was about to sow was far greater than the money behind it. The truth was she liked Bruce Cable, his beautiful smile and easy manner, his good looks, his unique wardrobe, his wit and intelligence, his admiration of writers, his skill as a lover, his presence around others, his friends, his reputation, his charisma that at times seemed magnetic. She was secretly thrilled to be so close to him, to be considered among his inner circle, and, yes, to be just another in his long line of women. Because of him, she'd had more fun in the past six weeks than in the last six years.

One option at the moment was to simply keep quiet and allow things to run their course. Elaine and her gang and perhaps the FBI would continue doing whatever they had to do. Mercer could go through the motions, feigning frustration at not being able to accomplish more. She'd made it down to the basement vault and delivered plenty of evidence. Hell, she'd even slept with the guy and might again. She had done her best so far and would continue to play along. Maybe Bruce would unload *Tycoon* just as he said, without a trace, into the murky vastness of the black market, and his vault would be clean when the Feds rolled in. Before long, her six months would be over and she would leave the island, and do so with fond memories. She might even return, for summer vacations at her cottage, or, better yet, on a book tour one day with a fine new novel. And then another.

Her agreement was not contingent on a successful operation. She was to be paid regardless. Her student loans were already history. Half the fee was in the bank. She felt certain the other half would arrive as promised.

For a long time that night she convinced herself to stay quiet, let the lazy summer days pass, don't rock the boat. Fall would be there soon enough and she would be somewhere else.

Was there a moral right and wrong? She had agreed to take part in a plan with the ultimate goal of piercing Cable's world and finding the manuscripts. This, she had finally done, though only because of an unbelievable blunder on his part. The operation, with Mercer in the center, had just succeeded. What right did she have to now question the legitimacy of the plan? Bruce had deliberately entered the conspiracy to get rid of the manuscripts, to sell them for profit and keep them away from their rightful owner. With Bruce Cable, there was no moral high ground. He had a reputation for dealing in stolen books and had admitted as much to her. He knew the risks and seemed to eagerly accept them. Sooner or later he would get caught, either for this crime or for a later one.

She began walking at the edge of the water, the tranquil waves pushing the sea foam quietly onto the sand. There were no clouds and the white sand could be seen for miles. On the horizon, the lights of a dozen shrimp boats glimmered on the flat sea. Before she realized it, she was at the North Pier, a long wooden walkway that jutted far into the water. Since her return to the island she had avoided the area because it was where Tessa had washed ashore. Why was her granddaughter there now?

She climbed the steps and followed the pier to its end, where she leaned on a railing and gazed at the horizon. What would Tessa do? Well, to begin with, Tessa would never find herself in such a predicament. She would never allow herself to be compromised. She would never be seduced by the money. With Tessa, right was right and wrong was wrong and there were no gray areas. Lying was a sin; your word was your word; a deal was a deal, regardless of the inconvenience.

Mercer anguished back and forth as the battle raged. She finally decided, at some awful hour of the morning, that the only way to stay quiet was to return the money and walk away. Even then, though, she would keep a secret that rightfully belonged to others, to the good guys. Tessa would be scornful if she backed out now.

She got in bed around 3:00 a.m., with no chance of sleeping.

At exactly five, she made the call.

15.

Elaine was awake, quietly sipping the first cup of coffee in the dark while her husband slept beside her. The plan called for another trip to Camino Island, her tenth or eleventh so far. She would take the same flight from Reagan National to Jacksonville, where either Rick or Graham would be waiting. They would meet in their safe house on the beach and assess things. There was excitement because their girl had spent the weekend with their target. Surely she had learned something. They would call her in for a late afternoon meeting and get the scoop.

At 5:01, however, all plans went out the window.

When Elaine's phone vibrated and she saw who was calling, she eased out of bed and went to the kitchen. "It's a bit early for you."

Mercer said, "He's not as smart as we thought. He has the manuscript for *The Last Tycoon* and he showed it to me last night. It's in his vault, just as we thought."

Elaine absorbed it and closed her eyes. "Are you certain?"

"Yes. Based on the copies you've shown me, I'm pretty certain."

Elaine sat on a bar stool at the breakfast counter and said, "Tell me everything."

16.

At six, Elaine called Lamar Bradshaw, the head of the FBI's Rare Asset Recovery Unit, and woke him up. His plans for the day were also tossed. Two hours later they met in his office in the Hoover Building on Pennsylvania Avenue for a full briefing. As she expected, Bradshaw and his team were irritated that Elaine and her company had secretly put together such an elaborate scheme to spy on Bruce Cable, a suspect they had discussed only in passing a month earlier. Cable was on the FBI's list, along with a dozen others, but only because of his reputation. Bradshaw had not taken him seriously. The FBI detested private, parallel investigations, but at the moment bickering in a turf battle would not be productive. Bradshaw was also forced to swallow his pride because Elaine Shelby had once again found the stolen goods. A quick truce was found, peace prevailed, and joint plans were made.

17.

Bruce Cable awoke at six in his apartment above the store. He drank coffee and read for an hour before going downstairs to his office in the First Editions Room. He turned on his desktop and began reviewing his inventory. The most unpleasant part of his job was deciding which books were not going to sell and must be returned to their publishers for credit. Each book returned was a failure on his part, but after twenty years he had almost grown accustomed to the process. For an hour he roamed the darkened store, pulling books from shelves and off tables, piling them into sad little stacks back in the stockroom.

At 8:45, as always, he returned to the apartment, quickly showered and changed into his daily seersucker, and at nine sharp turned on the lights and opened the front door. Two clerks arrived first and Bruce set them to work. Thirty minutes later, he went to the basement and unlocked the metal door leading to Noelle's storage area. Jake was already there, tapping small nails into the back of an ancient chaise. Mercer's writing table was finished and off to one side.

After the pleasantries, Bruce said, "Our friend Ms. Mann will not be buying the table after all. Noelle wants it shipped to an address in Fort Lauderdale. Knock off the legs and find a crate."

"Sure," Jake said. "Today?"

"Yes, it's a rush job. Hop on it."

"Yes, sir."

18.

At 11:06, a chartered jet took off from Dulles International. On board were Elaine Shelby and two of her associates, and Lamar Bradshaw and four special agents. En route, Bradshaw spoke again to the U.S. Attorney in Florida, and Elaine called Mercer, who was holed up in a local library trying to write. She said she was finding it impossible to be creative at the bed-and-breakfast. Elaine thought it best if she stayed away from the bookstore for a couple of days, and Mercer assured her she had no plans to go near it. She had seen enough of Bruce for a while and needed a break.

At 11:20, an unmarked cargo van parked on Santa Rosa's Main Street across from the bookstore. Inside were three field agents from the Jacksonville office. They aimed a video camera at the front door of Bay Books, and began filming every person who entered and left. Another van, with two more field agents, parked on Third Street and began surveillance. Their job was to film and monitor every shipment in and out of the store.

At 11:40, an agent dressed in shorts and sandals entered the front door and browsed for a few minutes. He did not see Cable. With cash, he bought an audio version of *Lonesome Dove* and left the store. In the first van, a technician opened the case, removed the eight CDs, and installed a tiny video camera and a battery.

At 12:15, Cable left with an unknown person and walked down the street to lunch. Five minutes later, another agent, a woman also in shorts and sandals, entered the store with the *Lonesome Dove* audio case. She bought coffee upstairs, killed some time, returned to the ground floor, and selected two paperbacks. When the clerk went to the rear, the agent deftly returned the *Lonesome Dove* case to the audio rack and took the one next to it, *The Last Picture Show*. She eventually paid for the paperbacks and the audio and asked the clerk about a good place for lunch. In the first van, the agents stared at a laptop. From the inside, they now had a perfect frontal view of everyone entering the store. They could only hope that no one would want to listen to *Lonesome Dove* anytime soon.

At 12:31, the chartered jet landed at the small airport on Camino Island, ten minutes from downtown Santa Rosa. Rick and Graham were there to meet Elaine and her two associates. Two SUVs picked up Bradshaw and his crew. Because it was Monday, hotel rooms were avail-

able, for a few days anyway, and several had been reserved at a hotel near the harbor, less than a five-minute
walk from the bookstore. Bradshaw took the largest
suite and set up his command post. Laptops were arranged on a table, and the video surveillance from the
cameras ran nonstop.

After a quick lunch, Mercer arrived at the suite and a
flurry of introductions followed. She was startled at the
show of manpower, and felt ill with the thought that
she had unleashed all these people on an unsuspecting
Bruce Cable.

With Elaine in the background, she was interrogated
by Bradshaw and another special agent named Vanno.
She retold her story, leaving out nothing but the inti-
mate details of her long weekend, a rather romantic
little fling that now seemed like a nostalgic romp from
long ago. Bradshaw walked her through a series of high-
density photographs of the Fitzgerald manuscripts taken
years earlier by Princeton. Elaine had the same set and
Mercer had seen it all before. Yes, yes, in her opinion,
what she had seen last night in the basement vault was
the original *Tycoon*.

Yes, it could be a fake. Anything is possible, but she
didn't think so. Why would Bruce be so protective of a
fake manuscript?

When Bradshaw repeated a question for the third
time, and did so with a tone of suspicion, Mercer bris-
tled and asked, "Aren't we on the same team here?"

Vanno eased in with a soft "Of course we are, Mercer,
we just need to get everything right."

"I got it right, okay?"

After an hour of back-and-forth, Mercer was convinced that Elaine Shelby was smarter and much smoother than Bradshaw and Vanno. Elaine, though, had handed her off to the FBI, and there was no doubt they would run the show until the end. During a break, Bradshaw took a call from an Assistant U.S. Attorney in Jacksonville and things got tense. It seemed as though the federal magistrate there was insisting on a closed hearing with "the witness" present, as opposed to allowing "the witness" to testify by video. This upset Bradshaw and Vanno, but they got nowhere.

At 2:15, Mercer was loaded into a car with Rick behind the wheel and Graham riding shotgun and Elaine in the rear seat with her. They followed an SUV loaded with FBI agents off the island and in the direction of Jacksonville. On the bridge over the Camino River, Mercer broke the ice with an unpleasant "So, let's have it. What's going on?"

Rick and Graham stared straight ahead and said nothing. Elaine cleared her throat and said, "It's all federal crap, your tax dollars at work. Federal Agent Bradshaw is pissed off at the U.S. Attorney for this district, he's federal too, and everybody seems pissed off at the federal magistrate, who does the search warrants. They thought they had an understanding whereby you could stay on the island and give your statement by video. Bradshaw says they do it all the time, but for some reason this federal magistrate wants to hear you in person. So, we're headed for court."

"Court? You never said anything about going to court."

"The federal court building. We'll probably meet with the magistrate in private, back in his office or something. Don't worry."

"Easy for you to say. I have a question. If Cable is arrested, can he go to trial, even though he's caught red-handed with the stolen manuscript?"

Elaine looked up front and said, "Graham, you're the lawyer."

Graham snorted as if it were a joke. "I have a law degree but never used it. But, no, a defendant cannot be forced to plead guilty. Therefore, anyone charged with a crime can insist on a trial. It won't happen, though, not in this case."

"And why not?"

"If Cable has the manuscript, they will put enormous pressure on him to squeal. Recovering all five is far more important than punishing the thieves and crooks. They'll offer Cable all manner of sweet deals to spill his guts and lead them to the others. We have no idea how much he knows, but you can bet he'll start singing to save his ass."

"But if by chance he went on trial, there's no way I would be called as a witness, right?"

All three were silent as Mercer waited. After a long, uncomfortable pause, she said, "Look, Elaine, you never mentioned anything about going to court, and you damned sure didn't tell me I might have to testify against Cable. I won't do it."

Elaine tried to soothe her. "You won't have to testify, Mercer, believe me. You're doing a great job and we're very proud of you."

"Don't patronize me, Elaine," Mercer snapped, more harshly than she intended. No one spoke for a long time but the tension remained. They were on Interstate 95 going south and entering the sprawl of Jacksonville.

The U.S. Courthouse was a tall modern building with many levels and lots of glass. They were waved through a side entrance and parked in a small reserved lot. The FBI agents practically surrounded Mercer as if she needed protection. The elevator was crowded with her entourage. Minutes later they entered the offices of the U.S. Attorney, Middle District of Florida, and were directed to a conference room where the waiting began. Bradshaw and Vanno yanked out their cell phones and began muted conversations. Elaine was talking to Bethesda. Rick and Graham had important calls. Mercer sat alone at the massive table with no one to chat with.

After twenty minutes or so, an earnest young man in a dark suit—hell they all wore dark suits—entered with a purposeful air and introduced himself as Janeway, an Assistant U.S. Attorney of some variety. He explained to the crowd that the magistrate, a Judge Philby, was tied up in a life-or-death hearing, and, well, it might take some time. Janeway said he would like to cover Mercer's testimony, if that was all right.

Mercer shrugged. Did she really have a choice?

Janeway left and returned with two other dark suits who offered their names. Mercer shook their hands. A real pleasure.

They whipped out legal pads and faced her across the table. Janeway began asking questions and it was immediately obvious he knew little about the case. Slowly, painfully, Mercer filled in the blanks.

19.

At 4:50, Mercer, Bradshaw, and Vanno followed Janeway to the chambers of Magistrate Judge Arthur Philby, who greeted them as if they were trespassing. He'd had a rough day and seemed irritable. Mercer sat at one end of another long table next to a court reporter who asked her to raise her right hand and swear to tell the truth. A video camera on a tripod was aimed at the witness. Judge Philby, minus his black robe, sat at the other end like a king on his throne.

For an hour, Janeway and Bradshaw asked her questions, and she told the same story for at least the third time that day. Bradshaw produced large photos of the basement, the vault, and the safe inside. Philby interrupted repeatedly with his own questions, and much of her testimony was repeated more than twice. But she kept her cool, and was often amused by the thought that Bruce Cable was far more likeable than these guys, the good ones.

When she was finished, they wrapped things up and thanked her for her time and efforts. Don't mention it, she almost said, I'm being paid to be here. She was excused and hurriedly left the building with Elaine, Rick, and Graham. When the federal building was finally behind them, Mercer asked, "So what happens next?"

Elaine said, "They're preparing the search warrant now. Your testimony was perfect and the judge is convinced."

"So, when do they attack the bookstore?"

"Soon."

CHAPTER EIGHT
THE DELIVERY

1.

Denny had been on the island for ten days and was losing patience. He and Rooker had tracked Cable and knew his movements, a monotonously simple task. They had tracked Mercer too and knew her habits, another easy chore.

Intimidation had worked with Oscar Stein in Boston, and perhaps it was their only plausible tool. Direct confrontation with the threat of violence. As with Stein, Cable could not exactly run to the cops. If he had the manuscripts, he could be coerced into cutting a deal. If he didn't, then he almost certainly knew where they were.

Cable usually left work around six in the evening and went home. At 5:50 Monday afternoon, Denny entered the store and pretended to browse around. As luck would have it, Cable's luck that is, he was busy in the basement and his clerks knew not to divulge this.

Denny, though, had just run out of luck. After months of moving seamlessly through airports and customs and security checkpoints, and using fake IDs and passports and disguises, and paying cash when possible for rooms and rentals, he was thinking of himself as quite clever, if not invincible. But even the smartest cons get busted when they drop their guard.

For years the FBI had been perfecting its facial recognition technology, software it referred to as FacePrint. It used an algorithm to calculate the distance between a subject's eyes, nose, and ears, and in milliseconds applied it to a bank of photos relevant to a particular investigation. In the "Gatsby File," as the stolen manuscripts case had been nicknamed by the FBI, the bank was comparatively small. It included a dozen photos of the three thieves at the front desk of the Firestone Library, though Jerry Steengarden and Mark Driscoll were in custody. It also included several hundred photos of men known or suspected to be active in the world of stolen art, artifacts, and books.

When Denny entered the store, the camera hidden in the *Lonesome Dove* audio case captured his face, as it had routinely captured the face of every other customer since noon that day. The image was sent to the laptop in the rear of the van across the street, and, more important, to the FBI's mammoth forensic lab at Quantico, Virginia. There was a match. An alarm alerted a technician. Within seconds of entering the store, Denny was identified as the third Gatsby thief.

Two had been caught. Trey, the fourth, was still decomposing at the bottom of a pond in the Poconos, never to be found nor implicated. Ahmed, the fifth, was still hiding in Europe.

After fifteen minutes, Denny left the store, walked around the corner, and got into a 2011 Honda Accord. The second van followed it at a distance, lost it, then found it parked in the lot of the Sea Breeze Motel, on the beach, a hundred yards from the Lighthouse Inn. A stakeout began.

The Honda Accord had been rented from an agency in Jacksonville that advertised "rent-a-wrecks" and didn't mind dealing in cash. The name on the application was Wilbur Shifflet, and the manager admitted to the FBI that he thought the Maine driver's license looked bogus. Shifflet had paid a thousand dollars cash for a two-week rental and waived the insurance.

The FBI was stunned at this development, at its incredible good fortune. But why would one of the thieves hang around the bookstore some eight months after the theft? Was he also watching Mercer? Did he have a connection to Cable? There were many baffling questions to be dealt with later, but at the moment it was a strong indication that Mercer was right. At least one of the manuscripts was in the basement.

At sunset, Denny stepped out of room 18 and Rooker stepped out of the room next door. They walked a hundred yards to the Surf, a popular outdoor bar and grill, where they dined on sandwiches and beer. While they were eating, four FBI agents walked into the office of the Sea Breeze and handed the manager a search warrant. In room 18, they found a gym bag under the bed. It contained a nine-millimeter pistol, six thousand dollars in cash, and fake driver's licenses from Tennessee and Wyoming. Nothing, though, revealed Wilbur's true identity. The agents found nothing of value in the room next door.

When Denny and Rooker returned to the Sea Breeze, they were arrested and driven, in total silence and in separate cars, to the FBI office in Jacksonville. They were processed and fingerprinted. Both sets of prints were pushed through the data bank, and by 10:00 p.m. the truth was known. Denny's military prints revealed his name: Dennis Allen Durban, age thirty-three, born in Sacramento. Rooker's criminal record nailed him: Bryan Bayer, age thirty-nine, born in Green Bay, Wisconsin. Both refused to cooperate and were put away. Lamar Bradshaw decided to bury them for a few days and sit on the news of their arrests.

Mercer was with Elaine, Rick, and Graham in the safe house, playing gin rummy and killing time. They had been told of the arrests but did not know the details. Bradshaw called at eleven, spoke with Elaine, and filled in most of the missing pieces. Things were obviously happening fast. There were a lot of unanswered questions. Tomorrow was the big day. As for Mercer, Bradshaw said, "Get her off the island."

2.

They watched the store even more closely throughout Tuesday, and saw nothing out of the ordinary. No more thieves lurking around, no suspicious packages shipped. A UPS truck delivered six boxes of books at

10:50, but left with nothing. Cable was upstairs and down, helping customers, reading as always in his favorite spot, and of course he left for lunch at 12:15, returning an hour later.

At five, Lamar Bradshaw and Derry Vanno entered the store and asked Cable if they could have a word. Quietly, Bradshaw said, "FBI." They followed him to the First Editions Room, where he closed the door. He asked for identification and they whipped out their badges. Vanno handed over a search warrant and said, "We're here to search the basement."

Still standing, Bruce asked, "Okay, and what might you be looking for?"

"Stolen manuscripts, from the collection of F. Scott Fitzgerald, property of the Princeton library," Bradshaw said.

Bruce laughed and without missing a beat said, "Are you serious?"

"Do we look serious?"

"I guess you do. Mind if I read this?" He waved the search warrant.

"Go right ahead. And as of now, we have five agents in the store, including us."

"Well, make yourself at home. There's coffee upstairs."

"We know."

Bruce sat at his desk and read the search warrant. He took his time, flipped pages, and gave a good impression of being unconcerned. When he finished, he said, "Okay, it's fairly straightforward." He stood and stretched and thought about what to do next. "It's limited to the vault in the basement, right?"

"That's correct," Bradshaw said.

"There's a lot of valuable stuff down there, and, well, you guys are famous for trashing a place when you go in with warrants."

"You watch too much television," Vanno said. "We know what we're doing, and if you cooperate no one else in the store will even know we're here."

"I doubt that."

"Let's go."

Clutching the search warrant, Bruce led them to the back of the store, where they were met by three more agents, all dressed casually. Bruce ignored them and unlocked the door to the basement. He flipped a light switch and said, "Watch your step." In the basement he turned on more lights and stopped at the door to the vault, where he punched in the code. He opened the vault, turned on its light, and when all five agents were crowded inside he waved at the walls and said, "Those are all rare first editions. Nothing of interest, I suppose." One agent removed a small video camera and began filming the interior of the vault.

"Open the safe," Bradshaw said and Bruce complied. When he opened its door, he pointed to the top shelves and said, "These are all very rare. Do you want to see them?"

"Maybe later," Bradshaw said. "Let's start with those four drawers." He knew precisely what he wanted.

Bruce pulled out the first one. It contained two cedar boxes, just as Mercer had reported. He lifted one, placed it on the table, and opened the top. "This is the original manuscript of *Darker Than Amber,* published by John D.

MacDonald in 1966. I bought this about ten years ago and I have the invoice to prove it."

Bradshaw and Vanno hovered over the manuscript. "Mind if we touch it?" Vanno asked. Both were experienced and knew what they were doing.

"Be my guest."

The manuscript was typed and the pages were in good condition with almost no fading. They flipped through it and soon lost interest. "And the other?" Bradshaw asked.

Bruce removed the second cedar box, placed it beside the first, and lifted the top. "This is another MacDonald manuscript, *The Lonely Silver Rain,* published in 1985. Got an invoice for this one too."

It, too, was neat and typewritten, with notes in the margins. To help matters, Bruce added, "MacDonald lived on a boat with little electricity. He used an old manual Underwood typewriter and was meticulous about his work. His manuscripts are incredibly neat."

They really didn't care but turned a few pages anyway.

For a bit of fun, Bruce said, "I'm not sure, but didn't Fitzgerald handwrite his original manuscripts?" There was no reply.

Bradshaw turned back to the safe and said, "The second drawer."

Bruce pulled it out as the two inched closer, straining for a look. It was empty. Same for the third and fourth. Bradshaw was stunned and shot a wild look at Vanno, who was gawking at the empty drawers in utter disbelief.

Reeling, Bradshaw said, "Empty the contents of the safe."

Bruce said, "No problem, but it's obvious, at least to me, that someone has fed you guys some bad information. I don't trade in stolen stuff and I wouldn't go near the Fitzgerald manuscripts."

"Empty the safe," Bradshaw said again, ignoring him.

Bruce returned the two MacDonald manuscripts to the top drawer, then reached to the top shelf and removed a clamshell holding *The Catcher in the Rye*. "You want to see it?"

"Yes," Bradshaw replied.

Bruce carefully opened the clamshell and removed the book. He held it up for them to see, and video, then put it back. "And you want to see all of them?"

"That's right."

"It's a waste of time. These are published novels, not manuscripts."

"We know that."

"These clamshells are custom made for each book and much too small to hold a manuscript."

That much was obvious, but time was not a factor and a thorough search was required. "Next," Bradshaw said, nodding at the shelves in the safe.

Methodically, Bruce removed the books one at a time, opened the clamshells, displayed the books, then set them aside. As he happily went about his business, Bradshaw and Vanno shook their heads, glared at each other, rolled their eyes, and in general looked as baffled as a couple of hoodwinked agents could possibly look.

When all forty-eight were stacked on the table, the safe was empty, but for the two MacDonald manuscripts in the top drawer. Bradshaw stepped closer to the safe, as if looking for secret compartments, but it was obvious there was no room for one. He scratched his jaw and ran his fingers through his thinning hair.

Vanno asked, "What about these?" and waved at the bookshelves against the walls.

Bruce said, "They're rare first editions, books published a long time ago. It's a collection I've spent twenty years putting together. Again, they're novels, not manuscripts. I suppose you want to see them too."

"Oh why not?" Vanno said.

Bruce pulled out keys and unlocked the bookshelves. The agents spread out and began lifting the glass doors to the shelves, inspecting the rows of books, finding nothing even remotely resembling a bulky manuscript. Bruce watched them carefully, eager to step in if a book were removed. But they were careful, and very professional, and after an hour in the vault the search was over and had yielded nothing. Every inch of it had been examined. As they filed out, Bruce pulled the door shut but didn't lock it.

Bradshaw looked around the basement and took in the shelves stuffed with old books, magazines, galleys, and advance reading copies. "Mind if we take a look?" he asked in one last, desperate attempt to find something.

Bruce said, "Well, according to the warrant, the search is limited to the vault, but what the hell. Have a look. You're not going to find anything."

"So you consent."

"Sure. Why not? Let's waste some more time."

They fanned out through the junk room, and peeked

and poked for half an hour, as if trying to delay the inevitable. Admitting defeat was unthinkable, but they finally gave up. Bruce followed them up the stairs and to the front door. Bradshaw offered a hand and said, "Sorry for the inconvenience."

Bruce shook hands and asked, "So, is this it for me, or am I still a suspect?"

Bradshaw pulled a business card from his pocket and handed it to Bruce. "I'll give you a call tomorrow and answer that question."

"Great. Better still, I'll get my lawyer to call you."

"Do that."

When they were gone, Bruce turned and noticed two clerks behind the front counter, staring.

"DEA," he said. "Looking for a meth lab. Now get back to work."

3.

The oldest bar on the island was the Pirate's Saloon, three blocks east of the bookstore. After dark, Bruce met his lawyer, Mike Wood, there for a drink. They huddled in a corner, and over bourbon Bruce described the search. Mike was too experienced to inquire as to whether Bruce knew anything about the stolen manuscripts.

Bruce asked, "Is it possible to find out if I'm still their target?"

"Maybe. I'll call the guy tomorrow, but I assume the answer is yes."

"I'd like to know if I'm going to be followed for the

next six months. Look, Mike, I'm going to the South of France next week to hang out with Noelle. If these guys are going to track me all over the place, I'd like to know it. Hell, I'll give them my flight numbers and call them when I get home. I have nothing to hide."

"I'll tell the guy, but for now assume they're watching every move, listening to every phone, and reading every e-mail and text message."

Bruce feigned disbelief and frustration, but in reality for the past two months he'd been living with the assumption that someone, possibly the FBI or perhaps someone else, was watching and listening.

The following day, Wednesday, Mike Wood called Lamar Bradshaw's cell phone four times and was sent straight to voice mail. He left messages, none of them returned. On Thursday, Bradshaw called back and confirmed that Mr. Cable was a person of interest, but no longer a target of their investigation.

Mike informed Bradshaw that his client would soon be leaving the country, and passed along his flight number and the hotel in Nice where he would be staying for a few days with his wife. Bradshaw thanked him for the information and said the FBI had no interest in Cable's foreign travels.

4.

On Friday, Denny Durban and Bryan Bayer, also known as Joe Rooker, were flown to Philadelphia, then driven to Trenton, where they were again processed and placed in separate cells. Denny was then taken to an interrogation room, sat at a table, given a cup of coffee, and told to wait. Mark Driscoll and his lawyer, Gil Petrocelli, were led by Special Agent McGregor to the hallway outside the interrogation room, and through a one-way window they took a look at Denny, sitting all alone and looking bored.

"We nabbed your buddy," McGregor said to Mark. "Caught him in Florida."

"So?" Petrocelli said.

"So we now have all three of you, the three who were inside the Firestone Library. Seen enough?"

Driscoll said, "Yes."

They walked away and entered another interrogation room two doors down. When they were seated around a small table, McGregor said, "We don't know who else was involved but there were others. Someone outside the library created the diversion while the three of you were inside. Someone else hacked the campus security system and electrical grid. That's five, could be more, only you can tell us. We're closing in on the manuscripts and we'll soon have a fresh batch of indictments. We are willing to offer the mother of all deals, Mr. Driscoll. You sing and you walk. Tell us everything and your indictment is forgotten. You enter witness protection and we'll set you up in some nice place with new papers, a good job, whatever you want. If there's a trial, you'll have to come back and testify, but frankly I doubt that'll happen."

For Mark, eight months in jail were enough. Denny was the dangerous one, and now that he was neutralized, so much of the pressure was off. The threat of retaliation was greatly diminished. Trey was not the violent type and lived on the run anyway. If Mark gave up Trey's real name he might soon be caught. Ahmed was a wimpish computer nerd who was afraid of his shadow. The thought of him exacting revenge seemed quite remote.

"Give me some time," Mark said.

"We'll talk about it," Petrocelli said.

"Okay, today is Friday. You have the weekend to make a decision. I'll be back Monday morning. After that, all offers are off the table."

On Monday, Mark took the deal.

5.

On Tuesday, July 19, Bruce Cable flew from Jacksonville to Atlanta, boarded an Air France jet for a nonstop flight to Paris, then killed two hours before connecting to Nice. He arrived there at eight in the morning and took a cab to the Hôtel La Pérouse, a stylish boutique hotel at the edge of the sea, a place he and Noelle had discovered during their first trip to France ten years earlier. She was standing in the lobby, waiting and looking very French in a short white dress and smart wide-brim straw hat. They kissed and embraced as if it had been years, and walked hand in hand to the terrace by the pool, where they sipped champagne and kissed again. When Bruce said he was hungry, they went to their room on the third floor and ordered room service. They ate on the terrace and soaked in the sun. The beach stretched for miles below them, and beyond it the Côte d'Azur simmered in the morning sun. Bruce had not taken a day off in months and was ready for serious relaxation. After a long nap, the jet lag was gone and they went to the pool.

As always, he asked about Jean-Luc and Noelle said he was fine. He sent his regards. She asked about Mercer, and Bruce told all the stories. He doubted they would ever see her again.

Late in the afternoon, they left the hotel and walked five minutes into the Old Town, a triangle-shaped section dating back centuries and the city's main attraction. They drifted with the crowds, taking in the busy outdoor markets, window-shopping at the boutiques along streets too narrow for automobiles, and having ice cream and coffee at one of the many outdoor cafés. They meandered through alleyways, got lost more than once but never for long. The sea was always visible just around the next corner. They were often hand in hand, never far apart, and at times seemed to cling to each other.

6.

On Thursday, Bruce and Noelle slept late, had breakfast on the terrace, and eventually showered and dressed and returned to the Old Town. They strolled through the flower markets and marveled at the spectacular varieties, many of them unknown even to Noelle. They had an espresso at another café and watched the throngs around the baroque cathedral at Place Rossetti. As noon approached, they eventually drifted to the edge of the Old Town, to a street that was slightly wider with a few vehicles jostling about. They ducked into an antiques store and Noelle chatted with the owner. A handyman led them to the rear, to a small workshop packed with tables and armoires in various stages of repair. He pointed to a wooden crate and told Noelle it had just arrived. She checked the shipping tag stapled to one corner, and asked the handyman to open the crate. He found his drill and began removing two-inch screws that secured the top. A dozen of them, and he worked slowly, methodically, as he evidently had for many years. Bruce watched him closely while Noelle seemed more interested in another old table. When he finally finished, he and Bruce lifted the top of the crate and set it aside.

Noelle said something to the handyman and he disappeared. Bruce removed thick packing foam from the crate, and suddenly he and Noelle were staring at Mercer's writing desk. Below its surface were the facings of three drawers that had been removed to create a hidden space. With a claw hammer, Bruce gently pried open the surface. Inside were five identical cedar boxes, all custom built to his specs by a cabinetmaker on Camino Island.

Gatsby and friends.

7.

The meeting convened at 9:00 a.m. and gave every impression of becoming a marathon. The long table was covered with paperwork already scattered as if they had been working for hours. At the far end, a large screen

had been set up, and next to it was a platter of dough-
nuts and two pots of coffee. Agent McGregor and three
more FBI agents took one side. Carlton, the Assistant
U.S. Attorney, took the other, flanked by his entourage
of unsmiling young men in dark suits. At the other end,
in the hot seat, sat Mark Driscoll, with his ever faithful
lawyer, Petrocelli, at his left elbow.

Mark was already savoring delicious thoughts of
life on the outside, of freedom in a new world. He was
ready to talk.

McGregor went first and said, "Let's start with the
team. There were three on the inside, right?"

"That's right. Me, Jerry Steengarden, and Denny Durban."

"And the others?"

"Right, well, on the ground outside the library was Tim
Maldanado, went by Trey. Not sure where he's from because he's lived most of his life on the run. His mother
is a woman named Iris Green and she lives on Baxter
Road in Muncie, Indiana. You can go see her but I doubt
if she's seen her boy in years. Trey escaped from a federal pen in Ohio about two years ago."

"Why do you know where his mother lives?" McGregor
asked.

"It was all part of the plan. We memorized a bunch of
useless stuff to convince ourselves to remain silent in
the event somebody got caught. The threat of retaliation, which sounded real smart back then."

"And when did you last see Trey?"

"November 12 of last year, the day Jerry and I left the
cabin and drove to Rochester. We left him there with
Denny. I have no idea where he might be."

On the screen, a mug shot appeared and Trey was smiling at them. "That's him," Mark said.

"And what was his role?"

"Diversion. He caused the commotion with his smoke bombs and fireworks. He called 911, said there was a guy with a gun shooting students. I made two or three calls myself, from inside the library."

"Okay, we'll get back to that. Who else was involved?"

"There were only five of us, and the fifth was Ahmed Mansour, an American of Lebanese descent who worked out of Buffalo. He was not on the scene that night. He's a hacker, forger, computer expert. Long career with government intelligence before he got booted and turned to crime. He's about fifty years old, divorced, lives with a woman at 662 Washburn Street in Buffalo. To my knowledge, he has no criminal record."

Even though Mark was being filmed and recorded, all four FBI agents and all five grim-faced young men from the U.S. Attorney's office scribbled furiously as if their notes were important.

McGregor said, "Okay, if there were only five, then who is this guy?" Bryan Bayer's face appeared on the screen.

"Never seen him before."

Petrocelli said, "That's the guy who slapped me around in the parking lot a few weeks back. Warned me to tell my client to keep his mouth shut."

McGregor said, "We caught him with Denny in Florida. A career thug, name of Bryan Bayer but went by Rooker."

"Don't know him," Mark said. "He was not part of our team. Must be someone Denny picked up to look for the manuscripts."

"We don't know much about him and he's not talking," McGregor said.

"He was not a player," Mark said.

"We'll get back to the team. Tell us about the plan. How did it get started?"

Mark smiled, relaxed, took a long sip of coffee, and began his narrative.

8.

Deep in the Left Bank of Paris, in the heart of the 6th arrondissement on Rue St.-Sulpice, Monsieur Gaston Chappelle ran a tidy little bookshop that had changed little in twenty-eight years. Such stores are scattered throughout the center of the city, each with a different specialty. Monsieur Chappelle's was rare French, Spanish, and American novels of the nineteenth and twentieth centuries. Two doors down, a friend dealt only in ancient maps and atlases. Around the corner, another traded in old prints and letters written by historic figures. Generally, there was little foot traffic in and out of these stores; a lot of window-shopping but few customers. Their clients were serious collectors from around the world, not tourists looking for something to read.

On Monday, July 25, Monsieur Chappelle locked his shop at 11:00 a.m. and stepped into a waiting taxi. Twenty minutes later, it stopped in front of an office building on Avenue Montaigne, in the 8th arrondissement, and he got out. As he entered the building, he gave a cautious look at the street behind him, though he expected to see nothing unusual. There was nothing illegal about his mission, at least not under French law.

He spoke to the lovely receptionist and waited as she called upstairs. He shuffled about the lobby, admiring the art on the walls and taking in the breadth and reach of the law firm's ambition. Scully & Pershing, announced the bold bronze lettering, with offices in, and he counted them, forty-four cities in every important country and a few lesser ones. He'd spent some time with its website and knew that Scully boasted of having three thousand lawyers and being the largest firm in the world.

Once his presence was approved, the receptionist cleared him to proceed to the third floor. He took the stairs and soon found the office of one Thomas Kendrick, a ranking partner chosen solely because of his undergraduate degree from Princeton. That was followed by two law degrees, first from Columbia and then from the Sorbonne. Mr. Kendrick was forty-eight years old, originally from Vermont but now with dual citizenship. He was married to a French lady and had never left Paris after the Sorbonne. He specialized in complex litigation of an international nature and, at least on the phone, had seemed reluctant to grant an appointment to a lowly bookshop owner. Monsieur Chappelle, though, had been persistent.

Speaking in French, they got through the rather stiff formalities and soon enough Mr. Kendrick said, "Now, what can I do for you?"

Monsieur replied, "You have close ties to Princeton University, having once served on its board of trustees. I assume you know its president, Dr. Carlisle."

"Yes. I'm very involved with my school. May I ask why this is important?"

"It is very important. I have a friend who has an acquaintance who knows the man in possession of the Fitzgerald manuscripts. This man would like to return them to Princeton, for a price, of course."

Kendrick's professional, thousand-dollar-an-hour facade vanished as his jaw dropped slightly, his eyes bulged, and he looked as though he'd been kicked in the gut.

Chappelle continued, "I am just the intermediary, same as you. We need your assistance."

The last thing Mr. Kendrick needed was another task, especially one that would pay him nothing and devour his valuable time. However, the appeal of getting involved in such a wonderfully unique transaction was almost overwhelming. If this guy could be believed, he, Kendrick, would play a vital role in bringing home a prize his beloved university treasured above all others. He cleared his throat and said, "The manuscripts are safe and still together, I take it."

"Indeed."

Kendrick smiled as his thoughts raced away. "And the delivery would take place where?"

"Here. Paris. The delivery will be carefully planned and all instructions must be strictly adhered to. Obviously, Mr. Kendrick, we're dealing with a criminal who is in possession of priceless assets, and he prefers not to get caught. He is very clever and calculating, and if there is the slightest misstep or confusion or hint of trouble, the manuscripts will disappear forever. Princeton will have only this one chance to retrieve the papers. Notifying the police would be a grave mistake."

"I'm not sure Princeton will get involved without the FBI. I don't know this, of course."

"Then there will be no deal. Period. Princeton will never see them again."

Kendrick stood and stuffed his fine shirt deeper into his tailored slacks. He walked to a window, glanced out at nothing, and said, "What's the price?"

"A fortune."

"Of course. I have to give them some idea."

"Four million per manuscript. And not negotiable."

For a pro who wrangled with lawsuits worth billions, the amount of the ransom did not faze Kendrick. Nor would it scare Princeton. He doubted his university had that much mad money lying around, but there was a twenty-five-billion-dollar endowment and thousands of wealthy alumni.

Kendrick moved away from the window and said, "Obviously, I need to make some calls. When do we meet again?"

Chappelle stood and said, "Tomorrow. And I caution you again, Mr. Kendrick, that any involvement by the police here or in the U.S. would be catastrophic."

"I hear you. Thanks for stopping by, Mr. Chappelle." They shook hands and said good-bye.

At ten the following morning, a black Mercedes sedan stopped on Rue de Vaugirard in front of the Luxembourg Palace. From the backseat, Thomas Kendrick emerged and began walking along the sidewalk. He entered the famous gardens through a wrought-iron gate and drifted with a throng of tourists to the Octagonal Lake, where hundreds, both Parisians and visitors alike, whiled away the morning, sitting and reading, taking in the sun. Children raced their toy boats across the water. Young lovers sprawled and groped on the lake's low concrete walls. Packs of joggers hustled about, talking and laughing. At the monument to Delacroix, Kendrick was joined without a greeting by Gaston Chappelle, briefcase in hand. They walked on, ambling along the wide pathways and moving away from the lake.

"Am I being watched?" Kendrick asked.

"There are people here, yes. The man with the manuscripts has accomplices. Am I being watched?"

"No. I assure you."

"Good. I assume your conversations went well."

"I leave for the U.S. in two hours. Tomorrow I will meet with the folks at Princeton. They understand the rules. As you might guess, Mr. Chappelle, they would like some type of verification."

Without stopping, Chappelle pulled a folder from his briefcase. "This should suffice," he said.

Kendrick took it as they walked. "May I ask what's inside?"

Chappelle offered a wicked smile and said, "It's the first page of chapter 3, *The Great Gatsby*. As far as I can tell, it is authentic."

Kendrick stopped cold and mumbled, "Good God."

9.

Dr. Jeffrey Brown practically jogged across the Princeton campus and bounded up the front steps of Nassau Hall, the administration building. As the director of the Manuscripts Division at the Firestone Library, he could barely remember his last visit to the president's office. And, he knew for a fact that he had never been summoned for a meeting described as "urgent." His job had never been that exciting.

The secretary was waiting and escorted him to the grand office of President Carlisle, who was also standing and waiting. Dr. Brown was quickly introduced to the university's in-house counsel, Richard Farley, and to Thomas Kendrick. For Brown, at least, the tension in the room was palpable.

Carlisle gathered the four around a small conference table and said to Brown, "Sorry for the short notice, but we've been given something that needs verification. Yesterday, in Paris, Mr. Kendrick was handed a single sheet of paper that is said to be the first page of the third chapter of F. Scott Fitzgerald's original manuscript of *The Great Gatsby*. Take a look."

He slid over a folder and opened it. Brown, gasping, looked at the page, gently touched the top right corner, and buried his face in his hands.

10.

Two hours later, President Carlisle convened a second meeting at the same table. Dr. Brown had been excused, and in his chair sat Elaine Shelby. Next to her was Jack Lance, her client and the CEO of the insurance company with twenty-five million on the line. She was still smarting from her brilliant but botched scheme to nail Bruce Cable, but she was also rallying quickly with the hint that the manuscripts might be in play. She knew Cable was not on Camino Island but did not know he was in France. The FBI knew he had flown to Nice but had not followed him. They had not shared this information with Elaine.

Thomas Kendrick and Richard Farley sat opposite Elaine and Lance. President Carlisle handed over the folder and said, "This was given to us yesterday in Paris. It's a sample from *Gatsby* and we have verified its authenticity." Elaine opened the folder and took a look. Lance did too and neither reacted. Kendrick told the story of meeting with Gaston Chappelle and laid out the terms of the deal.

When he finished, Carlisle said, "Obviously, our priority is getting the manuscripts. Catching the crook would be nice, but right now that doesn't really matter."

Elaine said, "So, we're not including the FBI?"

Farley said, "Legally, we don't have to. There is nothing wrong with a private transaction, but we'd like your thoughts. You know them much better than we do."

Elaine shoved the folder a few inches away and thought

about her response. She spoke slowly, every word measured. "I talked to Lamar Bradshaw two days ago. The three men who stole the manuscripts are in custody and one has cut a deal. The two accomplices have not been found but the FBI has their names and the search is on. As far as the FBI is concerned, the crime has been solved. They will frown on such a private deal, but they will understand. Frankly, they'll be relieved if the manuscripts are returned."

"You've done this before?" Carlisle asked.

"Oh yes, several times. The ransom is secretly paid. The goods are returned. Everybody is happy, especially the owner. And the crook, too, I suppose."

Carlisle said, "I don't know. We have a great relationship with the FBI. They've been superb from the beginning. It just doesn't seem right to exclude them at this point."

Elaine replied, "But they have no authority in France. They'll be forced to bring in the authorities over there and we'll lose control. A lot of people will get involved and it could get messy. One small mistake, something no one can predict beforehand, and the manuscripts are gone."

Farley asked, "Assuming we get them back, how will the FBI react when it's over?"

She smiled and said, "I know Lamar Bradshaw pretty well. If the manuscripts are safely tucked away in your library and the thieves are in prison, he'll be a happy boy. He'll keep the investigation open for a few months and maybe the crook will make a mistake, but before long he and I will have a drink in Washington and share a good laugh."

Carlisle looked at Farley and Kendrick, and finally said, "Okay. Let's proceed without them. Now the sticky question of the money. Mr. Lance?"

The CEO cleared his throat and said, "Well, we're on the hook for twenty-five million, but that's for a complete loss. This is shaping up to be something far different."

"Indeed it is," Carlisle said with a smile. "Assuming the crook has all five, the math is easy. Of the twenty, how much might you be willing to kick in?"

Without hesitation, Lance said, "We'll do half. No more."

Half was more than Carlisle was hoping for, and as an academic he felt somewhat off balance trying to negotiate with a hardened CEO of an insurance company. He looked at Farley and said, "Arrange the other half."

11.

On the other side of Rue St.-Sulpice, and less than forty feet from the front door of Librairie Gaston Chappelle, was the Hôtel Proust, an old, quaint, four-story place with typically cramped rooms and a single elevator barely large enough for one adult and his or her luggage. Bruce used a fake Canadian passport and paid cash for a room on the third floor. In the window he set up a small camera aimed at the front of Gaston's shop. He watched the live footage on his iPhone in his room at the Hôtel Delacroix, around the corner on Rue de

Seine. Noelle, in her room at the Hôtel Bonaparte, watched it too. On her bed were the five manuscripts, each in a different type of bag.

At 11:00 a.m., she left with a shopping bag and went to the lobby, where she asked the front desk to keep the maids away from her room because her husband was sleeping. She left the hotel, crossed the street, and stopped at the window of a dress boutique. Bruce walked by and without stopping took the bag. She returned to her hotel room to protect the remaining manuscripts, and also to watch what happened at Gaston's shop.

Strolling by the fountain in front of the classical church St.-Sulpice, and trying hard to blend in with the other tourists, Bruce burned some clock as he fortified himself for what was ahead. The next few hours would change his life dramatically. If he was walking into a trap, he would be hauled home in chains and sent away for years. But if he pulled it off, he would be a rich man and only Noelle would know it. He walked a few blocks, always circling back and covering his trail. Finally, it was time to begin the delivery.

He entered the bookstore and found Gaston poring over an old atlas, pretending to be busy but watching the street. There were no customers. His clerk had been given the day off. They stepped into his cluttered office in the rear and Bruce removed a cedar box. He opened it then opened the archival box inside, and said, "The first one, *This Side of Paradise.*" Gaston gingerly touched the top leaf and said, in English, "Looks fine to me."

Bruce left him there. He opened and closed the front

door, glanced up and down the narrow street, and walked away, as nonchalantly as possible. Noelle watched the video from the camera in the Hôtel Proust and saw nothing unusual.

Using a prepaid cell phone, Gaston called a number at the Credit Suisse bank in Geneva and informed his contact that the first delivery had been completed. As instructed by Bruce, the ransom war chest was sitting in a Zurich bank, waiting. As instructed, the first installment was wired to a numbered account at AGL Bank in Zurich, and upon its arrival it was wired to another numbered account in a bank in Luxembourg.

Sitting in front of a laptop in his hotel room, Bruce received an e-mail confirming the two wires.

A black Mercedes stopped in front of Gaston's and Thomas Kendrick got out. He was in and out in less than a minute and left with the manuscript. He went straight to his office, where Dr. Jeffrey Brown was waiting, along with another Princeton librarian. They opened the boxes and marveled at the prize.

Patience was required, but the waiting was torturous. Bruce changed clothes and went for a long walk. At a sidewalk café on Rue des Écoles in the Latin Quarter, he managed to choke down a salad. Two tables away, Noelle sat down for a coffee. They ignored each other until he left, with a backpack she had placed in a chair. A few minutes after one, he entered Gaston's again and was surprised to see him chatting with a customer. Bruce eased to the rear and placed the backpack on his office desk. When Gaston managed to slip away, they opened the second cedar box and looked at Fitzgerald's scrawl.

Bruce said, "*The Beautiful and Damned*. Published in 1922 and perhaps his weakest effort."

"Looks fine to me," Gaston said.

"Make the call," Bruce said and left. Fifteen minutes later the wire transfers were confirmed. Not long after that, the same black Mercedes stopped in the same place, and Thomas Kendrick fetched number two from Gaston.

Gatsby was next in order of publication, but Bruce was saving it for last. His fortune was coming together nicely, but he still worried about the final delivery. He found Noelle sitting in the shade of an elm tree in Luxembourg Gardens. Beside her was a brown paper bag with the name of a bakery on it. For good measure, the end of a baguette protruded out the top. He broke it off and chomped away as he headed for Gaston's. At 2:30, he entered the bookstore, handed over the bag and what was left of the baguette, along with *Tender Is the Night*, to his friend, and hustled away.

To mix things up, the third wire went to a Deutsche Bank branch in Zurich, then to a numbered account in a London bank. When the two were confirmed, his fortune went from seven figures to eight.

Kendrick appeared again to pick up number three. Back in his office, Dr. Jeffrey Brown was giddy as the collection grew.

The fourth manuscript, that of *The Last Tycoon*, was hidden in a Nike gym bag Noelle carried into a Polish bookstore on Boulevard St.-Germain. While she browsed, Bruce carried it away and walked four minutes to Librairie Chappelle.

The Swiss banks would close at five. At a few minutes

before four, Gaston called Thomas Kendrick and passed along some somber news. For *Gatsby,* his acquaintance wished to be paid in advance. Kendrick kept his cool but argued that this was not acceptable. They had an agreement, and so far both sides had behaved.

"True," Monsieur Chappelle said politely. "But the danger, as my contact sees it, is that he makes the final delivery and those on your end decide to forgo the last installment."

"And what if we wire the final payment and he decides to keep the manuscript?" Kendrick replied.

"I suppose that's a risk you'll have to take," Gaston said. "He is rather adamant."

Kendrick took a deep breath and looked at the horror-stricken face of Dr. Brown. "I'll call you back in fifteen minutes," he said to Gaston.

Dr. Brown was already on the phone to Princeton, where President Carlisle had not left his desk for the past five hours. There was really nothing to discuss. Princeton wanted *Gatsby* far worse than the crook needed another four million. They would take their chances.

Kendrick called Chappelle and passed along the news. When the final wire transfer was confirmed at 4:45, Chappelle called Kendrick back and informed him that he was holding the *Gatsby* manuscript in the rear seat of a taxi waiting outside his office building on Avenue Montaigne.

Kendrick bolted from his office with Dr. Brown and his colleague giving chase. They sprinted down the wide stairway, rushed past the startled receptionist and out the front door just as Gaston was emerging from the taxi. He handed over a thick briefcase and said that *Gatsby* was all there, with the exception of page 1 of chapter 3.

Leaning against a tree not fifty yards away, Bruce Cable watched the exchange and enjoyed a good laugh.

EPILOGUE

Eight inches of overnight snow had blanketed the campus, and by mid-morning crews were hustling with plows and shovels to clear the walkways and doorsteps so that classes could go on. Students in heavy boots and coats wasted little time between classes. The temperature was in the teens and the wind was biting.

According to the schedule he'd found online, she should be in a classroom in Quigley Hall, teaching a class in creative writing. He found the building, found the room, and managed to hide and stay warm in a second-floor lobby until 10:45. He slipped back into the winter and loitered on a sidewalk beside the building, pretending to chat on his cell phone to avoid any suspicion. It was too cold for anyone to notice or care. Bundled as he was, he could have been just another student. She came out the front door and headed away

from him in a crowd, one that swelled as other buildings emptied with the change of classes. He followed
at a distance and noticed she was accompanied by a
young man, one with a backpack. They turned here and
there and appeared to be headed for the Strip, a row of
shops and cafés and bars just off the campus of Southern Illinois University. They crossed a street, and as
they did her companion took her elbow as if to help.
As they walked on, even faster, he let it go.

They ducked into a coffeehouse and Bruce stepped
into the bar next door. He stuffed his gloves in a coat
pocket and ordered black coffee. He waited fifteen minutes, time enough to knock off the chill, then went to
the coffeehouse. Mercer and her friend were huddled
over a small table, coats and scarves draped over their
chairs, fancy espresso drinks in front of them, deep in
conversation. Bruce was beside the table before she saw
him.

"Hello, Mercer," he said, ignoring her friend.

She was startled, even stunned, and seemed to gasp.
Bruce turned to her friend and said, "I'm sorry, but I
need a few minutes with her. I've come a long way."

"What the hell?" the guy said, ready for a row.

She touched his hand and said, "It's okay. Just give us
a few minutes."

He slowly got to his feet, took his coffee, and as he
left them he brushed by Bruce, who let it go. Bruce took
the guy's chair and smiled at Mercer. "Cute guy. One of
your students?"

She collected herself and said, "Seriously? Is that
really any of your business?"

"Not at all. You look great, Mercer, minus the tan."

"It's February in the Midwest, a long way from the beach. What do you want?"

"I'm doing fine, thanks for asking. And how are you?"

"Great. How'd you find me?"

"You're not exactly hiding. Mort Gasper had lunch with your agent, who told the sad story of Wally Starke dropping dead the day after Christmas. They needed a pinch hitter this spring for the writer in residence, and here you are. You like this place?"

"It's okay. It's cold and the wind blows a lot." She took a sip of coffee. Neither looked away.

"So how's the novel coming along?" he asked, smiling.

"Good. Half-finished and writing every day."

"Zelda and Ernest?"

She smiled and seemed amused. "No, that was a stupid idea."

"Quite stupid, but you seemed to like it, as I recall. So what's the story?"

Mercer took a deep breath and glanced around the room. She smiled at him and said, "It's about Tessa, her life on the beach, and her granddaughter, and her romance with a younger man, all nice and fictionalized."

"Porter?"

"Someone very similar to him."

"I like it. Have they seen it in New York?"

"My agent has read the first half and is quite enthusiastic. I think it's going to work. I can't really believe this, Bruce, but it's nice to see you. Now that the shock is wearing off."

"And it's nice to see you as well, Mercer. I wasn't sure it would ever happen."

"Why is it happening now?"

"Unfinished business."

She took a sip and wiped her lips with a napkin. "Tell me, Bruce, when did you first suspect me?"

He looked at her coffee, some variety of a latte with too much foam and what appeared to be caramel squirted on top. "May I?" he asked as he reached for it. She said nothing as he took a sip.

He said, "The moment you arrived. At that time, I was on high alert and watching every new face, and with good reason. You had the perfect cover, the perfect story, and I thought it might be true. I also thought it might be a brilliant plan, hatched by someone. Whose idea was it, Mercer?"

"I'd rather not say."

"Fair enough. The closer we got the more suspicious I became. And, at the time, my gut was telling me that the bad guys were closing in. Too many strange faces in the store, too many fake tourists poking around. You confirmed my fears, so I made the move."

"A clean getaway, huh?"

"Yes. I got lucky."

"Congratulations."

"You're a great lover, Mercer, but a lousy spy."

"I'll take both as a compliment." She took another sip and handed him the cup. When he gave it back, she asked, "So what's the unfinished business?"

"To ask why you did it. You tried to put me away for a long time."

"Isn't that a risk all crooks take when they decide to deal in stolen goods?"

"You're calling me a crook?"

"Of course."

"Well, I think you're a sneaky little bitch."

She laughed and said, "Okay, we're even. Any more names to call me?"

He laughed too and said, "No, not at the moment."

She said, "Oh, I can think of a lot of things to call you, Bruce, but the good outnumber the bad."

"Thanks, I guess. So, back to the question. Why did you do it?"

She took a deep breath and looked around again. Her friend was sitting in a corner, checking his phone. "Money. I was broke, in debt, vulnerable. A lot of excuses, really. It's something I'll always regret, Bruce. I'm sorry."

He smiled and said, "That's why I'm here. That's what I wanted."

"An apology?"

"Yes. And I accept it. No hard feelings."

"You're awfully magnanimous."

"I can afford to be," he said and both chuckled.

"Why did you do it, Bruce? I mean, looking back, it was worth it, but at the time it was incredibly risky."

"It wasn't planned, believe me. I've bought and sold a few rare books on the black market. I guess those days are over now, but at the time I was just minding my own business when I got a call. One thing led to another and the plot gained momentum. I saw an opportunity, decided to seize it, and in short order I had possession. But I was in the dark and I had no idea how close the bad guys were until you came along. Once I realized I had a spy in the house, I had to make a move. You made it happen, Mercer."

"Are you trying to thank me?"

"Yes. You have my sincerest gratitude."

"Don't mention it. As we know, I'm a lousy spy."

Both were enjoying the conversation as they took another sip. She said, "I gotta tell you, Bruce, when I read that the manuscripts were back at Princeton, I had a good laugh. I felt sort of foolish, to get played like that, but I also said, 'Go, Bruce.'"

"It was quite the adventure, but I'm one and done."

"I doubt that."

"I swear. Look, Mercer, I want you to come back to the island. The place means a lot to you. The cottage, the beach, the friends, the bookstore, Noelle and me. The door is always open."

"If you say so. How's Andy? I think about him all the time."

"Sober, and fiercely so. He attends AA twice a week and is writing like a madman."

"That's wonderful news."

"Myra and I were talking about you last week. There were questions about your abrupt departure, but no one has a clue. You belong there and I want you to feel free to come see us. Finish your novel and we'll throw a huge party."

"That's very gracious, Bruce, but with you I'll always be suspicious. I might go back, but no more fooling around."

He squeezed her hand, stood, and said, "We'll see." He kissed her on the top of her head and said, "Good-bye for now."

She watched him ease between the tables and leave the coffeehouse.

AUTHOR'S NOTE

Allow me to apologize to Princeton University. If its website is accurate, and I have no reason to believe it is not, then the original handwritten manuscripts of F. Scott Fitzgerald are indeed housed in the Firestone Library. I have no firsthand knowledge of this. I have never seen that library, and I certainly stayed away from it while writing this novel. As far as I'm concerned, these manuscripts could be in the basement, the attic, or a secret tomb with armed guards. I made no effort at accuracy in this regard, primarily because I want no part of inspiring some misguided soul to get any felonious ideas.

I learned with my first novel that writing books is far easier than selling them. Since I know nothing about the retail side of the business, I leaned on an old friend, Richard Howorth, owner of Square Books in Oxford,

Mississippi. He reviewed the manuscript and found innumerable ways to improve it. Thanks, Rich.

The rare-book world is fascinating and I only dabble in it. When I needed help, I turned to Charlie Lovett; Michael Suarez; and Tom and Heidi Congalton, owners of Between the Covers Rare Books. Many thanks.

David Routh came through in the clutch at Chapel Hill, as did Todd Doughty in Carbondale.

Read on for a sneak peek at

The Rooster Bar

We hope you have enjoyed *Camino Island*.
We're pleased to present you with
a sneak peek of John Grisham's next novel,
The Rooster Bar, available now. Enjoy!

1

The end of the year brought the usual holiday festivities, though around the Frazier house there was little to cheer. Mrs. Frazier went through the motions of decorating a small tree and wrapping a few cheap gifts and baking cookies no one really wanted, and, as always, she kept *The Nutcracker* running nonstop on the stereo as she gamely hummed along in the kitchen as though the season *was* merry.

Things were anything but merry. Mr. Frazier had moved out three years earlier, and he wasn't missed as much as he was despised. In no time, he had moved in with his young secretary, who, as things developed, was already pregnant. Mrs. Frazier, jilted, humiliated, broke, and depressed, was still struggling.

Louie, her younger son, was under house arrest, sort of free on bail, and facing a rough year ahead with the drug charges and all. He made no effort to buy his mom anything in the way of a gift. His excuse was that he couldn't leave the house because of the court-ordered monitor attached to his ankle. But even without it, no one expected Louie to go to the trouble of buying gifts. The year before

and the year before that both of his ankles had been un-
burdened and he hadn't bothered to shop.

Mark, the older son, was home from the horrors of law
school, and, though even poorer than his brother, had
managed to buy his mother some perfume. He was scheduled to graduate in May, sit for the bar exam in July, and
begin working with a D.C. firm in September, which, as it
so happened, was the same month Louie's trial was on the
docket. But Louie's case would not go to trial for two very
good reasons. First, the undercover boys had caught him
in the act of selling ten bags of crack—there was even a
video—and, second, neither Louie nor his mother could
afford a decent lawyer to handle the mess. Throughout
the holidays, both Louie and Mrs. Frazier dropped hints
that Mark should rush in and volunteer to defend his
brother. Wouldn't it be easy to stall matters until later in
the year when Mark was properly admitted to the bar—he
was practically there anyway—and once he had his license
wouldn't it be a simple matter of finding one of those tech-
nicalities you read about to get the charges dismissed?

This little fantasy of theirs had some rather large holes
in it, but Mark refused to discuss it. When it became apparent that Louie planned to hog the sofa for at least ten
hours on New Year's Day and watch seven straight bowl
games, Mark made a quiet exit and went to a friend's
house. Returning home that night, while driving under
the influence, he made the decision to flee. He would return to D.C. and kill some time puttering around the law
firm where he would soon be employed. Classes didn't
start for almost two weeks, but after ten days of listening
to Louie bitch and moan about his problems, not to mention the nonstop *Nutcracker*, Mark was fed up and looking
forward to his last semester of law school.

He set his alarm for eight the following morning, and over coffee with his mom explained that he was needed back in D.C. Sorry to leave a bit earlier than expected, Mom, and sorry to leave you here all alone with your bad boy, Mom, but I'm outta here. He's not mine to raise. I got my own problems.

The first problem was his vehicle, a Ford Bronco he'd been driving since high school. The odometer had frozen at 187,000 miles, and that had happened midway through college. It desperately needed a new fuel pump, one of many replacement parts on the Urgent List. Using tape and paper clips, Mark had been able to wire and jerry-rig the engine, transmission, and brakes for the past two years, but he'd had no luck with the fuel pump. It worked but at a lower capacity than normal, so that the Bronco's max speed was forty-nine on level ground. To avoid being clobbered by 18-wheelers on the expressways, Mark stuck to the back roads of rural Delaware and the Eastern Shore. The two-hour drive from Dover to central D.C. took twice as long.

This gave him even more time to consider his other problems. Number two was his suffocating student debt. He'd finished college with $60,000 in loans, and no job. His father, who seemed happily married at the time but was also in debt, had warned him against further studies. He'd said, "Hell, boy, four years of education and you're sixty grand in the hole. Quit before it gets any worse." But Mark thought taking any financial advice from his father was foolish, so he worked a couple of years here and there, bartending and delivering pizza, while he haggled with his lenders. Now, looking back, he wasn't sure where the idea of law school had originated, but he did remember over-hearing a conversation between two frat brothers who were pondering weighty matters while drinking heavily. Mark was the bartender, the lounge was not crowded, and after the fourth round of vodka and cranberry juice they talked loud enough for all to hear. Among many interesting things they had said, Mark had always remembered two: "The big D.C. law firms are hiring like crazy." And, "Starting salaries are one-fifty a year."

Not long after that, he bumped into a college friend who was a first-year student at the Foggy Bottom Law School in D.C., and the guy gushed on about his plans to blitz through his studies, finish in two and a half years, and sign on with a big firm for a fat salary. The Feds were throwing loans at students, anybody could qualify, and, well sure, he would graduate with a mountain of debt but nothing he couldn't wipe out in five years. To his friend, at least, it made perfect sense to "invest in himself" with the debt because it would guarantee all that future earning power.

Mark took the bait and began studying for the Law School Admission Test. His score was an unimpressive 146, but this did not bother the admissions folks at the Foggy Bottom Law School. Nor did his rather thin undergraduate résumé with an anemic grade point average of 2.8. FBLS accepted him with open arms. His loan applications were quickly approved. Sixty-five thousand bucks were simply transferred from the Department of Education each year to Foggy Bottom. And now, with one semester to go, Mark was staring miserably at the reality of graduating with a combined total, undergrad and law school, principal and interest, of $266,000 in debt.

Another problem was his job. As it happened, the market wasn't quite as strong as rumored. Nor was it as vibrant as FBLS had advertised in its slick brochures and near-fraudulent website. Graduates from top-tier law schools were still finding work at enviable salaries. FBLS, though, was not quite in the top tier. Mark had managed to worm his way into a midsized law firm that specialized in "governmental relations," which meant nothing more than lobbying. His starting salary had not been established, because the firm's management committee would meet in early January to review profits from the previous year and supposedly jiggle the pay structure. In a few months, Mark would be expected to have an important talk with his "loan counselor" about restructuring his student debt and somehow repaying the entire mess. This counselor had already expressed concern that Mark did not know how much he would be earning. This concerned Mark too, especially when added to the fact that he didn't trust a single person he'd met at the law firm. As much as he tried to fool himself, he knew deep in his gut that his position was not secure.

Another problem was the bar exam. Because of demand, the D.C. version of the test was one of the more challenging in the nation, and FBLS grads had been bombing it at an alarming rate. Again, the top schools in town did well. The year before, Georgetown had a 91 percent pass rate. For George Washington it was 89 percent. For FBLS, the pass rate was a pathetic 56 percent. To succeed, Mark needed to start studying now, in early January, and hit the books nonstop for six months.

But the energy simply wasn't there, especially in the cold, dreary, depressing days of winter. At times the debt felt like cinder blocks strapped to his back. Walking was a chore. Smiling was difficult. He was living in poverty and his future, even with the job, was bleak. And he was one of the fortunate ones. Most of his classmates had the loans but not the jobs. Looking back, he'd heard the grumbling even in his first year, and with each semester the mood at school grew darker, the suspicions heavier. The job market worsened. The bar exam results embarrassed everyone at FBLS. The loans piled up. Now, in his third and last year, it was not unusual to hear students verbally spar with professors in class. The dean wouldn't come out of his office. Bloggers blistered the school and screamed harsh questions: "Is this a hoax?" "Have we been had?" "Where did all the money go?"

To varying degrees, almost everyone Mark knew believed that (1) FBLS was a subpar law school that (2) made too many promises, and (3) charged too much money, and (4) encouraged too much debt while (5) admitting a lot of mediocre students who really had no business in law school, and (6) were either not properly prepared for the bar exam or (7) too dumb to pass it.

There were rumors that applications to FBLS had fallen by 50 percent. With no state support, and no endowment, such a decline would lead to all manner of painful cost cutting, and a bad law school would only get worse. This was fine with Mark Frazier and his friends. They would endure the next four months and happily leave the place, never to return.

Mark lived in a five-story apartment building that was eighty years old and visibly deteriorating, but the rent was low and this attracted students from George Washington and FBLS. In its earlier days it had been known as the Cooper House, but after three decades of frat-like wear and tear it had earned its nickname as the Coop. Because its elevators seldom worked, Mark took the stairs to the third floor and entered his cramped and sparsely furnished flat, for which he paid $800 a month for five hundred square feet. For some reason he'd cleaned the place after his last exam before the holidays, and as he flipped on lights he was pleased to see that everything was in order. And why shouldn't it be? The slumlord who owned the place never came around. He unloaded his bags and was struck by the silence. Normally, with a bunch of students, and with thin walls, there was always a racket. Stereos, televisions, arguments, pranks, poker games, fights, guitar playing, even a trombone played by a nerd on the fourth floor that could rattle the entire building. But not today. Everyone was still at home, enjoying the break, and the halls were eerily quiet.

After half an hour, Mark was bored and left the building. Walking along New Hampshire Avenue, with the wind cutting through his thin fleece and old khakis, he decided, for some reason, to turn onto Twenty-First and stop by the law school to see if it was open. In a city with no shortage of hideous modern buildings, FBLS managed to stand out in its unsightliness. It was a postwar edifice covered with bland yellow bricks on eight levels slung together in asymmetrical wings, some failed architect's effort at making a statement. Supposedly, it once was an office building, but walls had been knocked out with abandon to create cramped lecture halls on the four lower floors. On the fifth was the library, a rabbits' warren of large, retrofitted rooms packed with seldom-touched books and some replicated portraits of unknown judges and legal scholars. The faculty had offices on the sixth and seventh floors, and on the eighth, and as far away from the students as possible, the administration carried on, with the dean solidly hidden in a corner office from which he seldom ventured.

The front door was unlocked and Mark entered the empty lobby. While he appreciated its warmth, he found the area, as always, utterly depressing. A huge bulletin board covered one wall with all manner of notices and announcements and enticements. There were a few slick posters advertising opportunities to study abroad, and the usual assortment of handmade ads offering stuff for sale—books, bikes, tickets, course outlines, tutors by the hour—and apartments for rent. The bar exam loomed over the entire school like a dark cloud and there were posters extolling the excellence of some review courses. If he searched hard enough he could possibly find a few employment opportunities, but at FBLS those had become scarcer by the year. In one corner he saw the same old brochures hawking even more student loans. At the far end of the lobby there were vending machines and a small coffee bar, but nothing was being brewed during the break.

He fell into a battered leather chair and soaked in the gloominess of his school. Was it really a school or was it just another diploma mill? The answer was becoming clear. For the thousandth time he wished he had never walked through the front doors as an unsuspecting first-year student. Now, almost three years later, he was burdened by loans he couldn't imagine paying off. If there was a light at the end of the tunnel, he couldn't see it.

And why would anyone name a school Foggy Bottom? As if the law school experience itself wasn't dreary enough, some bright soul had, some twenty years earlier, tagged it with a name that conveyed even more cheerlessness. That guy, now dead, had sold the school to some Wall Street investors who owned a string of law schools that were reportedly producing handsome profits while cranking out little in the way of legal talent.

How do you buy and sell law schools? It was still a mystery.

Mark heard voices and hurriedly left the building. He hiked down New Hampshire to Dupont Circle, where he ducked into Kramer Books for a coffee and a quick thaw. He walked everywhere. His Bronco lurched and stalled too much in city traffic, and he kept it tucked away in a lot behind the Coop, always with the key in the ignition. Unfortunately, so far no one had been tempted to steal it.

Warm again, he hustled six blocks north along Connecticut Avenue. The law firm of Ness Skelton occupied a few floors in a modern building near the Hinckley Hilton. The previous summer Mark had managed to weasel his way inside when he accepted an internship that paid less than minimum wage. At major law firms, the summer programs were used to entice top students to the big life. Little work was expected. The interns were given ridiculously easy schedules, along with tickets to ball games and invitations to fine parties in the splendid backyards of the wealthy partners. Once seduced, they signed on, and upon graduation were soon thrown into the meat grinder of hundred-hour weeks.

Not so at Ness Skelton. With only fifty lawyers, it was far from a top-ten firm. Its clients were trade associations—Soybean Forum, Retired Postal Workers, Beef and Lamb Council, National Asphalt Contractors, Disabled Railroad Engineers—and several defense contractors desperate for their share of the pork. The firm's expertise, if it had any, was maintaining relationships with Congress. Its summer intern program was designed more to exploit cheap labor than to attract top students. Mark had worked hard and suffered through the stultifying work. At the end of the summer, when he had received an offer that somewhat resembled a position upon passing the bar exam, he couldn't decide if he should celebrate or cry. Nonetheless, he jumped at what was being offered—there was nothing else on the table—and proudly became one of the few FBLS students with a future. Throughout the fall, he had gently pressed his supervisor about the terms of his upcoming employment but got nowhere. There might be a merger in the works. There might be a split. There might be a lot of things, but an employment contract was not one of them.

So he hung around. Afternoons, Saturdays, holidays, anytime he was bored he would stop by the firm, always with a big fake smile and an eagerness to pitch in and help with the grunt work. It was not clear if this was beneficial, but he figured it couldn't hurt.

His supervisor was named Randall, a ten-year guy on the verge of making partner, and thus under a lot of pressure. A Ness Skelton associate who didn't make partner after ten years was quietly shown the door. Randall was a George Washington law grad, which, in the city's pecking order, was a step down from Georgetown but several notches above Foggy Bottom. The hierarchy was clear and rigid, and its worst perpetrators were the GW lawyers. They detested being looked down upon by the Georgetown gang; thus they were eager to look down with even more disdain on anyone from FBLS. The entire firm reeked of cliques and snobbery, and Mark often wondered how in hell he wound up there. Two associates were from FBLS, but they were so busy trying to distance themselves from their school they had no time to lend Mark a hand. Indeed, they seemed to ignore him more than anyone else. Mark had often mumbled, "What a way to run a law firm." But then he figured that every profession had its levels of status. He was far too worried about his own skin to fret over where the other cutthroats had studied law. He had his own problems.

He had e-mailed Randall and said he would be dropping by to do whatever grunt work was available. Randall greeted him with a curt "Back so soon?"

Sure, Randall, and how were your holidays? Great to see you. "Yeah, got bored with all the holiday crap. What's up?"

"Two of the secretaries are out with the flu," Randall said. He pointed to a stack of documents a foot thick. "I need that copied fourteen times, all collated and stapled."

Okay, back to the copy room, Mark thought. "Sure," he said as if he couldn't wait to jump in. He hauled the documents down to the basement, to a dungeon filled with copiers. He spent the next three hours doing mindless work for which he would be paid nothing.

He almost missed Louie and his ankle monitor.

2

Like Mark, Todd Lucero was inspired to become a lawyer by booze-tinted conversations he'd overheard in a bar. For the past three years, he had been mixing drinks at the Old Red Cat, a pub-style watering hole favored by students from GW and Foggy Bottom. After college at Frostburg State, he'd left Baltimore and drifted into D.C. in search of a career. Finding none, he hired on at the Old Red Cat as a part-timer and soon realized he had a fondness for pulling pints and mixing strong drinks. He'd come to love the pub life and had a gift for schmoozing with the serious drinkers while placating the rowdies.

Todd was everybody's favorite bartender and was on a first-name basis with hundreds of his regulars.

Many times over the past two and a half years he had thought of quitting law school to pursue his dream of owning his own bar. His father, though, had strong opinions to the contrary. Mr. Lucero was a cop in Baltimore and had always pushed his son to obtain a professional degree. Pushing was one thing, but paying for it was something else. And so Todd had fallen into the same trap of borrowing easy money and handing it over to the greedy folks at FBLS.

He and Mark Frazier had met the first day, during orientation, back when they were both starry-eyed and envisioning big law careers with fat salaries, back when they, along with 350 others, were horribly naive. He vowed to quit after his first year, but his father yelled at him. Because of his commitment to the bar, he had never found the time to knock on doors around D.C. and hustle for summer internships. He vowed to quit after his second year and cut off the flow of debt, but his loan counselor strongly advised against it. As long as he was in school he did not have to confront some brutal repayment schedule, so it made perfect sense to keep borrowing in order to graduate and find one of those lucrative jobs that, in theory, would eventually take care of the debts. Now, though, with only one semester to go, he knew only too well such jobs did not exist.

If only he'd borrowed $195,000 from a bank and opened his bar. He could be printing money and enjoying life.

Mark entered the Old Red Cat just after dark and took his favorite place at the end of the bar. He fist-bumped Todd and said, "Good to see you, man."

"You too," Todd said as he slid over a frosty mug of light beer. With his seniority, Todd could comp anyone he damn well pleased, and Mark had not paid in years.

With the students away, the place was quiet. Todd leaned on his elbows and asked, "So what are you up to?"

"Well, I've spent the afternoon at dear old Ness Skelton, in the copy room sorting papers that no one will ever read. More stupid work. Even the paralegals look down their noses at me. I hate the place and I haven't even been hired yet."

"Still no contract?"

"None, and the picture gets fuzzier every day."

Todd took a quick sip from his mug stashed under the counter. Even with his seniority, he wasn't supposed to drink on the job, but his boss wasn't in. He asked, "So how was Christmas around the Frazier house?"

"Ho, ho, ho. I lasted ten miserable days and got the hell out. You?"

"Three days, then duty called and I came back to work. How's Louie?"

"Still seriously indicted, still looking at real jail time. I should feel sorry for him but compassion runs thin for a guy who sleeps half the day and spends the other half on the sofa watching *Judge Judy* and bitching about his ankle monitor. My poor mom."

"You're pretty hard on him."

"Not hard enough. That's his problem. No one's ever been hard on Louie. He got caught with pot when he was thirteen, blamed it on a friend, and of course my parents rushed to his defense. He's never been held accountable. Until now."

"Bummer, man. I can't imagine having a brother in prison."

"Yeah, it sucks. I just wish I could help him but there's no way."

"I won't even ask about your dad."

"Didn't see him and didn't hear from him. Not even a card. He's fifty years old and the proud papa of a three-year-old, so I guess he played Santa Claus. Laid out a bunch of toys under the tree, smiled like an idiot when the kid came down the stairs squealing. What a rat."

Two coeds walked to the bar and Todd left to serve them. Mark pulled out his phone and checked his messages.

When Todd returned, he asked, "Have you seen any grades yet?"

"No. Who cares? We're all top students." Grades at Foggy Bottom were a joke. It was imperative that the school's graduates finish with sparkling résumés, and to that end the professors passed out As and Bs like cheap candy. No one flunked out of FBLS. So, of course, this had created a culture of rather listless studying, which, of course, killed any chance of competitive learning. A bunch of mediocre students became even more mediocre. No wonder the bar exam was such a challenge. Mark added, "And you really can't expect a bunch of overpaid professors to grade exams during the holidays, can you?"

Todd took another sip, leaned even closer, and said, "We have a bigger problem."

"Gordy?"

"Gordy."

"I was afraid of that. I've texted and tried to call but his phone's turned off. What's going on?"

"It's bad," Todd said. "Evidently, he went home for Christmas and spent his time fighting with Brenda. She wants a big church wedding with a thousand people.

Gordy doesn't want to get married. Her mother has a lot to say. His mother is not speaking to her mother and the whole thing is blowing up."

"They're getting married May 15, Todd. As I recall, you and I signed on as groomsmen."

"Well, don't bet on it. He's already back in town and off his meds. Zola stopped by this afternoon and gave me the heads-up."

"What meds?"

"It's a long story."

"What meds?"

"He's bipolar, Mark. Diagnosed a few years back."

"You're kidding, right?"

"Why would I kid about this? He's bipolar and Zola says he's off his medication."

"Why wouldn't he tell us?"

"I can't answer that."

Mark took a long drink of beer and shook his head. He asked, "Zola's back already?"

"Yes, evidently she and Gordy hurried back for a few days of fun and games, though I'm not sure they're having much fun. She thinks he quit his meds about a month ago when we were studying for finals. One day he's manic and bouncing off the walls; then he's in a stupor after sipping tequila and smoking weed. He's talking crazy, says he wants to quit school and run off to Jamaica, with Zola of course. She thinks he might do something stupid and hurt himself."

"Gordy is stupid. He's engaged to his high school sweetheart, a real cutie who happens to have money, and now he's shacking up with an African girl whose parents and brothers are in this country without the benefit of those immigration papers everyone is talking about. Yes, the boy is stupid."

"Gordy's in trouble, Mark. He's been sliding for several weeks and he needs our help."

Mark pushed his beer away, but only a few inches, and clasped his hands behind his head. "As if we don't have enough to worry about. How, exactly, are we supposed to help?"

"You tell me. She's trying to keep an eye on him and she wants us to come over tonight."

Mark started laughing and took another sip.

"What's so funny?" Todd asked.

"Nothing, but can you imagine the scandal in Martinsburg, West Virginia, if word got out that Gordon Tanner, whose father is a church deacon and whose fiancée is the daughter of a prominent doctor, lost his mind and quit law school to run off to Jamaica with an African Muslim?"

"I can almost see the humor."

"Well, try harder. It's a scream." But the laughter had stopped. "Look, Todd, we can't make him take his meds. If we tried to he'd kick both our asses."

"He needs our help, Mark. I get off at nine tonight and we're going over."

A man in a nice suit sat at the bar and Todd walked over to take his order. Mark sipped his beer and sank into an even deeper funk.

Available now
from
JOHN GRISHAM

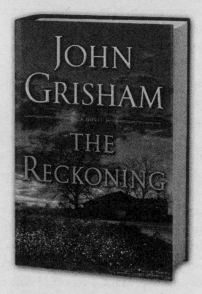

A shocking murder by a World War II hero threatens to tear a family apart in this unexpected, unforgettable novel.

"An original, gripping, penetrating novel that may be his greatest work yet."

—David Grann, *New York Times* bestselling author of *Killers of the Flower Moon*

jgrisham.com

Doubleday